LEGEND *of the* FIVE RINGS

The realm of Rokugan is a lan
and mystics, dragons, magic,
world where honor is stronge

The Seven Great Clans have defended
the Emperor of the Emerald Empire for a thousand
years, in battle and at the imperial court. While conflict
and political intrigue divide the clans, the true threat
awaits in the darkness of the Shadowlands, behind the
vast Kaiu Wall. There, in the twisted wastelands, an
evil corruption endlessly seeks the downfall of the
empire.

The rules of Rokugani society are strict. Uphold
your honor, lest you lose everything in pursuit of glory.

Legend of the Five Rings™

The Collected Novellas
Volume Two

THE GREAT CLANS
OF ROKUGAN

ROBERT DENTON III
DG LADEROUTE
MARIE BRENNAN

Tales of Rokugan by
MARIE BRENNAN • KEITH RYAN KAPPEL
CHRIS LONGHURST • ROBERT DENTON III
& DG LADEROUTE

ACONYTE

First published by Aconyte Books in 2022

ISBN 978 1 83908 132 3

Ebook ISBN 978 1 83908 133 0

Cover art by Mauro Dal Bo

Rokugan map by Francesca Baerald

Distributed in North America by Simon & Schuster Inc, New York, USA

Printed in the United States of America

9 8 7 6 5 4 3 2 1

ACONYTE BOOKS

An imprint of Asmodee Entertainment Ltd

Mercury House, Shipstones Business Centre

North Gate, Nottingham NG7 7FN, UK

aconytebooks.com // twitter.com/aconytebooks

CONTENTS

HIGH HOUSE OF LIGHT

FUCHI MURA

Unicorn Lands

Dragon Lands

Phoenix Lands

Lion Lands

TEMPLE OF THE FUTURE

YŌJIN NO SHIRO

FOOTNOTE VILLAGE

KITSU TOMBS

OTOSAN UCHI

Shinomen Forest

Northern Crane Lands

THE GREAT HOME

Scorpion Lands

GATES OF PERSISTENCE

Southern Crane Lands

Crab Lands

KUNI CASTLE

HIDA PALACE

The Shadowlands

Islands of Silk and Spice

Rokugan

DEATHSEEKER

ROBERT DENTON III

As I wrote this book, I thought often of those who stayed beside me when, hating myself, I lingered in a very dark place. Thank you for waiting with me. I wrote this for Christen, my wife, my love, my best friend.

Special thanks to James Mendez Hodes for his invaluable expertise and guidance on this story.

Content Warning:
This story contains elements of suicidal thoughts and ideation.

CHAPTER ONE

In the dim light, Shiemi regarded her latest death poem. She was no wordsmith, and her simple calligraphy was wasted on such fine ink and crisp mulberry paper. But, she admitted, this was her best effort yet. It was better than the one her father had left behind, even better than the one left by her brother. But then, they'd each only had one chance to write a poetic reflection on their imminent deaths. Unlike them, Shiemi had practice.

Tucking the paper away, she left the incense fog of the tent. The *ashigaru* were on the move, back banners fluttering in the crisp morning air. Samurai officers barked at them from horseback, herding them into rough units. She took her place among them, ignoring the *gunsō* that bowed to her. On the opposite side of the freshly plowed field, a single line of enemy defenders assembled on the top of the town wall. The vast field between them, a "death plain", as the Matsu called it, would give the enemy's archers ample time to shower arrows on any approaching force. The gates would likely be reinforced as well. A frontal charge would be costly.

It seemed someone in town had read Akodo's *Leadership*. Shiemi wondered who.

The gunsō looked over her shoulder, receiving orders signaled by kites, an innovation embraced by their general. She wondered if he was watching her now. He would be leading like an Akodo, from a hilltop in full regalia, command unit surrounding him, banner flying brazenly above his numerous organized forces. Whether or not they managed to seize the town, Matsu Katsuchiyo would irrefutably make his statement: he was a dangerous man to ignore.

The ashigaru parted, revealing Shiemi to their enemies. She imagined how she looked to them: a white-painted face with black lips, stiff hair cropped short, armorless except for lamellar guards on her forearms and legs, her threadbare kimono more patches than silk. And no sword.

Wordless shouts carried from across the field. The defenders broke into a frenzy, pointing, hastily stringing bows. A few vanished beneath the lip of the wall. Abandoning their posts.

The sight of a lone Deathseeker could do that.

She shut them out, tightening the straps of her iron claws as she focused on her objectives. *Cross the field. Scale the wall. Open the gates.*

And if anything went wrong, throw herself into the thickest fighting and let the ancestors decide her fate. Matsu's order, the one she commanded of herself.

Thundering drums. The signal. One final breath.

Go.

Shiemi burst into a run. Alarmed voices rose above the thudding of her heavy feet and the cascading *thwips* of the first volley.

They fell short. She pumped her legs and pivoted, zigzagging. Arrows dropped like daggers in disorganized clusters. They'd trained to fire on a marching column, but she was a lone target. They hadn't accounted for something crazy. Suicidal.

Their commander is sloppy, came her absent thoughts as she ducked past another volley. Why wasn't he coordinating their shots to cut off her path? But she already knew the answer; intelligence had suggested the local magistrate was away on business, leaving the town's defense in the hands of three young, untested deputies who often squabbled. Katsuchiyo had rewarded well the peasants who provided that information.

An arrow jabbed into her shin armor. She stumbled from the force but recovered. The archer should have been less hasty. *You're not drawing the bow far enough,* she thought. *You're not thinking!*

But a warrior wouldn't need to think. Incoming danger would not have altered their mindset or influenced their actions. And now she could see them clearly, eyes wide like flailing livestock, useless weapons thrashing as though they were drowning. These were papermakers and silkworm farmers. They weren't warriors. A sheep is still a sheep, even if it is taught how to roar.

The gate was close. Arrows rained down, near miss after near miss. She pushed herself in one last sprint beneath their commander's bewildered cries: "It's just one woman! It's only one!"

She leapt onto the gate with a bang. Iron claws raked the wood, clinging. This was why she'd foregone armor. She scrambled up. By the time she exhaled, she was over the edge.

She was greeted by an arrow, feet away, as the archer let it slip. It grazed her cheek. *Too bad.*

She kicked out his knee and tore out his throat.

Another rushed forward, machete swinging. She blocked and spun past, slashing open his heel. He screamed. Another scream, and he silenced.

More. Desperate opponents stumbled into her claws. A heavy thud at her side. She pulled, tossing him over. No time to hear him snap on the ground.

Drums. Katsuchiyo's advance. But they were too busy to deal with that, due to the unfortunate circumstance of a Deathseeker rampaging through their ranks.

They broke. Some pushed allies off the parapet. Their leader shouted, unheeded.

Now! Shiemi leapt down to the inner side. Cobblestone punched her knees. Were the town built for siege, this gate would be the first of two, and she would have another gate and a second column of archers to deal with. But it wasn't. She sprinted to the doors and slammed her shoulder into the massive plank barring them.

"Stop her!"

A loud thunk by her ear. An arrow. She spun, lashing out. The closest attacker wrenched back, red grooves in his face. The others flinched. She gave them no time, charging. They fell like wheat to her scythes.

Returning to the doors. Heaving the bar aside.

The gate burst open, the bang ringing in her ears. Soldiers poured in.

The wave of ashigaru wrapped around the town defenders like a massive snake in the square. The battle tide nearly sucked her up with it, but she swam against it, instead climbing the stairs to the parapets. Her gaze snagged on a man in ornate armor barking orders at the panicking defenders, attempting to organize them into a fish-scales formation, where spear-wielders formed a protective shell around a handful of strong combatants. This way, they could funnel opponents into the combatants at the front to be methodically dispatched. But the formation fell apart, the defenders scattering, leaving each other to their own fate. The armored man's face showed only confusion as he was pulled beneath trampling feet.

She shook her head. A town square, where existing structures would have better funneled attackers, was no place to deploy this formation, and fearful town conscripts could never maintain it. Experience would have taught him better. Experience he didn't have.

Akodo's *Leadership* couldn't teach him everything.

Heavy feet on the planks. A martial scream.

Pay attention! She reared back, catching a downward sword inches from her neck. Steel scraped against iron. She wrenched it away. The blade clattered at her feet.

Her attacker froze. With just the shadow of a beard, and the age of his helmet contrasting against the youth of his face, he couldn't even have been eighteen. He blanched, steeling himself. Accepting his death.

She waited until his eyes opened before stepping back.

"Try again," she said.

Hesitation. Slowly, he recovered his sword. "Th-thank you." His eyes never left hers.

He was one of the deputies, she realized. This may well have been his first assignment. Without experience, he'd inherited an impossible task. What was an untested youth doing in the middle of this fight? What had he done in his past life to deserve such poor luck?

His was such a young face, so full of promise, trying to look steel-eyed and brave in a helmet and armor that could have been his grandfather's. Hadn't her own brother looked just like that before he set off to war?

"You have the reach advantage," she reminded him. "Use it. Make me cross the line."

She had to be careful. He might think she was taunting him. But the boy nodded, settling into a two-handed stance that was far better than his first attempt.

"If... if I do as you say," he managed, forcing calm, "won't you just counter me?"

"There is no counter for the right action," she replied. "I cannot fight this battle for you, little cub. 'Think of your own safety, and you will fail–'"

"'–Be at peace with dying, and you will taste victory,'" the boy finished. His back straightened. He readied his blade and nodded for her to attack.

The gesture held the weight of a story just beginning. He was untested metal, and she the hammer. He would break, or be strengthened. If he defeated her, his blade would shine brightly. His forging would be remembered. As would she.

Maybe it will be him, she thought. She hoped so. The boy needed confidence. Killing a Deathseeker would certainly give him that. He would enjoy his lord's esteem, his reputation would increase, and she would live on in his legend. To play such a part in a young samurai's story would be a great service to the Lion. That would be the best possible outcome. Dust fell from the opening shutters of her heart as she allowed herself, for the first time in a long while, to hope for it. She raised her claws and breathed deep for her battle cry.

An arrow protruded from his throat.

Confusion flickered across his face.

And then he fell.

Shiemi blinked at the space where the boy once stood. The crunch of his landing punched her gut.

The ancestors might have favored him. He could have won. He could have defeated her. She could have played a part in his glorious story.

A story cut short. A future denied.

And another chance for her death to serve the Lion, torn away.

Who had dared to interrupt? Who–

Matsu Asayo. Katsuchiyo's *hatamoto*, his lieutenant and confidant. She stood just within range of her segmented bow, which she lowered in a gesture dripping with satisfaction. On her chest guard, the claw-arrowhead emblem of the Koritome, the vassal family from which she hailed, boasted of the archery prowess that made her family famous. Yet it was not half as boastful as the woman's smirk, nor her swagger as she stalked away.

So close. She'd been so close.

But why would Asayo interfere? Deathseekers were, by very definition, expendable. They volunteered for the most dangerous tasks, taking on the burden of risk so others didn't need to. Redemption through one final service to the clan was their goal. Why not wait until the duel had ended?

If only she would burst into flame! If only a collapsing wall would bury her! If only–

Taiko drums. A chorus of cheers. The defenders had fallen. Victory. Sweet, bitter victory.

Descending, she found the boy choking, eyes red, severed bones jutting out beneath the arrow. The fall had broken his neck.

He didn't deserve to die this way, on his back gasping at the sky like a hooked fish. So, she rolled him onto his stomach, which was far more dignified, and drew his short dagger, placing the tip where it would kill him instantly. It's what she would have wanted, if their roles were reversed.

"I'm sorry," she whispered. He was lucky.

Shiemi barely registered Katsuchiyo's voice as she sidestepped a stunned guard, batting aside the command tent flap. The eyes of his command unit turned away from the map on the command table to regard her.

"When the other towns fall," he was saying, "it will foster doubt among his vassal lords. If he cannot protect settlements this far in his own territory, then how can they trust he will protect their estates while they make war on his behalf?"

He paused, finally noticing her.

She slammed two sheathed swords onto the table. Tokens scattered to the floor.

Guards reached for their blades, but Katsuchiyo stayed them with a gesture. Only the crickets filled the lingering silence. No one moved, except the yokel Asayo, who idly picked her nose.

"It seems Lady Matsu wishes to speak in private," Katsuchiyo finally said.

The officers filed out. Even the guards left. Asayo remained at Katsuchiyo's side, as suited a lapdog like her.

As did Akodo Hiroki, Katsuchiyo's only other Deathseeker.

Shiemi was surprised when she first met Hiroki. He was easily the oldest Deathseeker she'd ever seen, a withered man whose wide frame suggested that he'd been a walking mountain in his youth. A thin scar cleaved a deep canyon into his wrinkled face, a lacquered patch covering his missing eye. His right kimono sleeve was pinned up at the shoulder to conceal the stump. She wondered if he resented whatever had taken these things from him, along with his ability to vanguard-storm the battlefield as demanded by his oath. She'd hoped he would tell her the story. She never passed up the chance to hear an elder's tale.

But he never did. He was always silent, just as he was now, gazing upon the map from the tent's far corner, a statue of quiet mystery.

As the last officers left the tent, Shiemi uncurled her fingers, willing herself to relax one tight back muscle at a time. That could easily have been her last breath. She'd gravely insulted the general, not only by disrupting the meeting, but by storming in armed, leading with her right foot. An extreme gesture, but what better way to get his attention than to threaten an outburst in front of his officers? And by showing that she did not fear reprisal, she demonstrated the seriousness of her intentions. Had Lady Matsu not done the same when she freed Akodo's captured lions and leopards into the Ikota plains, proclaiming them to be under her protection? Or when she answered the call of thunder, striking down Ikoma's son in front of her lord to claim what was hers?

Katsuchiyo lifted the smaller sword curiously. "It is unlike you to take battlefield trophies, Shiemi."

"It is the *daishō* of the boy who organized the village's defense," she said, emphasizing the word "boy".

"A regrettable loss," Katsuchiyo replied, almost sounding like he meant it. He stroked his beard and regarded her not unlike how he'd regarded his pieces on the strategy table.

"So then," he reasoned, "you intend to return his swords to his family, and you seek my permission." He shook his head. "Although you have served my forces well for some time now, it is not my place to give you leave, nor to compel you to stay."

That's not what this is about and you know it!

But she bit her tongue and chose cooler words. "It is customary for the one who felled the warrior to return their swords." At this, she stared pointedly at Asayo.

The woman shrugged. "Yeah, I'm the one who killed him. The boy would've taken her head if I didn't."

Shiemi inhaled deeply to cool the burning coals behind her eyes. "Then you admit to interfering in our duel." A flagrant violation of the unspoken warrior agreement: that the fight would be fair, one-on-one, no tricks. If *bushi* could not count on this assumption, then every match would devolve into chaos, no difference between samurai and brute. That way led to disorganized killing. It led to madness!

"Didn't look like a duel to me. Looked like you were teaching him how to beat you."

How about I teach you *a lesson, you uncultured hick?* After all, Asayo's country bumpkin teacher had apparently failed to instill when to keep one's nose out of another's affairs. But then, what good would come of such an outburst, when Katsuchiyo held Asayo's archery skill in such high regard, and losing her temper might undermine her point? Shiemi dug in her heels to prevent throwing herself over the table.

"Asayo only meant to spare your life," Katsuchiyo said.

Spare a Deathseeker's life? A *Deathseeker's*?

One whose breaths were drawn in atonement, whose tarnished reputation and stained past could only be washed clean at the end of a reddened blade?

When a Deathseeker joined an army, it was to be in the vanguard, to confront the fiercest fighting. Spurning reward or favor, they searched for a death so glorious, it would bleach away all memory of their crimes.

Death could come a thousand ways. Only a handful could be called "glorious". How many years had she sought them out, casting aside easier deaths in search of the one that would redeem her? The Deathseeker oath was as serious as coming-of-age or marriage vows, as sacred and binding as oaths sworn before the emperor! What place was it of this hayseed, of anyone, to meddle in them?

The worst cruelty is concealed by kindness. Asayo knew what the Deathseeker oath entailed. She knew exactly what she was doing when she'd released her bowstring.

It was an insult. A cruel prolonging of her punishment. Surely Katsuchiyo realized this.

And if he did not, then another Deathseeker would.

Shiemi turned to Hiroki on his stool. "Honored elder, please explain it to them. Tell them the nature of our oath, so that Lord Katsuchiyo might understand the full weight of the terrible thing Asayo has done." She glared at the archer. "So they might know what she stole from me."

Wind rustled the canvas of the tent. The dim lantern light cast irregular shadows across the old man's scarred face. When he finally spoke, Shiemi had to lean in so that she could hear him.

"In the fifth century, having committed herself to the path of redemption through service in the footsteps of Matsu Kirifu herself, the lone warrior Akodo Kakuime charged headlong into a force of thirty-four bandits. Impaled by their spears, she continued to fight until none of the bandits remained standing. Her incredible final act was witnessed by the poet Ikoma Ojirō who, so moved by her courage, was quoted as saying that as she dove into the wall of spears without regard for her own personal safety, it was *as if among her enemies she sought the face of death itself.*" He paused reverently. "Thus did the samurai who follow Kirifu's example come to be known as 'Deathseekers.'"

Yes, I know this already. Ikoma Ojirō was one of her favorite poets of the ancient styles. She'd studied his work, knew that play by heart. But she bit her tongue. Hiroki's age, reputation, and the grievous wounds he'd suffered, all demanded her silence and respect. Even Lord Katsuchiyo said nothing in the silence that followed, not daring to interrupt before the old man had finished his thoughts.

At last, he sighed. "It is a pity Ojirō did not have you there, Shiemi. You could have simply corrected him, that a Deathseeker's purpose was not to live without distraction in full recommitment to the clan, but instead to pointlessly throw their life away. But perhaps you have yet to learn what our oath really means."

The hayseed snickered.

Heat filled Shiemi's ears as she bit back a snarl. For how long now had she laid her very life upon the altar of battle, as generations of Deathseekers had before her? How many times had she nearly perished to snatch up yet another victory? Was he really defending Asayo's interference? Was he saying that in all these years of rushing headlong toward death, she was no closer to redemption than when her path began?

If so, then Matsu take his other eye!

"Even so," she argued. "It was single combat between us. She had no right to interfere. And if you will not reprimand her, then I demand–"

"Enough," Katsuchiyo spoke. "Asayo was following my orders."

Had she heard that correctly? Surely not. "You ... ?"

He nodded. "Yes, Shiemi. I told her to protect you."

The table steadied her against a disorienting wave. She blinked stupidly, opening her mouth for words, finding none.

Then it hadn't been Asayo who had just thwarted her. The archer was just the means. It had been Katsuchiyo. Her commander. Her *trusted* leader.

It was bad enough that he'd ordered Asayo to thwart her attempt at a glorious death. But he'd also insulted her martial ability with a simple implication: that she, a volunteer for the riskiest fighting, needed "protection" in the first place.

Katsuchiyo turned to the archer and the old man. "Give us a few moments, if you would."

Asayo brushed past Shiemi, flashing a smug grin, as a mouse skipping harmlessly between a lion's claws. She didn't even bother to help the old man rise; in the end, Shiemi lent her arm to help Hiroki stand. She fumed at him inside, smoldering from his reprimand, but age and experience still demanded her courtesy.

In the tent corner stood a sake jug and tray. When they were alone, Katsuchiyo uncorked the jug and poured not one cup, but two.

She could not focus on him. Flashes of their mingled past rushed through her mind in an endless stream. Him pulling strings in her first assignment so they might be near each other. Her drilling his ashigaru to his first military victory. Standing for him in a duel against a just accuser. Rooting out spies among his followers. Years of hand-to-mouth scrounging, wandering off only to return to his side, again and again as he needed her. An enforcer. A risk-taker. One who did not flinch. Her hobbies, her interests, fading slowly away with each of his requests. When he'd finally cast his dice across the war table to seize power, he didn't need to ask for her to join his forces. Through it all, there had always been Shiemi's same mute request: *let me die a glorious death in your service, and I will do whatever you ask.*

Then why the betrayal? Had she not served him well? As vanguard, as bodyguard, as…

The map stretched before her on the table. A layout of the next town. Her gaze flicked between wooden representations of his forces. Among them, at the forefront, a single figurine, painted white, representing…

His secret weapon.

Her.

Of course. She'd long lost count of the narrow escapes, the almost-deaths. How many times now had he foiled her redemption, just so he could deploy her again?

He'd been using her all this time.

She made no accusations. Why speak what no one doubts? Instead, she let her gaze, hot and narrow, speak on her behalf.

And his eyes, knowing and triumphant, made no denials.

So. Finally. They understood one another.

He approached, a full sake cup in each hand. "We are winning, Shiemi. The Matsu lords are abandoning my brother. We are proving that he isn't worthy to lead the family." He followed her gaze to the table, eyes lingering on the marker for Shiro Matsu. His intended prize.

Katsuchiyo's hatred for his brother Uniri was no secret to those who served under him. All his life he had been overlooked to lead the family. He was young, male, not famous enough, and too removed from Matsu's bloodline. He would never be considered, even if his aunt led the family. But now the Lion's Pride supported his brother's claim, and he was just as good as his brother. Why then, Katsuchiyo argued, shouldn't he take it himself?

"When my brother is cast down, and I am *daimyō*, I will need strong advisors. I intend to make you my hatamoto. I cannot do that if you are dead."

She searched for words. "A Deathseeker forswears all titles," she recited. "She refuses–"

"Shiemi, haven't you atoned enough?"

Atoned enough? She almost laughed. That was not for her to decide. It was up to her ancestors! She could not set aside the oath she swore all those years ago. It was unthinkable.

Yet he pressed, "How many years has it been? Eight? Nine? If your ancestors wished you dead, you'd be dead. Not even a Koritome arrow would save you."

Perhaps. She was no philosopher, but that made a sort of sense. There was no avoiding an ancestor's judgment. And it had been years, so many that all memory of another way, of a time before she ever dwelled three feet from death, was like looking through a mist at the battlefields of her past life.

"When this is over, and I am in my rightful place, many things will be within my power." He extended a cup, as one might to an equal. "Serve me, and I swear, you will be made whole."

History recalled a handful of Deathseekers who were pardoned their oath, their lands and titles restored, their disgrace forgotten. It was rare, impossible to hope for. But not unprecedented. Yet only the Lion Clan Champion could grant this. By implying that he would, Katsuchiyo revealed the full breadth of his ambitions.

And she almost believed him. Almost.

But he'd just uttered a promise. And the Matsu made no promises. Their deeds were their words. His had spoken volumes. She would be deaf to them no longer.

She smacked the cup away. He pulled back, lip curled like a hungry wolf. What had she ever seen in him?

"I know everything you've done, Katsuchiyo." She leaned in close. "You will never be worthy to lead the Matsu."

She could feel the heat of his gaze on the back of her neck as she turned away. He could not keep her here, for Deathseekers decided for themselves whom they would serve. But she knew that, if it was in his power, he would never let this slide. At his first chance, he'd avenge himself.

Or rather, he'd try.

Let him do what he wishes. She accepted whatever would come next.

Then she left to gather her things. There was nothing keeping her here anymore.

CHAPTER TWO

"You're leaving?"

Word traveled fast, it seemed. Shiemi had few possessions, just a handful of personal items always packed and ready. It took only minutes to grab her things and a share of traveling rations. And a book, her lone indulgence, randomly chosen from the stack she'd accumulated. Yet already, here came Ashi, red-faced and huffing, oversized bundle bouncing against his back.

She gave him several moments to catch his breath. A blacksmith should have more stamina than this.

"You're leaving?" he repeated, when he finally could.

"Lord Katsuchiyo and I had a disagreement."

He nodded. No need for anything further. "Where will you go?"

Good question. She wasn't quite sure. Wherever she went, it needed to be a place in conflict, a place with war.

Fortunately, that left many options. The ascendancy of Matsu Uniri, the first male daimyō in generations, had left the family conflicted. The endorsement of the Lion's Pride, without which no Matsu daimyō could claim legitimacy, had done little to convince those who sided with tradition. They bowed their heads in public but whispered behind his back. It was no secret; Uniri's worthiness would be decided by how well he could defend his position. Just as how Lady Matsu repelled vengeful ruffians who had once served her, or how she crossed swords with Akodo before she would bow to him, so, too, would the new daimyō be tested. And by his own brother, it seemed, who had been planning to usurp him for some time.

Shiemi could join the forces of any opportunistic lord attempting a land grab in the resulting instability. There were plenty to choose from. War had spread far across the southern lands. No province was left untouched.

But that would mean pledging herself to another ambitious lord. Another Katsuchiyo. There were so many like him. Her stomach lurched.

So that left just one option. "The Lion Champion is planning a campaign to recapture the Osari Plains. Those joining him gather at Yōjin no Shiro. There will be other Deathseekers there."

It felt right to say it out loud. Yes, that is where she would go.

"You weren't going to say goodbye?"

A rustle through the trees. Copper leaves fell like campfire sparks. "I would always be saying goodbye, Ashi."

He grinned sadly. "As you say."

He was like that, always forgetting what she was. Not all approved of the Deathseeker oath, and even among those who did, few saw past the white-painted face of one who chased death. They'd both been outsiders of a sort, hadn't they?

If she were to hesitate, it would be for his sake. But she could not change her mind now. There was no backward path for true samurai, and where she was going, he could not follow.

"Well, you can't leave without this." Ashi unstrapped the bundle from his back with difficulty. It was as long as he was tall. "It was requisitioned for you, after all."

She knew what it was. "Ashi," she began, "I am no longer in this army. You cannot—"

"No, *you* cannot!" he blurted. His voice bounced off the trees, resounding.

In the years she'd known him, had he ever shouted like that?

"You cannot," he repeated, slowly. "Not without this. I didn't spend two seasons hunched in the forge, wasting metal on prototypes and scarring up my forearm, just so you could leave this behind!"

He tossed aside the wrapping, revealing a massive, sheathed sword, its long handle wrapped in stingray leather, with a rounded iron handguard cast in the ancient style.

"None of the officers use the old blades, mistress. You alone requested a field sword. I won't see my greatest work melted down to make cookery utensils. Now take it, and if the notion so strikes you, thank me!"

He assisted her in removing the sheath. The blade was heavy with a barely perceptible curve. A gentle swing coaxed three low whistles in tandem. She understood now why the Matsu ancestors once believed such swords to be sacred. "You've outdone yourself," she said.

"You forget, these lands were once of the Kakita. Father made them many blades in his day." He shrugged. "I learned a thing or two."

What could she possibly say? Ashi knew this could land him in hot water. Her resignation voided any right to the army's supplies. But to refuse would disgrace him. And as she inwardly admitted, she wanted something to remember him by. "Thank you, Ashi."

"Walk with the Fortunes," he replied, bowing. "And let's meet again in our next lives."

The southern dirt road had just come into view when Shiemi heard the scream. She paused as the rustle of bamboo and brittle ferns engulfed the cry. At first, she thought it was a bird, or a fox practicing its human voice, as they were known to do. But then came two more on the wind. Deeper voices, demanding.

Leave it alone, she thought, just as she realized she couldn't.

Following the noise for several minutes, Shiemi spotted armored figures in a bamboo grove. They were too far away to make out distinctly, but she could see enough: three ashigaru fought vainly for their lives against five superiorly armed opponents wearing the armor of samurai.

Only they were not samurai, Shiemi realized, as details came into focus. A samurai strode like a mighty wolf, but these men fought like rabid dogs. Their blue laminar armor was of Crane make, yet pieces were mismatched and damaged; no Crane would allow themselves to be seen like that. They didn't wield their weapons properly, and since they couldn't be of the Mirumoto family, that meant they had stolen them. A crudely painted hatchet on an attacker's chest plate told all. These were Forest-Killers. Bandits of the worst variety. Animals without remorse.

This grove was far from the Forest-Killers' hidden base in the Shinomen Forest. But they had been spotted in Lion lands of late, due to the failure of the Scorpion Clan to keep them in check. Doubtless a calculated failure, as the Scorpion and Lion did not get along.

The ashigaru fighting the bandits were harder to place. They were not of Katsuchiyo's forces, of that Shiemi was certain. But they were not of the village defenders either. They were better equipped, and trained, unlike the hasty conscripts she'd faced that morning. They wore Lion colors, but no familiar heraldry.

Wherever they were from, they would die here. A spear tip scraped uselessly against armor before an ax cleaved into the defender's head. Emboldened brutes rushed over the dead man, driving a wedge between the remaining two ashigaru. They jabbed and shouted demands Shiemi could not make out. The ashigaru refused to give in. They seemed committed to death instead.

Brave. Especially for peasants.

I cannot help them, Shiemi thought. There was no getting to them in time. And without knowing who they were or who they served, she could be sticking her hand in a hornets' nest, becoming embroiled in matters not concerning her. And a death here, with an ax in her back, was no glorious passing. No, better to report this incident at the next waystation. She would go back to the road, find a magistrate…

There was a child in the clearing. She just now saw her: a girl, no older than nine, hands tucked uselessly into a swinging-sleeve kimono. An ashigaru swept defensively between her and the circling butchers, spear shaking in his hands.

Were the bandits attacking a child?

One rushed the girl, sword flashing. He would have killed her, had the ashigaru not leapt in the way. The sword slid into the peasant's belly, up to the hilt.

But rather than fall, the peasant straightened, meeting the bandit's bewildered face. Then, with a pained cry, he spun sideways, wrenching the sword from the bandit's hands. The last defender leapt before the child, replacing the one who fell. He'd protect her to the death.

Now it was impossible to walk away. In the face of such bravery, from mere peasants, how could she do nothing?

Shiemi sprinted as she shucked her new blade and cast the sheath aside. An ax head caught the sunlight ahead. The last defender fell. His eyes met hers as she crashed into the clearing, just as the light left them.

She roared. They spun.

The first lashed out with his blade. He lost his arms, then his head. She ducked a tossed ax and slashed the neck of the second. Arterial blood sprayed into the eyes of the third, who stumbled into her kick. She planted her sword like a flag into his back.

The last two hesitated. Bright fear danced in their wide eyes.

The fools. They'd wasted their opening. Now Emma-Ō would take them.

Leaving her sword, she batted aside a feeble punch. Then she drew the knife from his belt with her free hand, stabbing it deep into his eye. He crumpled.

The final bandit reached into his kimono collar. She wouldn't give him the chance to draw whatever was there. She flicked her wrist. The knife jutted from his throat. He fell, gurgling, to the dirt.

Silence. Shiemi exhaled and checked her surroundings. But no hidden attackers lunged from the brush. No arrows fell from the trees. There was only the call of the cicadas. The bandits lay still. Their blood would feed the wildflowers.

She finally relaxed, letting her conscious mind return. It was always better to let instinct guide the body in a skirmish, but now she had to tend to the child. Who, at this moment, was regarding the field sword with open wonder.

"Are you unharmed?" Shiemi asked, harsher than she'd intended. When was the last time she'd spoken to a child? She avoided children as a rule, ever since...

"That's the largest sword I've ever seen."

Not what Shiemi had expected. Unflinching, the child stepped over the fallen bandits to get a closer look at the *nodachi*. She didn't even cast her guardians' bodies a second glance.

It was only now that Shiemi noticed the fine condition of the girl's clothes, the red shimmer in her mop of unruly hair. A noble's child? The girl turned, and Shiemi's breath caught on the girl's eyes. Speckled, the shade of honey. Flecks suspended in amber.

The child's steps disturbed the last bandit, whose hand came free from within his collar. Shiemi saw what he'd reached for in his final moments: a sheet of paper, folded many times, like a fan.

And as it came free, she caught a glimpse of a familiar stamp. Only a handful would recognize the emblem, since its meaning was entrusted only to those who personally served the owner. A lump formed in Shiemi's throat: the secret chop of Matsu Katsuchiyo.

Why would Forest-Killers have a covert message from her former general? Why did this bandit think it would save him? Had they intercepted something damning, and somehow connected it to him? Was it blackmail, or something else?

The folds concealed whatever message it contained. Whatever it was, it didn't concern her. She should leave it be.

And yet she took the paper from his limp fingers. Should she open it? A repugnant thought: the letter was not addressed to her. She wouldn't trust someone who violated a private missive, so how could she justify doing that herself? And hadn't she just washed her hands of Katsuchiyo completely? She sensed in the folded paper a certain pull, a riptide that could yank her back into his current, marching beneath men who didn't respect her.

But then, the bandit had meant to show this to her, as if it would stay her hand. Could she make better choices if she knew what it contained? Could whatever secrets within protect her from his influence? From retribution?

Her thoughts bounced within her head. Decisiveness was virtue, but now…

"Hey!" barked the girl.

Shiemi tucked the message away, unread. Now was not the time.

"Are you a samurai?" the girl asked, golden eyes starry. "You look like one, except your face is painted like a geisha."

Heat rose in Shiemi's cheeks. *What a brat!* "What are you doing out here? Were these bandits robbing you?"

The girl smiled. An incisor, long like a fang, poked out from her lips. "You *are* a samurai!" she pronounced, then crossed her arms. "Then you will help me! My parents are also samurai, lords of their realm. You will take me home to Footnote Village!"

The lump in Shiemi's throat fell into her stomach. She could have avoided this. The road had been right there.

CHAPTER THREE

"What a pleasant surprise!" The village headman bowed as Shiemi approached. "You've returned much sooner than expected, Lady Matsu. Have you eaten?"

"Greetings, Kōza," Shiemi returned. "I am only passing through."

He did not press. As headman, the village's welfare fell on his shoulders. It was his job alone to deal with visiting samurai, seeing that they were fed, received whatever they wanted, and most importantly, were sent on their way. Other than recording their visit, and any expenses incurred, samurai business did not concern him.

He paused, noticing the girl for the first time. "I see you have a new... um... companion."

The girl spoke matter of factly. "Shiemi saved me from bandits. We are best friends now."

Kōza blanched, shooting Shiemi an alarmed look. "Bandits?"

"Forest-Killers," Shiemi said hastily. "Just a few. They're no threat anymore. Even so, I would suggest Magistrate Kenchi post a few extra watchmen along the outskirts."

"Magistrate Kenchi is not here," Kōza said with a shake of his head. "Answered a call to arms from the Lion's Pride. Took several assistant deputies with him as well, I'm afraid."

Shiemi tried not to frown. Another town without their magistrate. Especially bad, considering this was a marketplace town. No magistrate meant no oversight for crowded stalls.

But it was not as if he could ignore the Lion's Pride. Although technically landless, their sway was greater even than that of the Matsu family daimyō. Even if one disagreed with them on political matters, only honorless fools would refuse the Pride directly. What could be done about it?

"Kōza," she spoke quietly, "I am without traveling papers, and I need to go south."

"Say nothing more," he replied. "I will handle that. Please remain, in the meantime." He looked knowingly at a particular building at the end of the street. "Will you both require quarters for your stay?"

Shiemi smirked. "That will be up to Mistress Mirei."

"You brought a child in here?!" The matron's harsh whisper barely rose above the gentle music, but some of the customers still turned their heads.

Shiemi raised an apologetic hand. "It is nice to see you as well, Mirei."

A server ducked around them, carrying a bottle and cups. The sparse patrons watched the musicians, a zither player and a woman tapping an hourglass-shaped drum, which rested on her shoulder. A slow day for the House of Whispering Pines.

Another server approached, as if to inquire about food or drink. They were painted like *maiko*, geisha-in-training, white face and tidy red kimono. But they had no grace, waddling in their thick red kimono and balancing a drink tray. They, like the rest of this place, were part of a comforting illusion, one that proclaimed: *look what you can afford! You are more wealthy than you appear.*

Mirei sent them away with a look before turning back to the pair, jingling a few baubles woven into her elaborately styled hair. From her expression, one could believe Shiemi had brought a dog inside. "This is no place for children, Shiemi. You of all people should know this."

Some farmers nearby shifted uncomfortably, tensing like martins ready to take flight. If they had known Shiemi was a samurai, they likely would have. Peasants never spoke to samurai like that, not if they wanted to keep their heads. But Shiemi had left the trappings of her station at the door, alongside her weapons and sandals. Without them, in her threadbare kimono, she was just another stranger.

Which suited her purposes fine. Better no one should recognize her.

"It's OK," the girl chirped. "Shiemi's my bodyguard. I go where she does." She looked curiously at a hanging scroll, brow furrowing at the painted figures there.

Mirei blanched and spun it to face the wall before the girl could fully comprehend what it depicted. Her baleful look at Shiemi could have roasted a fish.

"Well," Shiemi replied, finding that was as far as she could get.

"This is a place for people to forget their troubles," the matron insisted. "Children have none, and so they shouldn't be here."

"This one has plenty, I assure you." The daydreaming girl had found something less *evocative* to stare at, so Shiemi gestured to a nearby screen. Mirei released an exasperated sound and slid it aside, revealing a sparsely adorned receiving room.

Shiemi remembered this cleverly hidden private meeting room. One never forgets a room where one once lost a month's stipend on a single Fortunes and Winds roll.

Behind the closed door, Shiemi explained what had happened in hushed tones. She only withheld the girl's unconcern about her guardians' deaths, despite how vividly she recalled the child stepping over the bodies, as though they were merely discarded clothes.

By the end, Mirei had cooled somewhat. "So, you are protecting this child now?"

Was she? There was nothing that obligated her, but she couldn't abandon the girl either. What cruel monster would leave a mere child alone to fend for themselves? "I had not planned to be," Shiemi finally said. In truth, she hadn't decided yet what to do about the girl.

"Why then bring her here?"

"She needs food and a room to stay." Shiemi lowered her head. "I knew nowhere else to go."

"I see."

Normally, samurai just took what they wanted, deferring costs to their lords, or leaving whatever payment they thought appropriate. It was not as if a peasant could haggle with a samurai's demands. But Shiemi could not do that to Mirei. She had been there when Shiemi was at her lowest, listening to words a samurai should never utter. She would never disgrace her friend.

But neither could she pay. Normally, the establishment would invoice Katsuchiyo and his war coffers. Now she had no lord to cover the bill, and nothing of worth to offer. Commerce was distasteful, and samurai society was arranged so bushi never had to consider monetary matters. But she was outside that now, and begging far beneath her...

Mirei rose and slid the door aside. "Don't worry about it. I'll see that you are both fed."

"I will repay–" Shiemi began.

Mirei raised a hand. "Enough. It's in my own interest. How could I allow a child to starve beneath this roof? People would say all sorts of things."

An excuse. Mirei *wanted* to help. Shiemi swallowed her reply. She wasn't in a position to protest.

She sat beside the child, who watched the performers and kicked her feet in tune to the music. A few patrons glanced at the young girl among them, but otherwise paid little mind.

Before long Mirei returned with a steaming bamboo basket, a bowl, and utensils. Deftly she scooped a ball of steamed brown rice and barley into the bowl, cracking an egg over the top and drizzling it with sesame oil. The child watched the bowl with growing eyes and a gurgling stomach.

Some farmers laughed nearby, clinking their sake cups drunkenly. Shiemi regarded them wryly. "So they really believe this is a geisha house, huh?"

Mirei sighed. "Perhaps they just like to pretend for a while."

A true geisha house would cater only to nobility. There would be no rowdy commons, no weaving servers, no bawdy pictures on the walls. Instead, there would be a sparse waiting room, perhaps one or two samurai catered to by white-faced maiko apprentices until they could be entertained in a private room, and only by appointment. They would be made to feel special, like human beings, and not merely weapons for their lords.

"I really was trained in the Flower and Willow world, you know." Mirei glanced at a nearby painting, smiling at the graceful woman depicted there. "Another thing the war took away."

Shiemi didn't ask which war. It could be one of dozens. War was the typhoon that fed the Lion every summer; as the stormy season fertilized crops and led to bountiful harvests, so, too, did war bring prosperity and purpose to the clan. It was easy for samurai to forget what these storms cost the peasants, what relentless wind and rain could tear asunder. Few ever seemed to care.

Mirei pushed the bowl forward, smiling as the child all but pounced on the meal. She procured a second bowl, thwarting Shiemi's protest with a look. "It is fine. I owe you more than this. I know you are not the sort to keep track, but I am." Amusement danced on her glossy red lips. "I still remember when you threw that ruffian out on his ass. I know you saw trouble for it. Not many samurai would stick their necks out for us, but you did."

Heat rose in Shiemi's face. "Thank you," she whispered.

"We all need help sometimes," Mirei replied. "There is no shame in accepting."

Then why did it feel so awful? She deserved none of this kindness. But neither could she refuse.

The matter settled, Mirei turned her attention to the girl. "What is your name?"

It only then occurred to Shiemi that she didn't know.

"Sute," the girl replied around a mouthful. Her bowl was already half empty.

"What a pretty name," Mirei remarked, casting Shiemi a knowing look.

Sute was a commoner's word from the rural dialect. It meant "foundling", suggesting she was adopted. Which was likely; wars made orphans in abundance. Each year, the Lion Champion renewed the command for married pairs to adopt at least once. No marriage was proposed without such a clause. To simplify the paperwork, would-be parents often named the child "Sute".

But it was just as likely that Sute was firstborn. It had become common for parents to name their first child "foundling" as a precaution, to protect their line from the vengeful spirits of parents whose own children were killed in war.

Mirei plopped a steaming stuffed bun in the empty space on Sute's plate. Her golden eyes glimmered as she reached for it.

"Where are you from, Sute?" Mirei asked.

Big bite. Puffed cheek. "Footnote Village."

Mirei looked amused. "There's a village named Footnote? Footnote. They named it that?"

"I've heard of it," Shiemi said. "It's south of here."

She wasn't sure what Mirei found so funny.

"Mom says it's not important enough to have a real name," Sute remarked.

"Your mother's right," said Shiemi.

A few heads rose at Mirei's sudden cackle.

Shiemi cocked an eyebrow. "Not a particularly graceful sound, Mirei."

The "geisha" turned her back to the pair, recomposing.

"Why were you so far from home?" Shiemi asked, pushing her water cup toward the girl.

Sute shrugged as she gulped it down.

She didn't know? How was that possible? "What of the

men who accompanied you?" The ones who died, whom she'd watched die, without emotion.

"They were my bodyguards until you showed up." Matter of fact. Another bite.

Shiemi had seen much death in her years. Bodies torn open. Limbs severed. Last breaths shuddering, choking on blood. She'd seen enough death to last many haunted nights, to conjure dreadful images whenever she closed her eyes. But for a child, lost and alone, to so casually dismiss a killing she witnessed firsthand? To recall it without any emotion at all? Something about that disturbed her. It wasn't normal. It wasn't right.

Mirei leaned on the table. "You have pretty eyes, Sute."

"Thank you."

"Such an unusual color." She ducked her head, bringing her face to Sute's eye level. "Are you of the Kitsu, by any chance?"

That would explain much. The Kitsu family, revered *shugenja* of the Lion, drew their lineage from feline *yōkai* of the same name. Those who could trace their bloodline to the catfolk bore signs of their heritage, golden eyes and elongated fangs. And their gifts, if the bloodline was strong enough.

The girl shook her head. "My parents serve the Ikoma." One of the great Lion Clan lineages, alongside the Matsu, Akodo, and Kitsu.

"But that is your adopted family," Mirei said carefully. "What of your birth parents?"

Sute seemed to shrink. She set down her chopsticks. "I never knew them," she admitted. Suddenly she burst out, "But Mom says that doesn't matter! I'm their daughter!"

"Of course," Mirei agreed. "Sute, what is your favorite type of music?"

"*Buri-buri!*" she exclaimed, any offense forgotten.

The two continued as Shiemi chewed her rice. Something wasn't adding up. It was likely Sute had Kitsu heritage but wasn't aware of it. Even so, she wasn't telling them everything. Perhaps the letter would illuminate matters.

If she were willing to open it. She had just washed her hands of Katsuchiyo. Even if it revealed his secrets, she didn't want anything to do with him.

The musicians finished as a middle-aged man with watery eyes stumbled onto the stage. His elaborate flanged shoulders and pointed cap designated him as an *omoidasu*, "one who remembers", a warrior-bard of the Ikoma. Several patrons cheered before he'd even said anything.

"Who is that?" Sute chirped.

Mirei rolled her eyes. "That's just Lord Nakabara. Pay him no mind."

"Friends!" he called out, voice filling the room. "I come with grave news. The spirits of this house are angry, befuddling the senses of those who discount them. Even now they loosen tongues, demanding stronger proof!" He paused, as if noticing confusion. "Oh sorry, I meant the sake."

Many good-natured groans. Shiemi rubbed her forehead.

"He's funny!" Sute remarked.

"He's drunk," Mirei replied. "Again."

"But enough of that!" He sat, tucking his feet beneath him. "I tell you now a tale of brothers divided, one shouldered with a duty he never asked for, the other driven by ambition to claim it for himself. Yet are either of them deserving, when their ancestors turn away?"

Shiemi didn't care for *rakugo* storytelling, where the

performer sat alone and presented a complicated tale from multiple perspectives, ultimately just to set up a terrible pun. But the Ikoma championed the style, and this man (Nakabara, she reminded herself) seemed rather good at it.

At the very least, the patrons seemed entertained. There were quite a few now, their drinks momentarily forgotten as the old man on stage unfurled his tale, each leap of perspective accompanied by a drastic shift of his facial expressions, a rise or drop in the octave of his voice. Why an Ikoma samurai would perform for commoners, even in a marketplace town…

But they weren't all commoners, were they? Now that their guards were down, Shiemi noticed new details. It was the subtle language of the body: sitting straight instead of slouching, drinking with their left hand so that the right was ever ready, holding their chopsticks farthest from the tips as if unconcerned with dropping food. And no matter how much they drank or laughed or enjoyed their surroundings, they never fully dropped their guards.

They were samurai. Disguised in peasant trappings, but samurai all the same.

As a student, Shiemi had snuck away from the dōjō on several occasions. She and her peers would pretend to be commoners or even rōnin, just to escape their stresses, if only for a night. It was a common pastime throughout the Empire, setting one's life aside to spend a night wearing another face.

But wolves cannot hide from wolves. To one from their walk of life, it was obvious what they really were.

…Which meant she would be noticed, too.

The realization struck her like a cold splash in the face. Even now she caught their knowing glances, more than one even flashing a subtle nod, as if to say, "Yes, I see you."

Dammit. So much for hiding out! She was a sore thumb sticking out among these hayseeds. Were any of them from Katsuchiyo's forces? Would they report back to him where she was?

She released a held breath. No. Katsuchiyo wasn't looking for her. He had bigger things to worry about. They had no reason to care. Right?

Someone in the audience didn't look away from her. Back to the omoidasu, he openly stared, right into her eyes.

She knew him. The years had streaked his topknot hair with silver veins, and there were new scars among those she'd watched him earn in sanctioned sparring matches beneath their instructor's eyes. But time and peasant trappings could not disguise him from her.

Her chopsticks slipped from her fingers.

He rose. She turned away, eyes down.

His heavy footsteps stopped just beside her. His shadow was cold.

Mirei and Sute's whispering came to a halt. Shiemi didn't look up, but she knew he was mere inches away. He just stood there, wordless, staring down.

Others were looking now. Whispering. Best to get this over with.

"Let us speak outside," she finally said.

Silence. Then, "Agreed."

He pulled away. Daylight flooded the room. She heard him take his swords from the doorway just as he left.

"Who was that?" Sute asked.

"Stay inside," she answered, then rose to follow.

•••

She met him in the dusty street, undoing the peace knots entangling his swords.

For a long time, they simply studied each other.

Until finally he nodded. "It *is* you."

His face had new wrinkles and scars, and a thin beard trailed his jawline, but it was unmistakably Akodo Ichisuke. How long had it been? Nine years? Ten?

He didn't bow. "I never thought I would see you again, Rikuyo."

"It is Shiemi now," she replied.

"Shiemi." He said her name slowly, testing it. "Very well, Shiemi. Fetch your sword and show me your stance."

She had no desire to do that. Perhaps he could see reason. "Ichisuke, you may not have heard; I have taken Kirifu's oath and now walk the path of a Deathseeker."

"What does that change?!" he barked. The village froze. Peasants gawked. Curious children were yanked indoors. Ichisuke lowered his voice. "I can never forgive you, Shiemi. No oath can erase the stain you left on the lives you ruined. Now, fetch your sword and show me your stance. I will give you the death you so crave!"

She couldn't talk him down. Had her time finally come? Would it be him?

She hoped so. He deserved justice. She nodded. "So be it."

Returning with her nodachi sent the onlookers scrambling. She heard windows slam shut and shutters clack open. Against her back pressed the collective gaze of the House of Whispering Pines. Mirei was probably watching, too.

"Is that your only blade?" Ichisuke asked.

"I swore off the daishō," she replied. All Deathseekers did.

He cursed. Scratched his neck, thinking. Finally, he extended his sheathed *wakizashi*. "Use this, then. I only need my katana." He thrust it forward. "Take it! When I defeat you, it must be a fair duel!"

His concern was the nodachi's size. The duel was *iaijutsu*, the art of the quick-draw. Combatants began within reach, swords sheathed. But a nodachi was too large to draw like that. It wasn't designed to be. Ichisuke would have an overwhelming advantage.

By extending his wakizashi, he was offering her the easiest of his blades to draw. The advantage would instead be hers.

She made no move to accept it.

"You'd prefer the katana instead? That would be fine as well."

"I swore off those blades," she repeated.

He grumbled, pacing, mind working, until he spotted the headman Kōza standing at a safe distance. Kōza, whose job was to witness the duel. Kōza, whose job was to assist samurai...

"You!" he jutted a finger at the peasant. "Come here! Hold her greatsword so she can draw it properly!"

All color drained from Kōza's face.

"Leave him be," she said. "I don't require–"

"I won't fight you on uneven ground!" he shouted.

Shiemi clenched her jaw. If he assisted her, there was the chance Kōza would be struck as well. He'd fall with her.

Unacceptable.

But he could not refuse a samurai, and she could say nothing. His shaking legs inched him closer.

"I'll do it." The omoidasu strolled into the street, waving Kōza back. He bowed as the peasant hastily withdrew. "I am Ikoma Nakabara. I would consider it an extension of my family's duty to assist your duel in this way."

Shiemi glanced at the man in bard trappings. It still meant an uninvolved party was at risk for her, but at least he was a samurai. Risk was his life.

Ichisuke nodded. "My thanks, Lord Ikoma."

"Fine," Shiemi said, relinquishing the massive sword.

The Ikoma held it out with flat palms. Shiemi sighed and corrected him, lowering the sword until it was just below her hip. Nakabara uttered an apology.

Then she settled her eyes on her opponent. She could feel his breath on her face.

"Should Lord Ikoma not be to your left?" Ichisuke said. "And the blade held higher?"

"I will not endanger a stranger for my own benefit," she replied.

"Oh?" he sneered. "Then you certainly *have* changed, Shiemi."

His words bit deep, found old wounds. But she could not dwell on them now. She had to focus completely on the task at hand. Even with assistance, quick-drawing a blade so long was a tall order. If she didn't give it her all, her death would not redeem her.

May the Fortunes favor you, Ichisuke.

They tucked their hands into their sleeves. She emptied her mind. The world fell away. There was only Ichisuke, his eyes a pond.

Arms came free. A blur. The pond iced over.

His hand whipped to his sword. A metallic ring.

Her fingers grasped the nodachi.

He alternated his grip. His sword plunged down.

She ducked and drew.

It was not enough to free her blade.

She jabbed the butt of the handle into his solar plexus.

He crumpled.

He missed.

She kicked off the ground. Darting past, dragging her blade free.

He spun as she rose. She brought the nodachi above her head.

He was faster. One-handed, katana up, to block.

She came down with all her weight.

A snap, like dried noodles. Then thunder.

Nails in her shoulder. Something hot and wet.

Ichisuke's cheek struck the dirt. His broken sword came after.

Shiemi blinked as the world rushed back. Pieces of his shattered katana left small pits in the road dust. He was sprawled facedown, a red pool growing beneath him. A warm sensation spread down her arm. A shard pieced her, perhaps. There was no pain.

Doors slid open. The crowd inched closer, mosquitoes drawn to blood. Shiemi knelt beside Ichisuke, feeling herself growing heavier, the sensation of being pushed into the ground. "You fought honorably."

But he was staring into the window of the House of Whispering Pines, dying eyes disbelieving. Red bubbles popped around his mouth but made no sound. He reached with a shaking hand.

It was Sute. The girl was in the window, looking out. She seemed so serene regarding his bloody form, his broken body. Fascinated, as if he were a blooming flower.

"It's her," he breathed. "It's her."

It's her?!

"Who?" Shiemi asked. "Who is she?"

His body deflated, words escaping in a low hiss. "If you truly wish to atone for what you've done, guard that girl with your life."

She said nothing. The Matsu made no promises.

He wouldn't hear if she had. Already, he was gone.

Sute hopped down from the window. But Shiemi stood there for a long while, staring at the space the girl had occupied, until at last Mirei took her by the sleeve and led her back inside.

CHAPTER FOUR

Shiemi splashed her face in the bowl, reveling in the unpleasant shock. The water grew opaque and gray with shed layers of makeup. She dipped her handcloth into the dish of cold cream Mirei provided and rubbed her cheeks and forehead, scrubbing into the crevices of her eyes and the roots of her hair, until the white veneer was fully peeled away, revealing a wet face with dark rings beneath tired eyes. So very tired.

Another splash, like icy daggers.

How many more old friends must die before your honor is restored?

She splashed her face again. Watched cream-colored droplets fall back into the bowl. No reflection.

Just hold your face under.

She scrunched her eyes against the thought, but it only grew louder. *Just hold your face under. Who cares if it's undignified? Just plunge into the water and wait until—*

Her backhand sent the bowl crashing.

The thoughts silenced. She breathed slowly. In and out.

Not yet. Not until it was time.

The noise upset the horses. She approached the nearest one, gently cupping his chin and stroking his muzzle until he settled. "It's OK," she lied, over and over. "It's OK."

Returning to the makeshift nightstand in the empty stall, Shiemi finished her evening rituals, scraping her teeth and arranging her things. Then she sat on a hay mound in the dim lantern light, wishing she had a book or something. There were pillow books inside, but she wasn't willing to enter and ask for one. Distantly came the sounds of revelry, bottles clinking, laughter, playful drumming. She wondered if Sute, alone in her room, would sleep through it.

Mirei had wanted to provide Shiemi a room as well, but the stables suited her fine. She deserved nothing more.

Sute. That child was probably sleeping soundly in a pile of cushions. Nothing bothered her, after all. Not even a slaying right before her eyes.

Shiemi remembered her first brush with death, an accident in the dōjō that had resulted in a senior's expulsion and the abrupt retirement of the instructor. She remembered how still the body was, laying on the dōjō floor, like a limp doll.

Shiemi glanced at the letter on the nightstand, Katsuchiyo's stamp peeking between the folds. Reading it would answer her questions. And did she not have an obligation, as his former vassal, to uncover the truth?

She began to unfold it.

No. You don't deserve to know.

She set it aside. Peeking at a missive not meant for her, that was for Scorpions and Cranes. The Lion did not conduct themselves that way. She was ashamed to have considered it. She needed to be better than that. Her oath demanded it.

She'd dispose of the letter tomorrow. That was what honor demanded.

Wasn't it?

Guard that girl with your life.

Shiemi pinched her nose against the start of a headache. Why had Ichisuke said that? Now she was honor bound. To do otherwise would disgrace Ichisuke's dying wishes. Reading the letter might better equip her, if the child was somehow connected.

But she couldn't care for a child! Not like this! Even now she was tugged south, to the Osari Plains, where armies gathered beneath the Lion Champion's banner. She couldn't drag a child into a war camp!

Then again, didn't the previous Matsu daimyō do just that with her own children?

A hand on the stall door. She spun. How hadn't she heard anyone enter the stables? Was she that distracted? Beneath the animal instinct that sent her grasping for her knife, her rational mind reminded her that not every footstep was a threat.

Ikoma Nakabara, the omoidasu, slid the door aside. He blinked with confusion. "This isn't where I left my horse."

Shiemi relaxed. "Funny."

He entered, hands tucked, looking around. His eyes lingered on the folded letter, but then passed over. "May I sit?"

She nodded. The bard had the air of one who'd sprinted into his forties. He'd enjoyed himself too much when he was young and was paying for his fun now, mostly in the knees, judging from how he took his time.

He settled on a block of hay and dug out a long pipe.

"Not in here," Shiemi said.

He sighed like a dog watching his master eat. "No smoke, no geisha, no sake, and no bed. But at least the Deathseeker Matsu Shiemi has good company." He gestured to the nearby horses.

Had she introduced herself to the bard? She regarded him carefully. "You've heard of me?"

"Absolutely not." He chuckled. "But I saw you write your name for the matron. Recognized the character for death. Your name is bad luck." His eyes wrinkled when he smiled. "Do you really think that will catch the Fortune of Death's attention? You should have named yourself, 'I'll-Live-Forever.' He'd see you perished in days."

"Good advice," she replied. "Got any more?"

He shrugged. "Don't sleep in the stables?"

"Anything else?" He was plucking her nerves like the strings on a *biwa*. "Then tell me why you're here."

"For your story," he said. "A Deathseeker comes into a geisha house with a child in tow. She is recognized and challenged by an angry duelist, someone she used to know. I've seen much in my short years. I know when I've stumbled across a story for the Tengen Wing of the Ikoma Libraries."

"The only part of my story that matters is how it ends."

He tilted his head. "Really? Other Deathseekers have told me what matters is how they lived."

The last thing she wanted was her shame recorded. Wasn't the entire reason she'd taken up this oath so that her past would be forgotten? "Not interested."

His eyebrows went up. "Not even for future generations that might walk Kirifu's path?" He grunted, rising slowly. "I could be a useful friend, you know. A death is not glorious if no one hears about it."

For a dread-laden moment, she thought perhaps he intended to follow her south. But no, she was in no danger of this. She could outrun him.

Again, he looked at the folded letter, a little longer this time. "Perhaps you came from the army camping nearby? The one led by Lord Matsu Katsuchiyo?"

She skipped a breath. Did he recognize the seal? No, he couldn't know Katsuchiyo's secret stamp. He'd deduced it, probably. Why else would she be here?

He smirked. Her reaction had told him everything. "What do you think of him? He's caused quite a stir."

He's worm dung. She swallowed her thoughts. "It is not my place to say."

He inspected her massive field sword. "I have heard it said, soldiers do not abandon armies, they abandon generals. Yes, we are born with ancestral duties, but loyalty is not inherited. A samurai chooses their lord, if only with their heart, wouldn't you say?"

Her martial instincts were roaring. Who was this bard? Did he work for Katsuchiyo's brother? Was he trying to recruit her in the daimyō's struggle to remain in power?

If so, he was wasting his breath. She was done with their feud. She would fight for the Lion Champion, for her own redemption.

"You know," he remarked, "as it turns out, the matron accidentally provided me with a larger room than I need, one with a partition. Instead of the cold stables, you are welcome to stay there."

Or maybe he was just a dirty old man, and she'd given him too much credit.

"I will do you a kindness," she replied, "and pretend you never said that."

He held up his hands. "Just a thought! I'll leave you be. But if you change your mind, my door will be open."

If he believed she would change her mind, then he did not know the Matsu.

Her eyelids parted into a moonbeam. Someone had opened the stable doors.

Shadows flickered across the crack. Quiet steps.

She breathed slow and deep, both to fully awaken and to remain calm. They could just be inebriated guests seeking more "private" quarters, no reason to do anything rash. But midnight lovers were rarely so quiet, so aware of their surroundings.

The feet stopped at her stall's door.

Even muffled, she knew well the sound of blades being drawn.

The stall door slid aside. Shiemi felt them enter, listening for a rustle of paper or a floorboard creak, anything to help her guess where they were. As they approached the haystack bed, her right hand found and then curled around the handle of her iron claws, her other tightening the strap.

Someone whispered. The hair on the back of her neck stood on end. She knew that voice. But from where?

A presence pausing by her bed.

Shiemi counted to three.

She rolled and struck. Steel scraped against iron. She smashed into a body. Her fist stopped at a belly, warmth pouring over her knuckles. He went limp.

Second attacker. Wide arc, screaming. She countered and crushed his nose with her forehead. He gurgled as she stood. She struck. He blocked.

Too slow. Her claws came back dripping. A wet thud.

Moonlight highlighted the intruders, but revealed no details, just shapes and noise.

There was a third, retreating to her nightstand, vaguely familiar...

The letter, a thin white bar. In the open.

The intruder grabbed for it.

Shiemi lunged. The claws came down.

A bloody scream, freezing Shiemi's blood. The figure jerked back. A heavy bang, ramming into the doorframe.

Another scream, heavy with loss. Vengeful. A woman's cry.

Matsu Asayo's.

The realization was like waking from a vivid dream. Matsu Asayo, who'd thwarted her duel just that morning under Katsuchiyo's orders. Had Katsuchiyo ordered this as well?

Shiemi's eyes adjusted. The note was in jagged pieces. Blood splattered across the floor, leading outside. Her gaze rested on the gouges her claws inflicted on the nightstand, and a few bloody fleshy lumps. With fingernails.

Asayo wouldn't be drawing a bow anytime soon.

Shiemi stalked out into the cold night air. The sky was bright with the swollen moon. The wind pierced her nightwear, pricking her mind with the reminder that she was completely exposed. She loathed the thought of giving Asayo an opening, but she had to be sure.

The blood trail led into an alley, where it vanished. The would-be assassin was gone.

Above, a balcony door opened. Mirei leaned over the rail, white painted faces peering over her shoulder.

"Lady Shiemi!" she exclaimed. "What happened? Are you–"

She cupped her mouth. The others gasped. Aglow in Mirei's lantern, Shiemi realized she was splattered in blood, iron claws dripping on the cobblestone.

"Good evening, Mirei," she said. "You need better security."

When the headman arrived, Shiemi gave her statement, then watched the undertakers drag the bodies away. They wore nothing revealing their connection to Katsuchiyo. Kōza recorded them as "thieves" and asked no questions.

Part of Shiemi hoped Asayo would dare to return to avenge the injury. But even that yokel was not so foolish. Perhaps Asayo's orders were to assassinate Shiemi, but somehow she doubted that. It was more likely that Asayo had seized a chance to kill a hated rival.

No, the letter had been her actual goal. That's why she'd made a grab for it, after all. And that meant Katsuchiyo wanted it back.

Or destroyed. The fibrous paper was in ribbons, much of it missing. Shiemi couldn't read it if she wanted to.

But then, its contents no longer mattered, did they?

If Katsuchiyo was willing to go to these lengths to retrieve it, then the contents were damning. If he thought Shiemi knew whatever secrets it contained, then this would not be the last attempt on her life. Not a glorious redeeming death, but an obscure, shameful death by assassins' blades.

And she would endanger anyone nearby.

Guard that girl with your life.

Her worthless life. That was precisely what endangered Sute now. Indeed, anyone near her could get caught up in the violence. She could not risk that. Not with what Ichisuke had wished with his last breath.

Had Sute's guardians not stumbled upon the Forest-Killers, they would still be alive, and Sute would be on her way to her parents. Fate was cruel that way. Shiemi would never learn why Sute was special, or how Ichisuke recognized her. But such knowledge would be wasted on her anyway. She was racing toward a glorious death. She only hoped she could reach it before assassins brought her one far less desirable.

Shiemi bowed her thanks as Mirei placed a bundle in her hands. Travel supplies, and a pickled fruit breakfast, wrapped in a patterned blanket.

"You won't tell me what this is about?" Mirei tried one last time. She wasn't happy.

Shiemi remained silent. The less she knew, the safer she was.

"Then, what should I tell Sute?"

A warm wind. Seasons were changing. Green would turn to gold, and the southern plains would bring drums and banners.

"Tell her to obey the caravan guards," Shiemi said. "Tell her to remain with them until they reach Footnote Village."

"You don't want to say goodbye?"

The sun's first rays lit the southern path. The color of Sute's eyes.

Shiemi sighed. "If so, Mirei, I would always be saying goodbye."

CHAPTER FIVE

The trade road south was startlingly empty, even when traffic should have been at its highest. From the morning until Lady Sun reached her zenith, not another soul crossed Shiemi's path, not even a traveling merchant or a road patrol. It was as if no other soul existed in the featureless stretch of swaying grain, like she'd somehow crossed into Meido, the afterlife Realm of Waiting, without realizing it.

Abruptly the fields gave way to a wall of thick red-bark pines. Shiemi became engulfed in forest, thin shafts of sunlight raining on the dirt road before her. There were not many woods left in Lion lands, but she'd walked this wood before and knew it to be one of the thickest.

She was being followed. Her trackers – she knew not how many – were sloppy enough to be heard even this far ahead. But she continued her pace, giving no sign that she'd noticed, considering how she would handle them. A counter-ambush, perhaps? A direct confrontation, sword drawn and ready?

No. Better to learn about them first.

When the road forked, Shiemi took the less-maintained

herald path, one originally cut for scouts and mail carriers. The rocks would make it hard for her trackers to maintain their pace. She smiled. She'd have a good lead.

The path opened up before a sudden gorge. The forest continued on the other side, the tall trees entangled so that the canopy formed a thin ceiling of green needles. Beneath, the cavern yawned deep. If she tumbled in, they'd never find her body.

Two parallel ropes, one low and another suspended at chest-level, connected the opposite sides of the gorge. It was a simple two-rope bridge meant for scouts; one crossed by shimmying sideways, grasping the top rope and stepping on the bottom one. It had been erected in haste, a stopgap before the better bridge – on the path she hadn't taken – was constructed. Now it was abandoned, old, rotting.

There was no way she would cross those ropes. It was ridiculously unsafe. But she wagered her pursuers thought she might.

Donning her claws, Shiemi climbed the tree closest to the edge. She soon broke through the needle canopy and felt warm sunlight on her face. Tilting forward she gazed down into the ravine. She couldn't guess how deep it went.

Just fall.

An urge to let go. To spread her arms. To feel the wind.

Just fall in. Wouldn't that be better, to end with a flash of excitement, to strike the earth like a lightning bolt? It would be over quickly. Painless.

She didn't want the thoughts to make so much sense. But they did.

Do it. Just–

"Shut up," she growled.

Only the whistle of the wind through the branches. Only the singsong call of the bush warbler.

Carefully she reached across to the canopy on the other side. Gripping a branch, she swung, clinging to the second tree as it dipped from her weight. She felt like a water droplet suspended above a vast pool, her heart floating in her chest. But the tree righted itself, and when it stopped bobbing, she carefully made her way to the safety of the upper trunk.

Then she waited, watching the other side of the ravine. To follow, they would need to come out into the clearing. She'd get a good look at them.

And if they did use the two-rope bridge, she would wait until they were halfway across, then hop down and put her claws to the ropes. If this inclined them to answer her questions, she could confirm her suspicions, maybe even discover what was in the letter. If they said nothing, she would just cut the ropes.

Assuming they didn't just snap on their own.

The crunching approach grew steadily louder. She waited.

Two noodle legs with too-big sandals crashed out of the brush. Long tan sleeves and a mop of hair that shimmered red. A child.

Sute.

Shiemi nearly lost her grip. What was Sute doing out here? Had she run away from the caravan?

Of course she had.

Shiemi's blood boiled. Idiot rōnin! What could you entrust them with?

"Sute!" she shouted. "Stop!"

The girl halted, head bobbing about, searching. "Shiemi? Where are you?"

"Don't follow me! Go back to the House of Whispering Pines!"

Sute finally spotted her. "Oh. You're over there. Hold on." She gingerly tested the bottom rope for tautness with her sandal.

Shiemi's heart leapt into her throat. "No! Sute, it isn't safe!"

But the girl had already begun, gripping the upper line with both hands and shimmying sideways across the bottom. The ropes bowed as she inched toward the center, like a bow being drawn, and she the arrow.

Dammit! Shiemi bolted down the tree, unstrapped and dropped her claws, and sprinted to the edge, where the ropes were knotted around an ancient pine. Only now did she see exactly how moldy and frayed they were.

"I said, stop!" Shiemi barked.

Sute halted, dead center. She blinked obliviously, suspended over the death drop.

A sweat bead traced down Shiemi's cheek. She tried not to think about how, if Sute fell, she'd never find her body. "Actually, keep going. Just… just slowly, carefully…"

"I am!" Sute replied, rolling her eyes, and resumed.

At first, Shiemi thought the snap was a stick, signaling another intruder. But then came another, and several more. Her eyes darted to the opposite side, where frays in the upper rope were starting to break.

"Sute," she spoke, more urgently than she'd meant, "grip that rope and don't let go."

An echoing crack. Sute vanished into the ravine.

The rope went taut. It snapped. Shiemi dived. Her chest slammed into the dirt. Both hands clasped the rope. Hot pain seared through her palms, as if she'd gripped an iron rod right out of the forge. Violently jerked, her body kicked up dust as she was dragged, rapidly, toward the edge.

She jammed her knees and elbows down, pressing against the ground for friction. Dirt cloud stung her eyes. *Stop*, her mind roared. *Stop! Stop! Stop!*

She stopped, suspended over the edge of the ravine. The girl looked up, clinging at the bottom of the rope, swinging gently.

"Sute," Shiemi said slowly, trying to ignore the spearhead treetops far below, "do not panic."

Sute nodded. No expression. "I'm not."

You can panic a little! Shiemi thought. Did nothing bother this child?

She dug in her feet, seeking leverage. No good. Her elbows were on fire. Her back felt like it would snap. Any moment her body would fail. Even now, it begged her to let go. She gritted her teeth.

"You need to climb up," she said.

"I can't. I'll fall." No fear, just matter of fact.

"Use your legs," Shiemi instructed. "Tuck them to your chest. Hold the rope with your knees."

Incredibly, the girl did as instructed.

"Now, reach up with one hand, and pull."

She did, supporting herself by her knees, and then again with the other hand. A surprised smile flickered across her face. Realization, her body making the connections.

"That's it!" Shiemi encouraged. Her arms were numb, her legs shaking, but she kept her voice level. "Inhale when you reach, then exhale when you pull. Do not rush. You're doing well."

But she wished desperately that Sute was faster. Her strength drained with each tug of the child's movements. Any minute her arms would rip from their sockets, or her feet would lose hold and they'd tumble over, or the rope would slip, or—

Sute grabbed her arm. Shiemi stiffened. Using her for grips, Sute scrambled over Shiemi's shoulders and onto safe grass.

Shiemi let the rope go. She rolled back, gasping. Her arms were brittle sticks. She felt like they would break if she bent her elbows. Slowly she straightened, limbs shaking, and looked at her hands. Rope fibers, like thin needles, covered her palms. Blood beaded between thin slits on raw flesh. She couldn't move her fingers.

Sute bent over her. "That looks like it hurts!" she remarked. She blinked innocently. "You know there's a safer bridge not far from here, right? You should've taken that one."

Shiemi's eye twitched. *Just toss her off the cliff.*

After Sute plucked the fibers embedded in Shiemi's hands, she stomped into the woods and returned with an armful of thick roots, plants Shiemi didn't recognize. The girl twisted one in half, revealing a sticky, pale, pulpy interior. She rubbed the pulp against the flesh of Shiemi's palms.

They went numb. Shiemi exhaled a gust of relief as the pain evaporated. She leaned her head against a tree and closed her eyes, relaxing in the chattering pine needles and the echoing taps of distant woodpeckers.

When she opened them again, Sute was fiddling with her traveling kit, procuring a roll of cloth bandage from within. Shiemi whispered her thanks for Mirei's foresight. *May her ancestors bless her a thousand times!*

The child worked deliberately, whispering instructions, self-reminding. She did better than some medics Shiemi had known, people twice or even three times her age.

"Good thing I'm here to patch up my bodyguard," Sute remarked.

Shiemi grunted. "I am not your bodyguard."

Sute jerked the bandage. A cascade of needles pricked Shiemi's palm. "You promised!" she insisted. "You promised that man with the broken sword!"

His deflating body. Blood in the sand. His urgent face.

Guard her with your life.

She shook away the memory. "The Matsu make no promises."

"But you did promise." Sute leaned in close. "You promised with your eyes." Then she returned to her work, as if that was the end of that.

This child was definitely related to the Kitsu. Only Kitsu children were this weird.

Not that she had much experience with them. Younglings had only been entrusted to her care once before, and it hadn't gone well. But there were rumors about Kitsu children. They talked to themselves, drank lantern oil, and even chased the moon. Shiemi believed those rumors. The blood of feline yōkai pumped through their veins.

But Sute was right, wasn't she? Shiemi may not have spoken a promise, but she had made one, if only in her heart. They were Ichisuke's dying words. She could not set them aside. She felt ashamed that she'd even tried.

Yet that didn't change the circumstances. How could she care for a child when her sacred vow commanded her to seek glorious death?

They rested only long enough for a brief meal. Sute ate two of their three rice balls and the pickled fruits. Then they resumed their way along the thin path, Shiemi allowing Sute to carry her sword, which she managed with an unwieldy gait. Before long, she began to sing, some silly tune about a stumbling centipede.

Shiemi fully expected Sute to annoy her, yet she wasn't bothered by her skipping, her singing, or how she turned over every large stone they came across. It reminded her of her dōjō days, when all that mattered was getting stronger.

Before long, the shadows stretched across the road, and the rattle of cicadas overtook the songbirds' keening.

They set their camp away from the path, finding a small clearing that was near a thin stream. Shiemi had Sute gather kindling for a fire while she cleared away brush, then set her mind working on options for shelter.

Were they in an army encampment, the perimeter would be enclosed by a hemp curtain, a *jinmaku*, to keep out the elements and hide their numbers. Only higher-ranking officers would have tents. Unless they captured a temple or village, the rest shared their beds with crawling bugs on the hard earth, with only the open sky as their awning. The years had taught Shiemi to sleep this way, in a seated position. But Sute would need a bed, and shelter.

Unfolding the blanket and removing the drawstring, she fashioned a hammock between two trees. Then she removed her tattered outermost kimono, laying it across as further bedding. It had more holes than Shiemi had realized, but it would have to do.

By now the fireflies had begun their blinking dance. Sute's kindling pile was a decent size. While Sute hummed in the nearby stream, Shiemi struggled with her firestone and knife, scraping, trying to conjure a spark.

A loud splash, and Sute whooped victoriously. A cherry trout wriggled in her grasp. She grinned, holding it high. "I got one!"

Shiemi smirked. Sute had a few more surprises, it seemed. "Good job, little cub. You might be useful after all."

"Little cub?" Sute beamed. "Yeah, that's me. I'm little cub!"

A chuckle worked its way up Shiemi's throat. "Sure. But we'll be eating it sashimi-style if I cannot get the fire going."

"Can I try?" Sute asked.

The girl crouched by the kindling for only a few moments before smoke sprang from the wood. Sute cheered again as Shiemi disbelieved her own eyes.

They speared the fish through the mouth and blackened it by the flames. The cooked trout's skin peeled off in a sleeve, revealing pale opaque meat. It was dry, but fine with the last of the rice balls. Sute ate the lion's share.

"Where did you learn such woodlore?" Shiemi asked.

Sute gnawed the last bits from the bone. "My friend Kaoru."

"Ah. From back home?"

She shook her head. "No. She told me today."

Today? But there hadn't been another soul to cross their paths. An imaginary friend, perhaps?

The girl cast the bones aside. "Should I replace your bandages?"

Shiemi watched as Sute replaced the wrappings with deliberate movements, skill that far exceeded her age. The child paused now and again, as if listening to instructions. Was this "Kaoru" speaking to her now?

"Mirei called you a 'Deathseeker'," Sute said suddenly. "What does that mean?"

Shiemi looked up into a cloud of blinking fireflies. "It means

I'm atoning for a mistake. The only way to set things right is for me to die."

Sute thought about this. "Then why didn't you just jump off the cliff?"

"It doesn't work that way. It must be a meaningful death in battle. My death must win some victory for the Lion."

"Then why didn't you let that man kill you in the duel?"

A stab of annoyance. "I can't just let someone kill me. I have to try to win."

"Why?"

Her oath. Her pride. Because true warriors didn't cheat, no matter how unfair things were to them. How to convey these things to a child? How could she make Sute understand?

"Because that would be giving up. Because it would disrespect us both not to fight back. Because if I let him win, then he didn't earn his victory, and my death would be meaningless, absolving nothing." She took a deep breath. Her heart was pounding. She wasn't sure why.

"What did you do that was so bad?"

You should have died instead of them!

"Are you done yet?" Shiemi snapped. "Hurry up!"

Sute lowered her eyes and resumed her work. "Sorry," she murmured.

Shiemi braced against new guilt. It wasn't Sute's fault that she didn't understand. She was young. There was much about the world she just didn't know yet.

And even if she never knew, it would still not be her fault. True warriors did not need such things to be explained. They understood instinctively. All things acted according to their nature. Not everyone was born a warrior.

"I didn't mean to snap," she said. "I ... don't like to talk about it."

Sute nodded, finishing up. If her feelings were hurt, she hid it well.

"And besides, it doesn't matter. The only path for a Death-seeker is forward. There is nothing to gain from relentlessly dwelling in the past."

"But ... isn't that what you're doing?"

Shiemi stared into the flames for a long time.

"They should just forgive you," Sute murmured.

The heat of the fire reminded Shiemi of another campfire long ago, in a similar wood, where a story once tumbled from her teacher's lips.

Shiemi spoke. "These lands were once the domain of a rich lord. One day, the lord discovered one of his vassals was stealing from him. After some time, it was determined that a specific farmer was the culprit. The farmer claimed innocence, but the lord punished him anyway, taking the farmer's hands so he could never steal again.

"Without hands, the farmer could no longer work, resulting in a smaller harvest. The lord was made poorer, but even so, he felt vindicated that justice was done."

Sute looked incredulous. "Who cares about the lord's wealth? The farmer's life was ruined!"

"As you say. Several years later, the lord discovered that the true culprit had been one of his advisors, who had long since vanished. Thus, he had unjustly punished an innocent man. He summoned the farmer and apologized. But this did not console the farmer, for what could an apology return to him? So the lord had the farmer's hands returned. But what did that repair, as the flesh could not return to life? The lord had new hands crafted, golden hands, sparing no expense. But even this could not restore the farmer to wholeness, for though they glittered, they were unfeeling and lifeless. In the end, the lord had his own hands severed, then joined a monastery to live in atonement, for only blood can pay for blood."

Shiemi sat back, her story finished.

"So, did the farmer forgive the lord?"

Shiemi blinked. "Perhaps." She had not considered anything beyond the end of the tale. "But true atonement is the only thing that is just. Some sins cannot be forgiven."

She seemed to think about that. "But Ichisuke forgives you."

A cold wind pricked her flesh. She stiffened. "What did you say?"

"The man with the broken sword. The one who called you Rikuyo."

Shiemi stumbled to her feet. Her heart was pounding. Sute couldn't know that name. She couldn't!

Sute blinked. Oblivious. Innocent. "Ichisuke forgives you. He knows you didn't want to duel. He says it's not your fault." She tilted her head. "And I guess, if he can forgive you, then perhaps sometimes, one can atone enough!"

"It's time for bed," Shiemi whispered.

Sute shrugged and hopped in the hammock, leaving Shiemi standing with shadows at her back.

Shiemi didn't sleep. She sat against a tree and watched the fire die, listening to the crickets and Sute's snoring. The girl slept with her mouth wide open, elongated incisors gleaming in the dying firelight. Her words repeated in Shiemi's mind, over and over. She couldn't have overheard Ichisuke. She'd been inside during the duel. No, there was only one way for her to know what she knew.

The Kitsu family's connection to the feline *kitsu* people granted them a wondrous power, a power to invoke ancestral spirits. Those with the strongest connection could speak to the dead, casting aside the mortal veil to reach the Realm of Blessed Ancestors. They were known as "spiritcallers".

Only a handful in each generation were born with this gift. The Kitsu alone knew how to hone them, transforming them from simple mediums into full-fledged spiritcallers.

Now Shiemi understood why Ichisuke had uttered his last wish, why Sute's guards fought to their last breaths to protect her. She was a spiritcaller. She had to be. There was no other explanation.

And seeing her home, safe, was more important than whatever awaited on the Osari Plains. At least for now.

"Very well," Shiemi whispered, and turned back toward the fire.

CHAPTER SIX

Shiemi woke to a distant rumble. She must have dozed off just after the fire burned itself out. Her eyes adjusted to the dark. Her weapons were nearby. Sute slumbered peacefully in the hammock. Thunder echoed faintly, carrying the musky smell of rain.

Something was wrong.

She couldn't quite articulate it, but she'd learned long ago to trust her gut instinct, her *haragei*, when it told her danger was near. Even the crickets were silent, only the echoing patter of distant rain. Slowly she donned her claws.

Sute sat up, awake after all. She watched the dark. "We're not alone."

Shiemi turned a slow circle. No movement beyond the brush, no sound. Yet her haragei roared and spun like a rusted wheel in her stomach.

A blur burst from the brush. Sute screamed.

Shiemi spun, claws up.

A blast of air. Dust in her face. Fire in her eyes!

She stumbled back. Each gasp stung her nostrils. Her tears were acid.

Metsubushi. "Eye-closer." Pepper or ash powder, if she was lucky. But it could also be iron sands or ground up glass. The thought iced her blood. Blind, she'd be useless—

Solid weight slammed into her. Her legs gave way. Her cheek struck dirt.

Damn! Three attackers, maybe more? She couldn't keep track. Where was Sute?

Squinting through the burn, she caught glimpses of advancing blurry shapes. But they weren't pressing their advantage. She forced open the eye spared the brunt of the metsubushi. They were waiting, armed and armored. Across the lamellar plates, she barely spotted the character for "ax."

Forest-Killers. Of course! The woods would be infested with them. She and Sute were sitting ducks! How could she be so stupid?

She gripped her claws. Her hands were still injured, the flesh raw and tender. But she bit back the pain. Why weren't they attacking? Were they afraid?

Good. She'd make it simple for them. "Leave or die."

"A fair offer," a man replied.

That voice.

He appeared in her clearing vision, a middle-aged man in bard trappings. Ikoma Nakabara.

Beside him, Sute kicked and squirmed in a bandit's grip. "Let me go!" she screamed. "Let me go!"

"Calm down, little Sute," Nakabara soothed. "We are here to help you."

She screamed louder, thrashing wildly.

Shiemi's head spun. Nakabara was with the Forest-Killers? It made no sense. If he served Katsuchiyo's brother, as she initially guessed, then surely he could not be in league with bandits. The Lion's Pride would never endorse an honorless man.

Or perhaps he was just a turncoat deplorable bandit himself.

Sute's fist found the bandit's cheek. He swore and folded her arm against her back. Nakabara whistled. "I knew you had Kitsu blood, child, but maybe you've also got some Matsu."

Shiemi rose. Her left eye stung and was swollen shut, but she could still see from her right. "I hope you've lived a good life, bard."

He frowned. "I tried to warn you at the geisha house. You would not listen. You made your choice. Now, you can choose to walk away."

"And leave her to Forest-Killers?" Shiemi spat. "Fat chance."

His brows went up. "And I suppose your lord's clutches would be better? Can you really not see him for what he is?"

What did he mean by that?

He pushed. "I saw the letter. I know whose stamp that is. I know where you are taking her." His eyes steeled. "I will not let you."

Then the letter *had* pertained to Sute! But did that mean Katsuchiyo was in league with Forest-Killers? Did the Forest-Killers want Sute for some reason? Who exactly did Nakabara serve?

Did it matter? He'd thrown his lot in with bandits, followed her into the woods, and ambushed their camp. What did she care what his goals were, or who he served? She didn't need to know. She'd die before she let them have Sute, and by Matsu's ashes, she'd take Nakabara with her!

"If you do this," he said, "you play right into–"

Sute screamed. The bandit holding her burst into flames.

He collapsed soundlessly and burned.

Sute twisted away, unharmed. She hit the ground and bolted. Nakabara cursed and dashed after.

The bandits watched the flames roll off their comrade's body. Shiemi struck.

The first two fell like stalks of reaped barley. The others ducked back. A flash, a blur, and her arms came together. Bound. A tug, and she stumbled.

A rope weapon. She knew the kind, two weighted bulbs connected by cord. The bandit yanked. The coil tightened, lacing her arms with hot pain.

"Kill her!" he shouted.

The other hesitated, machete wavering, unsure. "We're supposed to spare her."

"That plan's wrecked!" the first shouted. "Do it!"

Death at a bandit's hands was not glorious, but it was still a death in battle. And if she could take them all in her final moments, that would leave fewer Forest-Killers to sow discord in Lion lands. It would be a good trade.

Except, if she died here, where did that leave Sute?

No. She wouldn't die here. Not yet.

"I'll do it!" Her captor cursed and, keeping one arm gripped around the rope, reached for her nodachi.

She waited until his hands graced the sword's handle.

She wrenched back with her full weight. The rope went tight, yanking him off-balance. He stumbled.

She rolled forward. He crashed into her, impaled on her claws.

She kicked his limp body away, freeing herself and then finishing him with a final slash. The remaining bandit seemed rooted to the spot, shaking, staring at her claws with horrified eyes.

She recovered her sword and approached.

He dropped his machete. "Wait! I'm not a Forest-Killer! None of us were!" He pressed his palms together, surrendering. "We're spies. We were doing our job when Nakabara called us here!"

Spies? Pretending to be Forest-Killers? Did he really expect her to believe…

Actually, that sounded like something an Ikoma might do. Such was their reputation. But this raised many questions. She voiced the first to spring to mind.

"Why?"

"The real Forest-Killers are working with a Matsu lord. Nakabara is trying to discover who."

Her mind leapt to Katsuchiyo, his letter plucked from a Forest-Killer's hands, his lackey sent to retrieve or destroy it. "If that is true, why didn't he just say that?"

"How should I know? He tells us nothing!"

Because you're peasants, she thought. The less they knew about such matters, the better. If an esteemed Lion leader made deals with bandits, especially the worst kind, it could shame the entire clan.

Of course, the pretend bandit disgraced the clan by even suggesting it. Some would kill him just for that.

"Please." Snotty tears streamed down his face. "I'm not ready. Please!"

Some, but not her.

"Go," she growled.

He bolted and was swallowed up by the woods.

Would she regret that? Would it come back to bite her? Maybe. But how could she kill someone unarmed and begging? She was no butcher.

And there were more pressing matters now.

Shiemi sprinted in the direction Sute had gone. Trees punched up in all directions, misshapen pillars in an endless hall. There was no trail to follow in the dark and the rain. But she had to try. She had to find Sute before Nakabara did.

But what did he even want with her? What was the child's connection to any of this? *I know where you're taking her,* he'd said. Did he think Shiemi was still in league with Katsuchiyo? Was he trying to take the child for his own lord? Shiemi had seen the child's powers firsthand, but how did anyone else know about her?

Dammit. The bard wouldn't shut up before. Now he was keeping secrets?

Then again, perhaps he'd never been as he appeared. He misled her, and she underestimated him. She'd never do that again.

And she wouldn't forgive him, either. It didn't matter whose side he was on. Her honor, her integrity and trustworthiness, was all she had left, and he'd jeopardized it.

And he'd jeopardized Sute. The child had no supplies and no defenses. Even if she could escape him, even if she could catch fish and start a fire, even if voices whispered in her ears, these woods hid countless dangers. It was perilous for grown adults! If she didn't find Sute, right now, there was no way the child would survive.

She stopped. The wood expanded into a kudzu grove, the vines and massive leaves carpeting the forest floor. No sign of anyone.

She called out. "Sute!"

Nothing.

"Sute!" More urgent. "Sute!"

Her voice echoed off the unmoving trees.

She kept running, kept shouting. Her cries bounced off the canopy, her own taunting voice. Her heart raced. Her head swam.

She didn't care. She called Sute's name until her throat was raw, heard nothing but the hammering of her heart, her voice fading as the woods spun around her, faster and faster.

She's gone. You lost her.

She fell. Her sword clattered into the brush. She sank to her knees.

You lost another one.

For a flash, she knelt before a tall dais, a small knife on a wooden stand glinting before her as dozens of eyes watched, expectant and judging. A woman cried for vengeance, for blood.

How many more, Rikuyo? How many before you finally come to your just end?

She collapsed. Rain filtered through the canopy.

If she held very still, perhaps her heartbeat would just stop. She should just lie here. Let the forest take her. Let the needles fall until they blanketed her body, let the kudzu entangle her and take her apart, piece by piece, until there was nothing, nothing and no one left, unwound and undone. She wanted to be nothing at all.

But when she closed her eyes, all she could picture was Sute, wondering why she was just lying there. And she swore she felt the brush of someone moving past, the faint energy of another sharing the space. Yet there was nothing there. Nothing and no one.

No one but her own voice, thudding in her head. *I can't just let someone kill me. I have to try to win.*

Her fingers dug into the dirt. Sute was gone. She'd lost again. Why not just die here?

Because that would be giving up.

That's what she had told Sute, just hours ago. Didn't she believe her own words?

Yes. She did.

She forced her leg beneath her and pushed herself into a kneeling position. Her eyes strained and stung, and her left was swollen shut, but she could still glimpse the winding kudzu, the pale trunks reaching up. She could still hear the wind scattering pine needles and hammering rain against the canopy above. She still had her senses. She could still draw breath.

So she drew one, until her lungs pressed swollen against her ribs, and shouted again.

"Sute!"

Her voice bounced off the trees, cascading, fading. Then silence.

"Shiemi?"

A round face peered from beneath a kudzu leaf. Timid, with wide golden eyes.

Alive.

Sute stood up from the kudzu patch, a large leaf stuck into her hair by its stem. Camouflage. Quick thinking.

The girl stomped across the patch and into Shiemi's chest, embracing her. Her arms whipped around Shiemi's flanks, tightening. Shiemi embraced her without a thought. Thunder rumbled low as she released a long breath. She thanked the Fortunes. She thanked anyone.

When had this happened? she wondered. When had she cared so much? The girl was stitched into her heart now. She couldn't let anything happen to her.

"Are you OK?" she asked.

She felt Sute nod. The girl didn't want to let go.

Had she been afraid? It seemed unthinkable. She'd never shown a hint of fear before now. Indeed, she'd done much of what Shiemi might expect of Matsu students, instincts a teacher might spend years trying to coax. Now they melted away, and she was just a young girl with her mop buried in her guardian's chest.

"We have to go," Shiemi insisted. "Grab my sword."

She did. Shiemi hoisted her onto her back. There came a stabbing pain in her midsection, but she ignored it. There were more important matters.

"You're hurt," Sute observed.

"I'm fine," she replied. "Can you hold on?"

Sute nodded. Shiemi sprinted, crashing through the brush. The rain picked up, breaking through the canopy in thick sheets. She relied on instinct, enduring the scrapes and battering of lower plants, keeping Sute above the brushline.

They couldn't risk returning to the camp. Others might be waiting there. It was a shame to abandon their supplies, but at least she still had her weapons. And Sute.

They would manage. What mattered was Sute was safe.

She stopped in a thicket to catch her breath. No sign of pursuers.

She didn't understand what was going on. But when one's mind and warrior instincts were aligned, one needed no explanations. Her own duty was clear.

"When we leave the forest," she said, "can you guide us to Footnote Village?"

Sute nodded.

"Good." She readjusted her grip. "Then hold tight. I am taking you home."

"Sute!"

A jolt. Nakabara's voice. From where?

There. Above, just visible on a cliffside, sleeves whipping crazily, his lantern setting his wrinkled face aglow. But he couldn't see them, not from this distance. His cries were consumed by the wind and rain.

"I can't hear him," Sute remarked.

Nakabara. The ambusher. The betrayer. A man without honor.

Shiemi turned away. "It does not matter what he has to say. He is a deceiver." She clenched her jaw. "I will kill him one day."

Sute squeezed. "Let's go."

One more chance, Shiemi. Don't blow it.

Shiemi carried the girl deeper into the woods. She didn't stop, even after Sute fell asleep against her back, her breath gentle and slow.

CHAPTER SEVEN

"Again," Shiemi commanded.

Sute, barefoot, stomped across the mossy log. Her gentle rakes and shin kicks were capped with pauses, except where her confidence shone through and they became one fluid motion.

Shiemi watched nearby, tending the fire beside the rushing cascades. The smell of roasting bamboo sprouts permeated over the bubbling of their thin stew of eagleclaw bracken, lemony knotweed, and angelica leaves. They could have done far worse, but Shiemi missed rice. *Patience.* A few more days, and they'd have real food again.

Her mouth watered. Rice. Fish. Real food.

Enough of that. She returned to observing Sute's form.

"You are still using your arms, little cub."

Sute blinked. "How else do I get my hands into position?"

"I mean, you are starting with your arms." She patted her stomach. "Your movements should start from the belly. Exhale when you strike, inhale when you withdraw. Like when climbing the rope. Find the rhythm."

Sute resumed the kata. It was still just choreography, shifting pose to pose without force or purpose. But she was catching on, and she wanted to learn. Patience and time would help. And she was growing stronger. She no longer strained to carry the nodachi.

"Does it feel right?" Fighting with the claws was essentially fighting unarmed. The principles were the same as the Tiger Claw Style.

Sute regarded the iron blades protruding from her wrists. They were a little big for her noodle arms. "It feels like doing those push-ups you showed me."

Shiemi's heart swelled. "That's because the punches are hidden in the push-ups. You've been practicing them all this time."

Realized connections danced across Sute's face.

I should have been a teacher, thought Shiemi. She had enjoyed these lessons over the last week. She pictured a dōjō full of Sutes, eager to learn, bright futures...

But then, the only reason she had anything to teach was her hardships, her sins. She wasn't worthy to guide the next generation. She wasn't worthy to be anything but what she was.

"Enough for today. Let's clean up and eat."

Sute nodded, extending her arms for help with the straps.

Shiemi stepped away to bathe in a shallow while Sute packed their things. It would not take long; abandoning the camp had cost them almost everything, and they'd had to scrounge and cobble together and make do with what they could find. But even meager tools were precious in the wilds.

With icy water splashing against her back, Shiemi wrung out her hair and thought about the men she'd killed days before. If the Ikoma had spies among the Forest-Killers, then those peasants risked much for the Lion. Something terrible could happen to them if they were discovered. That kind of risk for the benefit of the clan deserved respect.

She'd butchered them. Even if it was self-defense, it was still a loss for the clan inflicted by her hands. Could it have gone another way?

How pointlessly they threw away their own lives. What good did it do them?

She gasped at a cold splash against her bare neck.

Hadn't she been doing the same thing?

Until Sute. There was no glory in what she did for her. Death in this endeavor would not assure a victory; to protect Sute, to see her home safe, Shiemi had to live. This was not a task for a Deathseeker. And yet, in spite of their aching bones and their growling stomachs and nights spent mostly awake, didn't she feel more and more like someone she'd forgotten, someone she'd once been?

Shiemi finished and donned her undertunic, then returned to Sute. She found the girl hunched over her patchwork kimono, reading an old, stained letter, yellowed and grooved with a hundred creases. Sute must have discovered it in her kimono folds. Was she rummaging through her things?

At first, she thought it might be one of her death poems. But then she recognized the graceful dark calligraphy. She froze. She'd never let anyone else see that letter.

Sute noticed and guilelessly held it up. "Is this from your mom?"

Even after all this time, although the rough paper fibers were visible, and a portion had faded to indecipherable markings, the last words were still displayed as vividly as the day she received it: *come home, Rikuyo. We miss you so much. We don't blame you for what happened. We don't care what you've done. You can return to us at any time. Please, just come back home.*

Shiemi closed her eyes. She could almost hear those words spoken in her mother's voice.

"Do you miss her?" Sute asked.

"Of course I do. I even miss my idiot brothers." She smirked. "Whenever I would come home from the dōjō as a kid, which was only once in a while, Mother would make this rice and barley porridge with *shiso* leaf, and a steamed egg, because she knew it was my favorite."

Sute had gone wide-eyed and quiet. As though she were listening to something sacred, like an *agachi* bird's rare song, or the purr of a lion.

"I was a troublemaker, Sute. But no matter how much I messed up, they were always so happy to see me come home. Even if I was in trouble, Mother always made that porridge, just for me. And she and Father always supported me, defended me, even when I was wrong."

"Why don't you go home, then?"

A gentle current bubbled up inside her, through the calloused channels in her chest up into her face. She fought against the swell, clenching her jaw, as if to collapse herself, but she could not contain her trembling.

"I can't," she said. "I may want to. But I committed myself to a path, Sute. I cannot set aside my oath. I'd only have to leave again, and that would hurt them more. Better to make a clean cut whenever you can. Otherwise, I would always be saying goodbye."

But even after she'd folded the letter and tucked it away, even after they'd dressed and gathered their things and resumed their march across the teeming glens, Shiemi could still see her brothers playfully tussling in their narrow courtyard, still smell roasted barley and shiso leaf mixed with hot rice, and she heard her mother's soft voice carried by the crisp wind, calling for her to come home.

It was midmorning when the forest finally yielded to an abrupt hillside, the road dwindling beneath overgrown grasses. Sute broke into a run, nearly tumbling down the hill with Shiemi's sword. Her voice carried across the expanse, "We're home! We're home!"

Shiemi let the open wind brush her face for the first time in days.

Beneath her sprawled a verdant terraced valley. Tiered paddies spread across the hillsides, like the steps of a gold and emerald dais. Flooded sections shone like silver mirrors reflecting the sky. Figures hunched over and seeded these sections with sprouts drawn from heavy bags. Fog rolled across the receding slopes, emanating from a great river at the bottom of the valley.

The famous Three Stone River, Shiemi realized. Plays had been written about it, battles fought on its three banks. Within months the waters would be at their lowest, exposing the three boulders that gave it its name. For now, they were fast and high.

Clustered at the village's center was a complex of tightly packed houses with gabled roofs. The outermost were peasant huts raised on stilts, growing more elaborate as they reached the interior, culminating in a simple square flanked by a three-story building. A sake house, judging by the strings of red and indigo lanterns.

It seemed much the same as any farming community plucked at random from Lion lands. Yet there was something different about this secluded place, something she couldn't quite name.

"There!" Sute pointed toward the lower valley, near the winding river. There stood a square one-story building, with a thatched roof and open courtyard, elevated on a sloped foundation. "That is Father's estate," she remarked. "We're almost home!"

Beside it, against the riverbank, stood a two-story shrine. It was nonagonal, with two flanged rooftops in dark tile. Stone butterflies danced in relief across its bone-white walls, the visible supporting beams painted a contrasting midnight purple. It rose from a platform held aloft by numerous columns.

"Whose shrine is that?" Shiemi asked, masking her unease.

"Our family's," Sute replied. "That is the shrine to Emma-Ō."

The heavenly judge. The Fortune of Death.

Emma-Ō's domain was Meido, the Realm of Waiting. Departed souls appeared before him in his Court of the Patient, where he judged them according to their karma, to be sent to their appropriate realm of reward or punishment. Or perhaps to the karmic wheel, to be reborn.

For nearly half her life, Shiemi had sought honorable death. Now fate brought her literally to Emma-Ō's doorstep. The Fortunes enjoyed irony.

"The young lady is back!" came a voice from the flooded terraces. A crowd of farmers appeared, slowing as they caught sight of Shiemi. They knelt, eyes lowered in deference of her station. None spoke, not even to address her. They knew better. Samurai spoke first.

Shiemi looked to Sute. "Where is the headman?"

Sute met the question with a blank stare.

"The magistrate? The deputy? The assistant deputy?"

Nothing.

Shiemi sighed. Footnote Village, indeed!

"Everyone," Sute called out to the farmers, "this is Matsu Shiemi. She's my bodyguard."

They stirred, unsure, then opted for further deference, bowing even lower.

This is why every village needs a headman! Shiemi thought. But then, when had any samurai, other than their local lords, ever needed to come to such a remote place?

One dared raise his head. "Lady Sute, did something happen? We didn't think you were coming back, at least not so soon!"

Wait, what did he mean by that?

"Taki!" A woman in a patched kimono ran up the hill, coming to a halt before Sute. She bowed hastily. "My lady, where are the others? Where is Taki?"

"I'm sorry," Sute said.

The woman's expression cracked. She collapsed, like a felled tree. "No! Not Taki! No!" Her tears watered the grass. The others looked away.

Shiemi had nearly forgotten about the ashigaru that protected Sute. Taki must have been one of them.

The woman wailed, head back, pleading. Shiemi watched in a fog. She'd seen this before, in another place, another time, circumstances not unlike this one. She'd only watched back then. But now, could she do something?

"He died with honor," Shiemi uttered.

They all turned. The woman stared, wet-faced, red.

"He gave his life to save Sute's. They all did."

A new voice. Velvety and dark. "Then they will be rewarded in the next life."

Shiemi had never seen a priest of Emma-Ō before. She'd only seen depictions in plays: white robes, a thin *shimenawa* rope belt, rectangular shoulder armor, and a featureless mask hanging loosely like an amulet. They'd failed to capture the real thing's foreboding stark peacefulness. With her curtain of raven hair, porcelain face, and sunken eyes painted black, the priest looked like she'd crawled out of a tomb.

"Masumi!" came Sute's happy voice. She buried her face in a patch of embroidered butterflies, embracing the priest like a grandmother.

The woman's mouth twitched in a smile. "Hello, little Sute. What a surprise."

The priest helped the sobbing woman to her feet. "We will honor his memory," she said, her voice both eerie and comforting.

"What will I do?" the woman asked. "How will I care for our children?"

"A village's fate and a child's are the same," said the priest.

The others murmured their agreement. She wouldn't raise her children alone. They would support her. They would come together.

She bowed. "Thank you, Lady Masumi."

The woman regarded Shiemi with an appraising air as the villagers left. She felt naked in the woman's unblinking gaze.

"This is Lady Masumi," Sute introduced. "She serves my parents."

"I serve Emma-Ō," Masumi corrected. She bowed deep.

"Welcome, Deathseeker. A friend of little Sute is always welcome here."

Masumi listened to Shiemi's story without interruption. Or so it seemed; at times, she seemed only to be half-listening, dark eyes glittering as they followed the dust motes, or invisible shapes against the sitting room wall. The smell of agarwood incense hung like thick cobwebs. Perhaps that accounted for Shiemi's unease.

The guesthouse was just austere enough not to impede her sensibilities. It was a repurposed teahouse, a two-room hut in the manor's interior courtyard. Sute had run ahead to see her parents while Masumi led Shiemi to the bath, lent her a fresh change of clothes, and provided lunch. Shiemi accepted each offer as the sun crawled across the sky. She assumed she would be called upon by the manor's lords soon enough. They would want to meet the samurai who saved their daughter.

Yet she could not still her stomach's churning. Her arms remained goose-pimpled since crossing the threshold, and her mind stuck on certain details. For one, there were few servants in the manor, even for a rural samurai family. Entire sections were just empty, furniture pristine and unused. No matter where she went, the shrine to Emma-Ō was always within view, ever looming.

And curiously, a portion of the manor, a blackened, ruined wing that had partially collapsed, was blocked off by standing screens, like a bandage over a burn that was too small to hide the scars. Had there been a fire? Why hadn't this ruin been cleared away?

The priest refilled Shiemi's teacup as she finished her tale. "It is a good thing you happened by. To think Sute may be in the hands of Forest-Killers were it not for you." Yet she didn't seem particularly alarmed, pushing the teacup forward with an air of knowing. "What do you think they wanted with her?"

The tea was strong, bitter, with a hint of anise. Quite good, actually. "I had assumed it was because of her lineage. But perhaps you know better than I can guess."

Masumi stirred the contents of the kettle. "Yes, she is quite special, isn't she?"

"She's a Kitsu." May as well lay the cards on the table. "She hears spirits. She knew a name I left behind years ago. And I watched her set a man on fire by screaming, so yes, I'd say she's 'quite special.'"

"I see."

Stir, stir. There was no denying what Sute was, but perhaps the priest was considering how well Shiemi could be trusted. She waited until Masumi nodded to herself, setting aside the ladle.

"It is as you deduced. Sute is of Kitsu lineage. She was found on the riverbank as a baby. She was starving, the poor thing, but never cried. The wardens of this manor took pity on her, adopting her as their own daughter. Of course, soon her unique lineage made itself apparent."

Found by the bank of the Three Stone River. Had she floated down its current, abandoned or left to drown? Shiemi gripped her cup tightly. How could anyone do such a thing?

Masumi continued, "One day, some men came and made inquiries about lost children, asking if one had been found here. But the manor wardens distrusted those men and kept Sute a secret. Or perhaps they'd grown to think of her as their own, and so she was never 'lost.'" The woman shrugged gracefully, a rippling motion that made Shiemi uncomfortable for reasons she couldn't explain. "All inhabitants of Footnote Village swore to keep her existence a secret from outsiders, at least until she was old enough to be trained."

She remembered the farmers' hesitance. Perhaps this was why. Sute was a village secret. They hadn't known if they could trust her with it.

"Fortunately, there is little reason for outsiders to visit. Footnote Village is a newer settlement, founded just a few generations ago. It was established as a sentry point, to keep watch over the nearby mountains." Scorpion mountains. "But it was never finished."

"What happened?"

"War happened," she replied. "More important matters arose. This village was forgotten." She sighed. "How short our memory. The country is in ruins, but the mountains and rivers remain."

That didn't explain why Sute was so close to a war camp with only a handful of ashigaru for protection. Yet another question pecked her brain. "You said, 'the wardens' adopted her. Not, 'the lords'. Am I to understand Sute's parents are not the lords of this manor?"

She laughed. "Heavens, no! This manor and the surrounding farms belong to the illustrious Ikoma Ujitōya, although he rarely visits these days."

Shiemi knew the name. He was a famous diplomat with a prestigious lineage, who was arranged to marry the great warrior Matsu Yunaki until the current Matsu daimyō won her heart. Ujitōya even had a child with her out of wedlock, although their combined reputations squashed any resulting scandal.

"However," the priest continued, "Sute's parents are Lord Ujitōya's seneschals. They rule in his absence."

Something wasn't right. Why didn't this priest call them by name? Why did she get the sense information was being withheld? Had she not earned the woman's trust? Was she not an honored guest?

"May I see the Most Honored Lords?" she risked, defaulting to the most formal mode of address in the absence of a proper name.

"Perhaps, if Sute accompanies you."

A flicker of annoyance. Of course she expected to be introduced!

"I have offended you," Masumi remarked. "Rest assured, my lords will see you soon. For now, they wish to see to their daughter's welfare."

But why keep her waiting? It was not as if Footnote Village was particularly bustling. How busy could they possibly be?

It was because she was a Deathseeker.

She was familiar with such polite excuses. Few lords wished to meet with such controversial and unpredictable figures. She'd severed herself from her lord; she could be anyone, have committed any crime, be disreputable...

"It is nothing you've done," Masumi said suddenly. "The time is simply not right."

Shiemi's ears burned. How could this priest read her thoughts so easily?

"In the meantime, please stay in this guesthouse."

She shook her head. She didn't deserve such finery. "A room in your stables will be fine. Or–"

"That would displease my lord." Masumi refilled Shiemi's tea.

She wasn't sure if the priest meant Sute's parents, or the Fortune of Death. "A Deathseeker spurns material comforts, only the blanket of her guilt–"

"Guilt is a sword you give your enemy." Masumi stirred the dark liquid. "Is it not true that Kirifu's oath absolves the Deathseeker of their sin? Are they not forgiven?"

"Only ancestors can do that."

"And not mortals. Which includes you, Shiemi. Yet you seem to be your harshest judge. If the goal was to deprive yourself of life's comforts, why commit yourself to this path, instead of simply walking away?"

Shiemi bristled. "Perhaps I could have, but what good would that have done?"

"Ah. So, this is simply about balancing the ledger. Making it up to your lord."

Shiemi slammed down her cup. "My lord had nothing to do with this! He tried to talk me out of it! He–"

He'd said that it wasn't her fault. That even if she had been there during the attack, she would just have died with the rest of them.

What was this woman's game? What was she trying to prove?

Shiemi breathed slowly until she could speak again. "A lord does not ask for one to become a Deathseeker. It is a path one chooses for oneself. I chose this for redemption. Only death will wash away what I've done."

Masumi was smiling. "I know little of this 'Deathseeker' tradition. But I know much about the Fortune of Death. My master judges souls not by how they died, but how they lived."

Shiemi could say nothing. Outside, the moon had just begun to appear over Emma-Ō's shrine.

•••

Tapping at the guesthouse door woke Shiemi from her restless dreams. Old habits had her reaching for her claws before she remembered she was a guest in another's home.

It was Masumi. Her white kimono and glowing green lantern made her seem like a ghost in the night-cloaked courtyard. The mansion was dark. No servants.

"Do you wish to see Lord Ikoma now?"

Shiemi squinted down at the sleeping *yukata* she'd been provided. *Now?* They would receive her like this?

The woman's look suggested something was amiss. This wasn't a question. It was a strong suggestion. Covert urgency.

And like that, she was wide awake.

"Should I bring anything?" she asked, flicking her eyes pointedly to her sword.

"That won't help, I'm afraid."

Well, that was concerning.

Shiemi followed the woman in silence, through and out of the manor, into the night. The river was high, and she could hear the crashing waters, even though she could not see them in the distance. With growing dread, she recognized the spindly path leading them to the Shrine of Emma-Ō, passing under the torii arch and the row of stone lanterns. But instead of inside, Masumi led her around to the back, where another stone arch led into a bordered unlit garden.

Or so she thought, at first. When her foot struck a cut stone, and her eyes finally adjusted beyond Masumi's lantern, she recognized the close-clustered grave markers. Stone pillars and flanged sculptures rose beside flat wooden slats, forming narrow paths through the twisting pines and wild ferns.

"You said this village was new," Shiemi whispered.

"These tombs predate the village," Masumi explained.

Tombs containing ancestral ashes were afforded only to especially important samurai. Otherwise, the urn was buried beneath the marker. If this was a mausoleum, then there must be some signature of the heroes buried here, some sign…

Candles flickering ahead. Shiemi halted beyond their reach, spotting a thin form hunched over a web of incense smoke. Sute.

Before her were two graves, marked with stacked stones carved into a likeness of the shrine to Emma-Ō. Although there were no names identifying these markers, Shiemi still knew, with a sinking in her belly, that these were the graves of the manor's seneschals. Sute's parents.

The girl never mentioned that her parents had passed. On several occasions, she'd even referred to them as though they were still alive.

But then, the dead weren't truly gone for the Kitsu. Not when they whispered in one ear or appeared when they were summoned. At last, Shiemi understood why the girl didn't cry over her dead servants, why she didn't even flinch as warriors were cut down in her presence. She saw them still, heard their voices, felt their presence. She wasn't cold, as Shiemi first thought. She was haunted, in every sense of the word.

Shiemi's nose wrinkled at the smell of burning juniper and buckthorn. Tiny flares arose from the kindling at Sute's knees, falling stars in reverse. It wasn't incense burning in the offerings bowl, but herbs. Sute breathed them deep.

"Don't interfere," Masumi warned. "It can be unpredictable."

"What can?"

The candles burst. Flames poured from their wicks like torches, more fire than a mere candle should emit. The heat brought sweat beads to Shiemi's forehead, even at this distance. Smoke poured from the offering bowl, enveloping Sute in a black shroud. Her silhouette craned within the smog, and for a flash, her hands appeared clawed, and her shadow became something feral, something feline.

"How is she doing this?" Shiemi gaped. "You said she wasn't trained!"

"By instinct." Pride shone in Masumi's eyes. "She is very special."

The flames coalesced into a bonfire before shifting hue to a sickly green. Within, forms wriggled to the surface, the light reflecting, focusing, as if shaped by hundreds of invisible tiny mirrors. Shiemi blinked, and two bodies appeared in the fire. Indeed, they were the fire; ember sparks were their eyes, flame ribbons were their elegant robes. A man and a woman. The depiction of a riding crop gently glowed on their clothes. The man looked stern and quiet, while the woman's face shone with her despair.

"Sute?" The ghost's voices were the crackle of the flames.

Matsu's ashes, Shiemi swore. The girl summoned her own parents.

"Mom! Dad!" She bounced in her seat. "I missed you so much! I have so much to tell you! I met a Deathseeker! And we went to a geisha house and met a really nice lady. And I'm learning to fight with iron claws!"

The ghosts exchanged somber looks as Sute gushed. "But Sute," the voice of her mother's spirit echoed, "why are you here?"

She hesitated. Her head lowered. "To apologize. I didn't mean what I said. I–" Her voice trembled, then burst. "Please, I want to be your daughter again. Please take me back!"

Shiemi's heart fluttered. Sute always seemed so aloof, so playful, so stoic. How had she missed this pain she'd been carrying?

Sute's father grew brighter, concerned. "Sute, you were not sent away as punishment! Our duty was always to protect and raise you until you were ready. We love you dearly, but your destiny is among your own kind. That is why you were sent to the Kitsu Tombs, to become a spiritcaller and claim your birthright!"

The farmer's words from the morning came flooding back in a cold shock: *We didn't think you were coming back.*

Because she wasn't supposed to.

Sute's ashigaru guards were escorting her, covertly, to the Kitsu. They were ambushed before they reached their destination. Sute wanted to come home, against her parents' wishes. And Shiemi had never questioned it. Not once.

Nakabara's voice echoed in her head. *I know where you are taking her. I won't let you.*

Shiemi, you fool. Nakabara wasn't the kidnapper. You were.

Her mother's face twisted in the fire. "Sute, it's not safe here! You are in grave danger the longer you remain."

"I don't care!" Sute leapt up. "I just want us to be together again! I don't want to be a Kitsu! I want to be Ikoma!" She held out her arms, a child to her mother. "Please! Don't leave me behind!" Sute reached for them, but recoiled with a gasp, clutching her burnt fingers.

The woman sighed. "Sute, my treasure, you cannot."

"You must move on," the father insisted. "For the good of the family. For the good of the Lion! You must meet your destiny! Keep the promise we made for you."

Sute leapt to her feet. "I said, *I don't want to!*" Tears streamed down her face. "Everyone wants to get rid of me! I don't belong anywhere!"

She ran, kicking away the offering bowl. The ghosts extinguished. The fires shrank back to mere candlelight. Sute vanished into the maze of grave markers.

Shiemi already made to follow. It was instinct; she didn't know what she would say, or how she could make things better, or if it was even her place to try. But she could not leave the girl alone in such a state.

Masumi's arm on her shoulder. "That is dangerous."

Shiemi wrenched out of her grasp. How could this woman call herself Sute's guardian? She was just a child. She needed counsel.

Sadness washed over Masumi's features. "She is haunted by her ghosts. There are so many. Must you add yours, Deathseeker?"

What did this emotionless priest know about not belonging? What did this pampered lady with her fine teas and long-winded philosophies know about being cast aside? All this pain Sute dragged with her, and did anyone help her to carry it?

She spoke through clenched teeth. "The strength of the Lion is in her pack. I won't abandon her like you did."

Masumi smiled. "Then go."

Shiemi ran, heart pumping faster with every forward push.

CHAPTER EIGHT

Sute was not hard to find, even in the web of distorted shadows. She had crawled between the legs supporting a large stone lantern and hugged herself beneath it. She cried into her knees.

A dozen thoughts battled for dominance in Shiemi's mind.

She lied to you! Used you! Just like Katsuchiyo!

She's hurt. She missed her family. She wanted to see them again.

Shiemi didn't care if Sute had lied. The lie had brought them together. And how could she be angry with a sobbing girl who just wanted to go home?

Sute finally noticed her. Wet amber eyes glittered, peeking over her knees. "Go away."

Not a chance. She knelt beside the lantern. It was too small for her to crawl through, and Sute was too far in to reach. She would have to coax her out. This was no place for either of them.

But Shiemi could not think of anything to say. She'd spent so many years hammering herself into hard iron claws. Could she remember how to be soft?

Let her talk about it. She needs to.

"When did it happen?" she asked.

Sute sniffed. "Weeks ago. They wanted to send me away. They said I had to live with strangers. They didn't want me anymore." Guilt tore across her features. "I got so mad. I said I hated them. And then... the light..."

The false Forest-Killer in the glen, face locked in surprise as he burst into flames.

The burned-out shell of the manor. Had that wing been the seneschal's quarters?

"It was an accident," she whimpered.

So. That was how her parents died.

Children with the shugenja's gift could not control their own power. Accidents happened. Wasn't that why they were trained in the wilds, away from towns and villages? Wasn't this why the Kitsu kept their kin in deep tombs, away from prying eyes? Yet here, without anyone to teach her control, what other outcome could there be?

In the dōjō, a student went years before they even touched a live blade. An armed and untrained student was a threat to everyone. But a shugenja's weapon could never be sheathed. Calamity was inevitable. They adopted her anyway.

They must have truly loved her.

Shiemi spoke the words her lord had once told her. "It wasn't your fault."

It didn't work then. It didn't work now. Sobs wracked Sute's tiny frame. "I'm bad. I'm evil. I burn everything." Hot tears anointed the dust. "Everyone wants to get rid of me. No one wants me. I should just go away."

Cracks spidered across the callused flesh of Shiemi's heart, lancing her, robbing her breath. In that instant she was once again hovering over the forest cliffside, looking down at Sute as she swung from a tether in her failing grip. And she knew that tether was slipping, and if she did nothing, the girl would fall into that abyss, never to be found.

You're wrong, came her desperate thoughts. *Someone wants you. Someone does.*

Show her.

Shiemi crawled down and extended a hand into the hollow beneath the statue. "I'm reaching for you, Sute. Come to me. We'll talk about what to do next."

Sute sniffed. For a moment, she almost looked hopeful. "Can I stay with you?"

That tide, bubbling up inside her, grew cold. No. That wouldn't work. She was a Deathseeker. Her oath was to throw herself into the thickest fighting, to incur the risk herself so others did not have to. Her path was no place for a child to grow. Nothing could thrive in that parched soil.

The girl's face scrunched in pain. "You don't want me either."

No! You will lose her! "Sute," she began.

"Just shut up!" Sute slapped her hand away. "Leave me alone! I don't need anyone!"

She was gone. She scrambled out on the other side of the lantern, vanishing into the tangle of graves.

Shiemi darted up. Where had she gone? The graveyard extended in all directions. She chose one and ran, calling out for Sute. Her calls bounced back at her, a cascade of desperate voices.

One should never call a name in a graveyard. That's what her peers at the dōjō used to whisper in her childhood. Someone with that name might think you were calling them. They might crawl their way back from the realm of the dead.

She didn't care. She called for Sute, again and again. She

panted fog as she darted among the markers. Something was different now. Wrong. The air tasted funny, like stale water.

And there was new light. Hundreds of pinpoint tears in a paper screen. Fireflies holding still. Or embers. Only they cast the stone tombs in ghastly purple. And they grew, slowly, until they were glowing orbs floating, lighting the fog that exhaled through the dust.

Where was the stone lantern? Where was the graveyard entrance, or the shrine to Emma-Ō? Featureless stone teeth jutted out and stretched out in all directions, and she was at the center of its maw.

She had to find Sute. She couldn't abandon her. Not now.

That didn't stop you last time.

Her veins froze at the voice. The same inner voice whispering to her all these years, a faint background urging that she tried to bury deep inside.

It was her own voice. Perhaps younger.

Hold your face under.

Just fall. Just let go.

It was stronger now than it had ever been.

And then came the memory, and Ichisuke's voice. His words were burned into the surface of her heart. She'd been known as Rikuyo when he'd spoken them.

"*I think it is a good first assignment,*" he'd said back then. "*I'll rest well knowing my* doshi *will be there when my niece is born. She will be in good hands.*"

But she hadn't been there, had she?

Two figures coalesced in her sight. They were made of glowing smoke, gentle and cruel. It stung to behold them, but she couldn't close her eyes.

One was Katsuchiyo. Before he was a lord, claiming only the lofty rank of hatamoto. His handsome features were chiseled from the smoke, his charm pouring like the fog trails rising from his elegant hair. He'd always been so good at hiding what he was.

The other was a young woman with bright eyes. She wore the lamellar armor of an honor guard and radiated the excitement of the newly adult on her first real assignment, of a future stretched out before her. So naïve. So hopeful.

So stupid.

Had she really ever been that dumb? Seeing herself like that was like swallowing needles.

Because she knew what came next.

She was saying something to him. Basically skipping, bouncing even. Her eyes sparkled when she looked at him.

"Don't do it," Shiemi whispered. "It's not worth it."

But the post was so boring. Nothing ever happened this far from the front lines. What harm could it do?

His mouth moved elegantly. Shiemi couldn't remember what he'd said back then. Just that it made her blush, and her heart flutter with longing.

"He's lying," Shiemi hissed. "He's false."

But she didn't know that back then, did she? And besides, he was her superior. Couldn't she trust him?

Shiemi's fingers curled against the ground. Grasping to hold the world still. "Stay at your post. Stay there, you idiot. By Matsu's ashes, stay at your post!"

The woman took his hand. They vanished, cruel laughter in their wake.

She was the lone survivor of her unit. Not because she fought off the infiltrators. Because she wasn't there.

She'd expected a harsh punishment. Her lord took away her position and reassigned her to a distant post, one where she couldn't cause any more problems. It didn't seem like enough, not for the blood on her hands, or for everyone she'd failed. Her family. Her unit. Her best friend, Ichisuke. His newborn niece, the other lost children… and herself. She begged for something worse. But her lord was not swayed. The loss was not her fault, he'd said. The ambush had been so sudden, so remote. Had she remained at her post, wouldn't she just have died with them?

But wouldn't that have been the right thing to do?

She pressed her cheek against the cool ground. The underworld was down there, a realm of the dead, the resting place of those she failed. If only she could sink down to join them, down into that breathless dark.

It was Katsuchiyo who had mentioned the Deathseeker oath. That path had not occurred to her until he had said it. It was a good excuse, nice and convenient. Her lord tried to dissuade her, but he couldn't do anything once she'd taken the oath. Tradition bound his hands. He had to let her go.

And so, in a way, she *had* died that day. Had anything been the same since? Alone she'd haunted the cities and countryside, seeking the only thing she thought would redeem her. That was why she returned to Katsuchiyo, again and again. It was why she'd protected him with her testimony. He'd promised her, over and over, that if she served him, this time she'd find what she was looking for.

But even that had been a lie, hadn't it?

"I'm sorry."

This time, the voice had come from outside her own head. A woman's voice, oaky but young. A voice that once belonged to her. Looking up, Shiemi saw her own face staring back down. Tears traced down the young woman's face, comets falling from dark skies.

"*I failed you,*" the phantom Rikuyo said. "*I failed everyone.*"

Her voice, the old her, sounded so much like Sute's.

"Of course you did," she told herself, her past self. "You were just a dumb kid. A fool. You didn't know what you were doing. You didn't know–"

Her brow furrowed. That was true. She didn't see what was happening, back then. She didn't have what she had now. Experience. Insight. Years spent trying to make up for her misdeeds. Peasants that she pulled out of villages under attack. Hurt victims that she'd brought to monasteries. Drunk ruffians that she'd thrown out of Mirei's sake house before they could hurt anyone. Vanguard charges that gambled with her life, she'd taken so others didn't need to.

And now, she wasn't the same. Not the same person. That idiot, that lazy worthless fool that she had once been… that wasn't her now. Wasn't that the point of the oath? To cast aside all distractions and recommit oneself to a life of service for the clan? For others? Hadn't she struggled and clawed her way for all these years so that she could be better?

A wry smile wormed its way onto her face. The old Deathseeker in Katsuchiyo's camp… he'd been right all along. She hadn't truly embraced the Deathseeker tradition. She'd been embracing her own guilt.

And if she had died that day, what would have become of Sute?

She sat up, slowly. Her thoughts were sluggish, muddy, but a shaft of filtered light just barely broke through the fog of her mind. A clear thought. It was the Deathseeker path that had led her to that clearing at that exact moment. It was what allowed her to protect an innocent soul.

"Guard her with your life, Rikuyo."

She gasped at the familiar voice, emitting gently from a being of rolling flames nearby. Akodo Ichisuke. But as she once knew him; young, smiling, with joking eyes. Her doshi, dōjō sparring partner, friend and rival in equal parts. A sacred bond for life. And, perhaps, death as well.

Had Sute inadvertently summoned him? Or had his spirit followed her all this way, and by being in this place, been granted form? Shiemi didn't know. Did it matter?

Her chest tightened. She couldn't bear his smile. She looked away.

"How can you forgive me?" she asked. "I ruined your life. Our reputations were linked. I shattered your family, then I killed you. How can you just let that go?"

The ghost stared at an invisible horizon. Faint cherry blossoms blinked into existence, just to fall and vanish where the ghost faded away. "Seeds have no say where they are planted, they can only grow. Scattered leaves sometimes clash in the icy wind; they have no say where they are tossed. Destiny crossed our paths, fate set us against one another. In another life, another world, we would have remained friends."

"Yes. That is the life of samurai."

Ichisuke had made peace with that. He lived in accordance with his principles. His death was cast from the moment he drew his first breath, for every choice he made was the only choice his code would allow. Just as it was for her when their paths crossed.

He asked her, "How then can you blame yourself?"

Clouds parted from the heavy moon. The graveyard was bathed in silver.

That made a sort of sense, didn't it?

The graveyard wasn't endless anymore. A bonfire of purple light blazed among a tight cluster of markers down the path. Sute would be there.

"Help her," he said.

She didn't reply. She didn't need to. The Matsu spoke no promises. But they made them, if only with their hearts.

The orbs had grown from pinpricks to melon-sized fireballs. They floated on an invisible breeze, rotating around the circumference of the clearing. At its center, Sute sat in a crumple, bathed in a sickly violet glow. The spinning orbs cast shadows across her feral features, a nose padded in leather, a split lip with elongated fangs, hair billowing like a lion's mane. Whether this was a trick of the flickering light, Shiemi could not say. But her martial instincts roared for her to wrench Sute away from the flames.

She reached for her.

Fire. A hundred burning hornets.

She recoiled. It was like a furnace. How could Sute stand to be within it?

The girl lowered her head. "I'm no good," she whispered. "They are right not to want me. I should just go away."

Shiemi reached again. An orb swung by her, blinding her, scorching her face. They were growing brighter, hotter. Sweat beaded on her forehead. An explosion in slow motion.

"They're just thoughts," Shiemi whispered. "They can't hurt you."

Sute looked up. Behind the feline features, her sad amber eyes were without hope. "Why should anyone want me? I'm bad. I've never done anything good."

"You're wrong!" Shiemi shouted, and dove in.

Fire raked hot claws across her skin. Her vision bleached in the pain. The muscles in her chest were wrenched so tight, she thought she would tear in half.

But she swallowed the pain and pushed, falling forward, until her searing arms wrapped around the girl's thin shoulders, bringing Sute into her chest, drawing her into an embrace. The girl stiffened in her grasp. Stunned.

A door opened inside her. Words tumbled out.

"I wanted to die until I met you," she confessed. "I was the one who was lost in that wood. You are the one who found me. And you made my life better just by being in it."

At once, the lights extinguished.

Sute buried her face into Shiemi's shoulder. She felt the girl's trembling, her wet tears, her thin fingers digging into her kimono. She held her there, not caring how long it took, until Sute's sobs slowed and quieted, and the girl finally pulled back to look up into her face.

The feline features were gone. Just a girl with mussed up hair and wet eyes the shade of honey.

"I'm sorry," Sute whispered.

Shiemi looked up to the entrance of the graveyard. Masumi's lantern glowed there. Somehow, they'd only wandered a few yards within. For a flicker of a moment, she swore she could see the fading afterimage of the Ikoma seneschals smiling at them both.

"We cannot undo what we've done," she told the girl. "But

neither can we retreat. Our ancestors... your parents... they guide us. They leave us a world that is the result of their best efforts. It may be a broken one, but what are mistakes if not lessons? Their suffering is a gift to us. How shameful it would be to cast it aside!"

Beyond stood the specter of the woman she had once been. Young. Impulsive. So sure of herself. Full of knowledge, but no insights. Of course she'd mess up. She didn't know what she was doing. She didn't have what Shiemi had now.

Don't waste it, she seemed to say. *Don't waste what I gave you.*

"But I can never make it up to them," said Sute.

"Perhaps not," she agreed. "But you can do better. If only a little bit. There is no stain so dark that it cannot be cleansed by the right action. If there is one way toward redemption, it is to achieve a lasting victory before you are gone.

"That is the oath I swore... If you swear it too, swear to live for the benefit of others and be better than you once were."

"I do. I will." Sute sniffed and rubbed her nose with her knuckle. Her face shone resolutely. "I'll master this, so that it never hurts anyone again."

The vision of the woman Shiemi once was bowed before fading away. She couldn't bring herself to hate her anymore.

Your job is not to condemn. It is to learn. It is to walk. Forward.

If the dead had already forgiven her, she didn't require anyone else's forgiveness. She required her own. Failure was an event, not a state one remained in. Redemption was not the glorious death waiting at the end. It was the path itself, the striving for one final victory.

What mattered wasn't how she died, but how she lived. And for the first time in ages, she wanted to live. What an unfamiliar feeling, wanting to go on, to do something great with her brief time.

She laughed. Sute watched, confused at first. But then came that toothy grin, as if she understood the joke.

Death was not the goal. The goal was a better future. Not the glory earned, but the victory won. That was the true way of the Deathseeker.

It had only taken all her life to discover it.

Shiemi carried Sute beneath the torii archway, hearing her gentle sighs as she slept. Her bones ached and her steps dragged. Perhaps she would sleep until lunch, or let an entire day pass, like she had when she was Sute's age. When had she ever felt this tired? But it was a good tired, she admitted.

Masumi stood at the manor's edge, looking up. Shiemi stopped beside her. At first, she thought the priest was watching the sky. But then she glanced at the surrounding terraces and saw little pinprick lights on the hill, past and above the village cluster, near the tree line. She could barely make out the flutter of banners, and the taut hemp of a jinmaku, a war curtain.

An army encampment.

Masumi procured a small scroll from her robes. Shiemi's heart sank at the emblem of Matsu Katsuchiyo.

"This is for you," the priest remarked. "I think it might be urgent."

CHAPTER NINE

Katsuchiyo had written the letter himself. Shiemi recognized the brusque writing, thick-brushed and oppressive, slathering the page from corner to corner. Normally he would rely on his war poet to write something suitably artful and threatening. But this letter was in his own words, by his own hand. It was a reminder of their shared history. *"I honor you with my toil"*, it suggested. The first barrage, meant to lower her guard.

He knew about the requisitioned sword. He knew about the rations. That was his justification for marching his forces into his neighbor's province; he called it "an insult he could not overlook". Her mind conjured Ashi's grin, his callused hands presenting the nodachi. She hoped he escaped punishment.

Katsuchiyo had no choice but to attack, the letter insisted. After all, they were sheltering her, a traitor and a thief. But he was willing to spare Footnote Village if she instead came to him. He wanted to meet on the flooded paddy fields near the top of the hill, giving him the high ground. She had until sunrise to stay his hand. He warned her to come alone.

All things considered, it was a very convincing letter.

It was also a bluff. There was no way he would attack Footnote Village. If he did, he would be drawing a second, unrelated lord into his border conflict. He hadn't the forces to fight on two fronts. And he would lose the moral edge; the attack would be unprovoked, painting him as the unjustified aggressor. He'd lose all clout in his bid to lead the family. He wouldn't risk that.

But could she ignore him? At the House of Whispering Pines, he'd proven that he could get to her without an army. He would try it again. She thought of Masumi, of Sute slumbering in her bed. There could be collateral damage.

Why was he here at all? Why such a risk? Just to intimidate her? This couldn't just be about the requisitioned sword and some rice balls. What did he think she knew?

She stared through the guesthouse window at the early morning sky. Sunrise. She'd ask him directly then.

A gentle rap. Masumi at the door. Twice in one night?

A curt bow. "A visitor to see you." Straightening, she cast a look that might have been apologetic. "Just remember, Sute is sleeping. Shouts will disturb her." She stepped away before Shiemi could question.

Replacing her in the doorframe was Ikoma Nakabara.

Shiemi crossed the room in two strides. She tore her greatsword from its sheath. Steel flashed a brilliant arc toward Nakabara's neck.

She stopped the blade a hair's breadth away.

The old man didn't flinch. He didn't even break his gaze.

He'd have let me take his head. They stared at one another, a thin barrier of razor-sharp steel between them.

"You missed," Nakabara said.

"I stopped."

He shrugged. "Same difference."

Shiemi stepped back and lowered her sword. Such conviction demanded to be heard out. Still, she never took her eyes off him.

"Thank you for sparing my agent," he said, looking over the room. "Although I wish you had spared the others. We've been infiltrating the Forest-Killers for almost a decade now. They are difficult to replace."

"You are the one who attacked without provocation," Shiemi refuted. "Or explanation."

"We misjudged each other. So let us drop the veil." He crossed his arms. "Are you still in service to Lord Katsuchiyo?"

Why hold back? Keeping secrets was what led to this. "I never truly served him. I fought for him occasionally throughout the years, but Deathseekers follow only their oath." A thought occurred. "You serve his brother, then?"

"I serve the Lion," Nakabara said. He shrugged again. "But it is perhaps most accurate to say that I serve Lord Ujitōya. He sends his regards, by the way."

The same name Masumi had mentioned. So they served the same lord. "Why didn't you say this before? At the House of Whispering Pines? In the woods?"

"My orders," he replied. "I could tell no one outside the operation. That, and I couldn't be certain you weren't still in Katsuchiyo's service. The matter is delicate."

"But now you have permission?" Her eyes narrowed. "Explain."

"For years, my lord suspected a predominant Matsu was working with the Forest-Killers, turning a blind eye to their activities for his own gain. Recently he suspected the same lord might be hiring Forest-Killers as mercenaries, to sow discord in the realms of his rivals and conduct activities that would be difficult to trace back to him. He is now confident that lord is none other than the Matsu daimyō's own brother, General Matsu Katsuchiyo."

Shiemi nodded. "It's true. I encountered Forest-Killers when I rescued Sute. They were carrying a letter with Katsuchiyo's emblem."

Nakabara's eyes widened. "Do you still have it?"

"His lapdog destroyed it." She recalled the shredded paper, blood spatters on worn wood. "It cost her."

He tugged his beard. "One samurai's testimony won't be enough."

Yes, they would need much more before they could hold Katsuchiyo accountable. He was the daimyō's brother, beyond reproach in the court's eyes. To accuse him publicly would divide the Lion. Many would capitalize on such an opening, like the Crane, or the Scorpion...

"So that is why you kept this secret. To protect the Matsu's face. But why does an Ikoma care about the clout of the Matsu family?"

Nakabara snorted. "Is that not the foremost duty of the Ikoma? If this became public, the Lion would have no face to show the other clans."

As good a reason as any other, she supposed. "How does Sute fit into all this? You said you knew where I was taking her. That you wouldn't let me."

He dug around his sleeve-pockets for his pipe. "I thought you might be taking her to Katsuchiyo. That's why he's here, after all."

It was like realizing the correct move in Go. It clicked.

Her ashigaru defenders, falling to bandit axes. The Forest-Killer who tried to show her the letter, as if it would save him. As if he'd recognized her as one of Katsuchiyo's soldiers. A letter, with his covert stamp.

Orders to kidnap Sute.

Her mouth went dry. All along, it was always about Sute. How hadn't she seen that?

"What does he want with her?"

He looked like an exasperated teacher. Hadn't she figured that out yet?

"I know she's special," Shiemi continued, her mind racing. "She's a Kitsu. A powerful one. And I know the wardens of this manor sent her away to become a spiritcaller. They discovered her as a baby…"

Sute's adopted father's words echoed in her mind: *our duty was always to protect and raise you until you were ready.*

Realization. "They didn't discover Sute. Sute was entrusted to their care."

Nakabara smiled.

"But by whom? Ikoma Ujitōya?"

"No," he replied, lighting his pipe. "By me."

Shiemi gawked stupidly. What kind of web had she become entangled in?

"No more games, Nakabara," she said. "Just tell me everything."

He gathered his thoughts. Ever the omoidasu.

"It began in the Temple of the Future. Do you know that place?"

The Temple of the Future was where the clan's greatest heroes were born, equal parts birthing hospital and day care. Akodo's children were born within those halls, as were the children of most Lion daimyō throughout history.

Yes. She knew that place. Its halls were burned into her, the children's charcoal drawings and the echoes of soft lullabies.

Nakabara exhaled sweet smoke out the window. Far beyond, the river was high and roaring.

"Nine years ago, a group of newborns vanished from the Temple of the Future. Their guardians were slain, leaving only a few witnesses. The children of numerous important leaders were taken from their cribs, the very future of the Lion stolen away. They were never recovered. Although their hearts cried for justice, the Kitsu and Ikoma kept the incident secret to preserve the temple's reputation."

Shiemi forced her features into a motionless mask as Nakabara searched them, even as her heart began to race, and moisture coated her forehead.

"The raid was unprecedented. Although it seemed senseless at the time, the Ikoma investigated the incident over the years, and we are now confident that it was perpetrated by Forest-Killer bandits in the employ of Matsu Katsuchiyo." He watched for her reaction. "While we can only speculate as to his motives, we believe he was trying to accomplish a political goal, and something went wrong, resulting in an unforeseen escalation of violence."

"But you cannot accuse him," she said, voice wavering beneath her effort to remain calm.

"Not after so many committed to the secret. Even now, he can deny the entire thing, and those he wronged would side with him to protect the temple." Nakabara's eyes twinkled. "Ah, but there is one detail I have left out."

"You," Shiemi guessed.

"It so happened that I was present at the temple the night of the attack. By pure chance a servant escaped with one child, a Kitsu child." He raised his eyebrows pointedly. "She fell into my hands, Shiemi. And to create leads we could follow, to lower the guard of the perpetrator, I allowed her to remain lost, entrusting her to the seneschals of this manor. My request: to keep her safe until she came of age, then send her to train with her kind." He raised a hand in apology. "It is regrettable that such a thing was necessary, but had I revealed her, Sute could have been in greater danger, and Katsuchiyo's role may never have been discovered."

Shiemi's head spun. She felt like she'd fallen into a fraying tapestry without end. "That does not explain why he wants her."

"Political clout," Nakabara said. "He knows she was one of those lost on that night. If he were to return her to her birth parents, he could claim that he was the one who found her, securing their allegiance in his battle to become Matsu daimyō.

"I thought you had intercepted Sute's guardians and kidnapped her on Katsuchiyo's behalf. I was wrong. You were only trying to protect her. My orders now are to see her safely returned to the Kitsu so that she might fulfill her destiny. Katsuchiyo must not use her to gain any more leverage. The Ikoma cannot allow such a man to become the Matsu daimyō."

She said nothing. He risked a sympathetic hand on her shoulder. "A twisted tale, to be sure. Perhaps it is difficult to believe."

But she believed it. She believed every word.

She believed it because she was there, stationed at the Temple of the Future, the very night the children vanished, nine years ago. Led astray by Katsuchiyo's honeyed words, she was not at her post during the sudden attack. As the lone survivor, the children's assumed deaths were on her hands. She hated herself from that day forward, casting her name and titles aside, swearing the oath of the Deathseeker. That night would haunt her, as would the memory of her fallen comrades and the children lost beneath her care. Marked and ashamed, not knowing how to right the wrong, she'd tried blindly to follow them all into the misty jaws of death.

CHAPTER TEN

Sute slept soundly in the mostly empty bedchamber. She was snoring, mouth agape, elongated fangs glittering with drool. Her nighttime tossing had spun her blankets into a cocoon from the waist down, and she was sprawled diagonally across her mattress, hair a disheveled mop, hands balled into fists. Unruly even in sleep. A warrior's slumber.

Shiemi studied her for a long time.

There *had* been a Kitsu baby among them, hadn't there? In all the passing years, Shiemi had forgotten that. But then, a newborn Kitsu looked much like any other. Her fangs would not have grown in. Her eyes would have been brown, shifting to gold gradually as she aged. Her hair would have been wispy curls, not the proud thick mane with the reddish sheen. No, she would have been like all the others. An empty cup, waiting for a life to fill it. A vessel for infinite futures.

A future lost. Or so Shiemi had believed.

No, she would not have recognized Sute, even if she had remembered.

But Ichisuke did. In his last moments, as his lifeblood poured into the street, he'd seen her in the window and known.

Because Sute was his niece, born in the Temple of the Future. He'd recognized her, his own blood, in spite of all the time that had passed. Perhaps she resembled his sister, or another relative. It was the only thing that made sense, besides the clarity of death.

Shiemi squinted at Sute's snoring features. Could she truly be one of those children? Had fate really brought them together? It didn't seem possible.

Yet, throughout Rokugan's history, had fate not played greater tricks than this? Could she not recall dozens of instances, stories of folk heroes and farmers alike, whose life threads were entangled by destiny's great loom? Was it so hard to believe that the ancestors in Yomi had heard her prayers for death, brought her to the threshold of the Fortune of Death himself, and, in their wry humor and relentless mercy, given her a reason to live?

I'll tell her one day, she decided, and gently tousled Sute's hair. *When this is over.*

But first, she would have to deal with Katsuchiyo.

Shiemi rose and returned to the interior courtyard. A padded tunic awaited her there, left by Masumi. It wasn't much protection, but it was the best armor that could be scrounged on short notice. And she was used to fighting unarmored. A full suit would only hinder her. This would be good enough.

The crickets had grown quiet. Dawn was approaching. Yet the sky was still so full of stars. The cowherd star shone brightly on the far side of the sky river. Legends said that it was once a living soul that was lifted up and set into the Heavens. Yes, Fortunes did intervene from time to time.

Were the other lost children still alive? Had they all been scattered? Were they waiting, biding their time, beneath Heaven's dome? Children born in the Temple of the Future were fated to lead the clan. They were born to be heroes. Surely destiny was not so easily thwarted. The Fortunes had their plans, and mortals could only bow.

As if to answer, a star fell, tracing a line in the velvet. Her breath caught as it vanished in the reddening horizon.

Had all the years she searched for death, all the suffering and self-doubt, been some part of a greater work, a story that wasn't even hers? It seemed like such a coincidence otherwise, one she couldn't bring herself to believe. No, it had been fate, from the very beginning. A chance at redemption. Destiny kept no secrets.

As the roosters began to crow, Shiemi dipped her fingers into her bowl of white makeup and painted her face.

The dawn cast a red horizon as Shiemi climbed the path up through the stacked paddies. Her steps disturbed clouds of rice bugs, scattering away like dandelion puffs. In the pools, her white-painted face reflected a woman at peace with whatever came next. The cock's crowing fell away, but where normally a chorus of frogs and screeching birds would fill the void, there was only the wind and the peeping wheeze of the whistling teal.

Her fist tightened around her greatsword. Sute, indeed the entire Matsu family, wouldn't be safe until Katsuchiyo was gone. His ambitions were poison. They would spread as long as he lived.

Could she do it? He had been her commander. They shared the name of a great house. He could well be her daimyō one day. Was it not treason to draw steel against him?

Among the many lesser-quoted passages of Akodo's *Leadership*, her mind went instantly to one: "*If a lord has swayed from the virtuous path, it is the obligation of their followers to depose them and cast them down. A vassal that makes excuses for their lord blinds themselves.*"

It was how Katsuchiyo had justified himself. He'd swayed so many. Yet all this time he was simply a jealous brother, mistaking responsibility for a toy he wanted. That she'd contributed to his successes...

A sour taste coated her mouth. She spat. Her misguided interpretation of the Deathseeker oath, her selfish fixation on her own failures, were what blinded her to what he'd been doing. She hadn't cared what kind of person he was, what his goals were, so long as he kept giving her chances to die. How could she have been so utterly *stupid*? And for this long?

But she knew better now. This was the true Deathseeker path, to take on the risk for others.

The village was evacuated and empty, the villagers waiting on the other side of the Three Stone River. Masumi had seen to it personally, her esteem in their eyes acting as salve for their worries. The evacuation had been her suggestion. And a good one, because it meant Shiemi's plan didn't risk anyone.

Sute would be among them. Safe and watching. Waiting. Katsuchiyo would never lay a hand on her.

A girl who lived with ghosts. Fearlessly asking a Deathseeker if she was a geisha because her face was painted. Catching fish bare-handed. Practicing kata on a mossy log. Grinning, elongated fangs poking out from her smile.

Shiemi nodded inwardly. *OK then. When this is over, I will serve her.*

It felt good to have a future.

Katsuchiyo waited patiently, flanked closely by honor guards. They were armor-clad and brandished forked spears, the *magari-yari*, but he was only lightly mailed, carrying his katana and wakizashi. Nearby were several others, a few she recognized as lower-ranking officers. She glanced beyond, toward his army encampment on the top of the hill, and saw no movement.

But they were watching. She knew they would be.

Katsuchiyo had threatened to attack the village. The plan was to call his bluff. If she could incite him into attacking, it would allow the village's lord to bring a grievance into the Lion's courts. His efforts would be perceived as a rebellion to be quashed by the other families. His own vassals might even leave him to preserve their reputations. He would be ruined.

Yes, that was much better than just taking his head.

She repeated the plan with each step. *Incite him. Lead him to the village. Entrap him.*

And if anything went wrong, throw herself into the thickest fighting and let the ancestors decide her fate. As she had always done.

She just hoped she knew Katsuchiyo well enough for the plan to work.

She stopped several yards away. Neither of them bowed.

He wouldn't ask for her surrender. She wouldn't ask for his. They both knew it was pointless. It would just disgrace them both.

"A pleasant morning," he said. His voice carried no farther than her ears. "Have you had rice?"

"I have received Inari's blessing," she replied. "Are you seeking Emma-Ō's?"

His smile didn't match the seriousness of his eyes. "I'd wager you know exactly what I seek, Shiemi."

She glanced again to the encampment. "You've come a long way for some rations and this sword," she remarked. Her fingers curled around the handle. "You are welcome to come and take it, Honored Lord."

He shook his head. "You disappoint me, Shiemi. Brushing shoulders with peasants, accepting charity like some rōnin, hiding in backwater hamlets." He clicked his tongue. "I thought you might make a good hatamoto when this was all over. But now I see you are only dedicated to your own suffering."

"It is better than following a usurper," she replied.

He smirked. "It is only usurpation if you do not deserve the post."

She raised her voice, hoping it would carry to the encampment above. "Loyalty is not inherited. You truly believe the Matsu would bow to a man who would kill his own brother?"

The morning sun chiseled a dreamlike expression across his face. "Why shouldn't they? I am the one who followed in my aunt's footsteps. My brother is too emotional. Too naïve. He has his principles, but little else. He hasn't won anything of significance. He cannot command respect just because the mantle fell on his shoulders. If he cannot defend himself against me, then how can he hope to protect the Matsu? This campaign will separate the grain from the chaff."

"What of tradition?" she asked.

He scoffed. "What of it? My brother broke tradition when he accepted the position. The Lion's Pride broke tradition when they called him daimyō. Why then shouldn't I stake my claim, when I am so much the better? They will follow me when I cast him down. They will follow me for whatever comes after."

There. The full breadth of his ambitions, laid bare. He would not stop at his brother's position. He would reach for the highest office in his clan, Lion Clan Champion.

"But first, you must mobilize your army against a lone Deathseeker."

"Not if she will listen to reason."

She knew better. "You can't have her, Katsu."

For a moment, she thought she caught him off guard. "No harm will come to her. To the contrary, I intend to present her to the Kitsu. They will be so grateful, they will eagerly support my bid."

Was that why he'd arranged for the attack on the Temple of the Future all those years ago? For political leverage? To stage his own heroism?

"You will need to kill me first."

His eyes flashed with familiar cruelty. "And suddenly you care about protecting children, Shiemi? You certainly didn't seem to care about it before."

With a splash, a flock of whistling teals took flight.

"Do you really think this will erase what you've done?" He took a few steps forward, no farther than the tips of his honor guard's spears. "Does she even know that you ruined her life? Does she know that, if you had been at your post, if you had actually cared for your duty then as you claim to do now, she would be living among her people, and not in some waterlogged shithole?"

His eyes narrowed. "If she did know, do you think she would forgive you? A few days of kindness against everything you've done?" He bared his teeth in a wolfish grin, as if his hunger was stirred by his own cruelty. "You're still the reason she lost everything. It is still your fault."

That would have worked before. It would have rent her in two, sent her screaming with her blades drawn. But now, they were just meaningless words. She didn't seek forgiveness. She sought to make things right. He couldn't hurt her that way anymore. He couldn't hurt her at all.

Confusion flickered across his face as she smiled. "You must have believed I was the only one who could have stopped your hired thugs," she said. "After all, that is why you led me away."

"Choose your next words carefully," he whispered. "There are still precious things one can take from Deathseekers."

"It was you who suggested I become a Deathseeker. You offered me chances to redeem myself, used that to pull me along. Knew that if I kept on surviving, I would always come back." She shook her head. "I was quite the fool. You had me convinced that you had nothing to do with what happened that night. That I should be protecting you. The truth is, you needed me. But I didn't need you, did I?" She leaned in. "But perhaps I should be thanking you. You've made me stronger than I ever would have been otherwise."

She glanced up. There were his officers, his soldiers, and the lords that backed him. The army was listening.

"The Matsu will never follow a man who cast his lot with bandits," she shouted. "My only shame is that I ever fell for your poison words. I never will again."

The others exchanged looks. Frowns. She imagined his army doing much the same, taking their weapons and walking away. *See what he is,* she thought. *Look upon your leader and be ashamed!*

"Enough," he hissed. "When I ascend, you will kneel. You will serve your daimyō! You will serve the Lion Clan Champion!"

She brandished her claws. "I will serve the Lion."

Was that doubt in his eyes? Was that fear that curled his lip?

"They are one and the same!" he barked.

She met his eyes. "You will never be worthy."

The first guard swept his spear low, to trip her. She countered. Her claws splintered the shaft and sent him reeling. The second came from the side before she could capitalize. Two thrusts, two close calls. She passed his reach and came close, just to strike empty air.

She drew a calming breath. These were honor guards. No pushovers. And they were fully armored. But she didn't need to kill them. Just buy some more time, time enough to–

A lance through her armpit. Sharp pain. A rusty taste flooding her mouth.

An arrow. She knew without looking that she'd been struck.

The guards rushed her. Their swords came down. She caught their blades and scraped them away, grazing a face and sending another splashing into a paddy.

Katsuchiyo pointed. "Take her head!"

Got him.

She ran. Down the hill, nearly tumbling. Back to the village, a slew of attackers hot on her heels.

She ignored the warm trickle running down her side, her blood mingling with the dawn-reflecting waters.

CHAPTER ELEVEN

The first who dared attack met their ends in the narrow streets. She encountered two more in an alley, sending them to Emma-Ō with her claws. The pain of her wounds had fallen to a dull itch as she crashed through a seller's stall, thwarting an ambusher and leaving him to bleed out on the planks.

A moment to breathe. She cast around.

Empty. No one in the tavern, no one in the streets.

They would know the village layout. They would have had time to map it from their vantage. They could organize ambushes. She just had to keep moving, lure them out–

An ear-splitting thwack. An arrow jutted from the wall beside her. She felt where it had struck her cheek, tracing a thin red line.

Matsu Asayo already had another arrow readied. Hate broiled on her face as she drew. Her mutilated hand shook as it struggled to hold the bolt.

Shiemi froze. Waited.

Only their shadows moved across the narrow street.

There was no way she could reach Asayo before the archer released. But Asayo couldn't hold the arrow for long. Her only hope was to wait, to watch for the exact moment to throw herself aside. But dodge too early, and the archer couldn't miss. They locked gazes. Asayo never looked away.

Not even as Shiemi slowly loosened the straps on one of her claws, until it was no longer affixed to her forearm.

The slightest widening of the eyes. A flash.

Shiemi ducked. The arrow came free.

As she fell, she flung the iron claw away.

It sank into Asayo's throat.

Asayo collapsed to her knees. Her hands grasped the claw's handle protruding beneath her jaw, mouth gaping like a fish. A crimson stream poured out. She gurgled and fell onto the planks. She was still.

Shiemi blinked at the fallen archer. She hadn't been sure that was going to work.

She pushed herself up carefully, hissing at the new stabbing pain in her hip, where Asayo's arrow had sunk deep.

Keeping her breath steady, she grasped the arrow and gently twisted.

Shockwaves of blinding pain.

She gasped and let go. The unyielding arrow hadn't turned at all.

That was bad. Unlike the first one, this arrow was embedded in bone. Only skilled hands could remove it.

With a flick, she drew her knife. Holding the arrow steady, she cut the shaft close so it wouldn't protrude, discarding the fletching, as she had done with the first.

How odd. Normally she wouldn't even care whether or not she survived a battle. But she had to make sure Sute made it back to the Kitsu. Emma-Ō could have his due after.

The streets were still empty. Where she expected to hear the sounds of woodblock sandals in pursuit, setting up more ambushes in the streets, she instead heard only the sounds of the morning wildlife. She shifted between two houses and cast her gaze back up to the encampment on the hill.

No movement. Just rippling banners and the jinmaku curtain.

Shiemi cursed. The plan hadn't worked.

Of course it hadn't. Katsuchiyo's emotion wouldn't overtake his strategic sense. That was why only a few had followed her down. It couldn't be a full unprovoked invasion if it was only a handful. This barely warranted a rebuke!

Fine. It was a gamble anyway. What mattered now was meeting Nakabara at the shrine, so that she could cross the river, reunite with Sute–

A familiar voice. A child's cry. "Shiemi?"

The voice, normally welcome, sent icy dread down her spine.

"Shiemi? Are you here?"

No.

She ran. Her heart thudded in her ears. She ignored the painful tearing sensation conjured by each step. She left red dots in the sand as she passed the manor, the shrine to Emma-Ō coming into view, its high towers draping the path in cold shadow.

There. Sute wandering down the shrine's steps, not a care in the world.

She could have tossed Sute headfirst into the river in that moment. Was there no guardian, no protector, that this girl wouldn't slip away from?

Shiemi stopped at the foot of the stairs and panted, hands on knees. She was too busy filling her tired lungs to say anything.

Sute's golden eyes widened. "You're hurt!"

"It's a battle," Shiemi managed. How had she even gotten here? Had she swum?

Sute hurried down awkwardly, sandals slapping against her heels.

Katsuchiyo's voice. "So that's her."

Shiemi spun. The nodachi was free before she knew she'd even drawn it. She held it threateningly to the side and snarled. She could hear Sute freeze up on the steps behind her, pictured her confused, unworried expression.

Katsuchiyo was not amused anymore. His face was that of a man tilting at *shōgi*, a man swinging in his own web, suspended midway between victory and defeat, and just a breeze to decide which way he would fall.

The honor guard at his side hurriedly strung their bows.

"Go inside," Shiemi growled. "Now."

She counted the sandal steps of Sute climbing back up the stairs, fading as she ducked within.

The honor guard nocked their arrows.

Katsuchiyo held up a hand. They paused. "You can't win, Shiemi. Look at you. There are funeral songs on all sides."

Her entire flank was bathed in red. Her kimono clung to her beneath the tunic. But she felt nothing. It didn't matter.

"Would you attack a shrine?" she asked, trying to hide her pain. "Is nothing sacred to you?" She looked from one hesitant face to the next. "Step one foot within, and Lord Ujitōya will hear of it. He will return the slight."

His eyes widened. His men exchanged looks.

She pressed. "How many lesser lords can you fight at once? Two? Four? Unified beneath your brother, with your treachery fully unveiled for the Lion to see?" She met his gaze. *Let him see your conviction. Let him see his own doom in your eyes.* Her whisper carried on the breeze. "Not even your Forest-Killers will save you."

Katsuchiyo cast aside his sheath. His naked blade flashed in the dawn light. "Such words call for blood, Deathseeker. I will grant you what you've always sought, a death in combat!" He raised his voice for his officers to hear. "You assail me with slander, but my conscience is clear! You will back your words with steel, or stand revealed a coward!"

Death in a duel against her most hated enemy, a man who had betrayed her. A death defending a child against insurmountable forces. A death at the foot of the shrine to the Fortune of Death himself. Even Nakabara could not have invented a more perfect way for a Deathseeker to die. And she was ready to die, if it meant Sute would live.

Even if she beat him, there would be an arrow for her throat. And another. If even one of his honor guards lived, Sute would be lost. They all had to die. Every single one of them. *So be it.* She closed her eyes and whispered a prayer. She hoped her ancestors were watching.

Katsuchiyo lowered his blade. His face turned up. His eyes were wide, disbelieving.

Smoke. She smelled it, and then saw it, pouring out from behind her.

It was rolling out of the shrine's entrance. From here, she felt the heat of flames.

A campfire had been nothing for Sute to light. She could conjure flame with just a word, even use it to give a body to ghosts. So certainly, immolating a shrine was just as easy.

"Put it out!" Katsuchiyo screamed. "The shrine cannot burn!"

Shiemi almost laughed. This would certainly be interpreted as an attack. Who could say that his forces hadn't started it? Perhaps Ujitōya could retaliate after all.

A sudden gust tore through the shrine. A sound like thunder burst out, and suddenly the walls were coated in spreading fire, stripping paint away in thin black strips. Katsuchiyo watched the conflagration in horror.

This was her chance. She could cross the path and take his head right now.

But that would leave Sute in the burning shrine. The fire spread too fast. She needed help.

Easy choice.

Shiemi spun and dashed up the steps.

A dozen bows snapped beneath the cracking flames.

She barely felt the arrows that planted themselves like flags in her back. She crossed the threshold just as the massive shimenawa rope fell, blocking the entrance behind her.

Each breath was like swallowing fire. The smoke stung her eyes. She ducked beneath sheets of flame and cast from room to burning room, coughing, hacking down flaming timbers, clearing her path.

There! Sute sat in a corner, a fallen banister blocking her. Shiemi threw herself beneath it and straightened, rolling it off her back. Distantly, she felt the sensation of an arrow shaft being pushed through her, feeling the head break the skin of her front. It was followed by a great pressure in her chest, as if a bubble inside her had collapsed.

Sute stood. Her head was just beneath the smoke curtain. "It got out of control," she said, matter of factly.

Yes, it had.

She took Shiemi's hand. "The old priest is laughing. He says there's a tunnel beneath the floor. It leads to the riverbed."

One of her ghosts. Shiemi coughed and tasted rust and ash. "Then tell him to lead."

She'd never been more thankful than she was for the cool damp air of the underground tunnel. She couldn't see, but Sute held her hand around barrels of aging sake and stacks of kōji bricks. *This must be where the alcohol offerings were kept,* she idly supposed. She fought the compulsion to pause and have a drink. She had many absurd compulsions right now, thoughts that didn't make sense.

The bank of the Three Stone River greeted them as they emerged in the daylight. Behind, she heard the flames running up the length of Emma-Ō's shrine. No sign of Katsuchiyo or his men. But they were nearby. They had to be!

She wanted to plunge her head in the river and gulp water down. Instead, she sat in the sand coughing black phlegm. Each time was like splinters coming up her throat. And she couldn't inhale all the way, like something took up the space where her air should go.

Sute knelt beside her, noticing the arrows for the first time. Her face broke into open concern.

"It is nothing," Shiemi rasped. "I've gotten worse scars."

Sute nodded, seemingly reassured. Even so, her eyes lingered on the wet crimson stains and the scratches on Shiemi's face.

From behind them came Katsuchiyo's distant scream. A voice filled with rage, of plans thwarted, of a world that was falling apart. They turned together and stared at the conflagration as his defeated cry echoed above the din of snapping timbers.

"Will that get the bad man in trouble?" Sute chirped.

Had she known about the plan? Had the priest told her?

Shiemi nodded. It would.

The fire danced in Sute's eyes. "Good."

A tiny riverboat broke through the fog, coming along the water. At the head was Nakabara, and two others that Shiemi didn't recognize. The old man raised a hand in greeting.

Sute moved protectively in front of Shiemi.

"It is OK," Shiemi said, voice full of ash. "He is a friend."

Reluctantly, Sute relaxed as the boat banked. "Hello, Sute," Nakabara said. "I know we had a rough first meeting. My name is Ikoma Nakabara. I'm here to help you."

When he saw Shiemi, his face went pale. And then sad.

Shiemi rose and made for the boat. Soon they would be away from here. After Sute was safe in Kitsu lands, she would–

Her legs gave way. She hit the sand.

Sute spun on her heel, shouting her name.

She tried to move. She couldn't. She couldn't even breathe. She could only suck air through gritted teeth, her arm going tingly, numb. Her throat was on fire, yet all she could feel was cold, like frost forming on her very bones.

Sute tugged at her collar. Shouted her name, again and again.

Nakabara pulled her back. "We can't help her," came his distant voice. "I'm sorry."

Shiemi felt herself going limp. She was shrinking. She couldn't tell what was killing her: bleeding out from her arrow wounds, her failing lungs, or the smoke inhalation.

She laid her cheek on the sand.

She'd pictured this moment many times before. This wasn't quite as she'd anticipated. Had this happened days ago, she might have felt cheated. But looking back on it now, all the times she'd thrown herself recklessly into battle, she'd been so ready to die for… what? Some lord's reputation? Fleeting military advances? Nothing. Nothing that would last.

This was better. Katsuchiyo, a threat to the clan, would be exposed for what he was. Sute was alive. She would go home to her people. She would live a full life.

Yes, this was a good death. A worthy death. One last step, a great victory.

The girl wrenched herself from the Ikoma's grasp. She planted herself on her knees beside Shiemi's body, as wet trails trickled down her chin. "I won't leave her," she whispered. "She shouldn't go alone."

But Katsuchiyo was nearby! They had to leave now, or this all would be for nothing! *Just go,* she thought. *Don't waste time!*

Nakabara knelt and laid a comforting hand on her shoulder. "We must go soon, little Sute. Your people want very much to meet you. They need you to lead them."

She looked up at him, uncomprehending.

"Your father was Kitsu Toju, daimyō of the Kitsu family. Your mother gave birth to you in the Temple of the Future. You were destined to lead your people, but in a twist of fate, you were lost. The Ikoma here… your parents," he corrected himself, "deemed you ready to return. I will take you home."

Of course. Daimyō's children were born in the Temple of the Future. Heroes of the clan. Those destined for greatness.

Like Sute.

Nakabara bowed his head. "Thank you, Deathseeker. You will live on in story and song. I will see to it myself."

A splash on her cheek. Then another, like timid rain. Sute's tears, perhaps? She wasn't sure. She couldn't focus on any one thought. She was sinking into the soil, spreading out into the grass, reaching the water.

Sute whispered, "Do I really have to leave you?"

Yes. She did. The only path for samurai was forward. Even if it was stumbling, even if it was the last step, even if you gained only an inch. If one must fall, fall forward! It was what they owed to anyone who would pick up the banner. It was everyone's duty in this life to win a victory, even in death.

Sute knew this. Deep down, she had to know. She possessed the warrior spirit, imprinted into her every cell. All she had to do was listen.

There was so much Shiemi wanted to tell her. That death held no power over one who lived with purpose. That guilt was a sword you gave your enemy. That Bushidō was not a binary choice between virtues, but a balance between them. Because the warrior path was not taught, it was simply walked. Bushidō existed long before Akodo ever gave it a name. She wanted to tell Sute that the true warrior never had to name their virtues, because right action embraced them all in equal measure. A path without guilt, a path without doubt, a path without fear.

And she would know it, because it was etched into her heart, an inherent universal truth, as it was with all warriors.

And perhaps, all human beings. The ashigaru who defied the bandits, even knowing they would die. The priest of Emma-Ō, who gave shelter without question. The omoidasu, who kept to his vows, even as they painted him a villain. The magistrate, the geisha, the farmer, the lord. All sentient beings, from Fortune to mortal. She understood now. They were the same. Just the husks were different. All fought their own invisible wars, seeking the path toward their own balance. A hundred thousand souls. All walking the Way.

She wanted to tell Sute. But she couldn't breathe. Every weak gasp pierced her with nails. Every exhale sank her deeper into the abyss.

Perhaps silence was for the best. Otherwise, she would have always been saying goodbye.

No.

What was she thinking? She hadn't given everything yet! This was her final step. It should be forward. *Forward!*

A twitch. All strength into her hand. Dragging, a trench in the dirt. Her greatsword, the nodachi. She would pass it on to her little cub.

How light it felt!

Sute's hands curled around the offering. Hugged it awkwardly to her chest. She raised her tear-streaked face. Her golden eyes shone with resolve.

Shiemi pushed with all she had left. She was no wordsmith, and her voice was raspy and torn, not good enough for such a momentous circumstance. But this would be her best effort yet.

"Go.

"Live.

"Roar."

Sute rose. She didn't have to say anything. Their hearts were the same.

Nakabara led her to the boat. He bowed, one final time. They pushed away. The fog consumed them.

Shiemi sighed.

Another of Katsuchiyo's screams, more distant this time, gently rolled over her, then withdrew like the river tide. She smiled.

Sute was going to be OK. It was all going to be OK. She didn't have to stay here any longer. She could let go.

How soft the ground. How gentle the wind. How merciful the flames. How cool the waters. How peaceful. How kind. This really was a beautiful place. A beautiful world.

She felt at peace.

And then, she felt nothing at all.

TRAIL OF SHADOWS

DG Laderoute

To Jackie, my wife, who is far more patient with me than I deserve.

And also to my friend Corbin, who greatly inspired the portrayal of Tale-Chaser the nezumi.

CHAPTER ONE

Remember. Remember all of this.

Ros'ku stopped and lifted his snout. Sniffed. Recoiled.

The air tasted the way a scream sounds.

Instinct shivered his whiskers and tail, made his paws press into the damp rock, ready to fling him into headlong flight toward the cave mouth. Instead, he grimly shifted the wicker basket slung on his back and resumed creeping along the rough tunnel. A pair of warriors scouted ahead of him, spears leveled. One carried a torch, but it guttered dimly, shedding sparks like dying fireflies. Ros'ku focused on following the warriors' scent trails, bright and hard with wariness and fear. But the scream-stink intruded, keeping him stuck on that knife edge of panicked getaway.

His paw touched icy water. It oozed between his toes in a way that made him think of blood. He flinched, but nonetheless tried to remember every terrible nuance of touch and texture.

Remember…

But why? Why am I here?

The warriors stopped abruptly, clouds of wary excitement

billowing around them. Ros'ku froze, but smelled only the scream, going on and on and on.

No. Something new. He made himself taste the air again.

It was fire. But not the torch. Or – it was, but not *just* the torch. It was many fires. And it was also rain. And wind. The acrid stink of lightning. The damp smell of a storm.

Ros'ku crept up behind his bulkier kin. "What is it?" He kept his voice to a soft hiss, but it still echoed against the rock like the snap of breaking bones. "What have you found?"

"I don't know, Rememberer," one of the warriors replied, his spear fixed ahead. The scavenged iron tip trembled in the fitful light. "There is something, though – just there."

Ros'ku followed the spear point and the dusky light toward something slumped on the cave floor. A figure? Lying on the ground?

Is this why I am here? Does my dream finally continue?

Beyond the prone figure was darkness. The warriors reeked of fear at the mere idea of pressing beyond it, farther into the cave. But they wouldn't have to. This fallen figure was the reason Ros'ku had come here.

Yes, my dream continues.

He had been a mighty warrior, clad in a great suit of armor made of many plates and straps, all in deepest gray, like the base of a thunderstorm. Even his face was covered by a ferocious, leering mask. Smells of fire and hot metal, wind laced with driving rain, a storm about to break emanated from this armor.

But this fallen man – because he was that, a human man – wasn't why Ros'ku's dream had brought him to this terrible place. His *armor* was.

Ros'ku leaned close, studying it. The plates and straps showed no damage or decay. The armor could have been placed there only moments ago. Ros'ku unbraided a stick from his fur and chewed on it, scraping wood away, gnawing a pattern of shape and scent that would embody this armor, this place, this moment–

"Rememberer," one of the warriors whispered, "have we found what you seek?"

Ros'ku spit out wood shavings. The warrior was right. Remembering all of this fully would take more time than he wished to spend here. He studied the memory stick, decided it would have to do, and wove it back into his fur. "Yes, we shall leave once we have…"

Have *what*, exactly? The Transcendent, his ancestor, had reached into Ros'ku's dreams and shaped the visions that had brought him here. But why? What was so significant about this armor?

Ros'ku touched it.

It was cold and smooth. The mixed scents of hot metal and wind and storm may have intensified slightly, but nothing else happened.

Still, he let the impulse keep guiding him, his touch becoming a grasp, paws gripping a large shoulder plate, tugging it to reveal lacings holding it to the rest of the armor. He picked at the cords, trying to loosen them. As he did, he studied a symbol emblazoned on the breastplate in pale gray, one that repeated on the shoulder plates – a circle inscribed with a clawed, many-legged creature. A crab.

Ros'ku recognized this sign as that of a human tribe. The humans he knew best, the spirit hunters called the Falcon Clan, spoke of them often. They lived beyond the forest, on a great stone wall, and were very gruff.

One lace left. A stubborn one. Ros'ku plucked at the knot with a claw. This piece, this shoulder plate, should fit in his basket. Perhaps both would fit. As for the rest, it would have to–

A piercing shriek tore at the air behind them, from the cave mouth. Ros'ku cringed, while the warriors spun about, terror swirling around them like smoke.

Another shriek, then the throaty blare of a horn.

"Alarm!" one of the warriors hissed. "We must leave, now!" Ros'ku yanked at the shoulder plate.

A warrior grabbed at him. "Rememberer! We must flee!" Ros'ku kept tugging at the plate.

"Rememberer–!"

The shriek keened a third time, as did the horn, but both cut off abruptly. The warrior dropped the torch and grabbed Ros'ku. He would force him back out of the cave, if he had to, or carry him out. Ros'ku yanked one last, desperate time at the armored plate–

It came free.

He jammed it into his basket, dropped to all fours, and ran. The warriors followed two-legged to keep their spears ready, but their longer gait let them keep pace.

Fetid pools splashed underfoot amid the damp rock. With no torch, Ros'ku used their scent trails to follow the return path. Now the rugged floor rose, and the tunnel turned. Turned again. Once more, and the cave mouth appeared, revealing skeletal trees, their branches like clawed fingers, black water and muck pooling among their gnarled roots. Beyond the trees, the world turned to mist.

Ros'ku slowed his mad rush, letting the warriors take the lead. They burst into the open and one warrior simply vanished, smashed into the mud by something vast. The other howled fury, fear and warning all at once and raised his spear, interposing himself between Ros'ku and whatever now towered above them.

The smell that was a scream was everywhere, everything.

Ros'ku raced past the warrior, splashing through brackish muck. Something huge smashed through the trees above him, showering him with splinters. The warrior howled again and lunged upward with his spear and then also vanished, swept away by a tsunami of darkness.

Ros'ku glanced back.

No warriors. Not the two who had escorted him, or the six who had remained outside. All were dead, gone.

Ros'ku ran, the wicker basket and the heavy shoulder plate inside it bouncing hard against his back. The swamps blurred past, an endless procession of moss-shrouded trees, of black water, of visceral terror. Wisps of light, as red as newly spilled blood, flickered and danced among the trees, offering a shortcut, a faster path, safety. He ignored them, fixing his eyes ahead and just running. Finally, the ground rose, becoming drier, the light brighter.

A thought, barely coherent.

Remember.

Now watery sunlight shafted down among ancient pines. Their resinous tang washed away the last of the scream-stink, but Ros'ku didn't slow his headlong flight.

Remember all of this.

CHAPTER TWO

A chill wind hissed across the drab stonework of Kuni Castle, prompting Hida Sukune to cinch his straw cloak. Lady Sun shone with summer splendor, but the wind still dragged the warmth from him. It blew from the south, from beyond the great Carpenter Wall. From the Shadowlands. Nothing good or wholesome ever came from that place. Not even the wind.

A horn sounded from a training yard below, a rapid string of shrill, staccato notes designed to slice through any din of battle. Sukune watched a company of Crab warriors, heavily armored *bushi*, swiftly shift their formation, heavy boots scuffing and clumping against the packed earth. Their movements had been impeccable: immediate, crisp, and precise.

Yes, impeccable. But– "Sukune-kun, there you are!"

Sukune turned and opened his mouth to reply, but had to pause and swallow the cloying aftertaste of nettle and lopseed, balsam and ginseng. The medicinal brew fortified his feeble lungs, his arrhythmic heart and aching joints. "I have been on this battlement for some time now, sister," he finally said, "in full view of most of the castle."

Hida O-Ushi strode along the rampart, her slate-gray *hakama* trousers billowing in that same cold wind. She wore no cloak, seemingly impervious to the chill that scraped his bones. "In case you had not noticed, dear brother," she said, "Kuni Castle is not small." She stopped and glanced down at the drilling bushi. "Although I actually *did* see you up here, from over there." She pointed at another battlement, one thrust out from the flank of the soaring keep. "But it would be unseemly, I think, for the daughter of the Crab Clan Champion to bellow across the drill yards for her brother's attention, no?"

Sukune smiled. "It is not like you to be worried about what is unseemly, sister."

"You may be the refined one in our family, but I do have *some* manners."

The horn shrilled again, prompting the warriors through another succession of maneuvers. O-Ushi favored them with an approving nod. "A demanding sequence, that one. They performed it well."

"I suppose."

O-Ushi turned a bemused look on Sukune. "Your standards are higher than mine, then?"

"You know that is not the case." He turned his frown from her to the bushi. "This morning, I read a report from the Wall, from the commander of the Fourth Tower. Three days ago, a company was conducting a patrol-in-force in the Shadowlands. It was attacked, mostly by goblins, within sight of the Wall. Another company was dispatched to support it. After a hard-fought battle, the goblins finally broke and fled. The two companies returned to the Wall with thirty-six dead, and almost twice that many wounded."

"A victory, then," O-Ushi said, but arched her brow in a way that expected Sukune to say otherwise.

He needed to speak his brooding thoughts, to vent them, so he ignored her indulgent tone. "A victory, yes. But to what end? What was accomplished, besides the loss of those warriors? If the first company had simply retreated, returned to the Wall, many of those dead and wounded would still be whole."

O-Ushi sighed theatrically. None of this was new to her. "Our nature is to stand and hold against our enemies, Sukune. The Empire counts on it."

"Indeed." He gestured at the force below them. "That is the bedrock upon which all these movements and formations stand. We stand. We hold. We do not retreat. We do not remain flexible or adapt. And so, we sacrifice ourselves. We die. Or worse." He looked back at O-Ushi. "Yes, we are the Wall. And that is the problem."

"Probably best not to say that where too many can hear it, brother," she replied, her eyes narrowing. "They might think you question our ancient duty."

"Again, you know I do not. The Empire endures because we endure, of course. But the Wall is, in the end, just stone." He touched the battlement. "It can only do what it does. But we are *not* just stone, *not* just a wall. We can adapt and become more flexible. We can defeat the darkness without just standing and holding and dying." He shook his head. "We can stop being so damned reverential of sacrifice."

Sukune looked back down into the drill yard. The bushi had formed into a tight battle line, each packed in close to the others, with just enough room to swing their weapons. The line was, indeed, meant to be as a wall to a foe, an immovable bulwark of armor and persistence against which attacks would break and fail. The companies whose battle was described in the report had no doubt stood in lines such as this against their goblin attackers. There were other, more open formations to employ against more monstrous enemies, like ogres, or trolls, or the demonic horrors called *oni*. But even those were designed to just stop these massive foes, holding them in place and eventually destroying them, always regardless of the cost. *We might not be mere stone*, he thought, *but centuries of acting like we are could be turning us into just that. "We are the Wall" might be on its way to becoming a literal truth…*

Sukune winced at a jabbing pain in his hands, now clenched in frustration. Deliberately, he opened and spread his fingers, and turned back to O-Ushi. "My apologies, sister. I'm sure you didn't come here just to listen to yet another of my tirades."

"One of these days, perhaps, you might say something different." She smirked. "Anyway, Lord Kuni Yori has finally deigned to appear. Father commands our attendance."

Sukune nodded as another cold gust whipped the battlement, stinging him with fine grit. Just as well; he'd be glad to get away from this damnable wind. Besides, perhaps now they would learn just what had prompted their father to suddenly bring them here from Hida Palace. They'd asked him about it, and only got the flat reply that he had to speak with Yori, the Kuni family *daimyō*, before saying anything more. Sukune and O-Ushi both knew one didn't press Hida Kisada on… well, anything.

"I would attack this place from the east," O-Ushi said as they started toward the keep.

Sukune gave her a blank look. "You what?"

"Oh, admit it, brother. While you were up here, you thought at least once about how best to attack this place."

He shrugged. "Whether I did or not, such mental exercises are never wasted." A few paces along, though, he glanced sidelong at her. "Why from the east?"

O-Ushi swept her arm around. "Because this place sits in the middle of the Kuni Wastes! In every direction, a perfectly flat plain! East, west, south… What difference does it make?"

Sukune opened his mouth, then looked around at the bleak flatlands surrounding them, and closed it again.

His sister laughed and clapped him on the shoulder – gently. "That is your problem, Sukune-kun. You think too much."

Sukune shot her a suitably insulted glare, but it wasn't entirely put-on. O-Ushi had meant *you think too much* in a teasing way, but to most Crab, all that mattered was action, swift and decisive, whatever the cost. To them, *you think too much* really was an insult.

Even by the utilitarian standards of the Crab, the meeting room was sparse – walls of gray stone, a pair of narrow windows to admit light, and a massive table of night-black teak surrounded by thin tatami mats. A sprawling map of the Empire covered most of one wall, while a small *kamidana* shrine was mounted high on the wall opposite the door. That was all.

Sukune dipped his fingers in a bowl of water placed beneath the shrine, an abbreviated form of the purifying ritual used in the rest of the Empire. He then bowed to a small piece of rough stone contained in the shrine. The stone had been retrieved from one of the long-gone bulwarks of the First Wall, one said to have been built by the Kami Hida himself. It provided Hida a place from which to watch over the proceedings in this room.

Sukune asked his divine namesake to guide and bless whatever transpired here, then moved aside so O-Ushi could conduct her own observance. In other parts of the Empire – say, among the Phoenix, or the Crane – the rituals of the kamidana would have been more elaborate. As with the purification, though, the Crab reduced them to their barest essentials, leaving more time for practical matters. Hida-no-Kami understood, of course.

Sukune was no stranger to the room, having attended many meetings there regarding strategy, the deployment of forces, their logistics. The top of the table could be removed, revealing a detailed model of the lands surrounding Kuni Castle and the nearest section of the Carpenter Wall. Many of those meetings had focused upon this miniature world, playing out attacks on the Wall and the Crab responses to them: responses that were invariably based on hundreds of years of similar scenarios all unfolding much the same. To do otherwise was to risk *thinking too much*.

Today, though, the tabletop remained in place. Sukune settled himself, waving away a servant offering dark, pungent tea from the Twilight Mountains. These harsh blends clashed with his medications and upset his stomach. In the meantime, he shared a glance with O-Ushi – who shrugged – then readied himself to wait–

The door, stout wood, squealed aside. Their father, Hida Kisada, strode through it, his muscular bulk and sheer presence suddenly filling the room in a way that made his nickname, the Great Bear, so apt. The man following him could scarcely have been more different: slight, wiry, and dour, Kuni Yori, daimyō of the Kuni family, seemed always brusquely purposeful, but with a hint of *knowing* about him, of secrets that were important, but could not be shared. Behind him trailed a much younger samurai bearing the crest of the Kuni family. He was clearly not long past his coming-of-age ceremony and caught in that awkward transition from gangly youth to young man. His name was Kuni Daigo, Sukune recalled, Yori's most recent apprentice.

After their own observances at the kamidana, Kisada knelt at the head of the table, Yori to his right, and Daigo to Yori's. The younger Kuni carried something large and flat wrapped in silk, which he placed on the table in a way that was almost reverent.

Sukune looked from the silk-wrapped something to his father, expecting him to begin speaking, but Kisada's attention stayed on the still-open door.

"Please," the Crab Champion finally said, "enter." His voice rumbled, but in a way that was uncharacteristically restrained, almost... gentle?

A figure appeared in the doorway. A short figure. *Very* short.

And...

Not human.

Whiskers, a pointed snout, fur. A *nezumi*.

"This is Tale-Chaser," Kuni Yori said. "He is a Rememberer of the Tattered Ear tribe, and our honored guest."

Tale-Chaser bent forward in an awkward approximation of a bow. "Name is Ros'ku," he said, the name incorporating a chirping squeak. "Tale-Chaser is my human name. The Falcon say I chase stories. But it is also a joke, yes?" His voice was soft, sibilant, his Rokugani strangely accented – unsurprising given that his mouth and throat were shaped to speak an altogether inhuman tongue.

The Crab returned his bow, then Tale-Chaser padded to the table and knelt. A pair of larger, bulkier nezumi followed, both scarred and bearing spears. Tale-Chaser introduced them as his escorts. Their still being armed raised Sukune's eyebrows. Etiquette dictated that, unless they were actually at war, guests would set aside their weapons, trusting their Crab hosts to protect them. But these guests weren't samurai, so normal courtesies, such as making reverence at the kamidana, obviously didn't apply.

Sukune turned his attention back to Tale-Chaser. Superficially, he seemed little different than the more familiar nezumi who lived near and even beneath the Carpenter Wall, from tribes called Third Whisker and Cracked Bone. Covered in sleek, red-brown fur, with eyes like orbs of black glass, he stood probably not quite as tall as Sukune's chest. Both he and his escorts wore simple, robelike garments of coarse cloth. Tale-Chaser also had things woven into his fur: sticks and twigs, some of which looked gnawed upon, and bits of twisted and braided grass. He struck Sukune as old for his kind, the fur of his muzzle graying in a way not too different from his own father's thinning hair.

None of which answered the immediate questions. The nezumi had a long association with the Crab, though particularly with the Hiruma, and particularly in the Shadowlands. Why did this Tale-Chaser's presence demand the attention of not just the Kuni daimyō, but the Crab Clan Champion himself? Yori had called Tale-Chaser a Rememberer, and Rememberers were important members of their tribe, custodians of detailed oral histories of their people, in this case, the–

"The Tattered Ear tribe?" O-Ushi said, frowning. "I am not familiar with them."

"They dwell in the Shinomen Forest," Yori said. "Our clan

records few dealings with them, though, because our people rarely enter past the forest margins. Such encounters as have been chronicled were, however, generally amicable."

O-Ushi glanced at Yori. "Generally?"

Yori offered a slight shrug. "Some of my family's ancestors had the misguided belief that, given their immunity to the Taint of Jigoku, useful information could be gained by–" he paused, "–studying the nezumi." Yori turned to Tale-Chaser. "However, that was long ago, such that I am hopeful we have put said matters behind us."

"Behind, yes," Tale-Chaser said, "but remembered."

Yori offered Tale-Chaser a bow of acknowledgment, but Sukune understood the hint of recrimination in the nezumi's reply. To have been *studied* in the gloomy laboratories of the Kuni had connotations he didn't want to even begin contemplating.

Silence. Sukune looked back at his father, assuming he would take charge of the meeting. To his surprise, though, he found Kisada watching *him*, as though waiting for Sukune to say something.

So he did. "You have come a long way, Tale-Chaser-sama. Whatever brings you here must be important."

"Important, yes."

"That," Kuni Yori said, "is a most dramatic understatement." He nodded at Kuni Daigo, who folded back the silk wrapping from the thing he had placed on the table.

It was a *sode*, a flat, armored shoulder plate from an *ō-yoroi*, a suit of heavy armor. This one displayed fine workmanship.

Remarkably fine. The lamellar strips of lacquered leather gleamed, the knotted cords lacing them together precisely and uniformly. It was colored a dark gray that reminded Sukune of the base of a thundercloud, the lacings black, the Crab Clan crest rendered upon it in pale gray-blue.

O-Ushi leaned closer. "That is magnificent work."

Yori offered a thin smile. "Faint praise, Hida-san, for something crafted by Lord Osano-wo himself."

Silence.

Sukune glanced again at his father. Again, he found Kisada already watching him.

"Crafted by Osano-wo?" Sukune said, turning back to Yori. "That is a remarkable claim, Kuni-sama."

And an unlikely one. Hida Osano-wo, the younger son of the Kami Hida himself, had lived, died, and ascended to become the Fortune of Fire and Thunder a thousand years ago. Anything truly crafted by his hands would be beyond rare. It would be a *nemuranai*, a sacred artifact, its spirit certainly awakened to potency by time and provenance. There was, in fact, only one such thing Sukune could think of, and it had been lost for hundreds of...

Sukune sat forward, his gaze locked on the sode, and whispered a single word. "*Kikyo.*"

Yori nodded. "We have researched this piece of armor since Tale-Chaser arrived here with it. We are certain that this is, indeed, a component of Kikyo, armor Lord Osano-wo made for Hida Atarashi."

Sukune sat back on his heels and bowed deeply to the sode. Practically the first story learned by every Crab child told how Hida Atarashi, the Kami Hida's elder son, had represented the Crab Clan on the Day of Thunder, when the Dark God Fu Leng was finally defeated. Atarashi died that day, but Osano-wo refused to believe it, and he made a magnificent set of armor for his older brother. Named Kikyo, the armor remained in Hida Palace, awaiting the day Atarashi would return to claim it. Then, almost two hundred years ago, a Crab Clan general named Hida Chuku donned the armor and led a great army into the Shadowlands, intent on ending its vile threat to Rokugan once and for all. The army, Chuku, and the armor were never seen again. The teak stand upon which Kikyo had rested in the halls of Castle Hida still stood empty in its place of honor.

O-Ushi stared at the sode. "But how can this be Kikyo?" She looked at Tale-Chaser. "Did you find this in the Shadowlands?"

Sukune glanced at the great map across the room, depicting both the Empire and the Shadowlands. Most Rokugani maps omitted the latter, for fear of attracting the attention of evil spirits. However, Jigoku, the underworld claimed by demons and evil spirits, encroached on the Mortal Realm through the Festering Pit at the center of the Shadowlands. Monstrous hordes emanating from that terrible place flung themselves without respite at the Empire – or, more to the point, at the Crab, whose ancient duty was to stop them. The Crab, therefore, had no need to try to avoid the attention of evil spirits. They already very much had it.

The map portrayed a long distance between the Shadowlands and the great Shinomen Forest, where Tale-Chaser's tribe lived. He might have made the journey, but–

"No," Tale-Chaser said, "never been to terrible place of Yesterday. I found it in the forest, in …" He stopped, then uttered a series of soft squeaks and chitters. "Must think to translate, yes? Found it in Cave of Blood… er, Bloody Ghost Fire."

"If this was not recovered from the Shadowlands," O-Ushi said, "then it cannot be part of Kikyo."

"I assure you," Yori said, "I am certain that it is."

Sukune pulled his eyes away from the piece of armor. "Tale-Chaser-sama, how did you come to possess this?"

The Rememberer didn't answer immediately. Instead, he untangled a stick from his fur, then spent a moment running his tongue across it, as though tasting it. Sukune and the others exchanged glances. When Tale-Chaser finally did speak, his voice assumed a rhythmic, sing-song tone. "*Began with a dream…*"

Despite the nezumi's halting Rokugani, Sukune found himself drawn into Tale-Chaser's tale. Sucking mud, cold water, hard stone. Darkness, brooding fear, then panic, as Tale-Chaser–

–*yanked one last, desperate time at the armored plate–*
–*dropped to all fours and ran–*
–*the cave mouth appeared, revealing skeletal trees–*
–*glanced back once–*
–*all dead–*

It took Sukune a moment to realize Tale-Chaser had gone silent, his story finished. He glanced around the table. O-Ushi and Daigo stared, as entranced as he had been. Yori looked intently at the sode. And Kisada…

Kisada watched Sukune again.

"Crab marking is clear," Tale-Chaser said, pointing at the sode. "So, we brought it to your town near forest… called Maemikake, yes? And Crab there said to find you. So we did, so you can help Tattered Ear."

Sukune looked back at Tale-Chaser. "Help with what?"

"Help rid Tattered Ear of darkness woken by…" He stopped and sagged slightly. "By me."

"It would appear," Yori said, "that the removal of this piece of Kikyo roused… something. Tale-Chaser described the area surrounding the cave as a bleak, dark swamp. We have long been aware of swamps in the Shinomen Forest that are Tainted, the lingering effect of events now lost to history. The Cave of Bloody Ghost Fire, where the Tattered Ear apparently found the armor, is located in these so-called Shadowed Swamps. And now, whatever their interference with the armor has provoked apparently threatens Tale-Chaser's tribe."

"So," Tale-Chaser said, "we will find the swamps again, take you to your armor. And you will help Tattered Ear."

Again, silence. Sukune glanced around and, yet again, found his father unusually focused on him. He made himself refrain from frowning or sighing. Such a silent, icy stare normally meant disapproval. How had he earned his father's ire this time? Had Kisada somehow learned about his diatribe to O-Ushi on the battlement? O-Ushi spoke up. "With all due respect, Kuni-sama, I find it difficult to believe that the nezumi found the lost armor of Hida Atarashi in a cave in the Shinomen Forest. This is a Crab piece, yes. But it must be part of something else. Kikyo *must* be somewhere in the Shadowlands." She directed her last words at their father. Yori opened his mouth to reply, but Kisada raised a hand.

"Sukune-san," he said, "what are your thoughts?"

Sukune stared for a moment. Father *wasn't* angry at him? He gave himself a mental shake. He hadn't formulated an opinion, but one didn't put off the Great Bear with, *I'm thinking about it.* So he said what came to him.

"If... if there is even a chance this is Kikyo, then... We must pursue it, my lord. And if it is not Kikyo, it is clearly still something important to our clan."

Kisada said nothing for a moment, then nodded, as though coming to a decision. "You are correct. An expedition must be mounted both to retrieve this armor and to assist Tale-Chaser's people."

Sukune looked at O-Ushi. This explained why Kisada had brought them here. His sister would command this expedition, and he would help her mount it. He considered what counsel he could offer her. Hiruma's *The Way of the Scout* offered useful insights into operating in difficult terrain, such as that of the Shinomen Forest. In fact, Sukune had blended Hiruma's work with that of a Lion tactician – a samurai of the Ikoma family whose name escaped him – in an effort to go beyond simply scouting and develop doctrine applicable to fighting battles in such a complex environment. His notes on the matter were back in Hida Palace, but he should still be able to offer O-Ushi some worthwhile advice–

"Sukune-san," Kisada said, "you will lead this expedition, as its commander."

Sukune stared, his absent notes abruptly forgotten.

"O-Ushi-san," Kisada went on, "will be your lieutenant. You may draw such forces as you deem necessary from the reserve army stationed here, at Kuni Castle. You will leave in no more than five days."

O-Ushi, Yori, and the others were staring at him, but he could not pull his gaze from his father.

I am commanding this expedition? Me?

Kisada met Sukune's frozen stare. In his father's eyes lay the truth behind his decision.

This is your chance to prove yourself, Sukune. To prove your ideas about how the Crab wage war. To prove yourself to your Empire, to your clan and family...

And to me.

Sukune finally remembered to bow. "As you command, my lord."

Sukune stood once more on the battlement and looked down into the drill yard. There was no wind; it had died a day ago. Absent its chill, Lady Sun's heat bore down unabated. Sweat sheened the troops marshaling in the yard, while they labored under the hard scrutiny of their sergeants. They had already completed a multitude of tasks, but a multitude more had yet to be done to prepare for the long march ahead.

Not *the* troops, Sukune reminded himself. *His* troops. Footsteps cracked against the stone behind him. Sukune recognized his sister's angry walk.

"What is this," O-Ushi snapped, "about Kuni Yori accompanying this expedition?"

Sukune could only shrug. "He discussed it with Father, who agreed. Yori's contention is that, given what we are seeking, and where we are seeking it, the effort requires someone of his–" He hesitated, recalling the words of the Kuni daimyō. "Of his stature and abilities, to help ensure our success." He shrugged again. "I think he simply wants to be there when we discover Atarashi's lost armor. Honestly, I can hardly blame him for that."

"I can. He is a daimyō. His place is here, overseeing his

family and all those in service to the Kuni. His presence risks muddying the chain of command."

"He has been very public about the subordinate nature of his role."

O-Ushi scowled. "I am still doubtful. He..." She stopped, biting back whatever she'd been about to say, then turned her scowl on the troops below. "Anyway, I still doubt that this really is Kikyo. How could it be, when all accounts say it was lost in the Shadowlands?"

"Excuse," a new voice said. "I cannot say if this armor is the one you name. But it is armor of samurai, of Crab. It is very special. Smells of fire and storm."

Neither of them had heard Tale-Chaser approach, the soft patter of his paws lost amid the martial clatter from below. His escorts – both his own nezumi guards and a pair of Crab warriors assigned to the duty – stopped a discreet distance away.

"Your pardon, Tale-Chaser-sama," Sukune said. "My sister does not doubt your sincerity. She is simply unsure that what you have found is truly what Kuni Yori believes it to be." He glanced at O-Ushi. "Although, if the nezumi believe it smells of fire and storm..."

O-Ushi just shrugged, but it lacked her earlier conviction.

"I understand," Tale-Chaser said. "But that is important only to Crab, yes? For the Tattered Ear, the dark thing woken by finding it is the most urgent of all."

The *dark thing*. Those two words, and the fact it had been *very, very big*, had been all Tale-Chaser could tell them of whatever apparently lurked near the armor. It said nothing whatsoever about what they might end up facing, which left them dangerously uninformed unless, and until, they actually encountered it.

Sukune turned back to Tale-Chaser. "Well, whatever this *dark thing* is, we shall help you deal with it, Tale-Chaser-sama."

The nezumi peered over the battlement. "Hope so. The dark thing was very, very terrible."

"We are the Crab," O-Ushi said. "Defeating terrible things is what we do."

Sukune admired his sister's confidence. Looking down at the – at *his* troops – all he could envision were the many things that could go so terribly wrong.

CHAPTER THREE

Once, as a boy, Sukune had snuck into the war room of Hida Palace. The massive map table there had fascinated him. It was not only a vast and detailed world in miniature, but one specifically intended for the design of military campaigns. He'd been sick yet again, his body wracked with aches, and the medicines he'd been given left his head pounding. But he'd been struck by an idea, something inspired by one of his tutors during a lesson about Akodo's *Leadership*, one of the Empire's most important treatises on war.

Clad only in a sleep robe, his bare feet cold against the stone floor, he'd taken up the colored wooden blocks representing companies and legions, supply trains and siege engines, and arranged them across the tiny hills and streams and mountains just *so*, in accordance with his great idea. His older brother, Yakamo, had caught him and immediately called for their father – of course. Sukune remembered that, too. Yakamo's contemptuous smirk as he'd held Sukune pinned, one arm bent painfully behind his back. O-Ushi had shown up first, though, and demanded that Yakamo release their brother. Before it once more came to blows between brother and sister, Kisada had arrived and thundered a command that sent them all scurrying back to bed.

The next day, Sukune crept back to the war room, desperate to resume leading his miniature wooden armies. He'd been surprised to find Kisada there, speaking to a pair of Crab generals and pointing at the map table, including Sukune's battle plan, still in place from the night before.

His father never said anything about the matter. But neither did he explicitly forbid Sukune from spending time in the war room. It soon became the boy's favorite place, his many hours alone there, waging epic campaigns across the little world, among his fondest memories.

He might be of little use as a warrior, the frail, sickly child having grown into a frail, sickly adult. But, when it came to matters of grand strategy, of the maneuver and logistics of armies, his ineptitude with a *tetsubō* no longer mattered. Sukune could command.

Or he could command armies of wood blocks, anyway, across battlefields that would fit into a single room.

He shaded his eyes against Lady Sun. These flesh-and-blood Crab warriors he now commanded were not just wooden blocks, and they deployed not onto a miniature field, but into the vast, primal wilderness of the great Shinomen Forest.

But he still must command them.

He glanced up at the massive stone *torii* gate looming overhead. Called the Gates of Persistence, the gate was said to have been carved from a single piece of stone, laboriously crafted and transported here by a samurai named Kaiu

Sudaro. Sudaro's young son had become lost in the Shinomen Forest and, after many weeks, was assumed dead. But the boy reappeared, unharmed, supposedly on this very spot, protected by some mysterious power of the forest. In gratitude, Sudaro had erected this great monument to the forest, a labor that took him many years and that, after his death, earned him ascension as the Fortune of Persistence.

Sukune read the characters graven into the stone vaulting overhead: *Nothing. Tomorrow. Forever. Today.* The simple script nonetheless conveyed despair preceding triumph, the need to maintain faith, to persist. Unless they had no alternative, Crab would always enter the Shinomen Forest only by passing beneath this gate. To do otherwise was not only to disrespect the Fortune, but to risk bad luck and the ire of the forest.

Every one of the more than two hundred members of the expedition, from the Kuni daimyō to the lowliest peasant retainer, would therefore enter the forest through the gate. Sukune had been first through them, with Tale-Chaser and his nezumi escorts immediately behind. O-Ushi followed, her favored weapon, a great *ōtsuchi* hammer, propped on her shoulder. With her came a pair of young Hiruma tasked to act variously as Sukune's aides, couriers, and guards. The Hiruma company followed. Lightly armored, and armed with spears and bows, they were mainly skirmishers, intended to engage and support from a distance. Still, each also bore a secondary weapon, bladed or blunt, inlaid with jade-infused resin in the Shirogane style for use against Tainted foes. Once through the gates, they detached scouts, who fanned out to secure the way ahead.

Now the Hida company trudged through the shadow of the

great gate, their faces grimly set against the burden each carried: heavy armor; a primary weapon, such as a massive *nodachi* sword or a club-like tetsubō; a jade-inlaid secondary weapon; and other gear and supplies. In the rear plodded a company of *ashigaru*, auxiliary peasant warriors, and finally a contingent of *hinin* Mudcrows, grubby corpse handlers who cleared the aftermath of battles. All the commoners bent under the weight of yet more supplies, essentially serving as the expedition's baggage train. Tale-Chaser had been clear that they should not eat or drink anything they found in the forest without his approval, so they must be as self-sufficient as possible.

A short distance away was the expedition's spiritual contingent. Kuni Yori stood by his apprentice, Daigo. With them was an intense woman named Kuni Kana, whose gaunt face and staring eyes made Sukune uneasy in a way he couldn't define. Her apprentice, a young Kuni named Naoyuki, was a stark contrast to Kana, grinning frequently and amiably. Sukune knew little about either Kana or Naoyuki, but if Yori himself had chosen them, he had no reason to doubt their facility with *shugendō*, the way of communion with spirits, and particularly those of the elements. He hoped this was true, anyway. Glancing at the gloomy forest ahead, he could easily envision myriad spirits eagerly awaiting them, for purposes he could only begin to guess.

Near the Kuni stood a trio of priests. Unlike the Kuni, who would deal with otherworldly forces directly, the priests would see to the ongoing spiritual needs of the expedition. They were doing so now, chanting prayers while one of them waved a wand of sacred *sakaki* wood hung with paper streamers over the passing troops. Inscribed with holy scriptures, the streamers would absorb *kegare* – spiritual impurity – from the expedition's members and eventually be burned. This, along with the positive energy of the gates, would ensure the expedition began its quest in a state of spiritual purity.

A hoarse shout erupted from further up the column. "You!" a man's voice growled. "Do you think you stroll through the gardens of some simpering Crane? Keep your attention on your duty, not on some pretty flowers!"

The speaker, a hulking brute of a lieutenant who commanded the heavy company of Hida, strode forward and cuffed one of the Hida warriors across the face. The man staggered, briefly disrupting the formation around him. This apparently further enraged the lieutenant, who shouted something else as he started dragging the unfortunate bushi from the ranks, a massive fist raised.

"Hida Amoro-san!" O-Ushi called out. "Hida Sukune-sama requires a moment of your time!"

Sukune shot her a sharp glance. The one she returned said, *you must deal with this.* She was, of course, correct. Sukune took a deep breath, bracing himself as the man approached.

Even more than his and O-Ushi's tempestuous brother Yakamo, Amoro was everything Sukune was not: slabs of muscle, uncouth and unkempt, with a reputation for going berserk in battle and simply attacking whatever he confronted until there was nothing left to die. Amoro was also their cousin, son of Hida Kisada's youngest sister, who had died giving birth to him. Some claimed that she was his first victim – but never where Amoro might hear it.

Amoro was also a powerful and supremely brave warrior who had never lost a skirmish or faltered in battle – hence Kisada's giving him command of the expedition's company of Hida, despite the fact that Sukune and Amoro despised one another.

Or more likely, Sukune thought, because of it. This was probably another way his father would test him in this, his first true command. Amoro made no secret of his contempt for Sukune's ideas about the Crab approach to warfighting, declaring them an insult to their ancestors, who had fought and died defending the Empire – successfully – using the Crab's ancient and well-established martial philosophies. Sukune's frailty, and his shortcomings as a warrior, only intensified Amoro's scorn.

Stopping and offering a perfunctory bow, Amoro said, "You wished to speak to me, Sukune… sama?"

Even a samurai freshly done with their *gempuku* would know how much silence could be placed between a name and the following honorific so as not to be insulting. Amoro either didn't or, more likely, didn't care.

Sukune glanced at O-Ushi, who returned a small nod. *Get on with it.*

"Yes," Sukune said. He had no words, no idea what to say to this massive, explosive man.

Amoro shrugged and started to turn away. "Very well, Hida-sama. Now that you have spoken, I shall return to my duties–"

"No," Sukune said, swallowing. "Wait. I am… concerned… about your treatment of that soldier just now."

Amoro turned back, his face suddenly all hard planes and angles. "Because I was too lenient with him?"

"No, because you were… too aggressive." Sukune's voice trailed off into the realization he had just accused a Crab bushi famous for his vicious bloodlust of being *too aggressive*.

Amoro took a step toward Sukune. Tale-Chaser, watching the exchange, quickly backed away, his guards tensing, but O-Ushi put herself in Amoro's path.

"As Hida Sukune-sama only just said to me," she said, "discipline is crucial, but reckless punishment is worse than useless. It risks rendering our warriors unfit for battle before it has even begun. It risks weakening us. And you would not wish to see us weakened, Amoro-san."

Amoro loomed over O-Ushi, a full head taller and far more massive. But O-Ushi made Sukune think of a sturdy oak, firmly rooted against an approaching storm. After a moment, Amoro grinned.

"Of course not, Hida Sukune-sama," he said, his gaze still on O-Ushi. "I appreciate your words and shall certainly heed them. Now, with your leave, I shall return to my command."

Sukune nodded. Amoro bowed and stalked back toward his company of Hida.

O-Ushi puffed out a sigh. "I am sorry, Sukune," she said, "but Amoro must be made firmly aware of who is in command here."

Sukune glanced around. His Hiruma aides had certainly heard her words, but they'd carefully kept their attention elsewhere. Tale-Chaser just seemed relieved the confrontation had ended.

"I think you have succeeded, sister."

O-Ushi opened her mouth, but Sukune just walked away. As he did, he glanced up at the towering torii.

Nothing. Tomorrow. Forever. Today.

Kaiu Sudaro had devoted most of his life to this monument, and he was named a Fortune for his devotion. But that was all the story of his ascension said. What of the multitude of obstacles and setbacks and difficulties he had undoubtedly faced along the way? The story said nothing about those – and that was unfortunate. After all, they were what really made his persistence matter, and where the true lessons lay.

Beyond the Gates of Persistence, scattered copses of red cedar and hemlock, of yew and poplar and maple, merged into a tangled wall of gnarled trunks, leafy undergrowth, and gloom. Birds flitted and piped overhead, but in the shadowed forest ahead, silence.

Left to their own devices, the Crab would simply have chosen a place to enter, then bulled their way through, their progress slow and laborious. Fortunately, they were not on their own. Tale-Chaser studied the bulwark of trees, as much with his twitching nose as with his eyes, then said, "This way, yes," and walked on. He led the Crab onto a narrow path that even the canniest of the Hiruma scouts had missed. Its width forced them to redeploy into a single file, but the way was relatively easy, the path winding among the trees, leading them steadily north and slightly east. Sukune, with Tale-Chaser immediately behind him, led the main column, preceded by the scouts who skirmished ahead and to the flanks.

The expedition had entered the Shinomen Forest.

Deep silence engulfed them. Birds – mainly larks, thrushes, and sparrows – still flashed and darted overhead, but uttered no calls. Even the flies and gnats seemed strangely subdued, as though wary of breaking the quiet. Dust motes floated through the still air, gleaming brightly when they drifted through a shaft of sunlight.

After only a few hundred paces, a slender figure stepped into the path, forcing Sukune to signal a halt. He tensed, but relaxed again as he recognized Hiruma Kazane, commander of the Hiruma company.

"Your pardon, Hida-sama," Kazane said, offering a quick bow. "Unfortunately, away from this path, the way is extremely difficult: the ground is rough and the foliage very thick. Our scouts are barely able to maintain their place ahead of the column, much less remain alert for threats."

Sukune nodded, about to respond, but Tale-Chaser stepped up beside him, shaking his head. "Excuse me, Sukune-sama. Best to stay on the path, or close enough to see the path."

O-Ushi leaned on her massive hammer. "That means we may only become aware of threats when they are upon us." Kazane nodded at her words.

Kuni Yori, a short distance behind, spoke up. "Hida Sukunesan, if I may... Tale-Chaser is our guide. If he believes straying from this path is perilous, then we should heed his words."

Sukune looked from one to the next as they spoke. Crab doctrine was clear: scouts were to be deployed, to provide early warning of threats. And although it was another, dogmatic convention, this one made sense. It had been developed and refined after hard experience in the Shadowlands, where not doing it would be suicidal.

But this was not the Shadowlands. The Shadowlands' barren, blasted terrain was generally open, the occasional stands of twisted forest usually easy to bypass. This place was entirely the opposite. Sukune thought about the doctrine, and about what he remembered from the notes he'd made from Hiruma's *The Way of the Scout*. He opened his mouth to speak to Kazane, but found he had no breath. Even their relatively slow pace had taxed him over the minuscule distance they'd covered. So he tried to appear as though he were considering the matter, without laboring too obviously at the heavy air hanging beneath the trees.

"What do…" he finally began, "what do you think–" but had to stop, betrayed by his lungs again, by an unavoidable coughing fit.

Kazane ignored Sukune's discomfiture. "I believe it is essential we continue to deploy scouts, Hida-sama. Even if they must remain in sight of this path, they will provide–" She paused as Sukune coughed again. "They will provide at least some warning."

Sukune nodded, catching his breath. "Very well. Redeploy your detachment accordingly."

Kazane bowed again, then turned and stepped away, whistling a signal intended to bring her skirmishers back.

Tale-Chaser muttered something, and Yori nodded. "I quite agree."

O-Ushi turned to him. "Do you have something further to offer, Kuni-sama?"

"No, but I believe our guide does."

"Crab beating their way through the forest instead of following the path slows us all down," Tale-Chaser said. "Speed and quiet are our best friends here."

"I appreciate your wisdom, Tale-Chaser-sama," Sukune replied, "but we have learned the value of–" He paused, but only briefly this time, his breathing finally having almost returned to normal. "Of maintaining security as we march."

They waited for Kazane to signal that her scouts had resumed their way. Instead, she eventually returned to the path. Sukune could see several of her scouts still crouching in place, while Kazane scanned the bushy wilderness beyond them, a frown creasing her weather-browned face.

"Is something amiss, Hiruma-san?" Sukune asked.

"Sayua-san is not here. She was scouting on the right flank but did not answer the return signal. No one has seen her."

Sukune now frowned. They were, what, perhaps five hundred paces into the forest? Hiruma Sayua could not be far away.

He glanced at Lady Sun, spearing down through the tangled branches in hard, bright beams. "I believe we can spare the time to find her, Kazane-san. She must be nearby."

Kazane nodded and dispatched scouts in pairs to locate the missing Sayua. The better part of an hour later, the last of them returned, reporting no sign of her. Hiruma Sayua had, it seemed, simply vanished.

Kazane's mouth was a hard, thin line. "Sayua-san was veteran of at least a dozen patrols into the Shadowlands." She glanced around. "It would appear I do not know this forest as well as I thought I did."

A bleak tone flattened Kazane's voice. Sukune should say *something*. Something encouraging. But he could think of nothing.

Kuni Yori stepped close to Sukune. "Perhaps," he said quietly, "you now see the wisdom in Tale-Chaser's words. I urge you to heed our guide."

Sukune glanced at O-Ushi. He could tell she wished to say something but, like him, had nothing to say.

He puffed out a breath. "Hiruma Kazane-san, recall your company to the path. We will forgo scouts, at least for the time being."

Kazane bowed. "As you wish, Hida-sama."

O-Ushi muttered something, but when Sukune turned to her, she simply shook her head and walked away.

The day wore on. As it did, the shadows deepened, and the forest changed.

The trees had been old – tall and hoary and thick through their trunks, even more so than their cousins growing on the foothills of the Twilight Mountains. Now, though, the trees looming over the expedition weren't merely old: they were *ancient*. Maples, firs, and poplars soared to impossible heights, their upper reaches lost in a canopy of branches so tangled and thick that no sky showed through them. Sukune marveled as he skirted a hemlock so massive its trunk could only be fully embraced by eight adults, perhaps, with arms outstretched and hands linked? Ten?

The undergrowth thickened as well. Willow, clethra, ferns, and flowering shrubs Sukune didn't even recognize pressed in on the path, compressing it into a narrow corridor walled by lush greenery. The air grew thick and damp, reeking of comingled growth and decay. Sukune had to work even harder to breathe as he plodded along. Several times, after climbing an incline or clambering over fallen trees, he had to call a halt – ostensibly to confer with O-Ushi, but really just to catch his breath and let his racing heart slow. His pack yanked at his shoulders. It was smaller and lighter than those carried by the rest of the Crab, an embarrassing reality his infirmities forced him to accept. Some of the weight was the sode Tale-Chaser had brought to Kuni Castle. There had been much debate about whether it should be brought along or left safely in Kuni Castle. Kisada had left the final decision to Sukune, who reasoned that it would be better to have it, and not need it, than to need it and not have it.

He frowned as they splashed across a stream, the murky water strangely tepid against his feet. Beyond it, the path ascended yet another hill. A strenuous march, with no scouts deployed, along a single, narrow path. One needn't have read any books of tactics or strategy to know this seemed to almost be *seeking* disaster–

"Tale-Chaser," O-Ushi said from behind Sukune, "who made this path? It appears well-used."

Sukune glanced back. His sister obviously shared his worries. "The Tattered Ear made some paths, like this one. Animals made others." Tale-Chaser paused to scratch an ear. "We are not sure who made some paths, though. They are just always there. Maybe other things made them, that even the Tattered Ear do not know. The forest is very, very big."

"Well," O-Ushi said, "as much as I do not like being constrained to this narrow path, if we are going to follow such well-worn routes all the way, then navigation will be one less thing to worry about, at least."

Tale-Chaser remained silent for a moment, then said, "It is a good path, yes, to the home of the Tattered Ear. Then not so good. Dark swamps are hard to find sometimes."

Sukune sighed and started up the hill. Tale-Chaser had already said the Tattered Ear's home was three days ahead. Then, at least two more days beyond that – perhaps more – to where the swamps *might* begin.

Yes, the forest seemed very, very big indeed.

The coming of night brought more changes to the Shinomen Forest. As the expedition halted and began its night routine, the forest assumed a watchful, brooding menace. Sukune, picking his way along the path to check on his command, found himself glancing quickly aside, each time convinced he had seen eyes staring at him. Each time, it turned out to be nothing more than vague patterns in gnarled bark. Darkness and his imagination had only made them seem like something more.

And yet, in each of those startled moments, they had definitely been eyes. Sukune was sure of it, in a visceral way. Eyes that regarded him with utter dispassion, the way he might look at an insect scuttling through the leaf mold – unworthy of consideration, unless it was to be crushed. And he would turn, and rationality would return, resolving them back into shapes in the bark. So Sukune would curse himself and turn away.

And again, in that instant before they were completely out of his sight, they would be eyes again.

Nor was he the only one, it seemed, who glimpsed unsettling things in the deepening night. Many of the Crab he passed, even his own aides, seemed to peer intently at things away from the path. No one spoke about what they might have seen, though, nor did anyone ask.

He passed a squad of Hida sitting along the path, their sergeant inspecting their feet by the flickering glow of a fire. At Tale-Chaser's insistence, their fires had all been placed only on the path, and then only fueled by dead wood that could be gathered within reach of it. After the disappearance of Hiruma Sayua, Sukune was not inclined to ignore the nezumi's counsel.

The sergeant bowed as Sukune passed by, then returned to her less-than-pleasant, but essential, task. Ensuring her soldiers were not concealing any injuries to their feet was just another of the myriad small things that kept an army functioning. Sukune could recall instances of warriors doggedly saying nothing until they were debilitated by feet so hugely swollen, they had to be cut free of boots, or toes gone so gangrenous they simply fell off. Even a simple blister could become crippling if left untreated. Worse, in the presence of the Taint, even a small wound increased the risk of implacable spiritual infection. It was the sergeant's job to circumvent that sort of stubborn endurance, so that all of her soldiers would be ready to fight, anywhere and at any time – or would answer for it if they were not.

On the way back, he met the priests, who were moving among the troops conducting their own inspection: one for spiritual contamination or burdens among the soldiers. Aside from a general uneasiness over the unfamiliar surroundings, they reported all was well. Sukune was glad for that. At least, until the next time he saw those watching eyes, and was left wondering if the priests might have missed something.

He finally returned to the fire where O-Ushi and the nezumi Rememberer sat. Yori and the other Kuni rested nearby. O-Ushi looked up from tightening the lacing on her armor, opening her mouth to say something, but a terrific, splintering crash wrenched apart the stillness of the night. Shouts of alarm went up; Sukune heard sergeants bark orders to their squads, while the hoarse shout of Hida Amoro rose above all of it, ordering his company to stand ready. Sukune snatched up his tetsubō – a smaller, lighter version of the weapon, more suited to his slight build – and peered into the darkness, flanked by his Hiruma aides, each wielding a short, brutal axe. O-Ushi crouched, armor forgotten, great hammer ready to swing.

Silence.

Tale-Chaser's voice rose from near the fire. "Caution is good for loud noises in dark, yes, but these loud noises only…" He trailed off into a series of squeaks and chitters. Sukune gave him a puzzled frown.

"Not sure of your words," the Rememberer said. "The sound of falling trees, happens in the forest at night…"

"*Furusoma*," someone said. Kuni Daigo stood a short distance along the path, his white-painted face lit a lurid orange by the firelight. The young shugenja offered a quick bow. "Your pardon, Hida-sama. I sought to learn what I could about the Shinomen Forest before we departed. The furusoma is mentioned by woodcutters, scouts, and even bandits who have spent time here. It is the sound of large trees falling in the distance. As Tale-Chaser said, it happens at night–"

Another great, shuddering crash ripped through the air. More shouts rose from the Crab.

"–and seems," Daigo went on, "to be more frequent and… intense here than in other forests."

"To what end?" O-Ushi asked. "If the intent is to lure us, then such dire noises in the night seems a poor choice."

"I am sorry, Hida-sama," Daigo said. "I do not know."

From the gloom beyond Daigo, an almost unseen Kuni Yori said, "It very likely has nothing to do with us at all. The forest has its own purposes."

O-Ushi leaned close to Sukune. "I know you have just walked among our people, but you should do so again," she said. "Explain this to them."

Sukune lowered his undersized tetsubō.

The forest has its own purposes, indeed. Had the priests accounted for that?

He sighed out a breath that tasted of damp leaves and started back along the path, eyes-that-weren't once more following him from the darkness.

CHAPTER FOUR

Sukune stopped at the top of a rise and looked back. He could see a good portion of the expedition trudging up the slope behind him – most of the Hida company, in fact. Few places had offered anything even close to such an expansive view since they'd entered the forest. Misgivings about being constrained to this single path still chewed at Sukune, but only when he actually thought to be worried about it. And that was the worst of it. This relentless march between tangled walls of foliage, through air that hung stale and thick, induced a sort of stupor, a soporific plod that sent the mind wandering off on journeys of its own. Such complacency was dangerous. Sukune would find himself lost in slogging reverie and yank himself back to the here and now. Then, he'd do it again. And again. Sun Tao had written, "Tired soldiers are a defeat waiting to happen." It was true. But a tired mind was worse, by far, than a tired body.

He must have said something aloud, because a passing warrior said, "Pardon, Hida-sama?" Sukune just shook his head at the man. The preceding night certainly hadn't helped. The crash of falling trees had persisted through the night, seemingly always just as sleep finally began to take him. One had sounded so close he'd actually shouted a warning and scrambled away from his bedroll. There had been no falling tree, of course, and O-Ushi and his aides had gaped in a way that said they'd heard nothing at all.

Sukune stifled a yawn. The rear of the Hida company marched into view, the bushi following a path winding among dark, still pools shadowed by massive pines. Looking at the water reminded Sukune that he should check on the expedition's supply. Tale-Chaser kept insisting they neither eat nor drink anything taken from the forest unless he–

A heavy splash and a sharp cry made Sukune jump. A bushi thrashed in one of the pools, the path skirting it apparently having collapsed under him. Sukune cursed and started back down the hill, pushing past the Crab warriors who had stopped at the commotion. His Hiruma aides hurried after him. By the time he reached the pool, the man was mostly submerged, his hands caked in black mud as he scrabbled frantically at the bank. Three of his squad mates reached for him, shouting encouragement. Hida Amoro appeared, dropping his tetsubō, shucking his pack, and leaping into the pool. As he did, the fallen warrior lost his grip on the slimy muck and slid beneath the water with a strangled gasp.

Amoro landed in the pool with a heavy splash, and stood there, the water barely reaching his knees.

Sukune and the others could only stare as Amoro reached into the water and swept his hands around, desperately grasping for the man who, somehow, had sunk out of sight in a pond that barely wet the Hida lieutenant's feet.

"He is… not here!" Amoro shouted, sloshing from one side

Legend of the Five Rings

of the pond to the other. He should have stepped on the missing bushi, even tripped over him. "Where has he gone?"

Amoro looked up at Sukune, his face a rictus of confused fury. "How in Bishamon's name could he be *gone*?"

Sukune could only shake his head.

Sukune kept his gaze on the fire his aides had set on the path. It guttered and smoked, as though struggling to stay lit. Like the expedition itself, it seemed tired and dispirited.

Sukune stared at the food he'd unpacked: rice balls, dried squid, and *umeboshi* pickles. Though he had been ravenous, he suddenly found himself with little appetite. He made himself eat anyway: chewing, swallowing, trying to ignore his aching joints, the arrhythmic flutter of his heart, the chronic shortness of breath that kept forcing him to pause and take a moment to breathe.

At least he was alive to feel miserable. The same couldn't be said for the Hida who had vanished into what was, in every discernible way, just a shallow pond. Nor could it be said for the ashigaru who had been crushed by a massive hemlock bough, the Hiruma archer who had plunged off a cliff whose edge no one had even realized the path skirted, or the pair of Mudcrows who, like the scout, Sayua, had simply vanished without a trace.

Sukune could feel unease permeating the expedition, as pervasive as their own grime and sweat. In his seminal work *Before the Strike*, the Lion general Akodo Tōma had written, "Know the minds of your soldiers before the first drum beat, the first horn signal, the first order to charge, because it is there that the battle has already been lost or won."

Sensible words, when read in the orderly confines of a dōjō.

Here, amid the ancient wilderness of the Shinomen Forest, they had a sinister edge, like a dire prophecy.

Something rushed overhead with a staccato beat of wings. A bird, flying low and fast. Hunting, probably, before darkness concealed its prey.

"The expedition has begun its night routine," O-Ushi said, stepping out of the gloom and crouching beside Sukune. "You should walk among the troops before it is completely dark. They are..." She frowned at the fire, as though searching for a word.

"On edge," Sukune said, and she nodded. He flicked a bit of rice off his kimono. "This has been a taxing journey. It will be good to reach the home of the Tattered Ear tomorrow. We could use the respite."

O-Ushi's eyes narrowed but remained fixed on the fire. "In my mind, I've been likening these things that have happened – this place, in fact – to the Shadowlands. Despite our best efforts, our most careful precautions, our people are lost or killed there, too, often in terrible and arbitrary ways." Her dark eyes turned to Sukune. "But this is different. The Shadowlands hates us. Every stone, every bush, every pool of water. All of it hates us. You can feel it when you are there, beyond the Wall." She plucked a twig that had caught in her obi and tossed it into the fire. "This place, though. It does not hate us. It does not feel anything about us." She glanced into the darkened forest beyond the firelight. "It does not care about us at all. I think that may actually be worse."

Sukune nodded. "I would rather be despised, I think, than treated with utter indifference–"

Another flurry of wings rushing overhead. Another. And another, making them both duck. O-Ushi said, "That was–" but another bird cut her off.

O-Ushi reached for her hammer, Sukune for his tetsubō. His two Hiruma aides took up their axes. Two more birds shot by. And another. And another.

Then the air became a storm of wings, a rush of feathered bodies. Sukune lost sight of O-Ushi, the Hiruma, even the fire. He dropped his tetsubō, useless against the swarming birds, and crouched, hands covering his face. Over a deafening thrum of wings, he heard O-Ushi shout. Other voices yelled over the blare of horns. All Sukune could do, though, was cower, his senses muffled, until the birds dispersed or were somehow driven off.

Eventually, the commotion of wings diminished. Stopped.

Sukune lifted his head and found a single bird perched on his arm. It was small, a sparrow with dark feathers. When its beady gaze met his, it shrieked once, then flung itself into the air and raced off after its fellows. The flock ebbed and flowed among the trees like smoke borne on shifting winds, then vanished into the tangled canopy.

Silence now, broken by the shuffle of feet, the creak of lacquered leather. A tight rank of Hida bushi stood grimly nearby, their weapons ready. A bulky figure snapped out an order to them, then stalked toward Sukune.

"Hida Sukune-sama," Hida Amoro asked, "are you injured?"

"I…" Sukune began, then stopped and considered the question. He seemed entirely unharmed. "No," he said, "I am… fine."

"Very well, then. The *yosuzume* seem to be done with you, so we will stand down."

Sukune stared. *Yosuzume*…

He huffed out a breath. The yosuzume were a dire portent.

A flock of night sparrows said to come from Chikushō-dō, the Spirit Realm of Animals, they would swarm about someone afflicted with ill fortune. The omen was far worse if the one being swarmed heard their call, but no one else did.

Sukune looked at O-Ushi. "Did you hear any of them utter a cry?"

"No," she said, giving her head a grim shake. "I will find the priests."

He looked at his sleeve. The yosuzume's feet had dimpled the fabric.

O-Ushi returned with the priests, who declared they could find no spiritual impurity afflicting Sukune. The expedition resumed preparing itself for the night. Something had changed, though, charging the night air. The wary tension of the Crab, which had been directed outward, at the Shinomen itself, had suddenly become focused inward – especially on Sukune. It bore down on him now, a new weight piled on the brooding menace of the forest.

He managed one more bite of the rice ball, then put his uneaten dinner away.

After the expedition members had eaten their morning rations, packed up their gear, and been purified under Lady Sun's dawn – as faint as it was beneath the vast forest canopy – the Crab prepared to march. According to Tale-Chaser, they would reach the forest home of the Tattered Ear sometime before darkness returned. Sukune strapped his tatami mat and blankets to the wooden frame of his backpack with a mix of anticipation and dread: anticipation that they would soon reach a place of relative safety, dread of the reality that there may yet be casualties and cost. And then, despite the declaration of the priests, there was the matter of the yosuzume. Heavy footsteps crunched behind him. He looked up to find Hida Amoro looming a few paces away.

"Hida Sukune-sama," Amoro said, offering a perfunctory bow, "a moment of your time before we march."

Sukune glanced at O-Ushi, who stood nearby with Yori and the other Kuni. Turning back to Amoro, he nodded. "What is it, Amoro-san?"

"I am requesting that you step down as commander of this expedition, in favor of Hida O-Ushi-sama."

Since they'd been children, whenever their brother, Yakamo, would torment Sukune over... something or other – it never seemed to matter – O-Ushi would ball up her fists, and her face would tighten in a particular way. Next would come the shouting, and then the blows. O-Ushi was doing those things now.

Taking his cue from her actions during his confrontation with Amoro at the Gates of Persistence, Sukune moved to place himself between them. At the same time, he took a deep breath and made himself look into Amoro's eyes.

"It is not your place to make such a request, Hida-san," he said, praying to the Fortunes his voice sounded more assured than he felt. "Now, return to your–"

"With all due respect," Amoro said, "I believe it very much *is* my place. Yes, you are our honored champion's son. And yes, your reputation for grand theory and logistics and the like is well-known." He gestured around them. "This is not theory. This is not a place to test your ideas of new ways to fight. This is real command, of real troops, in the field. In the Shadowlands, even the slightest wavering of a commander is cause for them to step down and surrender their place to a subordinate. We may not be in the Shadowlands, but this place is every bit as dangerous."

Sukune stood at the middle of a drama, like a stage play, except this was no fiction. All eyes that could see him were fixed upon him. Whatever happened in the next moments would be quickly known by everyone else.

Amoro lowered his voice to a deep rumble; this was, apparently, him being kind. "A preening Crane or narrow-minded Lion might see this as shameful, but we are the Crab. We do what is necessary, for the greater good. Your leadership has been... lacking. As the yosuzume pronounced last night, even this forest does not respect it. You are not up to this task, Hida-sama, and the most dangerous and difficult part is still ahead of us. So go back to your books and your theories, but leave command to the warriors."

O-Ushi's fury beat on Sukune's back like the heat of a midsummer sun. But, to her credit, she remained quiet, like the rest of the watching Crab.

None of the great tacticians had written about such a situation as this, because it had nothing to do with military theory.

Sukune swallowed again. "I will say it a second time, Hida-san. Return to your company and prepare to march."

Amoro's face hardened and he opened his mouth, but Sukune raised a hand. "If I am forced to say it a third time, I will not. Instead, I will expect you to perform the three cuts right here and now."

Sukune braced himself for an explosion of rage, or even an attack. Would that not make the Fortune of Irony proud? That, having survived the Shadowlands, the Wall, even the Shinomen Forest thus far, he was killed by another Crab samurai among dozens of allies?

Would O-Ushi or Yori or anyone else be able to save him?

Amoro, the muscles in his jaw clenched to hard knots, looked around, then back to Sukune, and finally gave a slow nod. "Very well, Hida-sama," he said, starting to turn away. Then he stopped himself and bowed. "As you command."

"Hida Amoro-san?"

"Yes, Hida-sama?"

"It would be a... a wasteful distraction to settle this as a matter of honor now. But when we return to Kuni Castle, you... will answer for this insult."

"Are you challenging me, Hida-sama?"

"I am."

Again, Sukune braced himself, this time for a derisive laugh, or some sort of dismissive scorn, anyway. But Amoro just said, "I accept your challenge, Hida-sama," and stalked away.

Sukune locked his knees, afraid he might topple over in the wake of what had just happened and not be able to get back up.

O-Ushi appeared beside him. "Sukune, that was..." She paused, then slammed her fist against his shoulder, an ancient ritual among Crab warriors in the aftermath of a hard-fought victory. The blow against his armor almost *did* make Sukune fall over. He staggered, recovered, then gave his sister a grimace.

"And here I was worried about Amoro hitting me," he said. He tried to make it sound flippant, but his heart still raced, making his voice brittle.

His sister leaned close. "If he had," she said, her voice pitched for only the two of them, "then we would have seen which was harder, these trees or his head." She smiled. "I am proud of you, brother."

As they began their march into the new day, Sukune found his breath still short, but his step surprisingly light.

The buoyant feeling soon faded. Tale-Chaser had turned onto a new path, one that traversed generally north and east. It seemed to Sukune no different than any of the other branching trails they'd passed, humbling him with the realization that, without the nezumi to guide them, the Crab would by now be hopelessly lost. The dense undergrowth actually thinned along this new way, the nearly impenetrable walls of willow, clethra, redvein maple, and ferns fading back, revealing vast tree trunks dwindling into the misty distance like the columns of some huge, primal temple. But the relief of more open surroundings was soon lost in the unending trudge of one foot ahead of the other, aches and pains flaring, breath rasping. Sukune's wooden pack frame ground against his shoulder blades; sweat stung his eyes. He wiped at his face, pulling away a hand smeared with black grit and leaf flakes.

A bird fluttered overhead. Sukune tensed, but it was only a lone bird, a wren, that flitted off among the dangling branches.

Behind Sukune, feet tromped against dirt and loam, armor creaked and scraped, the occasional sharp rebuke erupted from a sergeant. The boost of confidence Sukune had won from his clash with Amoro had faded, and now the dreary silence hanging over the expedition felt like something personal. Like an unspoken judgment of him as their leader. What had his "victory" over Amoro actually proven? That he could remain steadfast with the strictures of Bushidō and the weight of authority on his side? Crab warriors and retainers had died – or, in the case of those who had vanished, perhaps *worse* than died – and what had he actually done about any of it? What had he done to disprove the dire omen of the yosuzume? How had he even begun to try to address their faltering morale, or even to start to earn their trust and respect?

Really, who was he to question the way the Crab fought? To advocate innovation in strategies that had kept the Empire safe for generations?

As he levered himself over yet another fallen log, he couldn't help wondering if Amoro could have been right–

A shiver rippled through the forest, like a sudden breeze. But there was no wind. If anything, the air hung even more still, thick with a musty stink of growth and decay that stuck in Sukune's throat.

A hoarse shout rose from somewhere behind him. Another, then several more, followed by the blare of a horn, flat and muted in the heavy air. Sukune started back toward the commotion, his aides and O-Ushi in tow. As they passed the Kuni, Yori and Daigo joined them, while Kana and her apprentice, Naoyuki, readied bells and paper ribbons and similar tools of their mystical practice. Sukune found the Hida company taking advantage of the more open terrain, standing in a battle line, tightly ranked by squads. A short way off the trail, several figures stood apart from the rest: two warriors struggling to hold onto a third, Hida Amoro glaring at the three of them.

"Hida Amoro… san… what…" Sukune stopped, gasping and hating himself for it. "What is… happening?"

"This man," Amoro snapped, "wishes desperately to go…" he pointed at a gloomy stand of pines perhaps two hundred paces away, "…there. He cannot say why." His fists clenched. "Or he will not."

The man's eyes, wide and glassy, seemed to see something no one else could. He babbled something. Gibberish. There might have been words, but if so, it was a language Sukune didn't know.

Kuni Yori stepped close and looked into the man's eyes. "He cannot. He is clearly not in his right mind."

"Perhaps," Kuni Daigo offered, "it is *hitsu*."

Yori shrugged, stepping back as the man abruptly shouted and yanked against the warrior holding him. "Perhaps."

Sukune frowned at the unfamiliar word. "Hitsu?"

"A compulsion that emanates from the Spirit Realms," Yori replied, "where they intrude upon the Mortal Realm. It is rare, but almost impossible to deny when it happens."

"Can you stop it?" Sukune asked. "Take away this compulsion, this… hitsu?"

"No. Or… perhaps. But I do not currently know how to do so."

Another shivering wave rippled through the forest. The warrior suddenly yanked again, this time breaking free. Shoving Yori aside, he raced toward the pines. Amoro cursed and started after him, but stopped as a third, even heavier tremor shook the forest, the earth trembling under their feet. Amoro glared after the fleeing bushi, but he made no move to follow, instead ordering the others back into formation. Sukune watched the man stumble through ferns and willow fronds before vanishing into the blackish pines. As he did, a terrible howl tore through the forest, a cacophony of guttural roar and nerve-scraping shriek. It soared to a crescendo, then stopped, but the forest continued quaking, as though shaken by colossal footfalls.

"Sukune," O-Ushi said, "we must prepare!"

He stared at her. *Prepare for what? What is going on?*

Tale-Chaser appeared. "Sukune-sama, a terrible thing is coming!"

"Terrible thing? Wait. Tale-Chaser, is this the *dark thing* you warned us about?"

"No, no, not the dark thing! But still terrible, very terrible. It is… it is…" Tale-Chaser stopped, uttered a frustrated, squeaking chitter, then switched back to Rokugani with obvious effort. "What is the word… It is… yes! Your word… *onikuma!*"

Onikuma.

Demon-bear.

Sukune exchanged a look with O-Ushi, but Hida Amoro had heard *oni*, and that was enough for him. Hefting his tetsubō, he shouted, "Stand ready, children of Hida! Our ancient enemy is upon us!"

Sukune scoured his memory for the things he'd read in Kuni Castle about the Shinomen Forest, trying to recall anything about this onikuma, this demon-bear. But there had been nothing. Its approach shook the ground. It must be massive, but he could discern nothing else.

He turned back to Tale-Chaser. "What can you tell us about this onikuma?"

"It is very, very big!"

"Yes, I can tell that, but–"

Another howl spilled over the crest of a ridge to their left. Amoro shouted, the horn blared, and his company smoothly reoriented itself to face that way. At the same time, the bushi spread apart, opening their formation to one less tightly packed, and more suited to taking the charge of a massive foe.

Sukune took a breath. It was all happening so quickly, but he forced himself to take a moment and scan what had become a battlefield. The Hiruma scouts were already forward, and should give warning of the enemy's imminent arrival – of when and where it would appear–

–so the rest of the Hiruma company could move forward, to… *there*, a place roughly defined by a shallow ravine, where they would engage with archery and skirmish back, avoiding becoming decisively engaged, while weakening the enemy and covering the Hida–

–who would take a position *there*, well behind the Hiruma, ready to maneuver and engage the enemy–

–once the Hiruma had disengaged and withdrawn to the flanks, ready to support the Hida or react to other threats–

–and throughout, the ashigaru would stand and hold in the rear, in reserve, or to cover a general withdrawal if it proved necessary.

He turned to his Hiruma aides and rattled off a series of orders. They bowed and raced off to deliver them. Sukune turned to O-Ushi, to Tale-Chaser and Yori and the other Kuni. They could find their own places.

A rolling crash yanked his attention back to the ridge. Something the size of a siege engine shouldered the trees aside, cracking and splintering wood, leaves and dust swirling.

O-Ushi hefted her hammer and said, "That is, indeed, very, very big."

Sukune nodded. It was a bear. But it was a bear the size of a Kaiu stone thrower. It crashed into view, a mountain of fur and fury, shredding undergrowth with claws as long as a *wakizashi*. A trio of Hiruma scouts ran ahead of it, turning and firing arrows at the gargantuan creature without breaking stride. The arrows struck true, but only caught in the tangled fur.

Now the onikuma lumbered fully into view, slowing when it saw the Crab, its massive head swinging from side to side. Sukune could hear its breath, rasping like a forge bellows. Then, with a roar that made the air shake, it charged.

The Hiruma company loosed volleys of arrows and began skirmishing backward. The onikuma bore down on them, and they quickened their withdrawal. They aimed at vital spots, especially its eyes, but it moved much faster than its enormous bulk should have allowed, and the shots flew wide.

Something yanked at Sukune's sleeve. It was Tale-Chaser. "No, Sukune! Cannot fight the demon-bear! We must flee!"

Sukune looked across the battlefield. Another hundred paces, perhaps a little more, and then the Hiruma would be forced to disengage. That would leave the Hida free to engage...

And would end in disaster.

Sukune could see it: the onikuma slamming into the Hida, barreling through them, bowling them over, cracking armor, snapping bones. Tale-Chaser was right. Fighting it would be like fighting an avalanche, or an earthquake. Even if they could defeat it, victory would come only at a terrible, debilitating cost – one that would end the expedition, here and now.

They had to retreat. Sukune again placed himself above the map table, considering the wooden blocks of the expedition, including a new one, much larger and dominating the rest: the onikuma.

A simple, general withdrawal wouldn't work. The creature could just press after them, unrelenting. It *might* not, but Sukune had no gauge for its motives or behavior. So, he had to assume the worst.

Since it was already focused on the Hiruma, Kazane could detach part of her company, using it to keep the onikuma's attention, and attempt to lead it away from the rest of the expedition.

The rest of the expedition would disengage, the Hida company backing off, joining up with the reserve, quitting the field and regrouping well away from the threat of the demon-bear. After that…

There would be something to deal with after that. First, they had to break free of the onikuma. It was a terrible risk, especially for the Hiruma trying to divert the onikuma, but Sukune could see no other course–

Sukune's aides skidded to a stop, one and then the other, both sweat-grimed and breathing hard. He issued them new orders, and they raced off again. Turning to Kuni Yori, he said, "Yori-sama, your assistance in helping us to withdraw would be most helpful!"

"Indeed," the Kuni daimyō replied, "but, despite its being called a demon-bear, there is nothing demonic about it." He gestured at Kana and the other Kuni, huddled in urgent conversation. "Our intended invocations would therefore be of little use, so we must consider a new approach."

"We don't have time!" O-Ushi snapped. "We need you to do something *now*!"

Sukune opened his mouth to speak but caught himself. He knew nothing of shugendō, so he would have to trust the Kuni to determine what to do, and then do it. Instead, he turned back to the battle. Kazane's Hiruma had divided, roughly a third of their number angling to the right, still firing at the onikuma while backing away to stay unengaged. The rest retired to the left but loosed no arrows. Although the creature was not obviously harmed by the Hiruma's archery, the repeated impacts seemed to enrage it. It swung to follow the right-flank group, which was being led by Hiruma Kazane herself.

Good.

Now a sonorous chant rose from behind him. Kuni Kana knelt with her hands pressed against the ground, intoning an invocation, while Naoyuki tapped a small mallet against the earth in rhythmic time. Yori and Daigo stood to either side, hands raised in supplication, likewise chanting.

Better.

"Our esteemed Kuni finally take action," O-Ushi said, joining Sukune. "Although your plan appears to be working even without their—"

"Hida!"

Sukune and O-Ushi both spun toward the war cry. Sukune stared. He didn't understand. Instead of withdrawing toward the ashigaru and the tree line, the Hida company charged forward, weapons raised, closing on the onikuma—

The implication hit him like a tetsubō. Someone hissed, "No!" He thought it was O-Ushi, but then realized it was his own voice.

The onikuma swung its furious glare toward the onrushing Hida, then wheeled away from the Hiruma and charged this new threat.

How had they got his orders so wrong? Had his Hiruma aide misunderstood?

No. He could see his aide standing and watching the Hida company racing away, staring in limp horror.

"Amoro has disobeyed you!" O-Ushi said. "He ordered this charge!"

The expedition was about to slam headlong into catastrophe, and there was nothing he could do about it–

"Sukune," O-Ushi said, grabbing his arm, "we must do something to support the Hida!"

He gaped at her. "We must...?" He shook his head, shook loose the shock of blatant insubordination – of disloyalty, and betrayal. "Yes... we must support them." He looked around. The Hiruma company had disengaged and now raced to regroup behind the line of ashigaru. If Kazane wondered why the Hida now charged, rather than allowing her detachment to lead the onikuma away, she gave no sign of it and simply carried on with the plan.

Sukune plucked the wooden block of the Hiruma off the table, at least for now.

That left Sukune with little to influence the battle – his reserve, and the Kuni. But the lightly armed ashigaru had no hope of defeating the monstrous onikuma, and as for the Kuni...

Kana no longer chanted; she spoke urgently to Yori instead, shaking her head. Their invocation had clearly ended; there had been no visible effect.

He turned back to the battle just in time to see the onikuma slam into the charging Hida.

... bowling them over, cracking armor, snapping bones...

In a single breath, the Hida were locked in a swirling melee with the colossal bear, striking at it with their heaviest weapons. Through billowing dust, blows slammed home, but like the

Hiruma's arrows, they had little effect. It was like striking ancient hardwood trees or outcroppings of bedrock. The bear, though, flung bushi aside with swipes of its massive paws, tore through armor with its claws, seized screaming warriors in its jaws and shook them like a dog with a rag doll.

Yori appeared. "The *kami* refuse our entreaties. You must order the Hida to retreat."

"No!" O-Ushi shouted. "If you order a withdrawal, the Hida will be run down as they try to disengage!"

Yori glared at her. "They will be run down anyway."

Sukune looked from one to the other. Retreat. Yes. He scanned the battlefield but saw only chaos. O-Ushi was right. Retreat how? And to where? Where could they possibly go that the onikuma couldn't follow?

He spun around. No solution. No way out. But he had to find one. These were his troops, under his command.

A warrior stumbled backward out of the melee, blood dripping from a dangling arm. He made no move to reengage. Another followed. The Hida company was about to break. Perhaps that was the best they could hope for: that some would escape and survive–

A horn sounded, but it rang deep and resonant, unlike the shrill tones used by the Crab. A line of squat figures erupted from the trees to their right, spears leveled.

Nezumi. Dozens of them.

Tale-Chaser ran toward a nezumi following the spear-wielding warriors, one even more bent and gray-muzzled than the Rememberer and bearing a staff of twisted branches. A brief flurry of talk, an argument, then the older nezumi snapped something emphatic at Tale-Chaser and resumed his way, walking with grim purpose directly toward the battle. The Rememberer returned to Sukune, looking slumped and defeated.

"Please, Sukune, save the Crab," he said. "Moongazer, Dreamer of the Tattered Ear – he will make the demon-bear go away."

Sukune could read nothing in Tale-Chaser's eyes; as always, they seemed as blank as glass. But his tone was certain, if bleak. The nezumi would stop the onikuma and save the expedition from total disaster, but only at some terrible cost to themselves.

He glanced at Yori, whose own urgings had been clear and consistent: trust Tale-Chaser.

Sukune turned to O-Ushi. "Sister, I need you to rally the Hida and have them disengage."

She opened her mouth, protest tightening her face, but finally just turned and ran toward the melee, shouting.

For a moment, nothing changed. The onikuma continued to bellow and rage, Hida bushi fell, the battle crashed on. Perhaps Amoro would even refuse O-Ushi's commands and the company would fight on until they died.

But the Hida did begin disengaging, backing away from the combat, gasping, grimed with sweat and dust, spattered with blood. His sister struggled to re-form them into a battle line, trying to effect a withdrawal in good order and not just a rout. Sukune's heart sank further. Unless the nezumi acted now, it would be a futile effort, because the onikuma would just charge and savage them all over again. But the nezumi warriors hung back, spears arrayed in a defensive posture–

No. The old nezumi, Moongazer, moved to confront the onikuma with nothing but a staff of twisted branches. The huge bear saw it, spun, and reared onto its hind legs. It towered over the nezumi, who would now die. Sukune braced himself for it.

But the moment just went on, the rearing bear facing the old nezumi. Then it dropped back to all fours with a heavy thud. The nezumi stepped closer.

Silence, broken only by the gasps and clatter of the Hida as they re-formed... by the moans of the wounded. The onikuma didn't move, even when the old nezumi reached out and touched the top of its head.

Sukune turned to Tale-Chaser. "What is happening?"

"Moongazer is telling the demon-bear this is all Dream," the Rememberer said, his tone desolate. "He will lead the demon-bear away now – take it far away, deep into Dream, before it wakes up again."

Sukune stared. "I... I don't understand–"

"You do not need to," Kuni Yori said.

The Dreamer and the onikuma continued their wordless communion. A strange sense of unreality settled over Sukune: a disconnected, adrift feeling. It was as though the bear, the battle, all of it, had just been something he'd remembered upon waking up. He expected to blink and find himself still in his bedroll, Lady Sun just starting to reach through the trees, the day's march not yet begun. Moongazer placed his staff on the ground, then turned and began to walk. The onikuma shambled after him, the thump of its great paws muffled almost to silence. Sukune watched the Dreamer lead the onikuma back into the trees, where they both vanished.

And now, he found he had trouble recalling any details of what had just happened, only that it had.

Then the ponderous unreality dissipated like mist on a

sudden breeze, and the harsh reality of the moment crashed back in.

The Hida warriors stood gasping, leaning on their weapons. Sergeants shouted commands, re-forming the Hida into ranks, taking the roll to determine who, from their squads, remained alive and conscious. Every fighter had some skill in dealing with injuries, so those most unhurt were quickly organized into casualty parties, seeking out the wounded – those who could be treated, anyway – to offer immediate aid. It all happened without Sukune's intervention, the product of countless hours of drill and training. Instead, he looked through the organized chaos as he approached, searching for her familiar face.

O-Ushi rose from treating a fallen bushi. Blood spattered her from face to knees, but Sukune caught her eye, and she nodded. Relief flooded him like cool water. The blood wasn't hers. Or, at least, not all of it was.

Figures appeared around Sukune. Hiruma Kazane, Kuni Yori, the commander of the ashigaru. The next moments were a blur of reports and questions, more reports, orders. Sukune found himself facing one of his aides, the one who had delivered his orders to the Hida company. The man dropped to his knees, misery tightening his voice.

"Hida Amoro-sama… He heard the order you had given. He just said…"

Sukune nodded. "Go on."

"He said, 'The Crab do not run.' And then… he ordered his company to charge."

Sukune dismissed the man, then stepped through trampled and bloodied undergrowth to join O-Ushi. She stood over Hida

Amoro, who lay on his back, tetsubō still clutched in one hand, his chest caved in, a bloody claw-gouge furrowing his face.

"Why did he do this?" Sukune asked. "Did he really hate me so much, that he would risk ruin for his company, for this expedition, just to spite me?"

O-Ushi blew out a sigh. "I do not know."

"I do," Kuni Yori said, stepping around another fallen warrior. "He may have hated you, Sukune-sama, but more to the point, he did not understand you. You advocate new ways for the Crab to wage war." Yori shrugged. "He is – was – the epitome of how we have always done things."

Sukune sighed out a breath that tasted of dust and blood. *The Crab do not run.*

We are the Wall.

O-Ushi frowned at Yori, but said, "I will see to the Hida company, Sukune."

Both she and Yori walked away, already turning to other matters, but Sukune lingered, looking down on Hida Amoro. There would be no duel now. But it didn't matter. At a terrible cost in Crab blood, Amoro had proven Sukune's point. A stubborn refusal to yield or give way, to instead accept ever worse odds and revere the resulting sacrifice, would be the eventual doom of the Crab.

He looked at Kuni Yori, who, with the other Kuni, now moved among the injured, assessing those most in need of the kami's aid – assuming, of course, the elemental spirits would cooperate.

He did not understand you.

It hadn't been a criticism.

Sukune turned himself to the task of getting the expedition

regrouped. There were wounded to care for, dead to be burned. More than ever, though, he just wanted to get them to Tale-Chaser's home, where he hoped they might find respite, and a chance to rest. At one point, he thought to approach the nezumi, to thank Tale-Chaser and his people for essentially saving the day. But the nezumi were huddled among themselves in a way he didn't want to interrupt, so Sukune stayed away.

CHAPTER FIVE

Sukune sat on a fallen log and looked around at this place called *m-atikf 'chtr-foo*, which meant "the Great Home". It was, it seemed, the main settlement of the Tattered Ear. Others were scattered around the southern reaches of the Shinomen Forest, but those were apparently occupied only at certain times, or in relation to certain events Sukune didn't really understand. One such event seemed to involve some combination of Lord Moon's aspect, the time of year, and ... the color of the clouds? Tale-Chaser couldn't properly explain that last bit, there apparently being no other translation to Rokugani that came close to capturing the concept. But the Tattered Ear always returned to the Great Home, and apparently spent most of their year here.

Sukune craned his neck at the centerpiece of the Great Home, a vast camphor tree whose limbs shaded a glade at least two hundred paces across. He spied rough shelters of wood, bark, and leaves among the sprawling branches, but only because he already knew they were there. He had the impression that these were used more as defensive works, as lookouts, and for more esoteric purposes than as dwellings. It seemed the Tattered Ear actually lived in a sprawling warren of tunnels and burrows dug among the camphor's massive roots.

A comparison of the Tattered Ear and their Great Home to the nezumi who lived in the Shadowlands would normally have fascinated Sukune. But he just looked away, back at his battered expedition – the success of which was now in serious doubt.

A rhythmic chant rose from among the Crab encamped along one side of the glade. The priests moved among the company, sprinkling salt as they intoned prayers of purification. This would dissipate the spiritual grime that had accumulated from their recent exposure to battle and blood. Sukune had already walked among the troops himself, as a good commander should, but it had felt hollow–

"Sukune-sama!"

Tale-Chaser approached, accompanied by two other nezumi: one considerably younger, with tan fur; the second somewhere in between, and dark furred. The younger one carried either the same staff of twisted branches as had the nezumi who had led the onikuma away, or one very similar. Like Tale-Chaser, she also had things woven into her fur, but rather than sticks and twisted grass, these seemed to be flowers, and sprigs of plants. The dark-furred nezumi had nothing tied into his fur, but he stood taller and more imposing. Sukune took him to be a warrior.

The nezumi stopped. Sukune felt O-Ushi, Yori, and others watching him, but keeping their distance, having apparently decided he needed time alone.

Tale-Chaser gestured at the younger nezumi with the staff. "Sukune-san, please meet Mist-Walker. Since Moongazer went to Dream, she is now Dreamer of the Tattered Ear tribe."

Sukune offered Mist-Walker a bow. The Dreamer looked at Tale-Chaser, who chattered something to her, then gave an awkward bow in return.

"Tale-Chaser," Sukune said, "about your Dreamer. I have not yet had a chance to say this, but I am grateful beyond words for what he did. Indeed, all Crab are. Had he not–"

"Moongazer chose," Tale-Chaser said, raising a paw. "He wanted greater good for all. Crab help is important to defeat the dark thing, so the Tattered Ear will be safe. So, Mist-Walker is now our Dreamer, leader of the Tattered Ear."

"Your Dreamer is also your... leader? She now leads your entire tribe?"

"She does."

So the nezumi had not only lost their Dreamer, an obviously important member of their tribe, but also their leader.

More sacrifice. Am I a fool to think it can be otherwise?

Did Amoro prove me right, after all? Or did he actually prove me wrong?

Perhaps this is what the yosuzume were trying to tell me.

"Anyway," Tale-Chaser went on, "we talked. Mist-Walker agrees we must send warriors to help at the Bloody Ghost Fire Cave." He now gestured at the dark-furred nezumi. "This one, Tchickchuk, whose human-name is White Scar, will lead."

Tchickchuk – White Scar – stepped forward at the mention of his name. His pelt wasn't entirely dark, a single blaze of white shooting through it. Bulky and muscular, he moved with restrained menace.

He reminds me of Amoro, Sukune thought.

They spoke a moment longer, about the specifics of the Crab encampment and the way forward from the Great Home. Then Mist-Walker said something to Tale-Chaser, who told Sukune they needed to deal with other matters.

"The fight with the demon-bear was very hard," Tale-Chaser said as the nezumi turned to leave. "Very hard, very bad. The Tattered Ear will watch; the Crab may sleep now."

"Tale-Chaser-sama," Sukune said, "I am curious. Was it simply fortunate your tribe arrived at the battle when it did? Or did your Dreamer… did he *know*?"

Tale-Chaser stopped and offered Sukune a very human shrug. "I do not know. Does it matter?"

Sukune bowed as the nezumi left, then started the other way, toward the encamped Crab. He winced; at some point, he'd twisted his knee. Now it twinged as he walked.

O-Ushi intercepted him. She had washed off most of the blood in a cold stream that bubbled past the Great Home, but traces remained, faint crimson among the grime. "We have a final casualty count. Seventeen Hida bushi, including Amoro, are dead. Nineteen more are likely too badly injured to carry on and will have to remain here, with the nezumi, until we return. We also lost a Hiruma scout during the onikuma's approach."

"Lost?"

She shrugged. "Lost, dead. Vanished, anyway, into this accursed forest. We're not sure, and we don't have the time to look."

The Hida had lost thirty-six, a little more than a quarter of their strength.

O-Ushi's jaw tightened. "*Damn* Amoro for what he did."

Sukune said nothing. He shared her anger at Amoro's costly disobedience, but he couldn't shake a gnawing doubt. Could the Crab change? Or was "We are the Wall" just too deeply ingrained, too much a fundamental part of what the clan *was*? Would trying to change just cause more of what happened today?

And yet, if they didn't change, what then? How long could the Crab go on *being the Wall*?

Kuni Yori had said, "You advocate new ways for the Crab to wage war." Again, it hadn't been a judgment. But even if he had an ally in Yori, who was he to think he could bring change to the Crab?

Sukune frowned, realizing – with some surprise – he had made a decision. "Sister, would you walk with me?"

She nodded, and they turned away from the encamped Crab, heading for an emptier part of the great glade. Sukune's knee continued to twinge, but he made himself ignore it. Against so many dead and wounded, a sore knee seemed unimportant.

When they were well away from the Crab, Sukune began, "O-Ushi–"

"No."

"I haven't said anything yet."

"It does not matter. The answer is no."

"What do you think I am going to say?"

"That you want me to assume command of the expedition." She stopped and looked into the forest, shading her eyes against the glare of Lady Sun, who was shining in hard, ruddy sparks through the trees. "I will not do so, so it is pointless to ask in the first place." Sukune had never been closer to anyone than he was to O-Ushi, so for her to know his mind well enough to anticipate what he meant to say was no surprise. That didn't make her words right, though.

"You must," he said.

"Perhaps you misheard me. I said I will not."

"Sister–"

"Sukune, Father gave you command of this expedition and made me your second. Should you fall, then yes, I will assume command. But you do not look like you have fallen."

"O-Ushi… Sister… please. You know as well as I do that Father placed me in command to prove myself, or to fail. And … I am leading this expedition to failure."

"It was Amoro who failed today–"

"Because of me. Because I am in command. But the Crab are not ready to have me commanding them. They may never be." He looked back at the towering camphor tree. "Tale-Chaser said their Dreamer – the one who led away the onikuma today – did what he did for the greater good of all." He turned back to O-Ushi. "How can I do less? The message of the yosuzume was clear. I am not suited to lead. So, you must assume command in my place."

O-Ushi just stared at Sukune for a moment. Finally, she said, "Sukune, I owe you an apology."

"An apology? For what?"

"Shortly before your gempuku, both Yakamo and I offered to accompany you into the Shadowlands. Father forbade us from doing so. He insisted that you would retrieve the head of a Tainted beast on your own."

Sukune thought back to that time. As he was the son of the Crab Clan Champion, it was a foregone conclusion that he would train at Sunda Mizu Dōjō, the great school and training grounds for the Hida bushi. When the time came for him to pass the gempuku ceremony that would see him become an adult, the requirements of the dōjō were clear: he must venture into the Shadowlands and return with the head of a beast. He remembered the anxious days and sleepless nights leading up to his quest, then the terrible desolation and evil loneliness of that awful place. The dreary hunt seemed to go on forever before coming to an abrupt and terrifying end when he stumbled upon a troll feasting on the slaughtered remains of a pack of goblins. Before he could flee, the troll turned on him. Fortunately, the goblins had injured the troll enough that even frail Sukune and his undersized tetsubō had been able to dispatch it.

"He was correct, as it turned out," O-Ushi went on. The last shafts of Lady Sun's light began to fade; twilight crept in from the forest around them. "You returned with not one, but two heads: a troll's and a goblin's."

"The goblin's head had been clearly gnawed upon," Sukune countered, "so it was only to show that the troll mostly succumbed to them, rather than me."

"Not even the most seasoned Hida or Hiruma would hesitate to claim a wounded troll as a perfectly valid kill, Sukune. You should not, either. And," she continued, holding up a finger to stop his reply, "returning with the goblin's head as well, and an explanation why, showed an integrity that even impressed Father."

"I was just trying to manage expectations – as in, do not expect me to make a habit of killing trolls single-handedly." Despite Sukune's self-effacing words, O-Ushi's contention that he had impressed their father left him feeling just a little less morose.

O-Ushi rolled her eyes. "If there is a way you are unlike

most Crab, brother, it is your reluctance to brag about your exploits." She offered a fleeting smile, but her face became grave again. "Still, that is why I am sorry. Because we doubted you. Father did not. And that is why you cannot stand down from commanding this expedition, Sukune. Father may, indeed, be testing you, but not to simply confirm that you are incapable. Just as he believed you would find a way to bring back the head of a Shadowlands beast for your gempuku, he believes you will find a way to bring Kikyo back to our clan, and prove yourself a commander and a leader."

"Even after today? We suffered grievous losses today, and even if it ultimately was owing to Amoro's disobedience, I am still responsible. If you had been in command, I have no doubt he would have withdrawn as ordered."

"That is still his failing, not yours."

"Even so, I do not have the confidence of these troops, O-Ushi. Even the spirits balk at my leadership, as the yosuzume made so abundantly clear."

O-Ushi gave him a frustrated scowl but didn't immediately reply. When the answer did come, it wasn't from her.

Kuni Yori stepped out of the twilight gloom gathering under the great camphor tree. "Your pardon," he said. "I wished to speak to you, Sukune-sama, about an important matter, but meant to wait until you had finished speaking to O-Ushi-sama. I am afraid, though, I overheard the final portion of your exchange. If I may, I believe I may offer… if not insight, then at least something you may find of use."

Sukune glanced at O-Ushi. She gave Yori a hard stare, but said nothing, merely offering Sukune a small shrug. "Please, Kunisama," he said, "speak your mind."

"During the recent examination of a specimen retrieved from the Shadowlands, Kuni Daigo-san neglected to restore a ward, as it was his responsibility to do. Several hinin attendants were killed before the creature could be contained. It was only through good fortune that no one was seriously harmed. Now, I could justifiably dismiss Daigo-san from my service and name a new apprentice. That would be the end of his career and, quite likely, his life. But that would be a waste, and the Crab must waste nothing. Instead, I trust that he has learned from this failure, so that he not only never repeats it, but also learns a diligence he will apply to other areas."

"You believe I have learned from the events of today," Sukune said.

"No," Yori replied, making Sukune blink in surprise. "Or rather, I do not *know* if you have, just as I do not *know* that Daigo learned from his failure with the ward. But both of you have an obligation to continue fulfilling the duties you have been given, until it is certain, beyond any doubt, that you truly are incapable of doing so. Again, to do less is wasteful. The Crab waste nothing."

Sukune looked at O-Ushi. "Apologies, sister. Whatever I had meant to say, I have forgotten what it was."

"Well, if you do remember it, feel free to talk to me about it. Now, if you will excuse me, I must attend to repairing my armor." With a sidelong glance at Yori, she started back to the encampment, where several fires were beginning to shoot sparks into the growing darkness.

Yori watched O-Ushi until she was out of earshot, then said, "Hida-sama, as I said, there is a matter I wish to discuss with you. First, though, regarding what happened today, I believe your performance was exemplary."

"Kuni-sama, you needn't–"

Yori raised a hand. "I am not a politician. It is not in my nature to flatter. I state truths as I see them. If I believed you had performed poorly today, I would say that. If I believed you should step down as commander of this expedition, I would say that, as well. My statement that you performed well is simply a fact."

It was remarkable how Yori could drain anything remotely approving from a compliment, but Sukune simply offered a bow and his thanks.

"If this helps encourage you," Yori went on, "then that is a pleasant side effect. But it is not why I make this observation to you. Rather, I wished to tell you that I believe we share a basic belief, one upon which we base our essential philosophies, at least with regard to our clan." Yori had been looking into the deepening night, but now turned to Sukune. "What Hida Amoro did today was emblematic of our clan as a whole. He saw an enemy and sought to confront it and defeat it. He was incapable of doing otherwise. It is… was… who and what he had become."

Sukune's knee twinged again, and now a new ache flared in his hip. He ignored both and waited for Yori to continue.

"I also believe," Yori went on, "that you were correct in saying that, had your sister been in command today, Amoro would have conformed to her orders, whatever they might have been."

Sukune frowned at that. "You do not believe she would have ordered a withdrawal?"

"I do not presume to know what your esteemed sister might have done. I simply offer that, given your well-known stance regarding how the Crab wage war, Amoro balked. By behaving in such a contrary way, he avoided giving credence to what you represent."

"What do you believe I represent, Kuni-sama?"

"Change. It is the one thing our clan fears." Yori looked back into the growing darkness. "It is a fear I know well. I see it permeating our clan. It constrains us. It calcifies us. It is turning us into the same stone we use to build the Wall. Eventually, it will cause us to fail, and the Empire will suffer because of it."

One of the fires in the encampment suddenly flared, its abrupt light dazzling in the gloom. Sukune turned away from it, blinking.

We are the Wall. And that is the problem.

"In any case," Yori said, "I simply wished you to know that I, like you, believe that change is necessary."

"I… thank you, Kuni-sama." Sukune considered pursuing the matter further, exploring Yori's thoughts more deeply, but fatigue and pain pulled at him; he hadn't eaten since that morning, and there was still much to do before he could even consider settling into his bedroll. Further discussion on that subject could wait. "You mentioned another matter you wished to discuss?"

"Indeed. Since we have entered the forest, I, Kuni Kana, and our apprentices have made several attempts to commune with the elemental kami. The character and temperament of the kami in one place may be quite different than those in another. This place is new and strange to us, but I believe we finally understand something of the elemental spirits here."

"This is related, I gather, to your–" Sukune almost said *failure*, but the word seemed unnecessarily harsh, "–being unable to work on our behalf, today."

"It is. The kami here are wholly unused to communion with mortals. They are primal. Wild, even. And, therefore, they are unpredictable. Invoking them could be dangerous."

"Are you saying that, if you seek their aid, they will turn on us?"

"It is more nuanced than that. We Kuni have an affinity for the earth spirits in particular. But here, even communion with them will be difficult and demanding, requiring our full and uninterrupted focus. This will take time. I therefore request that you assign a squad of warriors to me, and another to Kana-san, to ensure that we can devote our absolute attention to the spirits without having to worry about our personal safety."

"Our forces sustained severe casualties today," Sukune said. "Diverting two squads of what remains to your protection may be... problematic. It will weaken our line of battle significantly."

"That is true. You must weigh that fact against our contributions in this spiritually fraught place. If you believe the line of battle to be more important..." Yori ended on a shrug, but his unspoken words were clear.

Then despite your words, perhaps you are, in the end, also afraid of change.

Sukune looked back into the darkness, now almost total beyond the flickering rings of firelight. The eyes in the night were back, more than just gnarled patterns in bark. He could feel them watching, staring out of a vast, primal forest where bears the size of battering rams prowled. A forest where people could lose touch with reality and vanish into gloomy pine groves, or sink and become lost in knee-deep pools.

The Art of Positional Warfare was written by Hida Banuken, Champion of the Crab Clan during the first construction of the

Carpenter Wall. *"Determine that which is most important to the integrity of your plans,"* Banuken wrote, *"be that a place, a thing, a person, even an idea. Then, make it the focus of your defense."*

"We shall assign one squad of Hida to protect you, Kuni-sama. Even with the addition of warriors from the Tattered Ear, I am reluctant to weaken our line of battle more than that."

Yori bowed. "I understand, Hida-sama, and appreciate your consideration."

The Kuni withdrew toward the encampment. Sukune stayed for a while, intending to enjoy a brief moment of solitude. But he still felt the eyes watching him, and they seemed closer now.

He returned to the fires.

By the time Sukune could finally settle into his bedroll, O-Ushi was already asleep. He admired her for that: her apparent ability to sleep anywhere, at any time. As he pulled his blanket around him, he expected sleep to be a long time coming for him. It vaguely surprised him it wasn't, a soft darkness closing over him almost as soon as he closed his eyes.

Sukune woke to unbroken darkness. He listened. Nothing: just silence. No… a sound. A flutter. Wings, beating in the night. Something darted overhead. A bird. A yosuzume. Another. Two more. Then many. A vast flock, their wings a rushing thrum that filled the night around him, filling his mind with the sound of their passage. Sukune wanted to cover his ears, block out the commotion, deny the awful portent of the night sparrows. But he couldn't. He couldn't move at all…

But the yosuzume had no interest in Sukune. They were fleeing. Fleeing something. The darkness wasn't absolute. Hints of shape and texture surrounded him: trunk and branch, twig and leaf, all around. All around, except in the direction of whatever it was from which the night sparrows fled. The darkness that way was... *more*. More than just an absence of light: a hole gaping in creation itself, pulling in light and warmth and life, consuming all. And the hole was growing, gnawing away the world.

Sukune desperately wanted to rise, to rouse the Crab against this awful corrosion of existence. He could see O-Ushi, sleeping within reach. He knew where Yori was, where all the Crab were. But he was struck speechless, frozen in place, a helpless witness to the end of everything.

Now, a vast, splintering crash, as the great camphor tree, the heart of the Great Home, slumped into ruin. It, too, was being consumed. The Tattered Ear were being destroyed, and so were the Crab. O-Ushi was ripped away, falling, dwindling, vanishing into blackness. Only Sukune was left now, alone in infinite darkness.

No. Wait. Someone stood near. Sukune turned, no longer paralyzed, and found a nezumi standing over him. He recognized the Tattered Ear Dreamer whose name had been Moongazer, until he led the onikuma away into Dream and saved the Crab.

"You must save my people, Sukune," Moongazer said. "No matter what it takes, you must save them. They have no other hope."

Sukune opened his mouth– Blinked.

Blinked again, at pale light gleaming through leaves.

He sat up and looked around. Dawn was becoming daylight, and the Great Home had awoken. Around him, officers roused their troops. Those already awake, who had been standing watch, kindled small deadwood fires to brew tea and warm meals of fish stew and rice.

Sukune took a shuddering breath. A dream. But it had seemed real. He expected to see the camphor tree fallen into wreckage and rot, but it still loomed as huge and hale as ever.

"Sukune, are you all right?"

He found O-Ushi sitting on a log beside her bedroll, applying salve from a small, enameled jar to a blistered toe. He shrugged. "I had a dream."

"Ah," she said, and that was all.

Among the Crab, dreams were considered deeply personal. One could choose to share one's dreams, but rarely with other than family and close friends. Even then, if one chose not to, that was that. You simply did not seek to pry into the dreams of others.

The nezumi were different, though. Yume-dō, the Realm of Dreams, played a much more central role in their lives. Perhaps they could offer insight that O-Ushi, Yori, or any of the other Crab could not. Over the course of the day, as the Crab rested, mended armor and gear, and otherwise prepared to resume their way, Sukune resolved several times to speak to Tale-Chaser about his dream from the night before. The fact that it had included the tribe's previous Dreamer, Moongazer, seemed of particular importance. If Sukune understood the concept of Transcendents – particularly wise and powerful Dreamers who had become a sort of ancestral dream-spirit – then Moongazer may have become such a being. And if *that* was true, then Moongazer had specifically implored Sukune to help the Tattered Ear, *no matter what it takes*. Consulting Tale-Chaser and the tribe's new Dreamer, Mist-Walker, would be the surest way to know.

Each time he approached the huge camphor tree, though,

he saw it again in his mind's eye as it appeared in the dream: a broken, rotting ruin lost to darkness. The image clashed so harshly with the busy thrum of life as the Tattered Ear climbed among the branches and burrowed among the roots that Sukune would turn away, unwilling to reveal something so dark and dire.

On one such occasion, as his nerve failed him and he turned back to the encampment, he saw a lone figure sitting apart from the rest of the Crab. From the slight build and dark kimono, he thought it might be Kuni Yori; curious, he moved that way, stopping a short distance away. It wasn't Yori, though. It was Kuni Kana. She didn't seem to notice Sukune, her attention fixed on something else: a trio of nezumi pups tumbling and roughhousing around a leafy shrub. Sukune had exchanged few words with the dour woman, and he didn't want to intrude now. But Kana turned, saw Sukune, and bowed.

"My apologies, Hida-sama. I'm afraid my mind was elsewhere."

"No apology is necessary, Kuni-san," he said, approaching. The pups paused as he moved, watching him with beady little eyes.

Sukune couldn't help smiling. "They truly are..." He stopped, searching for an appropriate word.

"Adorable," Kana said.

Sukune nodded. "Yes, they are."

Kana said nothing more; she simply stared at the pups, who launched themselves back into their antics. Again, Sukune felt like he was intruding and made to leave her be, but he noticed a wet streak on her cheek, gleaming against her Kabuki-style red-and-white face paint. The Kuni typically wore such paint, ostensibly so evil spirits would not be able to recognize them. Whether it actually worked or not, it did make it much easier to see her tears.

"Kuni-san, are you well?"

Kana glanced at him, then wiped quickly at her face, smearing some of the face paint onto her hand. "Again, my apologies. I am just ..." She stopped, cutting off whatever she had been about to say, and instead giving Sukune a thin, rueful smile. "I am not used to seeing something I would call... adorable. Which is unfortunate. It is important, I think, that we *do* see such things." She shrugged. "They are the things we protect. Great works of art, beautiful gardens. Children at play..."

She wiped her eyes again. "For the third time, I must apologize, Hida-sama. This display of emotion is most unseemly."

Sukune shook his head. "No, Kuni-san, it really is not. Please, forgive *my* intrusion."

As he walked away, and for a long time after, Sukune found himself returning again and again to what Kana had said, and to one word, in particular.

Children.

That single word was an entire story, carrying a novel's or stage play's worth of pain and regret and loss.

Like dreams, though, one did not pry into such things.

One after another, sergeants reported their squads. Sukune watched as Hiruma Kazane spoke to her second, then she came to him and bowed.

"We are ready to march, Hida-sama," she said, then paused.

"There is something else, Hiruma-san?"

"I am still... adjusting to the fact that we will not be deploying our own scouts."

Sukune looked toward the head of the column. A contingent of Tattered Ear warriors, almost a company's worth, would lead the expedition from the Great Home. Their commander, White Scar, had already dispatched scouts ahead. When Kazane had learned this, her face had gone hard; it had softened since, but not entirely. "This has nothing to do with the quality or abilities of our scouts, Hiruma-san. It is simply that the nezumi are far more familiar with this terrain than we are."

Kazane's mouth pressed into a thin line, but she nodded. "Of course, Hida-sama. We are fortunate to have them as allies."

"Indeed we are," O-Ushi said, arriving to report the Hida company ready. "Without their numbers to bolster us, we would be woefully understrength."

Kazane looked from O-Ushi to Sukune, then bowed quickly and returned to her company, which would march behind the Tattered Ear.

Sukune turned to O-Ushi with a sigh. "Sister–"

"I'll say it again. It is foolish and unnecessary. The Kuni do not need a squad dedicated to their protection."

"In *Leadership*, Akodo said a subordinate who questions you once seeks insight and should be answered. A subordinate who questions you twice seeks punishment and should be flogged."

O-Ushi glared at Sukune in a way that reminded him that while she usually saved him from the bullying of Yakamo and others, she wasn't above occasional bullying herself. But she finally puffed out a breath and shook her head.

"It is, of course, your decision. However, since you asked me to assume command of the Hida, I am duty bound to report the state of my command. Besides our dead, we are leaving sixteen of the most badly wounded here. With ten more now dedicated to protecting the Kuni, that leaves the company at just over half-strength."

Sukune gave a resigned nod. "It is what we have. At least, as you said, we have the nezumi reinforcing us."

"And I am sure they are capable and brave, and know this forest well. But they are also a contingent with whom we have only briefly drilled, and then only here, over the past day, and not in actual battle. Most do not even speak our language, and—"

"Sister," Sukune said, raising a hand, "I know all this. As I said, it is what we have."

He could tell O-Ushi wanted to say more, but she just bowed and returned to her company.

Sukune moved to his accustomed place at the head of the column. His aides, and Tale-Chaser and his two escorts, were already there.

"The Tattered Ear are ready, Sukune-sama," Tale-Chaser said. "We go to find the Crab armor, destroy the dark thing, and come home."

Sukune nearly said, *You make it sound so easy, Tale-Chaser.* But he did appreciate the Rememberer's simple faith. He even found it a little touching. So instead, he smiled and said, "So we shall, Tale-Chaser-sama."

He turned and looked back along the column. As he did, he couldn't avoid seeing—

—the great camphor tree, the heart of the Great Home, slumped into ruin—

Except it wasn't. It still towered against the sky, hale and strong. He turned back and nodded to one of his Hiruma aides. She bowed, lifted her horn, and sounded a short, sharp succession of notes. As one, the expedition began to move, heading in the same direction from which that terrible darkness had come in Sukune's dream.

CHAPTER SIX

The expedition marched on, through cavernous groves of towering maple and oak that gave way to tangled thickets of willow and birch that plucked and scraped at the trudging warriors. The thickets, in turn, opened into misty glades of fern, copses of moss-draped yew and hemlock, or silent, gloomy stands of black pine. The latter particularly made Sukune grit his teeth as his troops trudged through them, their feet silent on thick carpets of orange needles. He saw eyes again, but not only staring from the bark. They also stared in his mind, wild and empty. They were the eyes of the warrior who had succumbed to the strange compulsion called hitsu, the warrior who had been inexorably drawn to just such brooding pines as these, right before the onikuma attacked.

But the forest remained silent and the pines fell behind, replaced by something else. Day faded to night, night to dawn, and the expedition trudged onward.

What if the forest actually went on forever? What if there no longer were a Wall, a Crab Clan, an Empire – just forest to the ends of the world? For that matter, what actually happened to those who disappeared into the shadowy pines, or deceptively shallow pools, or were just seen no more at all? Could it have happened to all of them? Could they all have been swallowed by the Shinomen Forest, and become just lost souls wandering through an eternity of trees, now and forever?

He soon caught himself glancing around, trying to see things that he thought flickered and danced in the corners of his vision. But it was daytime, not night, and it wasn't just eyes staring at him from the forest: it was movement. Things stalked among the trees, keeping pace with them, never quite seen but always there.

And still, the expedition marched on.

Sometime on the second day out from the home of the Tattered Ear – or perhaps it was the third – Sukune found himself suddenly wanting to run, to shout, to do anything but keep up the dreary, rhythmic plod of their march. His breath caught in his chest; blood sang in his ears. *Hitsu*, he thought. *This must be hitsu, and now I'm afflicted… I cannot do this anymore, put one foot down, the other, over and over… I must run, I must go somewhere, anywhere else…*

"Sukune-sama, no! This way!"

He spun toward the voice. It was Tale-Chaser, and he stood on a rocky ledge that rose over the path. It rose even higher behind him, and Tattered Ear warriors were climbing it and vanishing over the edge. Sukune had winced and shaded his eyes, though, because the sky was so bright…

Wait. The sky. There were no trees above him. He could see the sky.

Sukune turned and scrambled up the rock face. The climb wasn't difficult – or shouldn't have been. But soon his heart fluttered and pounded, the breath rasped in his lungs, his joints burned. He climbed regardless, desperate to stand beneath that open sky, the way a drowning man might struggle for the water's surface, and the air beyond it, shimmering just above him.

And then he reached the crest. Now he heard – no, *felt* – a rumble through his feet. That made him stop, looking wildly about. The onikuma had also made the earth shake…

But this was different. It was a constant shudder, without rhythm or pause. Wheezing, he pushed himself over the crest, took a moment to catch at least some of his breath, then looked–

Gasped. Stared.

Sky vaulted overhead, dazzling blue behind pale, wispy clouds. The forest had given way to the course of a broad river whose dark waters cascaded down a series of massive stone steps. Sukune counted seven such drops, each an imposing waterfall in its own right. Together, they carried the river's flow into a chasm at least a hundred paces across and twice that deep, although its true scale was hard to discern through the drifting mist. At the very bottom, beyond the glowing arc of a rainbow, the river thundered into a yawning cavern and simply *vanished*.

Sukune kept staring. This must be, he thought, the River of the Sky, described in the journals of the famous cartographer Miya Riku. Riku had begun writing about the river in her usual dry, scholarly way, but soon switched to a far more lyrical style – more poetry than essay. Even her most eloquent words fell far short of… of *this*. This must, in fact, be the place Riku had called the Seven Trials; from here, the river flowed through deep places in the earth for many miles before emerging again.

Over and over, as it flowed southward through the forest, Riku had written, the river changed from an open watercourse on the surface to one hidden deep beneath the ground.

One by one, as the Crab surmounted the ridge and clambered up into view of the river, they paused for a moment to take in the panoramic glory of the scene. Sergeants and officers, who would normally snap their troops back to their duty, simply allowed it, each even taking their own moment to absorb the sight of river below and sky above. There was something more to it, though. Sukune thought about his mounting conviction that he'd become irrevocably lost in the forest, the flickers of panic it had provoked, the urge to run aimlessly and perhaps never stop. The rush of the thundering river had washed all that away. Now, he saw something similar on the faces of the other Crab, as each was cleansed of their own doleful thoughts.

But there was still no hint of the Shadowed Swamps and the cave within them that was their destination. They would have to leave this place and pass back beneath the trees. Just the thought made Sukune's stomach tighten.

He looked for Tale-Chaser. Surely the swamps must be near. The Rememberer stood a few dozen paces away, speaking to several other nezumi. Sukune started that way, but as he did, something on the far side of the river caught his attention. It was a regular shape, lines and angles, not organic at all. It was a slender, tapered spire. A tower.

He stopped near Tale-Chaser but still had to raise his voice over the rush and rumble of water. Pointing at the structure, he asked, "What is that?"

"Stone towers," Tale-Chaser said. "You see the tallest, but others are there. Many other buildings, too, all of stone."

"Who built them?"

"No one built them. They have always been there."

Sukune simply said, "Ah." Someone or something had obviously constructed the spire. In fact, a Hiruma scout named Kogoe had encountered mysterious serpent folk in the margins of the Shinomen Forest just several months before. Perhaps this was their work?

O-Ushi and Yori joined them. The entire expedition had now halted along the river.

"I thought this would be a good place to rest," O-Ushi said. On her face, Sukune saw hints – the last dregs of tension – that she had only just sloughed off her own demons.

He nodded. "Yes, a rest is a good idea." Turning back to Tale-Chaser, he asked, "We should reach the edge of the swamps sometime this day, should we not? How much farther do we have to go?"

Tale-Chaser didn't answer immediately. Strangely, he seemed hesitant. Sukune had become used to the Rememberer's unaffected bluntness, which sometimes rivaled that of the gruffest Hida. Now, though, he seemed to be reluctant to speak. That's all Sukune could tell; a nezumi's inhuman features didn't allow for much insight into their thoughts or feelings.

"Tale-Chaser, is something wrong?"

The Rememberer seemed to deflate slightly. "Yes, Sukune-sama. We should have reached the swamps before the river. But the scouts smell nothing but forest, see nothing but forest. The swamps are…" He paused and gave a very human shrug, "…are gone."

Sukune frowned. Gone? He exchanged looks with O-Ushi and Yori, but they seemed equally puzzled.

"It isn't uncommon for corrupted terrain to shift about and change," O-Ushi said, "but terrain does not simply change its location entirely."

"In our experience," Yori replied, "that is true. But we have little knowledge about these Shadowed Swamps in the Shinomen Forest, beyond the fact that their existence compels us, the Scorpion, and the Unicorn to all keep a wary eye on our respective clans' borders with the forest."

Tale-Chaser was not able to offer much more. The Tattered Ear avoided the swamps entirely. His own journey into them, which had led to the discovery of Kikyo, had been the first of any significance in nezumi memory.

"The swamps change," Tale-Chaser said, "even move. But not so much. They have always been…" He swept his paw back in the direction from which they'd come, "…that way, between the Great Home of the Tattered Ear and the river here. But not now. The swamps are just… gone."

It was Sukune's turn to feel deflated. To have come so far, and lost so many…

And now, it seemed, it had all been for nothing.

At least, Sukune thought, the open terrain around the Seven Trials gave the Crab a decent place to rest. And Tale-Chaser, who had been adamant about the Crab not eating or drinking anything that originated in the forest without his approval, declared the River of the Sky a perfectly good source of water. So, the expedition had just about everything it needed – for the time being, at least.

Everything except a purpose.

The Tattered Ear spent the next day scouting, dispatching small groups of nezumi to reconnoiter in every direction, even beyond the river. Each group returned having found no sign of the Shadowed Swamps. It was, indeed, as though they were simply gone.

The Kuni, in the meantime, attempted to commune with the elemental spirits, seeking to discern if they could provide some insight regarding the corrupted swamps. Like the nezumi, though, the Kuni uncovered nothing, leading Kuni Naoyuki to say, "Perhaps, when the nezumi disturbed the armor, they set into motion events that led to the dissolution of the swamps. Perhaps they truly are no more."

A strange thrill rippled through Sukune at Naoyuki's suggestion, a bizarre mix of hope and dismay. The disappearance of any Tainted land from the world would be a cause to celebrate. Except, would it not also greatly diminish any meaning of the deaths they'd incurred? And would Kikyo now be lost forever?

But Kuni Kana simply shook her head at Naoyuki and said, "No. That is not the way of these things."

When the last of the nezumi scouting parties returned, Tale-Chaser again just shook his head. Sukune called his subordinate commanders and the Kuni to a clearing away from the main body of the expedition. Tale-Chaser accompanied them.

"It would seem," Sukune said, "that we are at an impasse. Although we believe the Shadowed Swamps exist, they apparently cannot be found."

"The Tattered Ear will search more," Tale-Chaser said. "The swamps must be found. The dark thing must be defeated."

"The issue," O-Ushi replied, "is that we cannot sustain ourselves indefinitely. You have made clear, Tale-Chaser-sama, that much of what the forest could provide should not be consumed by our people. Our own supplies will last for only another two days, or perhaps three, if we are careful. After that, we must begin our journey back."

"There is also the matter of your own people," Hiruma Kazane said to Tale-Chaser. "Most of your warriors are here, with us. That leaves your home and tribe vulnerable."

Tale-Chaser stared at her, then lowered his head. "That is true, yes."

Silence, except for the distant sound of falling water. Sukune felt the others looking at him. He was the commander. The decision was ultimately his.

Would they persist, risk more loss, with no promise of success? Or would they give up, accepting what amounted to failure, leaving both Kikyo and the Tattered Ear to whatever fate decreed for them?

"The Shadowlands fears us," Kuni Daigo muttered bitterly, "and that is why it hides from us."

Sukune looked at the young Kuni. *He may very well be right.*

But Sukune thought about saying as much to his father when they returned to Crab lands. *We frightened the Shadowlands so much that the swamps would not even show themselves.* Never mind those who had died. It would make a great story to tell upon the Wall. One that glorified who and what the Crab were. And if this were true, what need had they to change?

"Hida Sukune-sama," Kuni Yori said, "if we cannot find the Shadowlands, then there may be a way of causing the Shadowlands to come to us."

Sukune glanced at O-Ushi, who narrowed her eyes at Yori, but said nothing.

He looked back to Yori. "What way is that, Kuni-sama?"

"These Shadowed Swamps may have unusual properties, distinct from what we have encountered before. Most notable, of course, is the apparent ability to simply vanish altogether. However, they will still have some inevitable commonalities with other expressions of the Taint. For instance, they will almost certainly cause the corruption of elemental spirits into *kansen.*"

Icy fingers touched Sukune at the mere mention of the word. Kansen, Tainted elemental spirits, were a scourge throughout the Empire, an ever-present menace to any who sought communion with the kami. Fortunately, they were rare outside the Shadowlands, whose pervasive, corrupting effects spawned the vile beings. But even the few who plagued the Empire proper could wreak terrible havoc, tempting those they impinged upon into heinous acts, including the practice of *mahō*, evil sorcery empowered by human blood.

O-Ushi's voice was like the sound of a sword being drawn. "What are you suggesting, Kuni-sama?"

Yori met her cold gaze squarely. "I am proposing that we draw such a corrupted spirit to us, then compel it to reveal the swamps."

Again, silence. This time, though, it was the quiet before a storm.

O-Ushi suddenly took a step toward Yori. "You have gone mad!"

Kazane placed a hand upon her own sword hilt. The other Kuni stared at Yori. Tale-Chaser tensed and looked ready to bolt.

But Yori was unfazed. "Hida O-Ushi-sama, when you stood in Kuni Castle, you were within a brief walk of a variety of

Tainted monstrosities in our laboratories, several of which were still alive. The Kuni are quite used to dealing with such things. This would be little different."

"Except kansen specifically seek to corrupt shugenja such as yourselves," O-Ushi shot back. "During missions in the Shadowlands, shugenja go to great lengths to avoid interacting with them. But now you propose to do just that, and in a place that you readily admit is spiritually..." She paused, seeking a word, finally settling on "complicated." She looked at Sukune. "I'll say it again: madness. We cannot allow this."

Yori clasped his hands in front of him. "Spurning interaction with kansen when it is not desired only makes sense, of course. That does not mean we cannot interact with them if there is good reason for it." Yori also looked at Sukune. "And this would seem to be such a time. Rest assured, Hida Sukune-sama, I do not suggest this lightly. We would take all necessary precautions to contain the Tainted spirit and prevent it from exercising its insidious influence on anyone present. Nor would we be bargaining with it, or seeking its favor. We would command its obedience." He offered a thin smile that didn't touch his eyes. "If it makes you feel better, it would be a *profoundly* unpleasant experience for the kansen."

Sukune looked again at O-Ushi. She expected him to reject Yori's proposal. And that was, in fact, his inclination. Recognizing the menace of the kansen was an early lesson for all Crab children, one repeated many times as they became samurai.

But Sukune thought about the missing and dead behind them, about the badly wounded they'd left with the Tattered Ear. As for the Tattered Ear themselves...

You must save my people, Sukune, Moongazer had said in his dream. *No matter what it takes, you must save them. They have no other hope.*

"If you do not accept this, Hida-sama," Yori said, "then I have nothing else to offer. The expedition either continues searching as we have been, hoping that the swamps show themselves before we begin to starve, or we leave now and accept the mission will be unresolved."

Unresolved. Not a failure, but it meant the same thing.

Sukune looked at the others. Kazane's expression mirrored O-Ushi's, while Daigo's and Naoyuki's were particularly bland. Kana merely looked resigned.

He took a deep breath. Something ached in his chest. It was just another ache among many.

I am so tired.

Sukune let out the breath and nodded. "Very well, Kuni-sama. Proceed as you suggest."

Yori bowed. "We will begin preparations immediately." Straightening, he added, "We will do this well away from the rest of the expedition. No one besides me, Kana-san, and our apprentices should even be within earshot of the invocation."

As the group dispersed, O-Ushi stalked over to Sukune. He resisted a sigh.

"I know, sister, that you find this objectionable. But it seems to be our only hope. I can certainly think of no other way to proceed. Can you?"

"Yes, I can. We accept that there is no good way forward and return home."

"Without Kikyo. And without having helped the Tattered Ear. In other words, return home in failure."

O-Ushi's eyes narrowed. "Is this about your ego, Sukune? Do you fear admitting failure to Father so much so that you would embrace something so dangerous?"

Sukune winced as the ache in his chest flared again. *So tired...* But he met his sister's gaze. "It remains to be seen what Father will consider failure, sister. Returning having accomplished nothing? Or returning having possibly succeeded thanks to Yori's plan? In either case, I will be accountable for the outcome, won't I?"

"Yes," she said, "I suppose you will."

As Yori had suggested, the Kuni removed themselves from the rest of the expedition completely, seeking a secluded place in which to perform their invocations. They also dismissed their protective squad of Hida. Sukune objected, worried about their safety, alone and immersed in a complex, dangerous ritual, but Tale-Chaser offered a compromise: a contingent of the Tattered Ear would escort and protect them.

Yori accepted grudgingly, as did O-Ushi, as Sukune reminded them both that the nezumi were immune to the Taint of Jigoku. They were less likely to be affected by the presence of the kansen, even if something did go wrong.

"There is one other concern, Tale-Chaser," Sukune said. "The greatest danger is that this evil spirit will corrupt one of the Kuni, even take control of them. If that happens, we would all be in great peril."

Tale-Chaser spoke to White Scar, who would command the escort. The nezumi warrior's reply was gruff, and brief. Tale-Chaser looked back at Sukune.

"Not to worry, Sukune-sama," the Rememberer said. "White Scar will not let the evil-Kuni live."

Sukune just stared for a moment, taken aback by the matter of fact tone of his reply, but finally nodded.

The Kuni and their nezumi escort departed, heading back into the forest in the direction from which the expedition had come. Sukune watched them disappear among the trees, then turned back to the main expedition, still encamped along the River of the Sky.

As he passed by the Crab warriors, he caught snippets of their conversations: practical discussions about weapons and armor, or scrapes and blisters, or the best way to eat dried fish; stories, almost always over-the-top in their telling; jokes and friendly, mocking insults. But all of it was shot through with a tense wariness, as speakers would go quiet and suddenly listen, or look quickly into the forest, or down into the river gorge. A few just stared at the enigmatic tower rising beyond the river, their expressions pensive. Sukune did his best to avoid eavesdropping, but most of the Crab muted their words, or went silent altogether, as he walked by.

It is because I am their commander, he told himself, and troops always go silent around their commanders. *But he couldn't help thinking back to the yosuzume, and how everything that had happened to the expedition since had essentially been one sort of failure or another.*

By the time he finally found O-Ushi, Sukune wanted nothing more to do with the troops, at least for the time being.

He corrected himself. *His* troops. Now, though, the phrase weighed him down, a burden, more than it inspired pride.

Neither Akodo, nor Sun Tao, nor any of the other great strategists had ever acknowledged that.

O-Ushi sat alone, near the lip of the gorge, staring into the plunging water. She glanced up as Sukune approached but said nothing.

"May I sit with you, sister?"

Her eyes stayed on the river, but her mouth hardened into a thin, pale line. Finally, though, she just sighed and gestured to the rock beside her.

He sat down. For a while, neither said anything. The roar of water soon began to chafe at Sukune, and he dithered between speaking, or just leaving. But O-Ushi spoke first.

"I am angry with you, Sukune. I think you have made a foolish, irresponsible choice."

"I know that."

She looked at him. "I want to be angrier. I want to be furious. Not only do I want to hate what you've done, but I want to hate you for it." She gave another sigh, a drawn-out one. "But I cannot."

"You should not let the bonds of family get in the way, if that is what you believe you—"

"That is not it," she said. "I cannot be angrier than I am because I am not sure you are wrong."

Sukune almost said, *Really?* But it would have come out incredulous and relieved and… just not right. So, he said nothing and simply waited.

"Back at the home of the Tattered Ear," she finally said, "when I said I was sorry for doubting you during your gempuku, I meant it. Still, I was surprised when Father named you commander of this expedition. I thought it was a mistake." She looked back into the gorge. "I told myself it was because this was an important but complicated mission, one not suited at all as the first major undertaking of a new commander. And that is true, at least to an extent."

"But?"

"But... part of it was me. I was... jealous."

"Jealous? Why?"

She took another breath, sighed it out and looked back at her brother. "Because returning Kikyo to our clan would be a glorious deed. I envied you that opportunity." She held up a hand as he opened his mouth to reply. "That is a petty thought, one of which I'm ashamed. And now, I am even more ashamed."

"Again, why?"

"Because I realize, now, that Father's decision was the correct one. So not only does it shame me to admit my wounded pride, but now I must accept that you were the better choice for command in any case."

"I don't understand–"

"I would have refused Yori's proposal!" she snapped. "I would have declared it foolish and irresponsible!"

"But you just did say it was that."

"I know! And now, because of that, this expedition would be on its way back home. We would not have found Kikyo, or helped Tale-Chaser's people, and that would be that. Father would accept it, and we would return to doing what we do, fighting the next attack upon the Wall, and our lives would go on."

"Perhaps not–"

"Do not patronize me, Sukune. You know it is true." She shook her head. "Would you have counseled me to consider Yori's idea?"

"I..." Sukune began, then nodded. "Yes, I would have."

"And would I have listened to you?"

"No."

"And there it is. I still believe that Yori's plan is foolish and irresponsible. But it might be all that works, and I would not have been brave enough to attempt it. So that is why I am angry but can't be furious. And also why I am so damned proud of you."

It was Sukune's turn to look into the gorge. He had only been able to imagine the Kuni failing, the way everything else about this expedition seemed to have failed. That was still the most likely outcome. But O-Ushi's words, and her pride in him, made his taut, gut-wrenching anxiety fade a little.

"Thank you, sister," he said. Then… that was all. They both knew there was nothing more to say. All they could do was what the rest of the main expedition was doing.

Wait.

A deep rumble woke Sukune from a fitful sleep. He'd been dreaming again, but this time, his dreams had been fractured and incoherent images, most barely remembered, but all vivid and disturbing. One had involved blood.

The rumble, though, was real. The rock around the gorge trembled, as though something gargantuan stirred beneath the earth. The Crab were roused to action, readying themselves for whatever was happening. At one point, Sukune even looked into the gorge, into the blackness where the river plunged underground. He braced himself, in case something like the onikuma came bursting out of the great cavern, water foaming around it as it dragged itself out of the depths.

But the percussive rumble soon faded, then died away altogether. The Crab remained alert, but nothing else happened. The eastern sky eventually lightened, heralding the arrival of

Lady Sun. Before she appeared, though, there was a commotion among the Tattered Ear contingent. A moment later, Tale-Chaser came to him, running excitedly.

"Sukune-sama, White Scar sent word! The Kuni succeeded! They found the way to the swamps!"

Sukune let out the breath he'd been holding. "Where are they?"

"The scouts White Scar sent back here will take us to them. We must start the travel from where they are!"

"Very well," Sukune said, turning and issuing orders to get the expedition moving. Sukune felt a pang as they left the mighty river behind them and plunged back into the gloom of the forest. He took a final look back at the sky, now blazing with Lady Sun's glory, wondered once more about that distant, enigmatic tower, then turned away.

They reached the Kuni and their nezumi guardians just before midmorning. The Tattered Ear had formed a ring of skirmishers, which collapsed and re-formed into a column of march at White Scar's barked commands. As the nezumi took their place at the head of the Crab column, Sukune moved to join the Kuni sitting and apparently resting a short walk away. O-Ushi followed at a distance. "Kuni-sama," Sukune said, "I understand you were successful."

In answer, Yori gestured in the direction of a fallen tree. There lay another beyond it, and another beyond that – a distinct path of toppled trees and uprooted foliage, in fact, following the trace of a jagged crack in the earth that dwindled into the mist of distance.

"That is our path," Yori said. "That will take us to the Shadowed Swamps."

Sukune glanced back at O-Ushi, but she remained several paces behind. He turned back to Yori. "And you had no... difficulties?"

"We had many difficulties. But if what you mean is, did we lose control of the kansen we called? No. It was obstinate, but we were finally able to compel it to our bidding." He pointed at the riven ground. "As a corrupted earth spirit, it used its natural medium to satisfy our demand and show us the path."

Sukune looked at the other Kuni. Both Daigo and Naoyuki sat on logs, drooping with exhaustion, but sporting determined looks, nonetheless. Kana stood apart, staring along the path the kansen had scoured through the forest.

"Very well," Sukune said. "O-Ushi-san, prepare the expedition to follow the path the Kuni have provided us."

O-Ushi bowed, hesitating before returning to the waiting troops.

The Kuni followed O-Ushi. As Kuni Kana passed Sukune, he saw her gaze fixed ahead of her, as though she saw something terrible and sad and far away. "Kana-san," he asked, "do you require time to rest? We can–"

"No!" she said, turning and blinking quickly. It seemed to take her a moment to recognize Sukune. "Thank you for your concern, Hida-sama, but... no." She glanced at the trail of fallen trees. "I would prefer that we simply do what we came here to do."

As Sukune followed her back to the column, he thought, *As would I, Kana-san.*

CHAPTER SEVEN

Sukune stared across a sodden crater-scape, a dreary sprawl of black muck, blacker water, and desiccated trees like great, skeletal hands. Pale vapors hung among them, sometimes drifting on unfelt currents of air, sometimes twisting into vaguely horrific shapes.

A dark pool yawned to his right. He glanced into it; despite the wan, gray light, he saw his own reflection. It was distorted, warped into something grotesque. His flesh liquefied, flowing like melted wax. A glimpse, maybe, of a future self, horribly maimed, perhaps by whatever horror waited ahead.

He looked away and kept walking. The sound of his boots in the muck made him think of corpses being piled after a battle, for cremation – a soft, damp sound.

"I almost welcome this," O-Ushi said, her voice flat in the dead air. Sukune looked back at her with a frown.

"I said *almost*." She shifted her great hammer from one shoulder to the other. "The Shadowlands is a terrible place, but it is a terrible place we *know*. In a way, I find it less disconcerting,

I think, than the forest." She glanced around. "This place hates us. I can understand hate, and hate it right back."

Something rolled under Sukune's foot. A fragment of dead branch, or maybe a bone. He shrugged. "I find it hard to choose–"

A shout, then a scream from ahead, from among the Hiruma company. O-Ushi said to him, "The Hida stand ready. Go!" and turned back to the company she led in Amoro's absence. Sukune hurried ahead, his aides close behind.

He passed Hiruma skirmishers standing ready, their weapons and full attention directed away from the commotion. If more threats appeared, they were ready. He finally reached Hiruma Kazane, who stood with two other fighters over a man whose leg had apparently dropped into a cavity among the tangled roots of a tree. He looked at Kazane.

"What is happening?" "He seems to be–"

The man suddenly screamed. "My leg! Something's biting; it burns! Please–!"

Kazane grabbed the man's leg and pulled. A skirmisher joined her. The man screamed again and again.

Kazane grunted. "Something… holds him…"

Another scream, piercing. Sukune reached and grabbed and began pulling as well. Finally, the leg came free of whatever trapped it, and they lifted the man away, then lowered him but kept his bloody leg elevated.

His flesh was gouged and torn, as though something had been chewing upon him. Fortunately, the wounds appeared shallow: the skin was shredded, but the gouges did not seem to reach the muscle beneath.

One of the other Hiruma, who had been peering among the roots, said, "There is nothing. If something was down there–"

The injured man groaned. "Something *was* down there!"

"In any case, it is gone."

Kuni Yori appeared, Daigo at his side.

Sukune turned to them. "Kuni-sama, can you assist this man?"

"We will try."

Sukune turned to an aide. "Pass the word. The trees are to be avoided as much as possible." As the aide bowed and hurried off, Sukune turned back to the Kuni. Daigo examined the wound, determining if conventional medicine would be sufficient, or if they must beseech the kami to mend the insulted flesh. Yori focused on the man himself, examining him closely, looking into his eyes, then extracting a slender finger of jade and touching it to the Hiruma's arm.

The man closed his eyes and shuddered.

"He is likely Tainted," Yori said, standing and looking at Kazane. "He will have to be watched."

Kazane nodded grimly. It wasn't common to become sickened with the Shadowlands Taint via such a relatively minor wound, but it did happen. And once a person was afflicted, there was no cure. The man might continue his service to the Crab for some time, but he would eventually be forced to join other Tainted Crab in the bleak ranks of the Damned. Eventually, he would die, or his suffering would be ended.

Sukune nodded at Yori as well. As he did, he thought about the number of times he had stepped near trees, even steadying himself against them recently – this past hour, perhaps? Since the path riven through the forest by the kansen had brought them to the Shadowed Swamps, anyway.

This could have happened to me. It still might.

Sukune pushed the dreary thoughts away. This was just a grim reality for the Crab. There was nothing more to say about it–

"Hida-sama," Yori said, "there is something else. Something potentially far more dire than one Tainted warrior."

Yori led him a few paces away from the wounded Hiruma, then held up the finger of jade he'd used to test the man for the Taint. Sukune looked at Yori, who simply nodded at the crystal, which almost glowed a luminous green in the cheerless gloom of the swamps.

Sukune looked more closely at the jade, and his frown hardened. Fine, dark tendrils were shot through it, like the tracks of burrowing worms.

He looked back to Yori. "Has this jade been previously exposed to the Taint?"

"It has not."

"This has happened since we entered the swamps?" Yori said nothing.

Sukune dug out the jade pendant hanging around his own neck. Like Yori's, its verdant clarity had been blemished by spidery veins of corruption. It would take at least a full day in the Shadowlands, perhaps longer, for such corrosion to occur.

"I have no immediate explanation for this," Yori said. "Like their seeming ability to disappear and reappear, it may be something particular to these swamps."

Daigo joined them, his own damaged jade on display. "There are also rumors that this jade was acquired by the Yasuki by... less than honorable means. If true, then perhaps that has diminished its spiritual purity."

"In any case," Yori went on, "it is a phenomenon worthy of further study."

Sukune shook his head. "This is far more than just an interesting *phenomenon*, Kuni-sama. If this continues, we have – what – perhaps two days? Less?"

"I am well aware of the gravity of the matter, Hida-sama. Of course, almost all our samurai carry jade-inlaid weapons, and those are – at least, so far – much less affected, and will still protect their bearers."

"Unless we have to actually use them," Daigo muttered, then winced and bowed an apology at Yori's glare.

Sukune rubbed a hand across his face. Dirt and grit scraped against his skin, but he ignored it. The jade-inlaid weapons were a good point, but Daigo was right. They had to assume the expedition would eventually confront Tale-Chaser's *dark thing*. And as soon as the inlaid weapons were used to strike a Tainted creature, those weapons would be severely degraded. Moreover, the ashigaru were not equipped with them. Ultimately, without jade to protect the Crab, the Taint would no longer only be a fear for the injured or wounded. Some would resist longer than others, but all of them would eventually be afflicted, their souls imperiled, even lost to the evil realm of Jigoku.

They would be safe if they turned back now, or at least soon.

The expedition would also be over.

Sukune told his second aide, still waiting nearby, to fetch Tale-Chaser. As he waited, he brooded over the failing jade. The thought of abandoning the expedition because of such a thing was crushing. And although he told himself he merely imagined it, the finger of jade seemed slightly more contaminated by the threads of darkness. But if they really only had a day before it failed entirely, then he could not allow them to proceed much farther into the swamps. It may have only taken them an hour or two to get this far, but the swamps were obviously unlike any previous experience they had with the Shadowlands. What if leaving the swamps took much longer? What if it took more than a day?

Tale-Chaser splashed through a puddle, stopped, and stared at the jade. "Pretty green stone," he said, then paused and cocked his head. "No, not so pretty."

"That is the problem, Tale-Chaser-sama," Sukune said. "We rely on this stone to protect us from the evil of this place–"

"Taint, you call it, yes?"

"Yes. But the jade stone is failing much faster than we expected. How far do we have yet to go?"

"Not far. But… I cannot say if not far is not far enough."

Damn.

He looked back toward the Hida, where O-Ushi waited. What would she do?

But he caught himself. What mattered was what *he* would do. Sukune looked from Tale-Chaser, to Daigo, to Yori.

"We will continue," he finally said. "But we will watch our jade closely, and once it seems as though we have gone as far as we can, we will turn back." He looked at the Rememberer. "I am sorry, Tale-Chaser-sama. That is all we can do."

Tale-Chaser bobbed his head once. "I understand."

Sukune resumed his place in the order of march. He prayed to the Fortunes that Tale-Chaser was right and they would soon reach the cave containing Kikyo. If they didn't, then his lofty words about the Crab eschewing sacrifice could prove to have been just empty noise.

Because he might have just sacrificed them all.

• • •

Sukune watched a man die.

The Tattered Ear scouted ahead of the expedition, but the Hiruma maintained a second line of scouts, for additional security. Two of them suddenly sounded an alert, pointing at a figure stumbling out of the mist. It was a third scout: Hiruma Sayua, the scout who had disappeared shortly after they had entered the forest on the first day.

He stopped. Frowned. How had she come to be here? She couldn't have. She hadn't.

Sukune drew a breath to shout a warning, but the dank air caught in his feeble lungs and emerged as a choking cough. Several other shouts rose from the Crab, but it was too late. When the nearest of the scouts reached Sayua, a crimson glare erupted from her eyes, her mouth. Her skin cracked, peeling back and exposing ruddy fire. What had been Sayua sloughed away like greasy smoke, and the red fire engulfed the scout.

He screamed. It went on and on.

The second scout stopped, raising his weapon. Kazane shouted orders, and a squad of Hiruma raced toward the horrible scene, ready for battle. But the crimson flame sped away, vanishing back into the mist.

Sukune, still coughing, maintained his place, as did the rest of the Crab. Kazane reached the fallen man. She looked back at Sukune and shook her head.

Sukune looked at the fallen Hiruma as he passed. Other Hiruma were scavenging his jade and anything else that might be of use. They carefully tried to avoid looking at the man, whose body had collapsed in on itself, desiccated skin stretched taut over bones, mouth still agape in that terrible scream.

Tale-Chaser finally halted them just short of a bleak expanse of oily, blackish pools and crouched, whiskers twitching as he sniffed the air. Sukune pushed back against his mounting dread. Had the blighted, sodden terrain stymied the nezumi? If so, and Tale-Chaser was unsure how to proceed, then Sukune would have to order a withdrawal and then pray that their remaining jade would be enough to see them back out of the swamps–

But Tale-Chaser abruptly turned and scuttled toward Sukune. "That way," he hissed, pointing. "Just past the trees and mist, just past seeing, is the Cave of Bloody Ghost Fire."

A ridge of barren rock rose from the muck, as though something massive had pushed it up from the Tainted earth below.

Sukune let out a breath. Relief flooded him, but new, even more acute tension thrummed in with it. They were here. If Tale-Chaser's *dark thing* still lurked near the armor, it would not be far away.

Sukune offered Tale-Chaser what he hoped was a reassuring nod, then turned to his aides and issued his orders. The scouts would proceed until they found the cave, then would fan out around it, isolating it. O-Ushi's company would advance next, accompanied by Sukune and the Kuni, securing the entrance to the cave. Kazane's Hiruma would support the Hida, covering their flanks and rear. The Tattered Ear, under White Scar, would stay in the rear as his reserve, along with the ashigaru. Once the expedition was fully deployed, Sukune, Tale-Chaser, the Kuni, and a squad of Hida would enter the cave to find and retrieve the armor, while O-Ushi would remain in command outside.

That was the plan, anyway. Many questions and uncertainties gaped within and around it, not least of which was the dark thing. If it didn't show itself, Sukune thought, then the threat to the Tattered Ear would remain – or would it? Could the menace of whatever had attacked Tale-Chaser simply have vanished?

You must save my people, Sukune... They have no other hope.

Sukune frowned at his brief optimism. Moongazer's dire message in his dream made it clear the Transcendent didn't believe the threat to the nezumi had ended, so neither did he.

His aides returned, confirming his orders had been delivered. Sukune scanned around one last time, then gave the order to advance. The scouts crept forward, vanishing into the mist. O-Ushi and the Hida moved next. Sukune fell in behind them, the Kuni and their wary escorting squad of Hida following. The Hiruma followed, bows ready, arrows nocked, though not drawn. Something bumped against Sukune's foot. An ancient helm.

Bits of armor, arrow and spearheads, fragments of bone.

The barren rock resolved into craggy outcroppings, the largest rising the height of four Rokugani warriors from the mud.

The advance continued. Sukune heard only the squelch of mud and water underfoot, the soft clatter of armor, the occasional hissed order from a sergeant.

The Hida company stopped. Sukune looked past them. At the base of the tallest outcrop, just ahead, a cave mouth gaped.

Sukune turned to Yori just as the world around him shattered into noise and chaos.

Only paces before the Hida company, something massive erupted from the mud, then rose, black water, muck, and slime cascading from it, until it towered over the Crab.

For one frozen moment, Sukune could only stare at... The *dark thing.*

A massive, humanoid figure, at least six times the height of the bulkiest Hida, it seemed made of the stuff of the swamp itself, of filthy water and mud and the decayed fragments of long-dead trees. But as it moved, the muck and slime sloughed away from it, revealing bone. A skeleton the size of a watchtower. It wasn't truly, though. This was a colossal agglomeration of skulls and femurs, spines and fragments of ribcage. An immense, humanoid construct of the bones of a multitude, melded into a towering whole and driven by a malign, destructive will.

Gashadokuro.

Only a handful of patrols had ever glimpsed what were probably gashadokuro, huge monstrosities stalking among the shifting mists of the Shadowlands near ancient battlefields. None of those patrols had lingered to learn more. Gashadokuro were said to be the embodied anger and resentment of those who died unknown, like those who fell in some forgotten battle or the massed, anonymous victims of a famine or plague. When the Taint of Jigoku fanned their bitterness, it gave rise to one of these, the most powerful and, thankfully, rarest of all horrors.

This one must have been spawned by whatever forgotten battle had formed the swamps in the first place. Or, with Kikyo here, could it have been the remains of Hida Chuku's lost army?

Sukune shook away his horrified inertia and focused. It didn't matter. What did was seeing the battle for what it was: an ongoing, fluid problem of deployment, of move and countermove, of seeking the decisive moment when the battle would pivot into victory, or defeat was imminent and a withdrawal necessary.

"Hida!"

O-Ushi unleashed a war cry, and the rest of the Hida took it up. The Hida opened their formation, presenting the gashadokuro with a multitude of smaller targets instead of packed ranks. They struck out at the monstrosity, inlaid jade and sheer mass smashing chunks out of it. Sukune took a breath to calm himself – wheezing, then coughing briefly – and looked to the Hiruma. Kazane's command had deployed to the flanks, some closing, seizing opportunities to slash and bludgeon the gashadokuro, fading back, avoiding blocking or fouling the Hida. The remaining Hiruma, mostly archers, remained alert for other dangers, since their arrows would do little to a construct of bone and malice.

Sukune forced his attention away from the battle, from his sister, who fought the gashadokuro almost head-on. He wanted to find the Tattered Ear, make sure he knew where the nezumi were deployed–

A heavy thud. Screams of pain. Sukune spun back as the gashadokuro's massive fist plowed through the Hida like a battering ram.

Their dispersed formation limited the harm, but at least two were smashed into the mud, unmoving. None of them were O-Ushi.

No. Focus. She would take care of herself.

The Tattered Ear crouched toward the rear. White Scar watched him, waiting for the order to engage.

OK. Good. Now, the Kuni…

Sukune found them directly behind him, perhaps twenty paces back. Rather, he had found Kana and Naoyuki, but either Yori or Daigo lay in the muck. The other – master or apprentice – had vanished. The Kuni had been attacked? But

Sukune saw no attackers, and neither, apparently, had their Hida protectors, who had formed a wide, protective ring around their charges–

Kana suddenly stumbled forward, rushing toward the gashadokuro and the Crab fighting it. Sukune stared, not understanding what was happening.

"Stop this!"

Kana's voice sliced through the commotion of battle as she ran, her feet slipping in mud, pitching her forward. She fell, but immediately drove herself back to her feet.

"No! Are you mad! Stop this! Those are children! *Children*!" Sukune didn't understand. What was she doing? Where was Yori?

Now Naoyuki charged after Kana, shouting her name. Kana just splashed onward, crying out about *children–*

Children.

Watching the nezumi pups playing, she had said, "They are the things we protect. Great works of art, beautiful gardens... children at play..."

After the Kuni had compelled the kansen to reveal the way to the swamps, Sukune had looked at Kana, whose gaze was fixed ahead of her, as though she were seeing something terrible and sad and far away.

And now she shouted, "Stop this! Those are children!" and ran at the Hida.

An icy fist clenched Sukune's stomach. He lurched toward the Hida, toward O-Ushi, shouting, "Stop her! She is corrupted!" so loudly his voice rasped painfully against his throat, but the roar and rush of battle washed it away – and it was too late in any case. Kana reached the rear of the Hida company, shouting, raising her hands. One held a bloody knife, the other dripped blood from a deep gash. She shouted again and the blood ignited like lantern oil, turning Kana to a pillar of roaring flame. The inferno quickly spread, immolating a Hida bushi, then two more, a Hiruma, all screaming–

Kuni Naoyuki lunged through the flames, knocking Kana into the mud. The fire engulfed him, but its spread slowed, faltered. Then a massive hammer shattered Kana's head, the blow so powerful it embedded a fragment of her skull in a nearby tree. O-Ushi immediately reversed her swing, crushing Naoyuki's head, killing him instantly. Without hesitating, she turned back to the Hida, shouting orders, struggling to re-form the company.

But their cohesion had shattered. No longer a coordinated unit, they fought as desperate individuals. The gashadokuro slammed left and right with its massive fists, striking a bushi, two more, bowling them over, while the rest frantically struggled to avoid being hit and find an opening to strike back.

The neat wooden blocks on the map table were just splinters and sawdust.

Sukune looked at the cave. If he could get past the gashadokuro...

If. And then, if he could find the armor, and if nothing else stood in his way... what would be left of the expedition when... if... *he returned?*

Sukune spun to his nearest aide. He had to grab the man, who stared, transfixed, at the smoldering remnants of the Kuni, and shake him.

"The retreat! Sound the retreat, now!"

The man gaped a moment, then nodded, lifted the horn,

and blew the notes that made the Crab stumble back from the battle, turn and quit the field. O-Ushi shouted something at him but fell back with her command.

The Tattered Ear stood their ground, covering the Crab as they retreated. Sukune waited until the survivors were entirely disengaged, looked one last time at the towering gashadokuro, the cave gaping behind it, then turned and joined the retreat.

CHAPTER EIGHT

Sukune sat on a fallen tree, apart from the rest of the Crab, and stared at nothing. His aides sat where they could watch over him, but otherwise left him alone.

A dozen bright spots of pain glowed across his body, myriad small injuries. But they were minor hurts; he didn't even know when most of them had happened. Nor did it matter, because he was used to his life having a pervasive background of pain.

Besides, there were others in far more pain than him.

They had fallen back to higher, drier ground not far from the Cave of Bloody Ghost Fire. The gashadokuro hadn't followed; it menaced the Tattered Ear while they covered the withdrawal, but likewise didn't pursue when Sukune finally pulled them back, either. For now, it seemed intent on remaining close to the cave – but even that seemed uncertain, given the Transcendent's dreamplea to Sukune. He certainly couldn't discount the possibility it would return and resume its attack.

Sukune rubbed his eyes. Yes, the expedition had regrouped, so they would not be taken by surprise. Now they huddled in a defensive ring, wary of the Tainted swamplands around them, ready to fight, or to further withdraw. But that offered no solution to the greater problem. They had suffered grievous loss – the Hida could barely field more than a third of their original strength – they were still mired in the swamps, their jade would soon be insufficient even to see them safely back to undefiled land – and not only were they were no closer to defeating the gashadokuro or retrieving Kikyo, but those things actually seemed even *more* out of reach.

At least they had recovered Kuni Yori. A Tattered Ear scout had found him stumbling through the swamp, dazed, a purpling bruise on his forehead. Kana had apparently struck him and Daigo before her delusional rampage, and then he'd become separated from the rest of the Crab during their retreat. It was a small piece of good news, as was Daigo's recovery from her attack.

Kana. Sukune sighed out a breath. Yori claimed he'd had at least some suspicion about Kana after they had summoned the kansen, and that he'd been prepared to deal with her – at least, mostly prepared. "What I had not anticipated," he said ruefully, "was that she would negate my most painstaking preparations by hitting me with a stick."

But Sukune should have suspected her himself. Whatever personal burden of pain she had borne had left her vulnerable to corruption, because such was the insidious nature of the Shadowlands. Indeed, instead of discreetly ignoring it, Sukune should have thought to find a way to help her. After all, did they not all have vulnerabilities, cracks through which the Taint could infiltrate? Did it really make sense to hide their respective pain behind a mask of determined strength, rather than sharing it, and dealing with it?

No one should have to be that strong.

But it didn't matter now. The damage had been done.

Sukune sighed again. Simply sitting here was not an option. Every moment that passed corroded a little more of their jade. They did still have a handful of jade-inlaid weapons that were substantially intact, but those would only protect a corresponding handful of the expedition's members. No, he had orders to give. The expedition must continue its withdrawal. They would leave the swamps, leave the forest, and return to Kuni Castle. Perhaps another expedition could be mounted. It was clearer, now, what they would face, so they would be better prepared. As for the Tattered Ear, perhaps they could leave the forest, too, or at least keep themselves safe, avoiding the gashadokuro, or whatever other monstrosities the swamps spawned, until a new Crab expedition was deployed.

But he would not be its leader.

Sukune started to stand, but hesitated. Once he did, and gave the final order to withdraw, his failure – which began with the omen of the yosuzume – would be complete.

He sank back down.

Will Father have any further use for me? My lofty ideas will have proven empty… just words. And I will be an object of scorn, a source of shame, nothing more.

I must spare Father that. He gave me a chance to succeed, and I failed. I must pay the price for that failure, one measured in three cuts–

He froze as a dark shape appeared from the mist. Frantically, he snatched up his tetsubō–

"No, Sukune-sama, it is me, Tale-Chaser! Please do not attack!"

Sukune released the tetsubō. "Tale-Chaser. You surprised me."

"Because you are alone. You should be with other Crab. It is always safer with your tribe."

"I prefer to be alone. I am afraid I have failed my... tribe. I do not feel I belong with them." Still sitting, he found himself looking directly into the Rememberer's wide, dark eyes. "I have failed your tribe as well. You asked us to end the threat to your people. So did Moongazer, the Transcendent who spoke in my dream. We have failed to do so. I am sorry."

Tale-Chaser just returned a glassy stare for a moment, then erupted in an excited chittering and started to bounce from foot to foot. Was this anger? Disappointment? If so, it was easy to confuse for buoyant happiness, because it looked like the Rememberer was dancing.

"Tale-Chaser," Sukune said, "what are you–?"

"Moongazer... Transcendent? And he spoke to you? What did he say?"

Sukune never had revealed that to Tale-Chaser or the Tattered Ear, had he? So now, Tale-Chaser was dancing – which was about the most out-of-place thing anyone could do in the midst of this bleak, despairing hellscape. Despite everything, Sukune couldn't resist a smile as Tale-Chaser capered about, squeaking and chirping. He waited for the Rememberer to finally calm a bit, then recounted to him what had happened in his dream at the Great Home.

By the time he had finished, though, Sukune's despair was fully back, a suffocating shroud. "All this means, of course," he finished, "is that I have failed your Transcendent as well."

"No."

Sukune's gaze had gone distant, looking into the dreary future he faced, but Tale-Chaser's single word snapped him back. "What do you mean, no?"

"You haven't failed. Just not succeeded yet."

"Tale-Chaser, I appreciate your–"

"We are still here," the nezumi said, gesturing around them. "Not dead." His black gaze bore into Sukune's. "It is not Tomorrow yet."

"Yes, we are still here. And no, we are not dead. But we no longer have the jade we need. And we've lost too many of our people to continue." Sukune shook his head. "I am truly sorry, but–"

"When you and scary-Kuni spoke at the Great Home, he said the Crab become stone, like the Wall, because they fear change. He said you think that, too. Do you?"

"Scary-Kuni?"

"Yori."

"Yes, I..." Sukune began, then waved the admittedly amusing moniker for Yori aside and frowned. Tale-Chaser had been eavesdropping on him and the Kuni daimyō? In Rokugan, that would have been a grievous breach of etiquette, one worthy of a challenge to a duel. But the Great Home was clearly not Rokugani, and Tale-Chaser just as clearly saw no problem with it. And, in any case, Sukune was intrigued by wherever the Rememberer was going with this. "What is your point?"

"Was scary-Kuni right? You believe this? If so, then maybe you are becoming rock, too."

Tale-Chaser's guileless insults were almost charming. But Sukune again pushed past it. "What do you mean?"

Tale-Chaser paused a moment. When he finally did speak,

his voice assumed the same singsong, storyteller cadence he'd used in Kuni Castle.

"Once, a poor nezumi was lost and alone in dry, barren lands. Hungry, yes, but worse, so very thirsty. Finally, he smelled water, deep underground. Desperate, he dug. But soil is hard, full of stones. The nezumi didn't reach water in time, so he lost his race against Tomorrow." Tale-Chaser glanced at Sukune. "That means he died."

"So I gathered."

Tale-Chaser said nothing. Sukune got the impression that whatever point he was trying to make should be obvious.

Except it wasn't.

"I'm sorry," Sukune finally said, "but I don't understand."

Tale-Chaser puffed out a jarringly human sigh. "The poor, lost nezumi can't reach water, so the answer is to give up, to walk away and die for sure?"

"Well, if he had no other option…" Sukune trailed off. No, Tale-Chaser hadn't told him this story for no reason. He must still be missing something.

"Wait," Sukune said. "He could try… to dig somewhere else?"

"Ah! Yes! He tries instead to find softer dirt, easier to dig, so he finds good water, instead of Tomorrow." Again, the Rememberer pushed his dark gaze into Sukune's. "He stops being like rock that does not think or change. Becomes a smart nezumi instead."

"Instead of giving up, he chose a different approach."

"Yes. Don't be rock. Be smart. Great-Bear-father, Kisada, thinks you can do this. Moongazer-Transcendent also thinks so. I trust both. You should, too."

Silence, as Sukune considered Tale-Chaser's words. The quiet was split once, by a brief, sharp yelp of pain from a wounded Crab warrior, probably having a broken bone reset.

The silence went on, until Sukune suddenly realized he'd made a decision. He no longer contemplated the ramifications of failure, but the possibilities for success. One possibility in particular stood out. It might still end in failure, of course, but it might not.

"Thank you, Tale-Chaser," he said. "You are very wise."

"Maybe. Maybe not. Anyway, I will leave you to think now." The Rememberer started to turn away, but stopped and looked back. "I think you can do this, too, Sukune."

Sukune watched the little Rememberer walk back into the mist. Being assured that he had the confidence of his father, and of Moongazer, helped immensely. But, somehow, neither buoyed Sukune as much as Tale-Chaser's faith in him.

"Almost two hundred years ago, a Crab general named Hida Chuku donned the armor called Kikyo and led an army into the Shadowlands, intent on ending its terrible threat to Rokugan once and for all. The army, Chuku, and the armor were never seen again.

"Because," Sukune said, "they never entered the Shadowlands. For reasons we may never know, Chuku brought his army here. They fought a great battle against something. Again, we may never know what. In any case, Chuku and his army were destroyed, and these swamps were corrupted by the battle, or perhaps by even older conflicts, lost to time."

"That does not sound unreasonable," O-Ushi said, glancing at the others gathered around Sukune: Yori, Daigo, Kazane, and Tale-Chaser. "But how does it help us?"

"All of those fallen Crab are still here," Sukune said. "They died, unremembered and uncelebrated. They *are* the gashadokuro."

This time it was Yori who spoke. "As your esteemed sister said, that does not sound unreasonable. Like her, though, I fail to see how–"

"Kuni-sama," Sukune cut in, "we have seen evidence throughout these swamps of battle. And yet, the gashadokuro does not seem inclined to leave the immediate vicinity of the cave. Based on Tale-Chaser's account of his first visit here, it did not even appear until he had already found Kikyo and removed the sode from it." As he spoke, Sukune removed the sode from his backpack. "I believe the gashadokuro is bound to the armor in some way. It seeks to protect it. Suppose that is some remnant of the loyalty of the fallen Crab? To their general, and perhaps even to their clan?"

"That is an unfounded supposition, Hida-sama," Yori said. "The souls of those unfortunate Crab have been exposed to the Taint for two centuries. At the very best, they will be quite mad. At worst, they will have been entirely consumed by corruption, now little more than *onryō*. Such vengeful ghosts would bear little similarity to the loyal Crab they once were."

"I must agree with Yori-sama," O-Ushi said, her sidelong glance at the Kuni daimyō hinting that their agreeing both surprised and annoyed her. "That is little more than a hunch."

"At this point," Sukune said, "unfounded suppositions and hunches are all we really have left."

"Very well," she shot back, "what, exactly, are you proposing?"

Sukune picked up the sode, looked at the Crab insignia upon it, and took a breath. "I will take one of the remaining jade-inlaid weapons and return to the cave, accompanied by Tale-Chaser and the Tattered Ear. In the meantime, the rest of the expedition will withdraw from the swamps under your command, O-Ushi-san, before their jade is wholly corrupted. Then, while the Tattered Ear engage and, hopefully, distract the gashadokuro, Tale-Chaser and I will enter the cave and find Kikyo. I will don the armor, then present myself to the gashadokuro as their commander and order the fallen Crab to stand down."

In the silence that followed, Sukune reflected that it had seemed like a reasonable plan until he spoke it aloud. Now, though, it felt charged with uncertainty and terrible risk. It really was based on unfounded assumptions and hunches. But he could think of nothing else that wasn't just giving up entirely, which *still* might be the best option. He looked back at the sode, waiting for the inevitable barrage of protests and objections.

Somewhere in the mist, something – maybe a bird, but maybe something else – wailed a miserable, mournful cry that ended on a piercing shriek, like a child screaming in pain.

O-Ushi glanced that way, then said simply, "That is a terrible plan."

"I must agree, Hida-sama," Yori said, taking his own turn to seem resentful of the fact. "The risk is far outweighed by the prospect for success. I urge you to just withdraw the expedition. Once safely back in our own lands, we can have a sober deliberation on other options."

But O-Ushi shook her head. "No, it is a terrible plan because I am not part of it. Between them, Kuni Yori-sama and Hiruma Kazane-san can lead the expedition out of these accursed swamps. I will come with you."

Sukune sat back, stunned. If he had wagered on which of Yori and O-Ushi would object, and which would be supportive, he would have got it exactly backward. Regardless...

"O-Ushi-san... Sister... there is no need for you to assume such risk. Because Kuni Yori-sama is correct, there is a great deal of it."

O-Ushi waved a dismissive hand. "Every time I enter the Shadowlands, or even stand upon the Wall, I accept risks that would make the most rabid Matsu quail. Besides, Kikyo is a suit of ō-yoroi armor, heavy and complicated. You will never be able to dress yourself in it." Sukune hesitated at that. She had a point; it was unlikely Tale-Chaser would be much help in donning the armor. Still...

"I can take someone else with me," he said. "We need not risk the both of us in this." He stopped and glanced at Yori, because what he was about to say wasn't about clan or duty; it was about family. "If we both fail to survive, then Father will have lost–"

"Father has already made that choice," O-Ushi snapped. "That is why we are both here, in this miserable swamp, having this conversation. Do not dishonor his decision by presuming to second-guess it."

Again, he sat back. Again, she was right.

"I am not going to dissuade you," he said to her, "am I?"

O-Ushi smirked back. "Why ask a question to which you already know the answer, brother?"

Kuni Yori scowled. "I must restate my objection to this. I am so opposed to it, in fact, that I am considering invoking my status as daimyō of the Kuni and ordering you to drop the entire idea."

O-Ushi turned her full glare on Yori, but he held up a hand. "I will not do so, however, because then *I* would be the one dishonoring your esteemed father's choices. I only say it to underscore how much I am opposed to this." The Kuni daimyō lowered his hand, but his hard stare remained on Sukune. Finally, though, he simply nodded.

"Your honored father made the correct choice. I must admit that the thought of allowing our ancient enemy to prevail galled me." He looked from sister to brother. "I pray that the Fortunes watch over both of you."

Sukune offered Yori a bow of thanks. O-Ushi was more direct. "Please do, Kuni-sama," she said, "because we will need all the help we can get."

CHAPTER NINE

Sukune crouched behind a skeletal tree, O-Ushi beside him, Tale-Chaser just behind. They'd come as close to the cave mouth as they dared, and now watched as White Scar led the Tattered Ear warriors forward. They advanced cautiously, spears and bows ready, heads swiveling, noses lifted to taste the air, ears pricked up...

Nothing. What, Sukune wondered, if the gashadokuro does not appear? The way to the cave would be open, but would it still pose a threat to the nezumi?

A wet plop of mud. Another. A patch of mud bubbled, then something massive rose from it, towering over the Tattered Ear. The gashadokuro loomed toward the nezumi, but at White Scar's command, they scattered and fell back, peppering the monstrosity with arrows. The missiles sank into muck and clattered against bone, but the huge creature surged forward, closing on the nezumi as they backed away.

"Now!" Sukune hissed, gripping the jade-inlaid *kabutowari* and starting for the cave. Something caught at his feet and he stumbled, gasping, sucking at air that seemed as thick as tree sap, desperately trying to keep his feet. But something else caught him. It was O-Ushi, pushing him splashing along through cloying ooze and black water, driving them both toward the cave. Tale-Chaser scurried along behind.

A terrific crash, then a shower of splintered wood. Sukune dared a glance. The gashadokuro towered over him, a colossal fist plunging toward him like an avalanche. O-Ushi yanked him toward her, but kept moving, practically carrying him now. A tremendous impact barely an arm's length away, where he would have been if O-Ushi hadn't pulled him aside, then an explosion of mud...

Now darkness. Sukune's feet no longer splashed into mud: they pounded against rock. He didn't stop running, though, until O-Ushi did. She leaned against the rock, looking back at the dim, gray patch of light that was the cave mouth.

"So much," O-Ushi gasped, "for the easy part."

Sukune could only wheeze and nod. Ahead, the cave turned and vanished into blackness.

While O-Ushi sparked a torch, Sukune croaked, "Tale-Chaser! Make sure... we... don't stray..."

"Don't stray, yes. Will do so."

The clamor of battle outside the cave faded as the Tattered Ear withdrew. O-Ushi, the torch in one hand, her own jade-inlaid kabutowari in the other, led them on, into the cave.

"It is, indeed, Kikyo," O-Ushi said, her voice barely more than a whisper.

Sukune nodded. There was no doubt. Like the sode Tale-Chaser had brought to Kuni Castle, the great ō-yoroi armor gleamed in the torchlight, its lacquered faces the deep gray of a thundercloud, its many lacings black, the symbol of a crab circumscribed by a circle emblazoned on it in pale blue-gray. Sukune leaned in, to study it more closely. He caught faint but distinct whiffs of rain-washed wind, of hot metal in a forge, of the way the air smelled after a lightning bolt.

There was no doubt at all.

Sukune knelt, bowing to the skull leering from inside the ornate helm. O-Ushi joined him. Tale-Chaser remained a respectful distance away, his nose twitching at the air.

"Hida Chuku-ue," Sukune said, "you have been lost to us. But now, your clan has found you. You and your loyal followers are remembered with honor and will never again be forgotten. As the son of our champion, Hida Kisada, I promise you that."

A moment passed in silence, then O-Ushi said, "There is no mempō."

Sukune looked at the armor. Looked around it. She was correct.

The face mask was nowhere to be seen.

He shrugged. "It might have been lost – well – anytime," Sukune said. "Perhaps somewhere out in the swamps, before Chuku-ue even entered this cave." He looked back at the armor. "In any case, the rest of Kikyo is here. That means we can carry on as we planned."

O-Ushi gave a grim nod and reached for the armor. "Which means," she said, starting to unlace the remaining sode, "that now it is time for the hard part."

Sukune had worn ō-yoroi armor before, during his training at Sunda Mizu Dōjō. He hadn't worn it since. It was simply too cumbersome for his slender frame. He'd expected Kikyo to similarly bear him down – and it did, indeed, hang heavy and bulky on him. But, as he walked along the dark tunnel, toward the seemingly perpetual gray light of the swamps, it didn't weigh him down anywhere near as much as he'd feared. He could actually walk, not simply waddle about as he had in the dōjō, prompting the other students to snicker and call him "the Armored Duck".

He banished the humiliating memory. It certainly didn't matter now–

"But it does," a voice said, booming across the raw stone like echoing thunder. Somebody now stood behind Sukune, a massive presence who would surely block the tunnel. He turned, but the speaker remained out of sight behind him. Its unseen nearness sent an electric thrill of anticipation rippling along Sukune's spine, like lightning about to strike.

Sukune opened his mouth to ask who this was but closed it again. He knew who this was.

"Lord Osano-wo," he said, forgetting even to kneel. "I am… beyond honored that you would appear–"

"Bah, no!" The voice roared like a furnace. "I am Kikyo. Osano-wo was my maker. If I seem to be him, that is because the creation is a reflection of its creator."

"My apologies. I–"

"More apologies!" The voice – which Sukune now realized was, indeed, that of Kikyo, the awakened spirit of the armor – crackled like electric discharge. "You have spent most of your life sorry. Sorry for being sickly. Sorry for your mother, who died bearing you. Sorry for being inadequate. Sorry for being weak. But weakness pervades you, Sukune. And I was not made to merely offset weakness. I was made to reinforce *strength*."

Something moved in Sukune's peripheral vision. He heard O-Ushi say, "Sukune, what is happening? Who are you–?"

He raised a hand, cutting his sister off.

"I have done my duty," he said to the spirit. "You may consider me weak, but I have done my duty–"

"Doing what is required of you is all that is required to be strong? Mere adequacy is enough?" The spirit gave a derisive snort. "Anything is impressive if you set the standard for it low enough. But I am not impressed. You are not worthy to bear me."

Sukune winced at the spirit's tone, harsh and recriminating. But it was true. He had spent so much of his life sorry, because his life *was* sorry, a life full of weakness.

He was sickly, but he'd fought an unrelenting war against his frail nature. His mother had died shortly after his birth, but he was not, could *not be* responsible for that. He'd thought himself inadequate, but here he was, bearing Kikyo, having done what he had been charged with doing. And that was despite all the setbacks, all the obstacles… It was despite every accursed thing the forest had flung at him and his followers.

Sukune was done with being found wanting.

"No," he said. "I will not be judged this way. To rise above my weakness *is* strength. To do my duty might be merely adequate for others, but for me, it is a triumph. You will not deny me that."

"You presume to gainsay me?"

"Yes, I do. Because, if you are a reflection of Lord Osano-wo, then so am I. My soul was fastened upon this vessel. His blood flows in my veins. If your creator judges me worthy enough for that, then who are you to say I am unworthy of bearing you?"

A moment passed, then the spirit said, "It seems that all this time alone in the dark *might* have affected my ability to judge a mortal's character. Very well, then. Let us remain together – for now – and see what you can do with this strength you claim."

The armor trembled, as though shivered by distant thunder, then went still.

"Sukune," O-Ushi said, "you were speaking to… no one." She glanced at Tale-Chaser, who nodded.

"Speaking to air, Sukune," the nezumi said. "Very strange. Good for the story, though!"

Sukune shook his head, the heavy helm wobbling against his temples. "I was not speaking to no one."

"You named Lord Osano-wo," O-Ushi said. "Was it really him?" She sounded both awed and disappointed, probably believing she had missed an opportunity to speak to one of their clan's most revered figures. But Sukune shook his head a second time.

"No, it was not Lord Osano-wo either. It was…" He sighed. "Someone else who wished to judge me. I am tired of being judged."

"So I gathered. Which means it is good it was *not* Lord Osano-wo, because you sounded rather…" Sukune looked at her, and she shrugged. "Not like yourself," she said. "Not like your usual self, anyway." She gave a tired smile. "I think I like the Sukune I heard speaking up for himself just now somewhat more."

"Yes, well, even that wasn't the hard part." He puffed out a sigh and gestured at the cave mouth. "That comes now."

Sukune gathered himself and walked toward, and then into, the wan gray light outside the cave.

Kikyo rattled and creaked as he splashed back into muck, waded through it a few paces, and stopped.

Nothing happened.

And then it did. Something massive suddenly loomed to his right. He turned to find the gashadokuro towering over him, a gargantuan pillar of mud and bone and malice, almost close enough to touch.

Sukune's heart raced, a pulsing rhythm hammering against his chest, and seeming to echo inside the heavy helm. O-Ushi shouted, but her words were lost in the rush and thunder of his own heartbeat.

When speaking to the armor's spirit, he'd thought, *here I am, despite all of our trials.* And, indeed, here he was.

But it wasn't going to be enough. He had believed the brave words he'd flung at the spirit, just moments ago. Believed them right until this moment, when they all suddenly sounded like nothing more than that single shriek of the yosuzume, just bad portents and noise.

Because this had all been unfounded suppositions and hunches. Nothing else. And it had all been for nothing anyway, because Sukune was about to die. He saw nothing in the gashadokuro that told him he could command it or do anything other than watch it kill him. He must tell O-Ushi to flee, save herself, Tale-Chaser, too, leave this place of death and despair and empty sacrifice, go home, find another way. He started to turn.

But the gashadokuro did nothing.

On instinct, Sukune had raised the kabutowari, ready to defend, to strike – but he lowered it again. O-Ushi still shouted, and so did Tale-Chaser, now. But Sukune ignored them. The gashadokuro just kept looming, a tower of menace.

The moment went on, heartbeat after heartbeat. Had something happened to the monstrous creature–?

Without warning, it moved, turning and raising a massive fist. Sukune looked for whatever had suddenly provoked it into action. There – O-Ushi and Tale-Chaser had been approaching. They crouched, expecting now to die, just as Sukune had a moment ago.

No. Enough. Sukune had come too far. The cost to get here had been too high. He would not lose anyone else.

"No!" he shouted, demanding the gashadokuro's attention. "You shall not harm them!"

Sukune's voice, emanating from Kikyo's helm, echoed like a coming storm. A tremor ran through the gashadokuro, as though it were riven by some internal conflict, caught between his words and a malign need to destroy. But the great fist finally lowered, the creature resuming a motionless place facing Sukune.

In the silence that followed, the thunder of his own blood in Sukune's ears sounded like marching feet.

Like an army.

An army. That's what the gashadokuro was. It was all of the fallen Crab of Hida Chuku's army. All of them. But they were corrupted by their centuries of entrapment, and by the Taint of Jigoku. They were irrevocably lost.

The truth made Sukune's throat clamp painfully. This was beyond a tragedy. He could do nothing for these Tainted, enraged souls – these lost, lonely Crab warriors. Jigoku had claimed them long ago.

He could do nothing for them. Except, that is, *command* them. That was why the gashadokuro did not strike him down, and why it refrained from attacking O-Ushi and Tale-Chaser when he so ordered it. Whatever remained of the Crab in these lost warriors recognized Kikyo, probably from their last moments alive, as a thing of inspiration, a rallying point. They still saw the armor that way.

Sukune now commanded an army. But it was an army like no other. It did not rest. It did not sleep. It needed no baggage train, no supplies. Virtually nothing could harm it.

It was an army that could not be defeated.

Back at the Great Home of the Tattered Ear, Kuni Yori had said the Crab waste nothing. Sukune could lead the gashadokuro on a great campaign into the Shadowlands, marching perhaps as far as the Festering Pit itself, destroying the threat Jigoku posed to the Mortal Realm once and for all.

With Jigoku's access to the Mortal World ended, there would be no more need for Crab to walk a katana's edge between corruption and death in the Shadowlands, only to end up slaughtered upon the Wall. No more such desperate need for jade that they must resort to dealing for it in the shadows, like an addict in some Scorpion opium den. No more waking each day in abject fear and ending it simply grateful to be alive. No more Crab souls Tainted and irrevocably lost to the insidious grasp of evil, simply because of a wound inflicted during a moment's inattention, or an instant of slowness brought on by deep, endless fatigue.

"Sukune," O-Ushi said, "what will you do?"

She half-crouched beside him, her eyes fixed on the looming monstrosity. Tale-Chaser remained well behind, his eyes bright with fear. Looking at him, Sukune heard another voice, that of Moongazer, the nezumi Transcendent.

You must save my people, Sukune.

He let out a long, slow sigh. A profound weariness fell upon him, far heavier than Kikyo itself.

Even if Sukune would simply dismiss these poor, tortured spirits and consign them to damnation, it was not within his power. But neither could he unleash the gashadokuro on the Shadowlands. Yes, it might save his clan, and the Empire – for now. But it would not stop there. No matter how good and noble the intentions in the beginning, such dark choices inevitably ended in greater darkness.

And yet, he must also save the Tattered Ear. To do this, he could see only one way.

"The armor returns, with us, to the Crab," he finally said. "But the gashadokuro will remain here, never to leave this place."

He then turned and started away from the Cave of Bloody Ghost Fire, and the gashadokuro standing silently outside it. He assumed O-Ushi and Tale-Chaser followed, but he never looked back to see.

EPILOGUE

Hida Kisada crossed his arms and studied Kikyo, which once more rested in the echoing halls of Hida Palace.

"You did well, Sukune," he finally said.

Sukune bowed. "You honor me, Father."

"Perhaps. But this also means that I will now expect even more from you."

"I understand."

"I do not think you do. But you will." The Great Bear turned away from the armor and looked at his son. "You shall assume command of the reserve army at Kuni Castle."

"Again, Father, I am... honored."

"The Wall remains strong," Kisada went on. "But I want you to prepare against the day it is breached. On that day, your army will be crucial, so it must be ready. How you achieve that is up to you."

"Yes, Father."

Kisada glanced back at the armor. "This armor will play a vital role in our war against our great enemy. It may even be decisive. However, there are those who believe it should be wielded in the forefront of our armies now. They believe that allowing it to be worn anywhere other than there – say, in command of the reserve army – is to waste it."

And the Crab, of course, waste nothing.

"Those are Yakamo's words," Sukune said, staring at Kikyo. "Even now, after all of this, he sees me as inadequate and unworthy." Perhaps, if he had come with the expedition instead of O-Ushi, he would have seen.

But no. Yakamo was not O-Ushi. Who knows what he might have done, were he there? What might have happened…

"All that matters," Kisada said, "is what you accomplish next." Sukune thought about all those lost during the expedition – and he included in that dreary count Hida Chuku's army, ordered by Sukune himself to just stand in place, forever damned. And yet, here they were.

"You are right, Father, of course," he finally said, then turned his gaze fully into Kisada's. "Whether you give me Kikyo to bear or not, the reserve army will be ready, when and where it is needed."

Hida Kisada held his own gaze on Sukune, then nodded. "Yes, it will."

Later, Sukune stood with O-Ushi upon a battlement of Hida Palace, staring down into one of many courtyards, their numerous complexity a part of the castle's defense. A chill wind blew once again from the Shadowlands, but Sukune barely felt it. His gaze was fixed on what was happening below. Priests stood before a bonfire, intoning funeral prayers. Among the flames were the few remains of Hida Chuku's army the expedition had recovered. The intent was to give the lost Crab army its final rest.

Sukune knew better. Chuku's army would never know rest. O-Ushi knew this, too. No one else knew this truth: not Yori, or Yakamo – not even Kisada.

The flames rose, splashing ruddy light across the stone. Tale-Chaser knew the gashadokuro remained, of course, but he…

Tale-Chaser. The Tattered Ear. It was the one thing about all of this that almost made Sukune smile. Almost.

The Transcendent knew you would succeed, *the Rememberer had said, before they parted ways at the edge of the Shinomen Forest.* So did I, Sukune. I am privileged to call you friend.

The memory brought a fleeting smile to his lips. The sad reality was that the nezumi were short-lived, and Tale-Chaser was already old for his kind. Helping them had been a patch of blue sky amid what, for Sukune, had become a thick, dark overcast of memories from the expedition. Yet even it was bittersweet.

Perhaps, Sukune thought, Tale-Chaser will be able to visit me in my dreams. I hope so, because they are mostly nightmares, otherwise.

"The yosuzume were wrong," O-Ushi suddenly said. Sukune looked at her.

"They seemed to portend disaster for you," she said, returning his look. "They were wrong."

Sukune looked back at the fire. Perhaps she was right. Perhaps they had been wrong.

Or, perhaps, the full weight of his choices hadn't yet caught up to him, and the yosuzume simply weren't right *yet.*

O-Ushi finally looked back into the courtyard below. Together, they watched the funeral pyre burn.

•••

Kuni Yori closed the heavy door to his private workroom and slid the locking bar into place.

Are you excited, Yori? Do you look forward to what you are about to do?

Yori glanced at the skeletal remnants of a spawn of Nairu no Oni, a Tainted, winged creature the size of a dog. It had been captured, studied, and eventually killed long ago, and now hung pinned with iron spikes to a large plank in the corner of the room. "Yes," Yori said, "because it is another step along the path to your ultimate destruction."

It is, indeed, another step along a path–

Yori turned his back on the spawn and worked at the complex Kaiu lock securing a stout, ironbound door of teak set into the stone wall. The lock required a precise – and secret – sequence of mechanical activations to open.

The lock snapped open and Yori swung the door aside, revealing a small vault lined with shelves holding many things: some ancient, all obscurely arcane. From among them, he retrieved something wrapped in silk.

If they only knew about these things, Yori. Your clanmates, your lord. What would they think? What would they do?

Yori placed the object on a worktable, beside a heavy mallet. "Eventually, they would celebrate my vision." Sukune, in particular, showed capacity for remarkably progressive thought.

And until then?

Yori pulled aside the silk, revealing a mempō – a scowling, full-face mask rendered in dark gray.

Yori studied it for a moment, then picked up the mallet and slammed it down on the mempō. Gray-lacquered ceramic cracked and splintered.

He struck it again. Again. With each blow, the slate-dark ceramic crumbled away, exposing something smooth and white beneath.

"Yes," he said, and looked back at the vault, at a thick sheaf of ancient papers on one of the shelves. "Great-grandfather, you were right."

He hammered away on what remained of the mempō, revealing a smooth porcelain mask. It was virtually identical to one already sitting in the vault, on the same shelf as the journals of Kuni Mokuna. He had found the first mask among his father's belongings when he had died, but had been able to discern little about it, aside from its having been infused with a potent, but latent, power. Mokuna's journals had hinted at more such masks, including one somehow associated with Kikyo's mempō. Yori had considered that little more than an interesting curiosity. And then Tale-Chaser had arrived with the revelation that Kikyo had been found.

Yori touched his new mask, feeling its cool, glassy smoothness. Yes, his clanmates would object, but only because they did not understand. They put their faith in stone and muscle, in courage and sacrifice. Those things were important, yes. In the end, though, they would not be enough.

Still, how had the mask come to be made part of Kikyo? Surely Hida Osano-wo had not deliberately chosen to incorporate it into the armor he made for his brother, Atarashi.

Had he?

Perhaps, Yori, you are not the first to believe that evil things can be turned to good purposes.

Yori placed the new mask in the vault beside the first, then closed and relocked the heavy door. He then returned to his worktable to begin transcribing the notes he had taken during the expedition.

But the vault kept snagging his attention. He finally put his writings aside, crossed to the vault, and opened it again.

The two masks stared back at him with dangerous promise.

THE
ETERNAL
KNOT

MARIE BRENNAN

To Terrance and Megs for introducing me to L5R, and to Kyle, Adrienne, Alyc, and Wendy, for a truly amazing campaign. 蝶 氏 八千代!

CHAPTER ONE

What do you remember?

Her breathing slows to a steady, unhurried pace, her stomach rising and falling, her shoulders relaxing and her spine lifting straight. It is a familiar habit, after so many years of training – but this time, she knows, will be different.

What do you remember?

Three sensei, facing her with unreadable expressions. The novices joke that they represent the three sins: desire for success, fear of failure, and regret for ever having started down this path. They never say it where the monks can hear, but she suspects that joke was old a century ago, and has been passed down through the generations, just like the teachings of their order.

Three sensei, and an afternoon of grueling examination. The nature of the elements and their role in the world. The power of the *kami*, from the seven Kami who founded the Great Clans to the animating forces of mighty rivers and mountains to the little *mikokami* that make up the physical world. The mysteries of the Void, the state of nonbeing, and the Spirit Realms that shimmer around and through mortal existence like the refracted light of a crystal. The Fortunes: seven great, ten thousand small. The Tao of Shinsei. All the spiritual wisdom the three sensei can wring from her, and no certainty whether it is enough.

What do you remember?

Before that, Migasha-sensei's fist hammering into her ribs. Just barely keeping her feet as he tries to hook one of them out from under her, retreating farther than she should, and the slight bend in his mouth that says he notices the error. Wading back in, feinting a kick with one foot and then lashing out with the other; it doesn't connect, but the bend in his mouth goes away. Breath grating in and out of her lungs, sweat stinging her eyes as it soaks through the white band tied around her forehead.

And all the while, knowing this is only the start. Of course, the trials begin with a test of fighting skill, so that novices go into the spiritual examination battered and exhausted.

If it were easy, it wouldn't be a trial.

What do you remember?

Years at the High House of Light, blurring and slipping together like overwatered ink. Learning *jūjutsu* from Sanaki-sensei, meditation from Ryōshō-sensei, theology from Shikkyo-sensei. Chores: chopping wood, carrying water, scrubbing the flagstones of the courtyards and the polished wooden floors of the halls. Raking leaves from the gardens and pouring tea for the senior monks. Hardship and resentment, serenity and satisfaction, and the constant song of the mountain wind, chill even in summer, sharper than a blade in winter.

What do you remember?

Seeing the thousand stairs for the first time, the impossible climb from the deep green of the valley below to the austere heights of the monastery above. The stories claim the High House of Light can only be found by those who are meant to be there: a person who seeks it without cause or merit might wander in the mountains for a hundred years and not come across the road even with a map to guide him, while one who thinks herself a hundred miles away might find herself at the base of its stairs – if that is her fate.

As a child of eight, she shivers at her own temerity, believing she is meant to reach the hidden monastery. And yet an unspoken certainty drives her, out of Phoenix lands, through the Great Wall of the North, away from her old life and into her new.

What do you remember?

Life with her mother. A market town at a confluence of roads, big enough to draw travelers, but not one of the famed cities of Rokugan – barely even famed within its own province. Aika braiding her hair, singing her songs, buying her sweets when they had a little money to spare. Giving her two sticks to care for, one longer, one shorter, both cut to a child's size, because someday – Aika assumes – she will inherit the two swords that ride at her mother's hip.

Until the day she sees an old monk, his left arm ending at the elbow but still corded with muscle and glorious with intricate tattoos.

What do you remember?

Back and back and back, through the whole of her life… and past it.

To what came before.

It is a rare thing, remembering a previous life. In Meido, the Realm of Waiting, the souls of the dead are washed clean of their memories before proceeding to their next life as decreed by Emma-Ō, the Fortune of Death. Only a few cling to any recollection, and even then it is only shreds.

But with time, training, skill, those shreds can be recovered.

Once *she* was the gnarled old *ise zumi* whose presence inspired a child to seek out the High House of Light. Once *she* was the sensei rapping young students across the shoulders with a stiff cane when they nodded off while meditating. She has raked these garden paths before, painted the walls of the dormitory with white lime, known the pines of the neighboring peak when they were not so tall.

How many lifetimes? She cannot say. Even now, with realization flooding her, she cannot summon the memories with perfect clarity. They remain fogged, like the valley below on a cold morning, when the sun first floods it with gold. She knows only that she has been an ise zumi before – that they learn to master the power of their intricate tattoos not only through a childhood spent training but through whole lifetimes. Taking that power into themselves, controlling it, refining it, until it flows through them like their own blood and breath.

What do you remember?

She remembers who she is, and who she was.

And she feels the power returning, dancing across her skin like lightning, striking into the marrow of her bones.

Mitsu entered the room silently, easing the door closed so he would not disturb Gaijutsu-sensei. It was courtesy more than practicality; he suspected the mountains could erupt in flame and ash and the blind old man would go on working without pause. But courtesy still mattered.

The room was small and plain – not the sort of place where one would expect to see momentous things happen. The wall panels displayed ink-wash paintings of the mountains in a minimalist style popular four hundred years earlier. Along the back wall stood a small shrine, at the center of which was a candle. Yanai knelt before it with her hands linked in a mudra, eyes half-lidded, gazing unblinking upon the flame.

But Mitsu knew from experience that Yanai wasn't seeing it, any more than she had heard him enter or felt Gaijutsu-sensei's hand on her skin. She had already passed the third trial of her *gempuku*, meditating under the guidance of Kotai-sensei until she recovered the truth of herself. Now she had sunk into a deeper trance, one that would sustain her until the tattoo master's work was done.

Gaijutsu-sensei's hands seemed to see what their master's eyes could not. One of his apprentices held the ink for him; his silk-bound needles found the mouth of the tiny pot without hesitation or error, then returned to the line in progress. A second apprentice held the skin of Yanai's bare scalp taut with one hand and wiped with the other, mopping away the blood that beaded up where the needles stabbed over and over again.

The tattoo along Yanai's right arm was already complete. Storm clouds and a serpent wound in thick curls around her biceps, with right-angled bolts of lightning spiking down onto her forearm. Something related to fighting, Mitsu suspected; she'd done well against Migasha. He had thrashed her, of course – nobody expected a novice going through their *gempuku* to hold their own against the senior jūjutsu sensei. The test was in how well she stood up to it.

Combat, spiritual matters, recollection of past lives, and finally this: the process that transformed a novice into an ise zumi, a tattooed monk.

Gaijutsu-sensei worked in a tireless rhythm, dipping and stabbing, dipping and stabbing. The outline grew even as Mitsu watched, but its shape ... that refused to cohere into something recognizable, no matter how he craned his neck. He wished he could approach and take a closer look, but even for a monk of his status, there were limits. The clan champion himself might hesitate to peer over the tattoo master's shoulder.

It was done sooner than he expected. Gaijutsu-sensei laid down his needles and did not pick them up again, and Mitsu realized the scalp mark was complete. An ordinary tattoo would be done in stages – first the outline, then the fill, giving the skin time to heal and the colors time to set before another layer was added – but Gaijutsu-sensei's needles were *nemuranai*. The awakened kami within them let him work without pause. If he was stopping now, it was because he was done. The storm-clouded serpent on her arm faded from bruise-dark to lightning blue, but the mark on her scalp would remain pure black.

The apprentices began clearing away their master's tools. None of them said anything, and Mitsu hadn't spoken, but that didn't mean anything where Gaijutsu-sensei was concerned. He spoke without hesitation as he wiped off his ink-stained hands. "Help me lay her out, Mitsu-kun."

Serving as novitiates in the High House of Light taught even the children of high-ranking samurai not to scorn chores. Mitsu had been born a peasant, and the habit of hard work hadn't gone away after he'd passed his gempuku. He slid one of the wall panels aside, took out a thin futon cushion, and laid it out on the mat before the candle. Then he took Yanai by the shoulders.

She went limp at his touch. Not meditating any longer, but unconscious. Her head lolled against his arm, giving him a good view of the entire symbol: an intricate knot of lines, crossing over and under each other in an abstract shape that made his vision swim the more he tried to make sense of it.

He laid her down and straightened her legs, then tucked a small buckwheat pillow under her neck, making sure it didn't press against the lines at the base of her skull. "What *is* this?" he asked Gaijutsu-sensei, now that there was no risk of disturbing anything. The Heavens themselves couldn't wake her now, not until she was done recovering. "I have never seen anything like it." Ise zumi tattoos were usually creatures like his own tiger and dragon and monkey, or sometimes natural images like bamboo and her storm clouds. Abstract forms like the knot of lines weren't unheard of, but they were rare.

And usually important.

Gaijutsu-sensei waved his apprentices out the door. They bowed and left, cradling their master's needles and inks in their hands. "It is what I saw."

Not with his blind eyes. He was the monastery's tattoo master not only because of his long years of experience, but because of his gift: the ability to see in visions what marks each ise zumi should bear. Mitsu had never quite dared to ask whether that gift came from one of Gaijutsu-sensei's own tattoos, which covered his body from neck to wrist to ankle, or whether he'd always had that gift – if, perhaps, that was the reason he'd come to the High House of Light in the first place.

"Of course, sensei," he said. "But… what does it *do*?"

The tattoo master shrugged and made his way to the door, one careful but confident step at a time. "That is for her to discover."

CHAPTER TWO

Yanai woke to stiffness the likes of which she hadn't felt since her earliest days at the monastery, when the grueling combination of chores and jūjutsu practice left her feeling like every inch of flesh had been beaten with a stick.

An involuntary groan escaped her as she sat up. It was as if every muscle had locked tight for hours... and maybe they had. The specifics slipped through her fingers like smoke when she tried to grasp them, but one glimpse of her right arm was enough to tell her that she hadn't imagined the feeling of lightning arcing through her skin.

I passed.

The thought made her dizzy – or possibly that was the lack of food. Monks were no strangers to fasting, but her last meal had come the morning her gempuku began, and who knew how long ago that had been. In between, she'd fought Migasha-sensei, answered endless questions, remembered her past lives, and received the first of her tattoos. It was enough to make anyone ravenous.

A sudden rustling of robes made her twitch away, but it was

only a boy coming to help steady her. A novice, perhaps halfway through his training – Hikkon, that was his name. She herself had sat a vigil like his, when Enshi had gone through her own gempuku.

"How long?" she asked.

Her voice rasped like grit under a sandal. Hikkon handed her a cup of water, which she downed in one gulp. He left her side long enough to pour her another, and this time he brought the jug back with him. While she drank, he said, "You have been asleep for a little over a day."

Since Gaijutsu-sensei had finished with her. She examined the tattoo on her right arm, not quite succeeding at repressing a smile. The storm-shrouded serpent was a little swollen to the touch, but not badly so. Once her skin finished healing, the image would be magnificent.

And her other tattoo...

The faint burning on her scalp guided her hand. Her questing fingers encountered stubble – a little over a day's worth; someone must have shaved her head again before Gaijutsu-sensei went to work – and a pattern of swelling whose details she couldn't make out. It extended from the top of her forehead to the base of her skull.

"What is it?" she asked Hikkon, hiding her frustration. Even with a good mirror, she wouldn't be able to see the top of her own head, which meant she couldn't admire her second mark.

Desire might be one of the three sins, but it would take a more enlightened soul than hers not to want to appreciate this moment.

The boy shrugged. "I do not know. It is... like a knot of lines? It makes my eyes swim if I try to look at it too closely."

A knot of lines. Every ise zumi tattoo was unique; there were some patterns, certain motifs that tended to map to certain effects, but no two were exactly the same. She'd never heard of a knot-like tattoo, though.

I wonder what it does?

She made herself stop poking at it. The skin was tender, and exploration wasn't making it feel any better. "Do you have any food?"

The question was reflexive, and foolish. She'd stood the same vigil for Enshi; she knew perfectly well what came next, and it wasn't a meal. Hikkon bowed in apology. "My instructions are to take you to wash when you are ready, and to notify Hassuno-sama that you are awake."

Because her gempuku wasn't entirely complete. She'd passed the trials, received her tattoos... but there was one thing left to do.

She drank the last of her water and said, "I am ready now."

Age had rendered Hassuno into an elegant skeleton, her flesh drawn as tight over her bones as the thin soil of the peaks over the stone below, but anyone who thought that made her weak was a fool. Tattoos covered both arms, both legs, winding across her chest and back; even in the cold environment of the mountains, she wore only a breastband and a loincloth. The clan champion was the *daimyō* of the Togashi family, but Hassuno was the *iemoto* of the school, the head of the Tattooed Order and the inheritor of its traditions.

Yanai had scrubbed herself from head to foot, not excepting her newly marked skin. That had been a form of self-inflicted torture, making her yelp a few words she must have retrieved from a previous life, because they certainly weren't anything she'd learned at the monastery. No bath, though – not until her tattoos healed. It left her feeling just the tiniest bit grubby... or maybe that was just in comparison to Hassuno-sama's presence.

Or the room they were in. The iemoto received her in a grand chamber whose walls depicted key moments from the life of Togashi-no-Kami: the fall from Tengoku, the Tournament of the Kami, his encounter with the Little Teacher, Shinsei. Hassuno-sama sat on a raised dais of mats, while Yanai knelt on the polished floor some distance away. Behind her was an array of monks in silent rows, and it was odd to think that she had probably known every single one of them in a previous life. They weren't just welcoming her to their ranks; they were welcoming her *back*.

Hassuno-sama read the formal phrases from a scroll, making official what the tattoos had already made a reality. Then one of her clerks laid a blank scroll in front of Yanai, spreading it flat with two jade bars, and set a stone, an ink stick, a tiny dipper of water, and a brush at her side.

She ground and mixed the ink, not hesitating. She'd made her choice before her gempuku began, and her experiences during it had only reinforced her decision – as if she'd known, even before she knew, what being here meant.

With bold strokes of the brush, she wrote her new name – *Togashi Kazue* – using the characters for "one eternity".

The clerk carried the scroll to Hassuno-sama, taking care not to smudge the fresh ink. The iemoto looked it over and nodded in satisfaction. "Togashi Kazue-san," she said. "Welcome to the order. May you serve the Dragon Clan well."

•••

When Kazue finally left the reception chamber, she found that most of the monks had dispersed, but one was still waiting outside.

"Mitsu-sensei," she said, bowing.

The movement proved to be a mistake. Her dizziness made her stumble forward a half-step, barely catching herself short of colliding with him. Embarrassment heated her cheeks. Mitsu was highly respected among the ise zumi; to the novices, he was nothing short of a legend. Having risen from peasant origins to senior status within the order, he traveled the Empire as freely as the wind, doing good and getting into trouble all in the same breath. He bore far more than Kazue's mere pair of tattoos, marked from scalp to calf with Gaijutsu-sensei's art: a walking example of what they all aspired to become.

Kazue had met him before, but now it was different. Now she was a monk, not merely a novice. She should conduct herself better. "Forgive me, Mitsu-sensei."

"*Senpai* to you, now," he said. His smile made it a friendly reminder, not a rebuke. "You are a full monk, Kazue-san. And one desperately in need of food, I think. Come with me, and I will talk while you eat."

She followed him to the refectory. In the normal way of things only two meals were served each day, and only the sick got food out of schedule. But perhaps the monks on cooking duty had been warned that she had just passed her gempuku, because she found herself holding a tray with hot soup, vegetables, and several rice balls that proved to be stuffed with pickled plum.

Mitsu-sensei – no, Mitsu-senpai; he was a senior colleague to her now – sat with her at one of the long tables. "Congratulations," he said.

Kazue swallowed an overlarge bite in her haste to clear her mouth. "It's nothing, really. Everyone says the sensei don't tap you for your gempuku unless they think you're ready." Not that this did anything to calm the nerves beforehand.

"But people do still fail," Mitsu pointed out. "And even if they were sure you were ready, that just means you passed your 'real' test weeks ago. So, take pride in your achievement."

The more food she ate, the hungrier she seemed to get. Kazue drank half her soup, then said, "What now?"

He tilted his chin toward her. "Do you know what those do?"

Her tattoos. Kazue moved her right arm, watching the marked skin shift over her muscles. "Not yet, no."

"Then that is what you do now. Find out. Not immediately, of course; you need to let them heal. A few days at least for the arm, and from personal experience, I recommend waiting two weeks before you try to shave your head again." He ran one hand over his scalp tattoo, grinning ruefully at what was obviously an unpleasant memory.

Two weeks of letting her hair grow. It would be the longest it had been since she arrived at the High House of Light, a wide-eyed child of eight. Long enough to interfere with the tattoo's power; they had to be uncovered for her to invoke them.

But the arm – that she could start on sooner.

"As my duties allow," Kazue promised.

But Mitsu shook his head. "That *is* your duty right now. You will need to move out of the novice dormitory, of course, and there will be a few other minor matters to take care of. But you should not do strenuous work or training for a little while. And until we know what your tattoos do, we cannot properly determine what *you* should do."

It sounded suspiciously like free time – a concept more alien to her than the gaijin lands on the other side of the mountains. "Just... poke at them and see what they do?"

"Poke at them, wave them around, concentrate hard, whatever seems like it might have an effect. Just try to do it someplace safe." Mitsu grinned again, tapping one finger against the magnificent dragon that covered his head. Kazue had seen him demonstrate its power, one bone-dry summer when a lightning strike caused a wildfire near the monastery. Mitsu had stood in the river and breathed his own flames onto the opposite bank, starting a counterfire that robbed the wild one of fuel and kept it from approaching too close.

She wondered if her own tattoo would send out bolts of lightning, and vowed to be nowhere near anything flammable when she tested that theory.

Her itching scalp reminded her of the unfamiliar figure inked there. "What if I cannot figure it out?"

"You will in time," Mitsu said, unconcerned. "It may take a while, but I have never heard of an ise zumi who went through their entire life with a tattoo they could not use."

"Have you ever heard of one like this before?" she asked, gesturing at her head.

Was it her imagination, or did his attention sharpen, like a hawk sighting prey? "No," Mitsu said, his voice still casual. "But let me know when you figure it out – I am very curious to know."

CHAPTER THREE

The tattoos would take some time to heal. There were spiritual techniques that could hurry the process along, but Kazue hadn't mastered any of them – and even if she had, Chasetsu-sensei, the monastery's senior physician, advised against using them. "Your body's ki is in flux right now," she said. "Best not to unbalance things further. You will heal soon enough."

On Chasetsu's recommendation, Kazue began her explorations gingerly. She'd had enough of sitting still, and since neither of her tattoos were on her legs, she undertook walking meditations, pacing slow circuits around one of the smaller stone gardens, her steps timed to her breathing. She could feel the latent power of the ink, just beneath the surface of her skin, but its nature and purpose remained opaque.

When this failed to produce insights, she grew bolder. Mindful of Mitsu's cautionary words, she left the High House of Light, descending the thousand stairs to the forest below. Running along the paths there showed her that neither tattoo had done anything for her endurance or her speed, but it went some way toward making her feel more like herself, after several days of forced inactivity.

On a bare crag overlooking one of those paths, she sat for a time in meditation, focusing on the sense of power in her right arm. Then she opened her eyes and exhaled.

Her breath joined the mountain wind and was lost.

So much for lightning.

Kazue got up, settled into a firm jūjutsu stance, and punched skyward. No bolt issued from her hand. Faintly disappointed, she leapt from the crag; after all, the tattoo showed clouds, and some ise zumi acquired the ability to soar as lightly as a feather. But she hit the ground with all the usual force and rolled to soften the impact.

When she rose to her feet, she saw a cluster of novices coming along the path, bearing new loads of firewood for the monastery. Their leader bowed in greeting, but said nothing as they continued on their way.

At the High House of Light, monks leaping off high rocks was hardly an oddity. And she, Kazue, was counted among their number now.

Again, she reminded herself. But that didn't make it any less satisfying.

By the end of the first week the swelling on her arm had mostly vanished. Kazue flexed it experimentally, gently brushing away the skin that peeled up from where Gaijutsu-sensei had inked her.

Then she punched the nearest tree.

Something flowed down her arm and into the wood. But nothing happened, and it felt like the time, early in her training, when she'd lost her temper and charged full force at Adaki, one of the senior students. Even at the age of twelve, he was built like the Great Wall of the North; he just stood there and let her bounce off his chest. After that, he'd called her Little Bean.

Kazue studied her fist, then the tree. Then she went back to the High House of Light and found Adaki.

His name was Shunrei now, having passed his gempuku several years before, but he hadn't gotten any smaller. "Why not?" he said, grinning, when he heard what favor Kazue wanted. "But let us go outside."

They went into the courtyard outside the jūjutsu dōjō. During the late afternoon it was nearly empty, with only a few monks passing back and forth. Short of leaving the monastery entirely, that was as private as they were likely to get, but Kazue didn't mind. In fact, she realized, part of her wanted an audience.

Chiding herself for that silly desire, she gathered herself again, remembering the feeling from before, attuning herself to the latent power in her arm. Then she set her feet and drove her fist at Shunrei's chest with all the force body and ink could muster.

He flew backward like an arrow shot from a bow, clear across the courtyard and into one of the beams supporting the walkway around the dōjō. Kazue winced, but Shunrei got to his feet with a roar of surprised laughter. "You've got the storm in you now, Little Bean!"

Not lightning, but something akin to it. With practice – not all of it aimed at Shunrei – she found she was able to deliver that power not just with her right fist but with her left as well. The effect was never again as strong as that first time, but when Kazue stopped for the day, glowing with pride and exertion, she found Mitsu watching her.

He acknowledged her efforts with a pleased nod. "I thought it might be related to fighting," he admitted as she approached.

Kazue thumbed sweat out of her eyebrows. "Why did you not tell me, senpai?"

"Because this is part of being an ise zumi." Mitsu tossed her a towel to dry off with. "Learning to find your own power."

It made her think of the third stage of her gempuku, the meditation to draw out her memory of past lives. Lowering her voice as they left the courtyard, Kazue said, "What about people who have just joined the order? All of us must have done this for the first time, once. How did we figure it out then?"

"Good question," he said, and seemed to mean it. "I do not remember my own first life in the order well enough to say. You?"

Kazue shook her head.

"Then it will remain a mystery for now. Tell me what you think of your tattoo."

He wasn't asking whether she liked it. The tests didn't end after one's gempuku; they continued onward, through not just this lifetime but all the ones to come. Kazue shook out her arm and said, "I think that, with practice, I will be able to channel its effect through kicks as well, and elbows and knees – any sort of blow. And it was stronger when I struck Shunrei for the first time, which makes me think I can learn to control how much force I deliver." *Maybe even enough to shatter a tree.*

Mitsu nodded. "Which is important, when you do not want to do too much harm. If you had hit someone other than Shunrei with that initial strike, it might have injured them badly. But his crab tattoo makes him resilient."

"He was like that before he got tattooed," Kazue muttered, causing Mitsu to laugh.

They were almost at the baths. Mitsu halted and faced her. "Practice with it for a while and see what you can do. But in a week's time, I will expect you to shave your head, Kazue-san."

She ran her palm across the stubble, long enough now to have softened. The skin beneath was still tender, and itchy with healing.

Not as itchy as she felt in her spirit, though. The exhilaration of using the storm-serpent tattoo for the first time was already fading, leaving her even hungrier to discover what the other one did.

She doubted it had anything to do with punching and kicking.

Mitsu seemed to read her impatience, even though she did her best to hide it. "A week, Kazue-san. Master one before you tackle the other. Or at least acquire basic competence with it."

She bowed to hide her embarrassment. "Yes, senpai."

The week passed with painful slowness. Kazue practiced with the storm-serpent tattoo, intermittently succeeding at channeling its force through something other than a fist, but failing more often than not. She knew that was at least partly because her heart wasn't in it: she wanted to be experimenting with something else entirely.

When the week was up at last, she got Enshi, the monk whose gempuku she had once sat vigil for, to shave her scalp. Kazue could do it herself, but it was common for the novices and monks to assist each other in the baths, and Enshi could more easily spot the areas that were still inflamed and take extra care around them.

"Any idea what it does?" Enshi asked when she had wiped away the last of the soap and trimmed hair.

The same question, again and again. Not everyone asked

it that openly, but Kazue knew every last monk in the High House of Light wanted to know the answer. "This will be my first chance to test it," she said. "Mitsu-senpai said not to until it heals. Thank you for your help."

Back out into the woods she went. This time it was less because she feared harming someone, and more because she wanted to work away from curious eyes.

The sunlight fell like gold dust through the pines as Kazue stood and thought through her various options. She told herself she was being thorough, giving the matter due consideration rather than flinging herself forward blindly.

But that was a lie, and she was a samurai. Honesty was one of the virtues of Bushidō.

The truth was, she was a little afraid.

Afraid that she might not be able to figure it out – which ought to make her try harder, but instead she shrank back. Afraid that it meant she had some significant destiny in the order, and she might not be equal to it.

Afraid of what the strange, interlacing lines of the tattoo might do.

Fear was one of the three sins. Kazue ran her hand over her scalp, a gesture she hadn't repeated so frequently since her earliest days as a bald-headed novice. Then she made herself take a deep breath and begin.

She swam in a mountain stream and proved she was immune to neither cold nor drowning. The same was true of fire. She tried to speak to birds, deer, and fish, and got ordinary noises in return. She listened to the wind and heard nothing but its usual sigh; she peered into the distance and saw nothing more than her own eyes could perceive.

Racking her memories from both this life and previous ones, Kazue thought of more unusual possibilities. But she couldn't whisper messages to someone at a distance. She couldn't change her shape. She couldn't heal herself or anyone else, climb walls like a spider, or read the traces of memory from objects people had once held. With the permission of her superiors, she asked a visiting Agasha *shugenja* to pray over her, beseeching the kami to heighten her senses; she had a brief understanding of what it was like to be a wolf, "seeing" the world through an intricate map of scents, but afterward the shugenja said it had been neither easier nor more difficult to affect her.

"No," Mitsu said when Kazue asked him hesitantly whether she should try more extreme tests. "The ability to come back from the brink of death has never taken any form other than a phoenix, and what you have is nothing like any kind of bird."

"What about spirits, then?" Kazue said. "I remember hearing of a tattoo from centuries ago that let its bearer trap spirits. The form it took was not like what I have, but–"

"But their shapes are not always the same," Mitsu finished. "Good point."

Kazue's pleasure at the praise dimmed in the face of practical concerns. "I do not know how to test it, though. I could wander the mountains for a month without chancing across a suitable spirit for me to test that theory on."

She could tell by the sudden light in Mitsu's eyes that he'd had an idea. "In that case, you need a guide."

CHAPTER FOUR

Kazue knew old Myobai-sensei. A whole generation of monks did, because they'd seen him wandering by as they labored in the gardens, raking or watering or pruning. He was one of the caretakers of those gardens, but his eyesight had failed him enough that his duties were light. The story among the novices was that his fern tattoo let him sense the health and wellbeing of plants, so his job was simply to walk around and tell the other gardeners what needed tending.

Mitsu laughed when she told him that. "I imagine stranger tattoos have happened – in fact, I know they have – but no. The fern does something else entirely."

They found Myobai clipping a tiny maple bonsai, feeling it gently with his hands before selecting where to apply his shears. "Sensei," Mitsu said with a bow, "Kazue-san here needs to find a spirit."

The old monk did not stop his study of the bonsai, tracing the line of one branch with a fingertip. "A particular spirit?"

"Just one that is not too dangerous."

"There are none here," Myobai-sensei said. Then he turned to

309

look at Kazue, and the delight in his expression made him look more like an eager boy than a wrinkled old monk. "But there might be in the forest. Young – er–"

"Kazue," she said, mystified.

"Young Kazue-san. Do you know how to get along in the wilderness?"

Mitsu gave her an encouraging nod when she glanced at him. "Yes," Kazue said. The uncertainty in her voice wasn't for the answer. She loved the mountains and had spent no small amount of time studying the plants and animals found there, how to read the weather, and how to create shelter.

She simply had no idea why he was asking.

But Myobai-sensei gave the tiny maple one last pat on its crown and bounced to his feet like she'd just taken twenty years off his age. "How soon can we leave?"

It turned out that Myobai-sensei's work in the garden was as much a concession to his love of nature as any kind of duty. In his day he had roamed the Empire, but unlike Mitsu, who spent most of his time around people and half of that around peasants, Myobai-sensei's purpose had lain in the wild parts of Rokugan.

And that was because of his tattoo. The fern inked along his left forearm had nothing to do with plants; instead, it allowed him to sense the presence of spirits. "All kinds," he said when Kazue hesitantly asked. "When I was young, I was not as perceptive, so I mostly only felt the bigger and more powerful things. But now, I can feel everything – even the mikokami that make up everything around us."

"How do you not become overwhelmed?" she asked, fascinated. "Feeling all of that?"

He shrugged. "How do you not become overwhelmed, hearing the air around you all the time? You learn to disregard it. Unless the wind is loud – and that is what a powerful spirit feels like for me. But I've learned to listen to the quieter whispers as well."

They had, with Mitsu's help, obtained permission to roam the valleys around the High House of Light in search of a spirit, so that Kazue might find out whether trapping them was her tattoo's purpose. With Myobai-sensei's failing eyesight, that seemed rather hazardous to her, but he blithely dismissed the risk. "The earth kami will warn me if I am about to step wrong," he said, which she suspected might be an exaggeration. Mitsu had made it clear before they left that she was supposed to look after the old man.

At least he was still hale enough. He made no complaint about camping with only a tarp to cover them, even though the air still held a spring chill. And he regaled her with stories as they walked, describing all the spirits he'd encountered in his travels: everything from the powerful kami of an ancient oak to a graceful *tsuru* shapeshifter to a vengeful *onryō*, a ghost that had tried to kill him. "Even a *dodomeki* once," he said. "She was a human bandit who had turned into a *yōkai* because of her greed. Had bird eyes all over her arms. Much more difficult to sense, yōkai of that sort – the ones who started out human."

"What did you do when you found those things?"

He shrugged. "Pacified the ones who needed it, banished the ones who needed *that*. Had conversations with a few, but most of them are not much for talk. They either attack you or make strange noises that do not mean much to a human."

Their goal out in the wilderness was to find something

relatively safe. "There is not likely to be anything dangerous nearby," Myobai-sensei said when they stopped to drink from a snowmelt stream. "Not much will venture this close to the monastery. I know a tree that is home to a *kodama*, but I do not want to disturb it; our best chance is to find some animal spirit for you to try."

True to his prediction, the first thing they stumbled across was a rabbit spirit. Or rather, Myobai-sensei's head came up and he sniffed at the air, then declared there was a rabbit spirit nearby. On his recommendation, Kazue built a free-running snare, which would catch but not harm whatever wandered into it. Then she set it along a rabbit trail with a small pile of clover as a combination of offering and bait, and they waited.

And waited, and waited. "It may take a while," Myobai-sensei said cheerfully.

Kazue settled into the lotus position and began to pray, asking the rabbit spirit to assist her in her attempt to learn the nature of her tattoo.

Either the spirit didn't hear her, or it didn't feel cooperative. It took several more days and Myobai-sensei alerting her to a monkey spirit, an otter spirit, and another rabbit – or possibly the same one – before they located a *kappa* in one of the mountain streams. Kazue, watching it from hiding, focused on the tattoo on her scalp and tried to direct its power at the turtle-like creature, but nothing happened.

"That is yours to decide," Myobai-sensei said when she asked him what she should do.

It didn't seem right to kill the kappa. They could be malevolent, but most of the time their mischief was harmless. Dredging through her memories from this life and those before,

Kazue went out and bowed to the kappa, forcing it to respond with the same gesture, spilling the water from the dish in its head. With the kappa thus weakened, she made it promise not to drown or otherwise harm any human beings.

When that was done, Myobai-sensei said, "Well, it *is* a yōkai. Possibly you need a proper spirit, something like a ghost."

"I don't think so," Kazue said, discouraged. "It felt... like I was trying to point with an arm I don't have at something that was not there. If this was meant to work on spirits, I think I would have felt more than that. Or maybe I'm wrong?" She slapped her thigh in frustration. "What do I know."

"More than anyone else does," he said gently. "Trust your instincts, Kazue-san. You are the only one who can say what you do or do not feel from your tattoo."

His words made her go still, thinking. "Maybe not the only one," she murmured. "What about Gaijutsu-sensei?" He was the one who had seen it in a vision and inked it into her skin. If anyone could give her insight, he could.

But Myobai-sensei shook his head. "I can tell you right now what he will say if you ask: 'That is yours to discover.'"

Much like Mitsu's advice not to shave her head too soon, it had the ring of personal experience. "How long did it take you to learn the use of your tattoo?" Kazue asked, nodding at the fern on his arm.

He patted the mark like an old friend. "Not long. But that is because an Isawa shugenja came to the monastery with the *bakeneko* she kept as a pet."

Trust an Isawa to keep a demon cat as a pet. Kazue squared her shoulders and said, "I know you would be happy to stay out here longer, Myobai-sensei, but I should return to the monastery."

He sighed in resignation but nodded. "Follow your path, Kazue-san. The Fortunes will bring you to understanding when it is time."

CHAPTER FIVE

"Enshi-san," Kazue said, "could I ask a favor of you? It is very odd to me that everyone else can see what is tattooed on my head, but I cannot."

"You still do not know what it does?" Enshi said sympathetically. "I do not know if seeing the shape of it will make anything clearer, but let me get my brush."

The monks of the High House of Light weren't renowned for any art form other than tattooing, but their order didn't discourage them from pursuing activities that might help their spiritual development. Enshi was a reasonably accomplished painter, and Kazue expected the process of sketching her tattoo would be a quick one.

After Enshi had thrown away three attempts, though, Kazue realized it wouldn't be so easy. "I am sorry. If I had known it would be this much trouble, I would not have bothered you. Do not inconvenience yourself any more, please."

"Stay right where you are," Enshi said, laying out another scrap of paper. "I do not know why this is so difficult – it is not as if the lines are moving. But I will get it right if it takes me all day. They say challenges are good for spiritual growth."

It didn't take quite all day, but they nearly missed the evening meal. Enshi's determination rewarded Kazue with a small, intricate painting, allowing her to see at last what Gaijutsu-sensei had inked into her scalp.

She felt none of the strange effects other people had described, but that wasn't surprising. The figure itself was not, she thought, in any way significant: it reminded her a little bit of one of the mandala scrolls given as a gift to a previous Dragon Clan Champion, now hanging in the eastern meditation hall, but apart from that it resembled nothing Kazue had seen before. Whatever sensation people got upon trying to study it closely must come from the tattoo itself, not the shape it took.

But its abstraction reinforced her feeling that the tattoo's unknown effect wasn't something material. It wouldn't make her stronger or faster, wouldn't allow her to perform physical feats beyond the human norm. Its power was more subtle than that, and to find it, she must look inward.

So, she returned to meditating. The next morning, she didn't join her fellow monks for the meal; she went instead to the eastern meditation hall, where she seated herself in front of the mandala scroll and focused her mind on its intricate figure. This hall was less often used because its floor needed replacing; here she would be undisturbed.

Kazue sat in a trance for hours. She knew already that the tattoo hadn't removed her need for food or water – she still got hungry and thirsty, just like before – but clearly she couldn't expect it to unfold its secrets with a few minutes' effort. She was determined to undertake a fasting meditation for at least three days before she gave up.

It didn't take that long.

Near sunset, she began to grow restless. Her mind, which had rested with perfect serenity on the mandala for most of the day, rippled with a nebulous and distracting sensation. Rather than fighting it, Kazue shifted her focus to that sensation, allowing it to become the object of her meditation. *What am I feeling?*

Gradually she realized the ripple originated from outside her own mind. Rising, Kazue formed one hand into a fist and covered it with the other in a meditative mudra, then began walking, as she had done before. Her steps were slow and perfectly balanced, three per breath. With her eyes half-closed and downcast, she moved toward the door of the meditation hall, out onto its veranda, into her sandals, and then down and around the corner into one of the gardens.

This garden was even less used than the hall. It lay in the shadow of a high wall and received very little sunlight; most things planted there died, and so it had been transformed into a rock garden not long after Kazue first came to the monastery. But no one had wanted to remove the enormous pine tree that grew in one corner, so the monk in charge of the transformation had attempted to design around it. The results were less than successful, and since then the pine had reigned over a forgotten expanse of gravel and small boulders.

The branches of the tree drooped nearly to the ground, despite the wooden crutches propping them up. Kazue's instinct led her toward it. When she knelt, the sensation vanished, and she saw that someone was hiding under the branches.

A boy, dressed in novice robes, and no more than nine or ten years old. His expression was more guilt than anything else – clearly, he wasn't where he should be, and now a monk had caught him shirking – but his posture, curled tight with his arms around his knees, and the marks still streaking his face, told Kazue that guilt wasn't the main thing on the child's mind.

She offered him a smile, unsure whether he could see it in the dim light. "What is your name?"

"Saburō," he said. Then he flinched. "Kanta."

New enough to the monastery that he wasn't used to his novice name. Saburō – that meant he was someone's third son. Unusual in Dragon lands these days; even in a monastery, surrounded by celibate monks, Kazue had heard about the infertility plaguing the people of the Dragon Clan. It must have gone hard with this boy's parents, if they were Dragon: seeing the Fortunes bestow such a blessing, then losing the child to a life among the ise zumi.

It was an honor, having one's child join the order. But even for dutiful samurai, honor of that sort could be difficult to bear.

The boy shamed himself, crying in a corner like this. But Kazue had done much the same when she first came to the monastery, as had many of her fellow novices – though her hiding spot had been behind a tall boulder in the southern garden. Other children grew up knowing they might follow in the footsteps of one of their parents, training as a *bushi* or courtier or shugenja, but ise zumi almost never had families of their own; everyone who arrived at the High House of Light came here a complete stranger, unfamiliar with anything more than legends. Even if they had sought it out of their own free will, the change went hard, and it would be many long years of training before most of them realized they had been here before.

She couldn't tell Kanta that. It was a secret revealed only during the gempuku, and then only to those who proved their readiness.

But she could try to ease his way. "I am Kazue," she said. "It does get easier, Kanta. I know that may be hard to believe now, and there will be times you will wish you had never set out for the High House of Light… but you would not have made your way here if you were not strong. The weak never find this place."

The light was fading fast. She could just make out Kanta's jaw tightening as he failed to hold back a wet sniffle. "Genzeki says it's weak to cry."

Not a name Kazue recognized; she assumed that was another novice. "Courage lies in knowing fear, and overcoming it; strength lies in knowing weakness, and getting up again. You will get up again. And when you do, you will understand strength better than Genzeki does."

Kanta shifted. "They'll beat me for running away."

Kazue held out one hand, palm up. "Yes. But that will only hurt your flesh. Separate yourself from it; learn to experience pain from outside. Then it will no longer rule you."

She knew her words weren't precisely comforting. Anything else would be dishonest, though – she and Kanta both knew the punishment he faced. The best help she could give him was instruction in the proper way to bear it.

He accepted her hand, and she drew him out from under the tree. "If you hurry," Kazue said, "you can return to the dormitory before dark." The consequences would get more severe after that.

Kanta started to run, stopped, flung an awkward bow at her, and took off again.

Alone in the pine garden, Kazue ran her hand over her scalp. A faint smile rose to her lips.

The tattoo had guided her.

Not in what she had said to Kanta. That had been all her own doing; she'd lost the tenuous thread of connection to her tattoo when she saw him under the tree. But it had alerted her to his presence.

Other monks could sense living creatures around them. She didn't know of any who could sense the distress of those creatures.

No wonder I had so much trouble figuring it out. This is a monastery; we're supposed to be serene.

Smoothing her own expression into serenity, if not her heart, Kazue went to find Mitsu.

CHAPTER SIX

"Distress." Mitsu tapped one finger against his knee, thinking.

Kazue couldn't tell what he thought of her tale. Her satisfaction over having figured out her tattoo's effect had faded while she described it; what had seemed in the moment like a great victory had grown smaller in the telling. When strange or unique tattoos appeared, it usually heralded some kind of destiny within the order. But what destiny could be linked to sensing the presence of emotional conflict?

She was glad they were talking privately, in one of the rooms used for individual instruction. Kazue had made herself wait until after the evening meal, because even when her discovery seemed momentous, it wasn't worth disrupting the monastery's routine. Mitsu must have seen the excitement in her bearing, though, because he had approached her as soon as the meal was done and led her to this room to talk.

His finger stilled. "Call on the tattoo now," Mitsu said. "Tell me if you sense anything. I want to see how far it reaches."

Kanta had been very nearby – just on the other side of the wall from where Kazue had sat in meditation. But just as her storm-serpent tattoo could be used to varying degrees, she might be able to get more from the knot. Kazue drew in a breath and exhaled it slowly, closing her eyes, attuning herself to the lines inked into her scalp.

Nothing. However far the effect extended, it seemed there was no one within range who felt distress.

"I am sorry, senpai," Kazue said. "I do not think it goes very far – at least not yet."

When she opened her eyes, a tear was slipping down Mitsu's cheek.

He wiped it away with a deliberate hand. "I do not think it is emotional distress that you sense, Kazue-san. Something similar, perhaps – but if that were it, you would have sensed me."

Startled, she said, "But you're one of the most–"

She stopped herself before she could finish the sentence, but Mitsu nodded anyway. "One of the most advanced monks in the order. Yes. But although I have learned to cultivate serenity, that does not mean I lack the capacity to feel."

"What were you thinking about?"

The question was beyond impertinent. Kazue realized, too late, what had troubled her about the tattoo's effect – or rather, its supposed effect. If she could sense other people's distress, then its function was to undermine their *tatemae*, their outward mask of composure. Though it might serve a useful purpose, it also shamed the target, exposing their true feelings despite their best efforts to keep those honorably concealed.

"Forgive me, Mitsu-senpai," she said, bowing to the floor. "I should not have asked."

"It is nothing, Kazue-san." She straightened in time to see him smile sadly. "Unlike most in our order, I have traveled the

Empire from one end to the other. We are samurai as well as monks, and both codes teach us the importance of compassion. I have seen enough suffering to make any compassionate heart weep."

Kazue's cheeks heated. "Yes, senpai." Even if the tattoo didn't actually undermine tatemae, she had succeeded in making Mitsu reveal more than he should have.

His finger went back to tapping against his knee as he thought. "Not distress, then, but something else. That which is hidden? No – if it were that, you would have figured it out long before now. Something rarer, then. Something more subtle."

Then he cocked his head to one side. "You have thought of something, Kazue-san."

"No," she said, shoulders tensing. "Not exactly. That is…"

He leaned forward. "Do not be reluctant to say it. This is quite a puzzle; any clue might be of use."

She dug her own fingers into her knees. "I think… just as the storm-cloud serpent can be used to greater or lesser degree, I think this one has more purpose than merely to sense – whatever it is I sensed. That is only the smallest part of what it does. I feel as if… as if there is a way for me to use it in a more directed fashion."

"Directed. You mean *on* someone."

She could read his thoughts as if a scroll had unrolled over his face. Sudden apprehension drove her next words out in a hurry. "Mitsu-senpai – I think it might be dangerous."

He eased back, not retreating, but considering. "How so?"

"I do not know," Kazue admitted. She would have preferred to leave this unspoken; it was all guesswork, vague fumblings toward an understanding of something she had only used once, and imperfectly at that. "Just that when I imagine trying to focus its power on someone, I feel like I am standing at the edge of a cliff. Or like *that* person is. And it would be irresponsible of me to push them over the edge without knowing what is at the bottom."

She phrased it in suitably sensible, dutiful terms. Calling the idea "irresponsible" was better than admitting what she really felt: fear.

When she thought about unleashing the tattoo on someone – not merely sensing something from them, but directing its power against them – what she felt then wasn't a cliff. It was a canyon. A crevasse leading downward into darkness. Ise zumi like Shunrei were trained to withstand all kinds of physical blows, but who would be able to resist this?

She had no way of knowing, because she didn't even know what *this* was. But one thing was certain: she wasn't going to try it out for the first time on one of the most respected monks in the order.

Given Mitsu's reputation for impulsive action, she almost expected him to insist on trying anyway. But he didn't command such respect simply for his ability to punch things; he nodded his agreement, and she tried not to sag in relief. "Leave it alone for now," he said. "I will consider what the next step should be. In the meanwhile, I think it is time you assumed your normal duties. Talk to Rōju-san and he will make the arrangements."

She bowed in obedience as Mitsu climbed to his feet. Embarrassment and gratitude warred in her heart. *I should have been able to figure this out by now. But at the same time… I'm glad not to keep pushing at it.*

If that was weakness, then she would have to remember the advice she'd given Kanta – and get back up again.

•••

Mitsu had expected it would take longer to receive an audience with the clan champion.

Like all his predecessors, Togashi Yokuni was reclusive. Whereas most clan champions lived in palaces at the hearts of major cities in their realms, surrounded by all the bustle of government and trade and art, the leader of the Dragon lived at the High House of Light, in a remote set of chambers connected to the rest of the monastery by only a single gate. He rarely appeared among the ise zumi, and he conducted most of his duties via messengers. A simple monk like Mitsu, however advanced, might wait for weeks or months before getting the opportunity to speak with him.

Instead, Mitsu was summoned the next day.

The degree of speed was surprising, but not the fact of it. Mitsu had suspected for some time now that he was being considered for some particular duty. After years of wandering the Empire without restraint, he'd come back to the High House of Light only to find Hassuno-sama ordering him to stay for a time. Then he was assigned to oversee Kazue after her gempuku – a task that had proven more complex than he anticipated.

Perhaps the clan champion had foreseen what was coming with Kazue. The legends said Togashi's heirs were blessed with a degree of his foresight. Who could say where their vision would guide them?

Mitsu climbed the narrow steps that led to the audience chamber. Anywhere else in the Empire it would have been a broad staircase, flanked by statues and banners, but the champions of the Dragon were chosen from the ranks of the ise zumi. While they lived in more splendor than the average monk, it was still ascetic by the standards of the other clans.

Two guards stood outside the chamber. One was a bushi of the Mirumoto family, armed and armored; the other was one of Mitsu's own senpai, a woman covered with tattoos for striking and defending, as well as for sensing possible threats.

They opened the doors for him, and he entered the presence of Togashi Yokuni.

Like the entrance outside, the chamber was austere, expressing its beauty through simplicity rather than opulence. The grain of the polished wooden floor shone gold in the light from the lamps, and the lamps themselves, though gilt, were elegantly spare. The wall panels changed with the seasons; now, in the trailing end of spring, they showed wisteria blossoms, with swallows flitting among them. The hangings around the dais were antique silk and matched the delicate shade of the wisteria.

Amid this elegance, the Dragon Clan Champion stood out like a mountain peak. Although he came from the ise zumi, he wore armor from head to foot, including a *mempō* that completely obscured his face. It should have meant he could not call on any of his tattoos, but Mitsu took it for granted that the armor was a nemuranai. Its awakened spirit might bestow all kinds of benefits on the wearer.

But it meant that the champion was reclusive even in person, his body and face entirely hidden from view. The samurai who acted as his body servants were the only ones who had seen Yokuni unmasked since his accession, and their discretion was as steadfast as stone.

Mitsu bowed to the floor. "You honor this unworthy one, Togashi-ue."

"Rise and speak."

Had all of Yokuni's predecessors been as terse as he was? The ise zumi cultivated many talents, but flowery rhetoric was rarely one of them. Mitsu had seen Crane courtiers in their domains; it could take them a quarter of an hour to get to the point. Here it was always brief.

Mitsu described Kazue's experience with Kanta, and the discussion that followed. "Unless she tests her tattoo's power on a subject," he said, "she will have no way of understanding its full effect. But since this may endanger the target, I feel that it should be used on someone possessed of great physical, mental, and spiritual strength, who might be able to withstand its force. Togashi-ue, I request permission to offer myself as that subject."

He'd almost said it the night before, when the idea first came to him. But although samurai weren't supposed to fear death, there was a very large difference between not fearing it and courting it recklessly. Like all his kind, Mitsu owed a duty to his lord, and that duty included not scrambling his mind like an egg without obtaining permission first.

"No," the clan champion said.

Mitsu had enough self-control not to rock back in surprise. *I was so sure...*

Why else would Hassuno have told him to stay, then assigned him to Kazue, if not for this? She had some purpose in mind for him, likely received from Yokuni; was it not to help Kazue discover the nature of her new power? When he was summoned so promptly to this audience, Mitsu had thought his suspicions confirmed.

"Togashi-ue—" he began, even though arguing was a breach of etiquette in this court as in any other.

"That is not your path," the clan champion said. "Nor is it hers. The tattoo Kazue-san received will show its true power in due course – but you must find some other for her to use it on."

Silence fell. Mitsu waited three heartbeats, to see if there would be anything more; in addition to being terse, Yokuni also paused for thought. But the clan champion said nothing else, and so Mitsu bowed again. "I understand, Togashi-ue."

It was both true and not. He didn't know where he was supposed to find a suitable target for Kazue – or what a suitable target would even look like.

But he did understand that finding the answer to that was a test for him as well.

CHAPTER SEVEN

No one spoke about it openly, but within a day Kazue was sure that every ise zumi at the High House of Light knew she had failed.

I haven't failed, she told herself. It's only been a few weeks. No one has seen anything like this before; it's reasonable that I might need more time to figure it out.

Reasonable, yes. But she still felt the collective breath the monastery had held, and the collective exhale of disappointment when they resigned themselves to not learning the answer any time soon.

She hadn't gone through years of training for nothing, though. Ise zumi, like all monks, like all samurai, were supposed to bear hardship with stoicism. Kazue walked through the series of three gates in the northeastern corner of the complex, symbolically stripping herself of desire, fear, and most of all, regret. Then she lit incense and prayed for wisdom, and when that was done, she applied herself to her duties.

Which for now consisted of working in the scriptorium, writing out copies of texts that had been requested by samurai elsewhere in Dragon lands, or even farther away. The library of the High House of Light was far from the most impressive in Rokugan, dwarfed by the archives of the Ikoma and the Phoenix, but it held a great many esoteric writings, including an assortment of legends and fables from which grains of truth might fall. The courtiers of the Dragon traded copies of those materials for political favors from scholarly monks, courtiers, and shugenja.

The work was straightforward and meticulous. It also locked her away from sunlight and fresh air – but that was a small price to pay for also being sheltered from the view of others. In the scriptorium, she could pretend that no one was waiting for anything at all. Here she didn't feel like a scroll was dangling around her neck, labeling her as *Togashi Kazue, the monk who can't use her tattoo.*

As the days went by, though, that shelter started to feel more and more like a hiding spot. Like she was Kanta, huddling under the tree. If she'd still been a novice, she would gladly have come out and taken her punishment, if it meant she could have a sensei tell her what to do. But she was a monk, and the lesson here was one nobody else could teach her.

Mitsu found her there a month later. Kazue almost botched the character she was writing, she was so surprised to see him. She didn't think he'd forgotten her, not exactly... but she'd convinced herself that "I will consider what the next step should be" had been a polite way of telling her to solve the puzzle on her own, and that the time elapsed since then was just more evidence of her failure.

She'd tried. And Mitsu clearly knew that, or at least guessed, because the first thing he said to her was, "How much dust did you get on yourself, digging out old records of strange tattoos past?"

"Very little," Kazue said with dignity. "The caretakers of the library are much too diligent to let dust gather."

"Did you find anything useful?" He shook his head before she could answer. "No, of course not, or you would have told me."

It wasn't quite true. She'd found accounts of ise zumi past who took far more than a few months to learn the purpose of their tattoos, because the effects weren't amenable to being revealed through ordinary experimentation. One man had spent decades at the High House of Light without ever knowing the purpose of the humble catfish tattoo on his right leg, until the day a catastrophic earthquake shook the mountains. He had slammed his feet down like a *sumai* wrestler and the ground beneath the monastery fell still, while the slopes all around them crashed down in landslides.

I just hope it won't take me fifty years to learn what this knot does. Impatience was a form of desire, but surely it wasn't too much to ask that she be able to use her tattoo sooner than half a century from now.

She said, "Do you need me for something, Mitsu-senpai?"

"Finish your work today," he said, "but tomorrow, someone else will have to take on that duty for you. We leave at dawn."

It was a good thing she had laid her brush down, or she would have dropped it. "Leave?" Her heart thudded. *They can't be casting me out.*

A foolish thought. "Fuchi Mura," Mitsu said. "I have arranged a way for you to test your tattoo. Whether it will be useful, who can say – but at least we can try."

Fuchi Mura. Was that one of the villages she'd passed through on her way to the High House of Light as a child? She couldn't remember, and hadn't left the monastery since. Short journeys into the surrounding wilderness for her training or tattoo experiments didn't count. The rest of Dragon lands – much less the rest of the Empire – had come to seem almost imaginary to her, like a story made up by visitors to entertain the monks.

More foolish thoughts. Kazue hoped neither her sudden excitement nor its accompanying apprehension had shown through. "Of course, senpai. Is there anything I should prepare?"

He studied her critically. "You have probably never been on a horse."

"My mother could not afford one, senpai. A bushi did take me on a ride once, though, during a festival."

"So, in essence, no." He considered it, then shook his head in humorous resignation. "Mortification of the flesh has its spiritual merits, but I do not want saddle sores distracting you when we arrive in Fuchi Mura. It is only a few days away; we will walk."

Summer had arrived in the Great Wall of the North. The peaks retained their caps of snow, but even the most sheltered valleys below were green and lush. The passes took them up through stony regions carpeted with mountain heath, then lowered them into dells of false hellebore and sturdy rowans, which the monks often cut for firewood. The cherry trees had long since shed their blossoms, but the rowans were studded with bursts of white.

Kazue breathed the air in deeply, tilting her face to the sun. She wasn't aware of Mitsu watching her until he said, "You enjoy being out here."

"I am happy at the monastery," she said hurriedly, composing herself once more.

"I did not suggest otherwise. But copying texts is the wrong duty for you, I think. Your calligraphy is good enough, and you seem to be diligent, but sealed away in the scriptorium is not where you belong."

They were traveling alone. Kazue remembered high-ranking samurai passing through the town where she grew up, accompanied by grand entourages: *jizamurai* vassals, peasant *ashigaru*, servants, whole caravans of people to assist them. The visitors to the High House of Light were usually much less ostentatious, but whether that was because the Dragon were a relatively poor clan or because they knew no one at the monastery would be impressed by displays of power and wealth, Kazue didn't know. Mostly their retinues consisted of armed escorts, because there were bandits in the mountains.

She pitied whatever bandits thought it a good idea to attack two lone monks. Mitsu on his own could probably rout an entire gang, and she wouldn't mind the chance to call on the one tattoo whose use she knew. But bandits were generally smart enough to avoid ise zumi, because they never knew what strange abilities they might face.

All the monks knew Mitsu was being considered for some kind of elevation or special duty. His own words had confirmed it, in a roundabout way: he had spoken as if he had the power, or at least the influence, to have her reassigned from the scriptorium. His frequent absences from the monastery meant he held no official title there, but if Kazue were asked to list the most important monks in the order, his name would be among them. Yet he was out here with her, walking along a narrow mountain trail, with no one to accompany them.

Then again, he usually traveled alone. She was already more escort than he was accustomed to.

"If you think that would be best, senpai," she said. "I am happy to serve wherever I can best be of use."

"A properly dutiful answer," Mitsu said. "But ours is a strange situation, Kazue-san. Like all samurai, ise zumi are expected to do as our lord commands, regardless of personal desire. But you have passed your gempuku; you know that you have been in the order before. What do you recall from that?"

Of specifics, very little. She knew Mitsu wasn't asking for the names she'd borne, though, or the deeds she'd performed. "We reincarnate into the order to hone our spiritual power across multiple lifetimes."

"Yes. Our discipline is not that of Brotherhood monks, whether they propitiate the Fortunes or seek Enlightenment through the Tao of Shinsei. We cultivate ourselves to better serve the Dragon Clan and its champion."

"And sometimes," Kazue said slowly, "cultivating ourselves takes us down… unusual paths."

Her restrained choice of words made him grin. "You must have remembered at least one lifetime when you went out into the world. You know our reputation."

For most Rokugani, the ise zumi were a colorful legend, as exotic as the yōkai that haunted the wilderness and far less predictable. Kazue hadn't attended a single play in this lifetime, but she knew that tattooed monks were a stock figure in certain kinds of stories, appearing out of nowhere to do something inexplicable that inevitably turned out to be important.

"We have more freedom," she said. "More opportunity to do whatever seems right or necessary."

"And at the same time, we have *less*," Mitsu said. "Because while we pursue our individual growth, we do so in the service of a single purpose – not only in this lifetime, but in many to come."

The paradox felt comfortable, like a well-worn pair of sandals. Kazue hesitated, wondering if she should speak her mind. The question that haunted her had been with her through more than one lifetime, and she'd never answered it to her satisfaction.

If there was anyone she could ask, though – anyone who might be able to answer – it was Mitsu.

"But what is that purpose?" she said. "Each of us spends most of our lifetimes in the High House of Light, meditating, training, strengthening ourselves – but then not employing that strength. There are monks with tattoos for attack and defense who will die without ever using them against an enemy. Some lifetimes we go out into the world, and then our abilities may make a difference... but those lives are rare. Why did Togashi-no-Kami establish the order, then instruct us to keep ourselves so much apart?"

Mitsu locked his hands behind his back, across the tail of the tiger that crouched in his skin. "Perhaps for those occasions when we *do* go out. The power we have is difficult to master; maybe all the lifetimes of seclusion are necessary preparation for those few moments when we make a difference."

That was one of the tenets of their order: to find the balance between contemplation and action. Learning to recognize the right moment to tip fate in one direction or another.

But Kazue, studying the line of Mitsu's shoulders, didn't believe that was all.

"You think there is more to it," she said softly.

He bent to dig a pebble out of his sandal, and for a moment she thought he wouldn't answer. When he straightened up, though, his smile was rueful. "I suspect so, yes. But it is a suspicion only."

"Togashi-no-Kami was famed for his foresight," she said. "If anyone would have established an order of monks, drawn back again and again through the cycle of reincarnation, honing their power for some decisive moment far in the future... it would be him."

"But what moment?" Mitsu said, finishing her thought. "I do not know, Kazue-san. Whatever it is, it may not come in this lifetime, or the next."

They were ise zumi. A thousand years from now, they would still be here – or rather, be here again – ready to serve the Dragon and the Empire.

Mitsu nodded at Kazue, and she realized he was indicating the tattoo on her scalp. "Something like that does not come at random. I think you have it because of your efforts in previous lives, because you have cultivated yourself to the point where you can bear whatever that is. So, while caution is good, Kazue-san... do not fear your own power."

She resisted the urge to duck her chin. "I will do my best, Mitsu-senpai."

He started walking again, and she hurried to catch up. Over

his shoulder, he said, "And I will suggest you be removed from duty in the scriptorium. I do not know what your fate is in this lifetime, Kazue-san, but I suspect it lies outside the High House of Light."

CHAPTER EIGHT

Mitsu had seen countless mountain villages like Fuchi Mura in his time wandering the Empire. Whether they were in Dragon lands, in the neighboring mountains of the Phoenix, on the Lion or Scorpion sides of the Spine of the World, or down in Crab territory, they consisted of a scattering of houses along a valley floor, usually near a stream that provided fresh water, the terraces of their fields rising on the slopes above.

But only a dismissive eye would assume the similarities meant they were all the same. Lion *heimin* grew rice in abundance; the Dragon and Phoenix, facing a harsher climate, grew more barley and buckwheat, and the reed-thatched roofs of their houses were steeply pitched to shed the winter snow. Crab peasants went armed to a degree that would make any other clan fear incipient rebellion.

So, when Mitsu looked at Fuchi Mura, he saw the things that marked this village as distinct.

He saw a village that would not be there for long.

The declining birth rates of the Dragon meant their population had been falling steadily for generations. As their numbers shrank, the daimyō who ruled the various provinces had made the decision to draw their people inward, abandoning villages in marginal areas and consolidating the population closer to the roads and fertile valleys.

It was a pragmatic decision. But it also meant uprooting the heimin from the places where their ancestors had lived for centuries, and not all of them accepted it with grace.

Fortunately, Fuchi Mura didn't seem poised on the brink of riot. The peasants went about their work with resigned patience, while their children – fewer than they should have been – played carefree along the paths, oblivious to the worries that hung like weights over their parents' shoulders. Several of the farmhouses already stood empty, their thatching damaged by winter's storms and not repaired. The village lay fairly deep in the mountains, not convenient to anything other than the High House of Light; within a few years, Mitsu suspected, the whole place would stand empty.

In the meanwhile, it was an ideal place for Jusai, the daimyō of the Kitsuki family, to send the man she'd selected for this experiment.

The two monks had been visible on the path descending toward the village for some time before they arrived, so it was no surprise that several people waited for them just beyond the last farmhouse. One was an old woman, gray-haired but straight-backed despite her age. The other two, judging by age and one's family resemblance, were her son and her daughter-in-law.

All three bowed to the ground as Mitsu and Kazue approached. "Greetings, and welcome to Fuchi Mura, honored monks," the old woman said in a clumsy approximation of formal language. "I am Yae, the headwoman of this village. We have received word of your coming, and the honored guests whom you are to meet are waiting here for you. Please allow me to offer you the use of my humble house for as long as you wish to stay. There is plenty of room, as my husband passed into Meido this past winter."

"Please, grandmother, rise," Mitsu said. "The others as well." Once they were on their feet, he said, "I am Togashi Mitsu, and this is Togashi Kazue. We will gratefully accept your hospitality but hope not to burden you for long."

The formalities took some time, because Mitsu didn't want to insult Yae by hurrying through them. Once he and Kazue entered the village, though, he sent the younger monk to bathe, while he sought out the people who had come to meet them.

It was a small group, just two ashigaru and a bushi, plus the man they'd brought. The bushi introduced himself with brief courtesy as Mirumoto Ujinao. "We have him in the storage shed out back," Ujinao said.

Such sheds were common in Dragon lands, where timber was abundant and the risk of burning down the main residence very real. They weren't generally used for sleeping, though, and Mitsu frowned. "'Have' him?"

"Were you not told whom we were bringing?"

Hassuno had written to Kitsuki Jusai to request someone suitable for Kazue to work on. Mitsu hadn't given a lot of thought to who that might be ... but he should have.

"His name is Heidoku," Ujinao said. "And he killed a samurai."

The shed might have belonged to the village headwoman, but it hadn't been repaired in quite some time, and it wasn't locked. Out there in the hinterlands, who would break in and steal anything? Whatever items of true value Yae owned, she undoubtedly kept close. The shed was for household tools and other things she didn't want to risk losing in a fire, not for coins or finery.

The bar holding its doors shut was a recent addition, placed not to keep thieves from breaking in, but to keep the shed's contents from escaping.

When Mitsu heaved the creaking doors open, he found the interior all but empty. The household tools had been cleared out; the only thing it held now was a man, curled up against the back wall with his bound hands before him.

Even if Ujinao hadn't told him the story, Mitsu would have known this man was a peasant. Samurai, better fed and cared for by skilled physicians, tended to grow taller and straighter than the heimin, and kept more of their teeth. The scars Heidoku bore weren't those of a bushi who had seen regular combat. And a samurai – even one stripped of their family name and cast out as rōnin – would have gathered themself upright at the sight of Mitsu, holding onto what scraps of dignity remained.

Heidoku remained slumped against the wall. Only the flinch of his eyes at the sudden flood of light betrayed any reaction.

Mitsu paused, considering. Then he sat down cross-legged on the threshold, resting his hands on his knees. "Tell me your story."

Silence fell. Finally, Heidoku said, "What?"

No courtesies. No attempt to bow, no polite invocation of "samurai-sama". Why should Heidoku bother? He'd committed murder; the penalty for that was death. If he hadn't been brought here, he would have been hanged by now. The man must know that this journey wasn't any kind of pardon, just a trip to some different punishment.

Whether that would prove true or not depended on Kazue's tattoo.

"Your crime," Mitsu said. "I want you to tell me about it."

The prisoner closed his eyes and turned his face away, doing his best to ignore his unwelcome intruder. Undeterred, Mitsu said, "I am told you killed a samurai. Mirumoto Oribe."

Heidoku spat. The insult was as deliberate as the lack of courtesy. Mitsu suspected he was hoping to outrage someone enough to provoke a swifter death. What had they told him about the reason for coming to Fuchi Mura?

"Yes, I killed him," Heidoku said. "I beat his head in with the handle of my millstone. Beat it to a broken, bloody pulp, and then kept on hitting long after he was dead."

"Why?"

If Heidoku had been walking, he would have stumbled over his own feet. The law didn't care *why* a peasant killed a samurai; the cause had no effect on the sentence. For a member of the lower classes to murder a superior was an unforgivable crime. So why should someone like Mitsu bother asking?

Mitsu waited.

Bare feet scuffed against the hard-packed dirt of the floor, as if Heidoku were trying to press himself into the wall. When he spoke, his voice was softer, thinner. "He… he was beating a lad. Overseer of our village, and he made all the young ones work for him as servants, but he beat them for every little thing. Took a cane to them if his tea wasn't hot enough, if his rice was too sticky, if he found a bug crawling across his futon. Taku, the lad, he- he asked to be let off duty so he could tend to his grandmother. The bastard started cursing and laying into him, and I... I stopped him."

This wasn't the bravado of a moment before, emphasizing the grotesquerie of the murder in the hope of getting a reaction. It was the truth, told with the hopeless air of a man who was certain no one would care.

Mitsu asked quietly, "Had you reported Mirumoto Oribe's abuses?"

He suspected the answer even before a bitter laugh answered him. "The word of a miller against his samurai overseer. Who would listen to me?"

No one. In the eyes of the law, a peasant could testify against a peasant, and a samurai against a samurai, but if two people of unequal status disagreed, credence went to the higher-ranking one. In theory this was because with rank went the burden of honor, of speaking honestly even when it was to one's own detriment.

In practice, Mitsu knew, it rarely worked out that cleanly.

Murder was not the answer, of course. The harmony of the world depended on each person fulfilling their role; it could not allow for men like Heidoku deciding to take justice into their own hands. But the first failure had been Oribe's, forgetting that Bushidō exhorted him to compassion, justice, and self-control. And the second had been that of Oribe's lord, whose responsibility it was to correct his subordinates when they strayed.

The weight of those first two failures had fallen on Heidoku and everyone in his village. Under that pressure, it was unsurprising that a soul might break.

Mitsu closed his eyes. He had no fear that Heidoku would

attack him, and he needed to detach himself from the sight of the man. Oribe was beyond human justice now; he would face Emma-Ō, the Fortune of Death, and reap the consequences in his next lifetime. Oribe's lord might yet be disciplined and made to reform. But Heidoku must answer for his own crime.

Compassion burned in Mitsu's heart. That must be balanced against the other virtues, though, and in this case, justice must win out.

He opened his eyes.

"You will soon face one of my sisters," Mitsu said. "Go to her with dignity. What will happen to you then, I do not know – it is in the hands of the Fortunes. You may die, as you would have done had you never been brought here. But it may be that the Heavens will choose to spare you. I recommend you spend tonight in prayer."

The flickers of life that had shown in Heidoku guttered out, and he slumped once more against the wall. This was a man who had given up on the Fortunes – or at least on their mercy for him.

Mitsu rose and left, barring the door once more. Then he walked a small distance away, struggling with himself.

Should I tell Kazue-san, or not?

He took a deep breath of the mountain air and exhaled it slowly. No. He didn't know what her tattoo would do, but now, of all times, he must not prejudice her thinking by telling her the specifics of Heidoku's crime. She knew he was a prisoner, condemned to death and then sent here, but beyond that, she must face him with nothing but instinct to guide her.

That would have to be enough.

CHAPTER NINE

Kazue declined breakfast the next morning, saying she had decided to fast. But the truth beneath the polite fiction was that her fast had its roots in a more mundane cause: she was too queasy with nerves to eat.

She had spent the night in the small structure that served the village as both shrine and temple. Here the people of Fuchi Mura came to make offerings to the Fortunes and hear what few parts of the Tao seemed to have relevance to their difficult lives. In this they were aided by a middle-aged monk who nominally served the Order of Ten Thousand Fortunes, but who espoused both Fortunist and Shinseist theologies without much differentiation between them. Kazue spoke briefly with him and found him unlettered yet good-hearted. Being asked to bless an ise zumi from the High House of Light reduced him to stammering, but he pulled himself together and did as she asked.

When dawn came and brought Mitsu with it, she hoped those blessings would be enough.

Her thoughts must have been not as well-hidden as she hoped, because Mitsu spoke gently, "If he had not been brought here, they would have hanged him. Even if he dies as a result of your actions today, you will have done no worse than the justice already passed down."

It wasn't much comfort. But Kazue knew her duty – and she would rather face an unpleasant answer than continue to live with uncertainty.

"Where would you like to test this?" Mitsu asked.

She almost wanted to name the little temple-shrine. If her tattoo proved lethal, though, she didn't want to defile the structure with death. And if it proved destructive... better to be somewhere well clear of the village.

"Up on the ridge," she said, shading her eyes with one hand. "Under that pine tree at the top." Her tattoo had first brought her to Kanta under a pine tree; she hoped the association would prove auspicious.

She climbed the slope ahead of the others, leaving Mitsu to notify Mirumoto Ujinao. Out in the sunlight, the wind was a welcome touch of coolness; under the pine's shading boughs, it bit more sharply. Kazue sat cross-legged in the dirt and waited, doing her best to clear her mind, and only partially succeeding.

No one spoke on the way up to her, but she heard them approaching: the muted rattle of Ujinao's armor, the soft thud of feet against the earth.

When they arrived at the top of the ridge, Kazue said, "Seat him in front of me."

The two ashigaru pushed Heidoku down. He knelt with his hands bound in front of him and his head bowed. It meant she couldn't see his expression – couldn't see his face properly at all, just a foreshortened sliver of forehead and nose – and she was shamefully glad of that. If he had looked her in the eye, she might have lost her nerve.

She could not allow such thoughts to disturb her. Kazue settled her breathing, focusing only on the rise and fall of her chest... and the power within her tattoo.

If Mitsu had asked, she would have told him the process might require hours of meditation, as it had before. This time, though, it came much more rapidly.

At first it was the familiar ripple. The sense that there was *something* in front of her – a presence, a disturbance. She could tell it came from Heidoku, and that was a relief: her tattoo's failure to work on Mitsu back at the monastery could have meant this entire experiment was in vain, Heidoku an unsuitable target. Maybe the problem before had simply been that Mitsu's distress was too deliberate, too distant, not immediate enough.

Or perhaps it was the three sins she sensed, not simply general turmoil. Kanta, hiding away under the pine tree, must have been feeling regret for the turn his life had taken. Heidoku, facing death, must be deeply within the grip of fear; peasants were not taught to face their own end with the same equanimity as a samurai.

But the three sins were fundamental because all human suffering ultimately arose from one of those sources. Mitsu might have wept out of compassion for the things he'd seen, but that was, in its own way, a form of regret.

She couldn't learn the truth by halting here. She had to draw more deeply on the tattoo's power and see what it did when directed against a specific person.

Kazue inhaled again, a sharp, deep breath. Then she let it out, a fierce hiss like she used when training in jūjutsu, and stopped holding back.

Fear. Regret. Desire. Yes, all three of those were there; they were in every person to one degree or another, and all three were strong in Heidoku right now. His head came up, like a puppet's on a string, and she saw his blunt, scarred face, two teeth missing on one side where they had been pulled or knocked out. He desired to see the samurai suffer as his own people did: not all of them, but the ones who reaped the benefits of their rank without caring for its burdens. He regretted not protecting someone, more than one someone, not protecting them sooner or better. He feared his death, but he feared even more what unknown thing Kazue was going to do to him.

She sank deeper.

Helplessness. That was fear and regret and desire all together: the wish to act, the awareness of how impossible it was, the terror of what would happen as a consequence. And lacing through it came white-hot strands of violence, the impulse to *hurt*, the horror at what he'd done, the bone-deep terror when he'd realized.

But what *had* he done?

Did her ability go beyond sensing his inner state, the *honne* behind the tatemae? Was the effect of her tattoo to read other people's minds – to strip away that last defense of privacy?

No.

She'd described it to Mitsu as a cliff, to herself as a canyon: the feeling that there was something more, an edge she could push her target over. Now that she stood poised at its brink, she felt it as an abyss. Not a vast gulf like the valley between two mountains, but just a crack, tiny and yet infinitely deep. A flaw, an opening, and not one she would push Heidoku into; rather, it was a gap into which something else might come.

There were mediums in the rural parts of Rokugan who claimed to become possessed by kami and speak with their voices. When Kazue spoke, she might almost have mistaken her speech for that – almost. She knew the words were her own. But they spilled from her tongue like water from a hidden spring, unforeseen until the moment of their speaking.

"The wheel without a hub, turning, stops for the hand of neither master nor no master."

She spoke in a mild tone, hardly louder than a whisper, but in her mind it struck like a thunderclap. And as soon as the last word passed her lips, Kazue sagged with sudden exhaustion. She felt as if she had lifted the High House of Light on her own back and carried it to a new peak. Mitsu moved a half-step forward, but stopped himself; Kazue caught her weight on one hand and refocused her eyes on Heidoku.

He blinked, brow furrowing into two vertical lines. Then he shook his head, like a dog trying to shake away a fly.

Mirumoto Ujinao said, "What happened?"

Kazue tested her voice, unsure if it would work. "I am – not sure."

"Did you do anything?" Ujinao asked, unaware of or unconcerned with his rudeness. He prodded Heidoku with one foot. "Speak! Tell us what has happened to you!"

Heidoku didn't respond. Kazue wasn't sure he'd even heard Ujinao.

She was grateful when Mitsu intervened. Kazue wasn't sure she could have stood right then if she tried, and she didn't look very commanding propped up on one hand. "Let me examine him," Mitsu said, and suited deeds to words.

But he found nothing: only that Heidoku would not, or perhaps could not, speak. "If he has only been struck mute," Ujinao said, "then that is not enough for his crime. I will take him down to the village and execute him."

"Wait," Mitsu said. "We do not know yet what the true effect of this was. Take him back but keep him under constant watch. I will be with you as soon as I have seen to Kazue-san."

Ujinao clearly thought Mitsu was putting off the inevitable, but he nodded and snapped a command to his ashigaru. When they were safely out of earshot, Mitsu knelt at Kazue's side and said, "Are you all right?"

She nodded, unsure whether it was true or not.

"What can you tell me?"

As if that one cryptic line had stolen all her eloquence, the explanation came haltingly. She finished her account by saying, "Those words – I do not know what they were."

Mitsu eased himself into a more comfortable position. "They sounded like a kōan. Or at least the ending of one."

The ise zumi used kōan as a teaching tool, a way to help novices break through into greater understanding. But what Kazue had said was nowhere in the collections of stories and dialogues she'd studied during her training. "I am not sure. It felt almost like…" One hand started to rise toward her scalp. She made herself stop. "Like a weapon," she whispered.

"Driven into the crack you sensed." Mitsu frowned, then

shook his head and rose, dusting his hands and knees clean of dirt. "Well, I suspect the answer to this question is waiting for us down in Fuchi Mura. If you can stand, we should go see."

CHAPTER TEN

Heidoku remained silent for the rest of the day, neither speaking to anyone, nor showing any sign that he heard them. If hauled to his feet he would walk, but he would halt as soon as his captors stopped pushing him along. When Mitsu insisted on providing the man with food, saying, "He hasn't been executed yet," Heidoku paid it no attention.

Kazue watched for a time, until she couldn't bear it any longer. Then she went back to the temple-shrine and prayed for wisdom. She had successfully used her tattoo; she still didn't know what it did.

She'd done *something*, though, and it struck a nameless fear deep within her heart. As if whatever had happened to Heidoku was... something she had seen before? Not from a similar tattoo – surely she would have found a record for it if the knot had ever appeared in ise zumi history. Something she remembered from a past life – only no matter how she reached for it, the memory slipped through her fingers like mist.

No. That made it sound inevitable, like it wasn't her fault. In truth her mind shied away from the memory, no matter how hard she tried to steel herself. Like a hand flinching away from a flame.

Because she knew that touching it would hurt.

But she made a point of thanking the Fortunes for putting Mitsu at her side. He showed no impatience or disappointment, and seemed content to observe until there was nothing more to be learned from Heidoku. By herself, Kazue didn't think she could have mustered the conviction to prevent Ujinao from hanging the prisoner, so that he could declare his duty complete and return home. Mitsu insisted they wait three days before they declared the experiment finished.

She had three days to figure out what she had done.

On the second day Heidoku began to speak.

"The wheel without a hub, turning, stops for the hand of neither master nor no master."

He mumbled it to himself, dazed at first, then thoughtfully, then with an increasingly frantic air. The words shifted, grew, as if he were attacking them from different angles: "The hubless wheel, the wheel that has no hub. It turns around nothingness, no hub, no center, empty, an empty wheel."

Mitsu and Kazue watched him, while she tried to pretend the sight wasn't making her gut twist. "How long will he go on doing this?" she whispered.

Heidoku couldn't possibly have heard her, but his head came up anyway, his gaze fixing – not on the two of them, she thought. *Through* them. "Master nor no master," he said. "No master or master. Masterless. The masterless wheel. What is the wheel with no hub?"

"At least Ujinao can't claim we're wasting time," Mitsu said. Which was not an answer, for her or Heidoku. "I'll persuade him to give us another few days."

But another few days were not needed. On the third day, Heidoku's mind broke.

Only the iron discipline of the High House of Light and Kazue's own sense of honor kept her from clamping her hands over her ears. The peasants of Fuchi Mura had no such compunctions; most of them hid inside their houses, while a few jostled to see the prisoner, held once more in Yae's storehouse. The door was open, Ujinao standing guard, and Heidoku's screaming laughter, laughing screams, broken shards of what had once been speech, echoed through the village.

Here and there, one could still make out a few words: "wheel," or "master." And, once, a clear sentence: "*Now* I understand."

Mitsu tried to calm the man, but half the time Heidoku didn't seem to notice he was there, and the other half he tried to claw at or cling to Mitsu's legs, while Kazue clenched her hands hard enough that her nails, short as they were, nearly drew blood. Finally, she couldn't stand it any longer. Not caring that it was a display of weakness, she turned and fled.

She made it to the far end of the village before her foot caught on a stone and she fell. Mitsu caught up a few seconds later and dropped to his knees at her side. "Kazue-san–"

"You know what this is," she said, the words barely making it out of her throat. "We both know. We've seen it before."

Not often. It was rare in the Empire, but more common in the Dragon; rare among the Dragon, but more common in the Togashi. Only a scattered handful of cases – perhaps one in a generation; perhaps less – but the ise zumi remembered shreds of their previous lives. Kazue had seen this before.

And so had Mitsu.

He murmured, "Enlightened madness."

The shattering of a mind that comprehended the truth of the world before it was ready. Heidoku, the illiterate peasant who knew no more of spiritual truth than a few rote lines from the Tao: it took only a single tap to break him forever.

No wonder it hadn't worked on Mitsu. And Kanta... Kazue's stomach heaved as she thought of what she might have done to him.

Mitsu's tattoos rippled as he set his shoulders. "He may recover."

She scrabbled backward through the dirt, lurching to her feet. "Recover? You know he won't. No one has ever come back from enlightened madness. I told you that what I felt in him was a crack, a flaw, and I drove something into it. Like driving a wedge into a block of wood so it splits. I broke him open and I *can't undo that.*"

She was losing her composure, her voice getting higher, her speech more rapid, but she couldn't hold it in any longer. She knew her power now, and it was the power to destroy minds.

For the first time, she saw Mitsu at a loss for words. It seemed almost by reflex that he said, "Our tattoos are a gift from the Heavens. They would not have given you such a talent for no reason."

"A *talent*?" Kazue jerked back, as if tearing free of a hold he hadn't tried to take. "This isn't a thing to celebrate, senpai! You told me that whatever I did to him, it wouldn't be worse than the sentence he already faced. But this is far worse than death!"

Mitsu flinched. "Kazue-san, remain calm–"

She was far past calm. She'd destroyed a man, shattered his spirit. Because she wanted to know what she could do.

"Whatever the Heavens intended me for," she said, her body shaking from head to toe, "I can't do it. I *won't*." Kazue spun and hurled herself up the slope, not toward the ridge where she'd broken Heidoku, but away from the shrieks of the broken man.

Mitsu knelt in the village's little shrine and tried to find tranquility.

Kazue's words had struck with more force than her storm-serpent tattoo. *You told me that whatever I did to him, it wouldn't be worse than the sentence he already faced.* He'd been a fool to make such promises – to assume that he'd seen the worst that could happen to a person. Watching Heidoku's mind splinter under the obsessive weight of Kazue's words had taught him otherwise.

If this was his test, as well as Kazue's, then he had failed.

Heidoku's voice was fainter now, worn thin by constant use. Mitsu instinctively tried to block it out, then made himself stop, letting the sound wash over him. If he hoped to find any wisdom by that route, though, he was disappointed.

Enlightened madness. If that was what had happened to Heidoku, then there was no guessing what he might do now. Men and women afflicted by that condition had done whatever their splintered minds thought best: drowned themselves, laid a thousand chopsticks end to end, devoured human flesh. Heidoku could be kept under watch, made to eat and drink, his life sustained for a time... but he would not recover.

And Mitsu was prepared to fight anyone who tried to claim this was a more fitting punishment for his crime than hanging. The only question was whether it should be now or later.

Now, Mitsu decided. The sound was tormenting the innocent people of Fuchi Mura, who had already suffered unexpectedly from the samurai presence; he would send a message with Ujinao, urging some kind of compensation for them in return. Ending Heidoku's torment wasn't cowardice, an attempt to protect himself or Kazue from the knowledge of their actions; it was compassion and justice.

He bowed to the altar and went outside to find Ujinao.

A little while later, the noise stopped.

Kazue didn't come back before sunset. Mitsu followed her tracks until he saw her in the distance, sitting cross-legged on a flat slab of stone. She looked like she was meditating, and he knew she found solace in nature. After a moment's hesitation, he went back to the village.

She needed time, he thought.

The next morning he awoke to find her futon still folded in the corner, unused. But a message was written on the floorboard in charcoal, in the same neat, tidy hand she'd used during her time in the scriptorium.

I cannot do it.

I am sorry.

CHAPTER ELEVEN

She walked at a steady pace, without direction, without any purpose other than to get away.

Ordinarily the wild beauty of the mountains brought peace to her heart. The bare stone cliffs and crags of the peaks, the tall pines and the hawks wheeling above, the icy streams cradling little pockets of wildflowers and teeming with fish. Now she barely saw any of those things. She only knew that this far north, villages were scarce. Shinseist monks of the Brotherhood came here for hermitage, to spend years contemplating the Tao without disturbance from the outside world.

She could do the same.

Just like your mother.

Kazue's sandal caught against a rock and she stumbled, catching herself with one hand on the trunk of a hemlock. She recognized it from the bark, which formed into distinctive square shapes, each one cracked away from its neighbor. Broken. The sight made her recoil, snatching her hand back as if stung.

She could run away from human society, but not from the memory of what she had done. Even the trees would remind her.

And it *was* running away. She didn't even attempt to pretend otherwise. Maybe Mitsu was right, and the Heavens had given her that tattoo for a reason; her duty was to use it for the benefit of her order and her clan. But she couldn't face the prospect of an endless line of Heidokus, people offered up as sacrifices or object lessons or things to be disposed of in the most horrifying way imaginable. However much she trusted the wisdom of her senior monks and her clan champion, she couldn't bring herself to do that again. And if Mitsu had guessed correctly about her going out into the world this lifetime, she might be ordered to serve some other lord – one with much less restraint about when she should use the tattoo.

So, in one swift move, she had renounced her duty and become rōnin.

Just like she'd been born.

I should have stayed in Phoenix lands.

Kazue started walking again, but now it was as if the ghost of her mother walked alongside her. Aika had never spoken of how she became rōnin – not directly, not to her daughter. Over the years, though, the outline of it had taken shape, from the countless little dropped hints. Aika had been born to a Shiba vassal family, though Kazue didn't know which one; she'd trained as a bushi in a minor dōjō and become a guard in some higher-ranking samurai's retinue.

Until the day she was given an order and refused to obey it. Aika had walked away from everything, rather than do as her lord commanded.

Kazue hadn't even waited for the command.

I would rather give in to fear, she thought, *than live the rest of my life with even more regret than I carry now.*

The only saving grace was that she now understood her tattoo well enough to be sure she wouldn't find herself using it out of reflex. And if she stayed away from people, she wouldn't even have any suitable targets to tempt her. Animals couldn't find enlightenment, and so they couldn't be broken by it.

So long as she remained out here, everyone would be safe.

Including her.

Kazue had been in the mountains for three days when she finally began to consider the pragmatics of her situation.

Even in summertime the nights were chill, especially for someone wearing only an ise zumi's minimal clothing. As soon as the seasons changed, she would need shelter, unless she meant to die of the cold. And Kazue knew enough of wilderness survival to realize that if she wanted any hope of staying alive past autumn, she should begin preparing right away – building a shelter, stockpiling food – and that still might not be enough. Even Shinseist hermits started their isolation with more in the way of supplies than she had.

She might have no choice but to visit at least one village and hope she could work in exchange for a few necessary items. Like warmer clothing.

But she couldn't face the prospect, not yet. Kazue kept moving, studying the landscape around her, trying to find a spot that boasted enough wild food sources to sustain her for a good long while.

Aika had taught her some of that, long before she ever became an ise zumi. They lived in a town, and Aika earned enough to get by, but life as a rōnin was hard. She'd had to survive in the wild before and wanted to make sure her daughter could do the same, in case it became necessary someday. When Kazue – Yanai, as she had been then – declared that she was going to the High House of Light, her mother must have thought such risks were behind her forever. *My daughter will be a clan samurai,* she had said, and buried her tears in Yanai's shoulder as they embraced.

Mother. I'm sorry. More regret for Kazue to bear, and she was only glad that the reclusive habits of the Dragon meant Aika would never know how her daughter had failed.

Samurai elsewhere in Rokugan would say that an honorable suicide was the only way for Kazue to redeem herself now. But she was an ise zumi: killing herself would only send her back to the order, a few years down the road when she was old enough to feel the call to the High House of Light. And then after they trained her again, she would undergo her gempuku, and perhaps remember the unspeakable shame of her previous life. Death was no escape from that.

On the fifth day, as Kazue was washing herself on the bank of a mountain stream, she scrubbed one hand over her scalp… then paused.

She hadn't shaved since the morning she destroyed Heidoku. Her hair was already beginning to obscure the tattoo. Soon it would cover the lines enough to prevent her from calling on its power. At that point she wouldn't have to fear using it, no matter the provocation.

At that point, no one would even know it was there.

But the storm-serpent on her right arm still proclaimed her an ise zumi. If she wore something to cover it, though – in a year or two, when her hair was long enough that nobody would realize it had once been shaved off–

She could rejoin society and be safe.

Was that what she wanted?

Kazue sat back on her haunches, shivering slightly as a breeze dried the icy water on her skin. Although she'd tried not to think about him since the day she fled, it was as if Mitsu sat at her side, picking up the thread of the conversation they'd had on their way to Fuchi Mura. About Kazue going out into the world, and about the practice of giving ise zumi tattoos that might never see use in this lifetime.

Ise zumi lived and died with the power to shatter bone, walk through fire, or leap over castle walls, without ever doing those things outside of training. Who was to say her own power shouldn't be the same? Their sensei trained them to find the balance between contemplation and action. Perhaps she'd simply tried to call on the knot of lines too early. Perhaps in this lifetime she was meant simply to live with it – and then in some future incarnation, she would be ready to use it.

Or perhaps that was cowardice talking, masquerading as wisdom.

"How can I tell the difference?" she whispered.

Her reflection, rippling in the stream, had no answer.

She reached for her knife and, with careful strokes, scraped the stubble away. It wasn't a decision – more like a decision not to decide yet. Not to fully surrender her identity as an ise zumi, as a Togashi, as a Dragon.

She could always let it grow again.

CHAPTER TWELVE

Mitsu waited another three days in Fuchi Mura after Ujinao left, hoping Kazue would come back.

He told the bushi that she was in seclusion after the execution of Heidoku – which was true, if not precisely honest. Mitsu was a reasonably honorable man, but if Kazue managed to pull herself together and come back, he didn't want her humiliated by a more accurate description of her absence.

He knew in his heart, though, that she wouldn't come back. Not to Fuchi Mura, anyway. He stayed three days just in case, praying in the little shrine and helping the villagers however he could. Then his own duties sent him back to the High House of Light, hoping every step of the way that he would arrive to find Kazue already there.

She wasn't.

Hassuno-sama paled visibly when he told her what effect Kazue's tattoo had on the condemned peasant. "Enlightened madness? Are you certain?"

"Yes," Mitsu said. "I remember when Togashi Shidai broke,

two hundred years ago. In his case it came about from reading too deeply in the restricted scrolls, but the effect was the same."

He'd never seen the iemoto at a loss for words. She sat for some time, her expression serene once more, but it was the kind of serenity that masked turmoil within. Then she said, "And Kazue-san?"

"She needs time to think, iemoto-sama," Mitsu said. "And I think it is better that she takes that time away from the monastery and its distractions."

Hassuno-sama's gaze sharpened. "Did you instruct her to do so?"

He couldn't bring himself to lie outright to the head of his order. Kazue hadn't been seeking contemplation; she had run away, overwhelmed by her fears. And those fears weren't the kind of thing one could resolve in a few days – maybe not even in a few months.

It was entirely possible they'd lost her, at least for this lifetime.

But maybe not. She was no newcomer to the order, enduring the weight of their teachings for the first or even third time; she might find her way out from under this one. And Mitsu was still not willing to be the one who shamed her.

So he merely said, "She needs time to think."

Hassuno-sama could read through that well enough. She knew both what he was not saying and why. Instead of pressing, she asked, "And you, Mitsu-san?"

This visit to the monastery was already longer than most. But Mitsu found himself with no urge to wander off again, seeking adventure and new things in the rest of the Empire. No, what he really wanted to do was to scour the neighboring mountains until he found Kazue, and then help her.

But until he had something more useful to say to her than what he'd already said, his presence would only rub salt in an open wound.

Mitsu bowed low. "If you have need of me elsewhere, iemoto-sama, command me. Otherwise, I will remain here."

"Stay," she said. "For now."

Silently, Mitsu sent a prayer of thanks up to the Fortunes. Because he could think of one person who might be able to help, and that person never left the High House of Light.

He found Gaijutsu-sensei in a tiny courtyard supervising three of his apprentices, who were hard at work grinding the pigments used to make tattoo ink. They had what looked like corroded bronze in their mortars, and the grinding seemed to be going very slowly.

A senior apprentice was kneeling nearby, ready to fetch anything his master needed. When he saw Mitsu at the gate, the apprentice rose to whisper in Gaijutsu-sensei's ear. A flick of the latter's fingers indicated that Mitsu should approach, so he bowed and obeyed.

"Sensei," he said, "I apologize for troubling you. May I speak with you privately?"

To his senior apprentice, Gaijutsu-sensei said, "Make sure they grind it finely enough." Then he stretched out his arm for Mitsu to support it and said, "Walk with me."

They moved at a slow pace out of the courtyard, into one of the gardens reserved for senior monks. Mitsu waited until they had passed into a stand of bamboo before he spoke. Elsewhere in Rokugan, he might have worried about someone eavesdropping from cover, but not in the High House of Light.

His report this time was briefer than the one he'd given to

Hassuno-sama. When he was done, Mitsu asked the question that had been seething in his mind since Heidoku's mind had broken. "Sensei – is it possible that some… outside influence has corrupted Kazue's tattoo?"

Gaijutsu-sensei halted on the path, turning his blind face toward Mitsu's in astonishment. "Corrupted it?"

"Warped its power somehow. Turned what ought to have been a beneficial effect into one of pure destruction." The tattoo master had to be able to feel the tension in Mitsu's arm, knotting his muscles tight. "I know you saw that image in a vision. But I cannot understand why Tengoku would afflict her with this – what honorable purpose it could possibly serve in the world."

"Ah." Gaijutsu-sensei stood like a stone, while a gust of wind made the bamboo sway around them. By the time it died down, he seemed to have made a decision. "Come with me, Mitsu-san. There is something I think you are ready to see."

Mitsu had known for many lifetimes that the pigments and other supplies Gaijutsu-sensei used were kept in a small, freestanding building in an out-of-the-way part of the monastery.

He had never realized there was a trapdoor in the floor, opening onto a steep staircase and a dark tunnel.

Gaijutsu-sensei paused at the top of the stairs. "Oh, yes. I imagine you will want to bring a light."

Mitsu fetched a lamp and followed the tattoo master silently. He didn't need to be told that whatever he was about to see wasn't common knowledge, even among the senior ise zumi. Or that it should be kept secret afterward.

The tunnel seemed to stretch on forever, though distances

became deceptive underground, with only a bobbing lamp for illumination. The stone around them was chill, and the passage narrow enough that Mitsu's shoulders kept brushing the walls. Then they came to a single door, held shut by a lock with no keyhole.

He didn't see what Gaijutsu-sensei did to open the lock. The man's body obscured it for a moment, then it clicked, and the door swung open.

The room beyond was small, and austere even by the standards of the monastery. The carvings that adorned the walls were in a style Mitsu recognized as ancient, and the cabinet that stood in the middle of the room wasn't much more recent. It was the sole object in the room.

"Ordinarily I come down here only when I am preparing to tattoo someone," Gaijutsu-sensei said. "But also, very rarely, to show someone this."

He bowed and clapped his hands as if approaching a shrine, then opened the lacquered doors of the cabinet. Inside stood a single vessel, carved from a pale stone so thin that Mitsu could see the dark liquid it contained. The stopper proved to be a long shaft, of the sort a physician or a perfumer might use to add just a drop or two to some other mixture.

In the light of Mitsu's lamp, the liquid at the end of the stopper was as red as blood.

"From Togashi-no-Kami," Gaijutsu-sensei said. "We use it in every ise zumi tattoo – every one that contains power. It is from this that the power comes."

Mitsu didn't need the explanation. The moment he saw the blood, his own skin sang in response, everywhere he had a tattoo. The resonance crawled along his arms and legs, across his chest and back, up his neck to the dragon head that spanned his scalp.

His ability to withstand blows, to transform his hands into claws, to run faster than the wind and breathe fire at his enemies... they all derived from the Kami who had founded his clan, his family, and his order.

No force short of Fu Leng himself could corrupt that.

The thought made Mitsu's skin shudder in a different way. He'd traveled from one end of the Empire to the other, and while he'd spent a good deal of that time among the common people, he'd also encountered certain kinds of Crab and Phoenix samurai: those who hunted the practitioners of a particular blasphemous art.

His mouth refused to shape the words *blood magic*. But Gaijutsu-sensei was alert to things other than sight; he must have heard Mitsu's breath catch. The tattoo master stoppered the vial. "We keep this secret for many reasons," he said. "There are those who would seek to exploit it, to capture this power for themselves... and there are those who would misunderstand."

Mitsu couldn't stop the puff of incredulous laughter that escaped him. Explaining to a Kuni Witch Hunter or an Asako Inquisitor that *this* blood magic didn't call on the power of Jigoku... yes, they would misunderstand. Quite a lot.

Whereas Mitsu himself was beginning to understand even more. "Your visions," he said. "They come from Togashi-no-Kami, don't they? So, whatever is happening with Kazue... is meant to be."

Gaijutsu-sensei inclined his head, then placed the vial back in the cabinet and closed the doors, bowing to them once more. This time Mitsu followed his lead.

His muscles ached, fighting themselves. He wanted more than anything to charge back down the tunnel and out of the monastery, into the wilderness where Kazue had vanished. The tattoo she bore – it wasn't just dangerous to other people. Enlightened madness appeared more often among the ise zumi because of their order's practices, because the power they carried in their skin was sometimes too much for them to bear. If she didn't find a balance with the lines inked into her scalp, they might wind up breaking her the same way they'd broken Heidoku.

But now Mitsu had information that could help her. If she knew the tattoo she bore truly was a gift, a sign of great honor from the Kami himself–

Would that help? Or would it make the danger worse?

He didn't know. And in some ways it didn't matter, because what Gaijutsu-sensei had shown him here was secret. Mitsu had no right to share that with anyone else. And as desperately as he wanted to help Kazue…

In the end, she would have to find her way out of the wilderness on her own. It wasn't enough for her to trust Togashi-no-Kami's wisdom; she had to trust *herself*. Without that, she would always be vulnerable.

Someone with that kind of power could not afford to be vulnerable.

A blind man's eyes did not fix themselves on any particular target, but Mitsu knew Gaijutsu-sensei was watching him. Waiting, just as Hassuno-sama had, to see what he would do.

Was the right answer to stay, or to go?

Ordinarily he would have gone in a heartbeat. But although his actions until now had brought him to the attention of the monastery's leaders, Mitsu suspected they were looking for more.

It doesn't matter what they're looking for. You need to do what is right for this situation.

As much as it galled him to admit it, what was right in this case was inaction.

The decision washed down his limbs like cool water. In every lifetime, this had been the hardest lesson for Mitsu to learn: not what to do, but what *not* to do. How to recognize when it was better to remain still, rather than to act. How to accept that inaction could be the right course.

They hadn't assigned him to Kazue to help solve her problems. They'd done it to teach him that those problems were hers to solve – not his.

Mitsu followed Gaijutsu-sensei back down the corridor and into the light. Then he extinguished the lamp, thanked the tattoo master, and went to pray.

CHAPTER THIRTEEN

Kazue kept shaving her head after that. It became her way of marking time, in a place where time seemed almost to become an illusion: the weather changed, sun to clouds and back again, and flowers bloomed and died, but it was easy to pretend the mountain summer would go on forever. The scrape of her knife over her scalp reminded her that the real illusion was that feeling of timelessness. Sooner or later, she would have to take steps to ensure her ongoing survival – or else return to the monastery.

But as the days went on, that second possibility faded further and further from her mind.

Her voice had destroyed Heidoku. The power came from the tattoo, but if that were the guiding hand, her voice was the weapon. The last words she'd spoken were in Fuchi Mura, before she fled; since then she had been silent. Even the mental conversations she had with herself were fading away, replaced by a state of mind that was neither meditation nor normal activity. She moved without thinking, following instinct as she searched for water, food, shelter. Like a bird, or the wolves that came down from the peaks when winters grew hard, preying on livestock and even people.

She wasn't going to become a predator, but that way of thought was comfortable. Birds didn't have to remember the past. Wolves didn't feel guilt for what they'd done.

Her movements loosened, abandoning the smooth control of a well-trained monk in favor of something more feral. When she heard the grunting of a bear, she sank reflexively into a crouch, then skittered like an insect from cover to cover until she was downwind of the creature and could flee. At night she curled tight for warmth and stayed like that until dawn, when she eased the kinks out with a few grunts of her own.

She was hungry all the time, even with her knowledge of how to find food in the wild. But it didn't bother her.

She kept washing herself in streams, though, and sharpening her knife, and shaving her head when her hair grew too long. She knew, without ever admitting it to herself, that the day she stopped doing that would be the day she surrendered her final link to the world of humanity.

Despite everything, she wasn't quite ready to do that.

Then, one morning when she had just shaved her head again, she smelled woodsmoke.

Wildfires were a danger in the summer months. If the season was too dry, a lightning strike could set the trees aflame, and then the winds would carry the sparks and the blaze faster than anyone could run without the aid of a tattoo.

Those thoughts made her think of Mitsu, for the first time in days – Mitsu whose centipede tattoo carried him faster than thought, Mitsu who had breathed fire against fire to deprive it of fuel and save the monastery from danger.

She lacked fire and speed both. But after one blank moment of animal alertness, human sense reasserted itself: the scent was a mere thread, the product of a small fire, not a blaze that would consume the mountains. And there had been no lightning strikes.

Someone was out here.

In my *mountains.*

That thought – the first articulate one she'd had in some time recalled Kazue to herself. It was absurd to think of the mountains as her own; she wasn't some territorial beast, and neither was she a bandit, trying to assert some kind of claim against samurai and the emperor. She was…

I'm human. That's enough for now.

But she remained wary as she approached the source of the smoke. It was coming from the direction of a bald-topped peak, but lower on its slope. Kazue took care to remain downwind and behind brush that would hide her from prying eyes. Finally, she crept close enough to catch a glimpse of the smoke itself and the fire it came from, burning in a shallow earthen pit in front of a hut.

Kazue crouched beneath the low-hanging branch of a tree, balancing herself with fingertips braced in the dirt as she peered around. She saw no movement, apart from the dance of the flames. No sensible person would leave a fire unattended for long, though, even if they had dug out the pit so nothing nearby would catch. That was the *other* way wildfires got started.

Then again, foolish hermits were always a possibility. Just

because someone decided to contemplate the Tao on the edge of the Empire didn't mean they knew the first thing about surviving in the wilderness.

The darkness inside the hut shifted, and Kazue recoiled further beneath the tree. The shift resolved itself into a human figure: a woman, ducking out from under the low lintel with a simple clay pot in her hands. She went to the fire and spread the branches with another stick until she could nestle the pot in the embers. Then she sat back on her haunches and waited.

A tantalizing scent rose from the pot. Nothing elaborate and no meat; Kazue hadn't tasted meat since she arrived at the High House of Light. But it was more than the simple roots and berries and mushrooms she'd been eating, and her mouth began to water.

To distract herself, she studied the woman. Her first assumption had been that the stranger was a religious hermit, but if so, she had forsaken the robes of her order, and hadn't cut her hair in years. She wore a homespun kimono that had been patched more than once, and leggings tied tight around her calves for practicality. Her feet were bare and her hair pulled back into a simple tail, bound at several points along its length to keep strands from escaping.

The woman wrapped her hands in her sleeves and removed the pot from the faded embers. Kazue twitched in surprise – she hadn't realized how much time had passed. Her sudden movement jarred the branch under which she sat, and the woman's head came up like a deer's, searching the trees.

Retreating would only risk giving her position away more clearly. Kazue remained where she was, scarcely breathing, until the woman relaxed. Once the stranger was fully absorbed in eating her meal, Kazue slipped away, going back to her roots and berries and mushrooms.

That should have been the end of it.

Wasn't the whole point of coming out here to avoid people? She had found a person; now the sensible thing to do would be to move onward, continuing her search for a place to settle down that would keep her fed.

Except the sight of that hut, ramshackle as it was, reminded Kazue that her current method of survival wasn't good enough. She needed shelter. She needed supplies, like a clay pot. And although she had absolutely no intention of trying to join forces with the stranger, perhaps that woman could offer her useful advice. It looked like she'd been out there a long time – longer than a single summer. She would know how to live through the winter.

It was like shaving her head. Kazue didn't make up her mind to leave, but she also didn't approach the stranger. She just kept going back to the hut, finding different hiding spots that still allowed her to see, watching the stranger go about her business.

That went on for days. *This is absurd*, Kazue told herself one morning, after she took shelter in the branches of another tree. *I have to make a decision.*

She touched her scalp. Her hair wasn't quite long enough yet to hide the tattoo, but in a few more days it would be. Once the knot was safely hidden, Kazue decided, she would speak to the stranger.

The woman was outside again, cooking in the pot, but she also had a pile of dandelion greens and other things Kazue couldn't make out at her side. She poked a finger into the pot to test its temperature and nodded in satisfaction.

Then she lifted her head and called out, "If you are hungry, you're welcome to join me. I have enough for two."

CHAPTER FOURTEEN

This time Kazue had more self-control. She didn't jerk or make any noise. After a moment, the woman added, "If not, I understand, and go in peace. But you are welcome here at any time."

It was the first human speech she'd heard in... Kazue realized she had lost count of the days. Lost count of the times she'd shaved her scalp, even. Long enough that the sound of a voice came as a shock, and she wasn't even sure her own would work in reply.

I told myself I would do this. It's coming a little early, is all.

Her body had locked tight with surprise when the woman spoke; now she made her muscles relax. One careful movement at a time, she descended from the tree, and came into the open.

Judging by the woman's reaction, she hadn't only known Kazue was present – she'd known exactly where Kazue was. She got up, dusting off her hands, and bowed. It had none of the practiced grace of a samurai's childhood training and her accent betrayed her peasant origins, but she carried herself with dignity, nonetheless. "I am Senzai. Please, join me. My hospitality may be simple, but I offer you everything I have."

Kazue bowed and opened her mouth to reply – and choked. *Togashi Kazue? Or just Kazue?* Her arms were still bare; Senzai could see the storm-serpent on her right biceps, even if she missed the knot half-hidden beneath the stubble. And Kazue's clothing was clearly that of a warrior monk.

But did she have any right to claim the Togashi name, when she'd walked away from her duty?

When the pause threatened to stretch for too long, Senzai said, "I am sorry that I do not have any kind of mat or cushion, but I promise you that the grass is soft."

Kazue could feel herself flushing in embarrassment and gratitude as she knelt without giving any name at all. Senzai portioned out the food, giving Kazue what appeared to be her only bowl, and eating her own meal directly out of the pot. The soup was thin, but rich in comparison to what Kazue had been eating since Fuchi Mura, and it was all she could do not to just pour the entire thing straight down her throat.

She made herself pause halfway through to ask, "Are you a monk?"

Senzai looked startled. "No. Why do you ask?"

Kazue gestured with the bowl. "No meat. You seem to be very good at surviving out here, so I doubt it's because you don't know how to set snares."

"Ah." Senzai divided up the greens, giving Kazue the larger pile. "No, I'm simply a peasant woman. From Seseki Mura, in Kinenkan Province."

Not a village Kazue had ever heard of, but Kinenkan Province lay to the south and east of the High House of Light, and was ruled by the Agasha family. "Why did you leave?" Then she flushed again. "I am sorry. It has been… some time since I had anyone to speak with."

Senzai's gentle smile made her feel less awkward. "It's an understandable question. A peasant like me isn't generally free to leave her village and make her home in the wilderness – not unless she first takes holy orders."

The smile faded. Kazue expected to see sadness beneath: whatever drove this woman forth clearly could not have been a happy event. But Senzai seemed to have found peace with her past, because she set the pot down, folded her hands in her lap, and spoke tranquilly. "I'm told by my elders that I was always an insightful child, even before I could talk. My father passed away when I was only a year old, but I seemed always to know when my mother was grieving for him, and what to do to comfort her – whether that was a hand on her cheek, a silly trick to make her smile, or some misbehavior, so that she would have something to chide me for."

Kazue inhaled, holding back the tears that threatened to prick at her eyes. She knew now why she'd been watching Senzai from the shadows: because she felt kinship with this woman, another hermit seeking solace in the isolation of the mountains. But she hadn't expected this additional step, both of them fatherless children with only their mothers to raise them.

She's a peasant. I'm a rōnin. Her father died; mine abandoned my mother. The similarity wasn't as great as she thought. After days of solitude, though, every whisper of connection felt like a shout.

"You may think this is coincidence," Senzai went on, "or just the bond of a daughter to her mother. But when I learned

to speak, it became more. I had a reputation in the village for
always knowing when someone was secretly angry at another
person or planning a surprise. The young people came to me
to ask whether the one they hoped to marry had any feelings
for them in return, and whether their parents would approve. I
didn't know everything – no matter what they said about me –
but I knew enough."

It wasn't difficult to see how that might have gone wrong.
"They came to fear you," Kazue said.

"What is charming in a child becomes more worrisome as
she grows. No one likes to have their guilt revealed – their little
adulteries and thefts, a man swearing to his wife that he has
stopped drinking when in truth he keeps a jug of sake behind
the woodpile. And I knew that…" Senzai's gaze was distant,
looking past Kazue to the trees, and beyond. "But it was difficult
for me to distinguish between insight and knowledge, to realize
that what seemed so plain to me was hidden from others."

Kazue's mouth was dry. "How – how did you know these
things?"

Senzai met her gaze briefly, then looked down before it could
become rude. "I'm not a shugenja, I promise you. And I didn't
know people's thoughts. It was simple observation – simple to
me, at least. The man who drank would bring in smaller loads of
wood than he was capable of carrying, so that he had to go out
to the woodpile more often. And he chewed more mint leaves
than anyone else in the village, to hide the smell of the sake on
his breath."

Not like her tattoo, then. Kazue hadn't spent enough time
around Heidoku to observe anything about him, and he'd been
silent and frozen when he came before her. What she knew had

come from the tattoo itself, sensing the vulnerabilities that could break him. But still, it raised the hairs on the back of her neck.

Especially when Senzai went on to add, in a thoughtful tone, "Even beyond those bits of evidence… I could tell he felt guilty. I saw it in his every movement. Just as you can see that someone's angry, when they clench their fists and walk heavily and glare at the target of their anger – it was always that clear to me, even when it wasn't so obvious. I knew he felt guilty about something by looking at him; I knew what he was guilty of by looking at what he did."

Another silence descended. Kazue might not have such natural insight, but she could tell the purpose of this pause was to give her a chance to speak. Senzai couldn't possibly fail to guess that an ise zumi living in the wilderness who choked on whether to give her name might have some weight burdening her heart.

But Kazue took long enough to find her tongue that once again, Senzai filled the breach before it could grow uncomfortable. She said, "In the end, I revealed one thing too many. My neighbors began to insist I wasn't a girl at all but a yōkai, masquerading in human form. I knew they were planning to hurt me, so I fled. I lived for a time as a beggar in a nearby town, until a yoriki came to arrest me for vagrancy. I told him that his superior magistrate would soon find out he was in the pay of a local gang, and while he was in shock from that, I ran again. Since then, I've been out here."

"And have you never thought about going back?"

It almost felt like the cryptic phrase she'd spoken to Heidoku, with her mouth moving as if of its own accord. But in this case, Kazue knew exactly why she said it.

She hoped that in Senzai's life, she might find some guidance for her own.

Without even a breath of hesitation, Senzai shook her head. "I am done with human society," she said. "It has no need of me."

CHAPTER FIFTEEN

Senzai might be done with human society, but without ever saying it outright, she invited Kazue to stay – at least for the night.

It began with her offering to build up the fire so that Kazue could wash properly, with gritty sand to scrub herself down. For the first time since Fuchi Mura, Kazue felt like she was truly clean, and without thinking she found herself shaving her head again. By now her scalp was red and irritated from shaving so often in cold water, though she'd tried to keep her knife in good condition; it would have been better to let her skin heal for a while. But it was habit now, until she made up her mind once and for all. And despite what Senzai had said, she hadn't done that quite yet.

She was one step closer to it, though. A life like Senzai's seemed appealing: no challenges except survival, no obligations except to herself. She might be fated to return to the ise zumi in her next lifetime, but in this one, she could find peace through solitude.

Heating the water used up a lot of the firewood. "I'll gather more later," Senzai said, but Kazue insisted on helping, in gratitude for her hospitality. Together they went out into the forest, collecting armfuls of branches and carrying them back to the hut.

"I apologize for lurking around like that," Kazue said as they walked.

"There's nothing to apologize for. I'm a stranger out in the woods; naturally you would be wary."

Kazue ran her thumb over the scab forming where she'd scraped her left forearm across a stone. "Wary, yes – but it was more than that. I… I have always enjoyed being out in the natural world. Left to myself, I think I enjoy it a little too much."

"What do you mean, too much?" Senzai braced her foot against a fallen branch and pulled, snapping it into two pieces of more convenient size.

The branch had a cousin, equally dead, but still attached to the tree. Kazue jumped and wrapped her hands around it, then hung there, bouncing slightly. "Even though I have not been out here as long as you, it has changed how I think."

"Is that a bad thing?"

Her weight finally tore the branch loose, and Kazue thumped to the ground in a shower of dead leaves. "It was like… nothing existed but the present moment. I was trying not to think about the past or the future, and the result was that they faded from my mind. I started to act more like an animal, on instinct."

Senzai bent to help her break the branch into pieces. "Yes, I know what you mean." She grunted as the wood gave way. "When there's no one to talk to, there's no need to put your thoughts into words. Without words, past and future lose their separate nature. You act based on your knowledge and according to your need, without conscious thought. But again – is that a bad thing?"

Kazue stopped in the midst of brushing bark from her hands. *Without conscious thought*: it was one of the lessons of jūjutsu, of any martial training. To fight with the conscious mind was too slow: perception, analysis, and decision paralyzed the body and gave the opponent time to strike. The movements of a true master were informed by past experience and by future intent, but the mind existed only in the present moment, and acted without conscious thought.

"I suppose not," she said slowly, collecting the pieces. "I had not considered it that way."

"The natural state of the mind is to be at peace," Senzai said, continuing onward. "It's only when we allow external things to trouble us that we lose that serenity."

That wasn't the only such thing she said during the course of the day. The branches they'd gathered were useful, but they would burn fairly quickly, and Senzai didn't have an ax to cut heavier logs. When they came upon an entire young beech tree that had fallen on a slope, Kazue offered to do what she could to break it up. After stripping the smaller limbs with ordinary strikes, she set her feet and breathed, focusing her attention, for the first time in weeks, on the storm clouds and winding serpent inked into her right arm.

Her first attempt produced a spray of bark and rolled the trunk halfway down the slope but didn't break the wood. While Senzai watched, Kazue descended and this time placed herself beneath the trunk, so that at least she would knock it upward, rather than down into an inaccessible gulch.

Laughter brightened Senzai's voice as she called out, "Don't try so hard! Strike without effort, like you did at the branches."

Kazue paused, shading her eyes with one hand as she looked up to where Senzai perched on a comfortably rounded boulder. "Are you sure you were not a monk at some point?"

"Quite sure! You would know better than me, but I assume becoming a monk is the sort of thing a person would remember."

"Maybe you were one in a previous life, then," Kazue said, lining herself up with the tree. "Or you are just living proof of what Shinsei said – that the Eternal Truth can be found anywhere, even in a single drop of water. You have never studied the Tao, but you understand its principles better than some monks I have known."

Strike without effort. She hadn't practiced enough with the storm cloud tattoo, her attention at first focused too much on the knot and its mysteries, then trying to avoid all thought of her tattoos entirely. But she already knew her use of the storm-serpent could be refined, and the only danger it posed right now was to the tree.

No, Kazue thought. *No danger.* And she struck.

She'd thought once that her tattoo might let her shatter a tree. She knew now that she could – but that wasn't what happened. Instead, she cleaved off a piece of the trunk about the length of her forearm, not as cleanly as an ax would have, but well enough to leave a usable log. A few strikes later, the whole trunk had been sectioned into useful pieces, good solid hardwood that could sustain Senzai's fire for many hours.

Senzai came down to join her and bowed in gratitude. "I'll come and collect these tomorrow."

"No need," Kazue said. "Let us take the smaller branches

with us, and then I will come back for these. And then–" She glanced down at herself and laughed. "I think I will need to bathe again."

She contented herself with rinsing off in a stream, rather than burning more wood for another hot bath. Once all the large logs were stacked up under a sheltering tree where they wouldn't get too wet if it rained, Senzai set about preparing the evening meal, with Kazue's assistance.

They didn't talk the whole time. Senzai was even more content than Kazue to work in silence, asking for things with gestures as much as words. But when Kazue drew her out briefly on this topic or that one, her impression of the hermit's wisdom deepened.

It wasn't that Senzai knew the Tao, not in the way people normally used the word. She didn't know the actual text of the Little Teacher's conversation with the Kami at the dawn of the Empire, the rules he set forth for monastic communities, and the later material written by the first abbots of the Brotherhood's orders, discussing the spiritual relationships between Shinsei's teachings, kami worship, the ancestors, the Five Elements, and the Spirit Realms. Senzai was illiterate; she couldn't have read that text even if she'd possessed a copy.

But Kazue knew full well that the book called the Tao was, as the proverb had it, not the Tao. The text was a guidebook; the Tao itself was a way. And whether it was because of her remarkable insight, or the trials she'd suffered, or her solitude in the mountains, Senzai understood that way very well.

It made Kazue wonder about her own path here. The similarities she'd noticed between Senzai's life and her own –

were those mere coincidence, Kazue craving fellowship after so much time alone? Or were they signs from the Heavens, that she had come to where she needed to be?

Here, perhaps, she had found the teacher she so desperately needed.

As dusk fell, Kazue asked why Senzai kept to a vegetarian diet, despite not being a monk. The hermit said, "I know it would be easier for me to keep myself fed if I were willing to eat the flesh of animals – fish especially. But I can't bring myself to say that my own survival should come at the expense of another creature like that. I'm just one woman; why should my life matter more than that of a rabbit?"

"You are higher in the Celestial Order than a rabbit," Kazue pointed out.

"That's both true and an illusion. In a previous life, I may have *been* a rabbit. Better to live in harmony with all things, so that when I find myself in such a position, I can hope for others to live in harmony with me." Senzai prodded the fire with a long stick and added a little more fuel. "Besides, it would tempt me to see the success of my snare as an achievement, and then I would be celebrating the death of another living creature. Every victory is a funeral."

Her words struck home unexpectedly. Heidoku would have died either way, hanged for his crime regardless of what Kazue did or did not do – but her victory, uncovering the true power of her tattoo, was from another perspective a thing to mourn.

"Senzai-san." Kazue hesitated, well aware that her tongue had almost shaped it into *sensei* instead. "There are many monks in the Empire with less wisdom than you have. I know you said that the world has no need of you… but in this one thing, you are wrong. I beg you to consider returning. I know the Brotherhood would welcome you with open arms."

The hermit woman's expression remained serene, but now it was the serenity of polished stone. "No. I have left all that behind."

Without thinking, Kazue edged back from the fire until she could bow with her forehead to the ground. It didn't matter that Senzai was a peasant and Kazue a samurai; here in the wilderness, such distinctions were as meaningless as those between a human and a rabbit. "Then please accept me as your student. Tengoku has sent me here, I am sure of it. Under your tutelage, I will learn how to carry the burden I have been given."

She heard nothing, only the crackle of the fire. Then a faint rustle, as Senzai stood.

"I have left all that behind," Senzai repeated. "I ask nothing of the world beyond this place, and I owe it nothing in return. You are welcome to stay the night, but in the morning, you should go."

CHAPTER SIXTEEN

Despite her cold response, Senzai's hospitality remained undiminished. When Kazue tried to say she could leave that night, the hermit insisted she stay; when Kazue tried to cede the hut's minimal comforts to her host, Senzai insisted that she accept them. The futon was merely a blanket over dried grass, but it was softer than the ground outside, and Kazue felt guilty as she stared into the darkness, broken by threads of moonlight that came through the cracks in the walls. It might not be luxury, but of the two of them, she was the monk. The hard ground should have been *her* bed.

And it wasn't as if the comfort of the hut were helping her sleep. She lay awake, listening to the wind, and wondered: *where did I go wrong?*

The question provoked a silent, bitter laugh. Where, indeed? There were so many points to choose from: not just here, but in Fuchi Mura, at the High House of Light, all the way back through her life – not just this one, but those that had come before. Mitsu thought the knot tattoo was a gift, earned by her merit in a previous incarnation, but maybe it was a punishment for some failing.

Looking at the recent past, though… she truly had believed she was meant to find and learn from Senzai. Instead, the hermit had rebuffed her, and Kazue couldn't understand why. How could someone with Senzai's compassion, her insight, cut herself off so thoroughly from the world?

The ise zumi studied the Tao, even if they didn't follow it as the Shinseist orders of the Brotherhood did. Kazue knew it advocated nonattachment – but surely there was a difference between renouncing desire and making oneself insensible to the good one could do.

Outside the ramshackle hut, the wind picked up. Kazue sighed and shifted position, arranging herself as comfortably as she could. It wasn't part of their gempuku, but one of the skills ise zumi were expected to master during their training was the ability to put themselves to sleep at will. She closed her eyes and was about to begin the meditative technique when she felt a draft and sensed a faint increase in the light against her eyelids. The blanket that covered the doorway had been pushed aside.

Senzai. Kazue drew breath to apologize… but a guttural whisper stopped her short.

"You are unworthy."

Kazue shot upright. A figure blocked the doorway, stoop-shouldered, wild-haired, its eyes glowing with the sickly light of swamp gas. One hand held the curtain out of the way; the other scraped down the edge of the doorway, claws against weathered wood.

"You scorn your gifts and lack the wisdom to use them well. You must be destroyed."

Hoarse and twisted though it was, Kazue recognized that voice. She breathed, "*Senzai-san.*"

There were stories of this in Dragon lands, and among the Phoenix, too. Anywhere wilderness and deep religious dedication came together. Female monks, shugenja, priestesses – women dedicated to their spiritual development – went out into the mountains and the forests to cultivate their inner power. And they succeeded.

But in cutting themselves off from human society, from their duty to the world, they transformed themselves. Gradually, one silent summer and frozen winter at a time, they lost their humanity and became yōkai.

Senzai was a *kobukaiba*: a hag of the deep woods.

Kazue scrambled to her feet. "Senzai-san," she said, her hands out in a defensive gesture. "Forgive me. I should not have disturbed you–"

"*You disturb the balance of the world!*" The hut's interior fell into shadow as the kobukaiba dropped the curtain. "*I feel it in your skin, little monk. The power you don't understand, the power you fear. You have failed. You are unworthy. And I will destroy you!*"

Her voice rose to an unearthly shriek. Kazue dodged instinctively and felt the air shift as Senzai's claws raked through the air where she'd been. She tried to twist past, gaining the doorway and the freedom of the night beyond, but wire-thin whips lashed across her face and arms – the kobukaiba's hair. It tried to wrap around her limbs, and Kazue, writhing free, slammed against the wall of the hut. The space was tiny; it gave her no room to maneuver. An instant later the hair had her trapped, ensnaring her arms so she couldn't pull loose.

The glowing eyes fixed on her, drawing nearer. "*You are full of fear, full of regret. How can a creature like you claim understanding? You are more ignorant than the most foolish child – and more dangerous.*"

"I don't want to hurt you, Senzai-san," Kazue said through clenched teeth. "But I understand this much: that the willow survives where the oak tree falls."

She stopped pulling away from the tangling hair and instead gave in, driving her fist forward – with all the power of the storm-serpent tattoo backing it.

A thunderclap broke the air. The kobukaiba shrieked as she flew backward, through the wall of the hut, into the moonlight beyond. The hair trapping Kazue went limp as it tore free from its mistress. She leaped into the new gap and saw Senzai rising at the edge of the trees, and offered up a brief prayer of thanks to the kami and the Fortunes. That blow would have shattered an ordinary woman, but yōkai were more resilient.

Because she didn't want to kill Senzai. The woman's spiritual power was very real; if it weren't, she never would have transformed into a kobukaiba. Come sunrise, she would be as patient and hospitable as before, with no memory of what she had done in the night.

But dawn was hours away. How could Kazue survive that long?

She ran up the slope, away from Senzai, wishing briefly that she had practiced the spiritual technique that would allow her to leap up the mountain in soaring bounds. If she could lose her attacker in the woods, then she might return by daylight and try to find a way to restore Senzai to humanity. Unfortunately, the scream that split the air behind her said it wouldn't be that easy.

Kazue ran harder than she ever had in her life, heedless of

the danger ahead, because the danger behind was worse. The shadows around her swam into sharper detail, as if she had borrowed the vision of a cat; once she had known how to invoke such blessings, and now the memory came back to her. It let her plant her feet with more surety, keeping just ahead of the kobukaiba, for whom the darkness was her natural home.

But it wasn't enough. Kazue would tire; the yōkai would not. She used every trick she could think of, every unexpected swerve into a narrow gully and leap down a sharp but survivable drop, rolling as she hit and coming to her feet nicked in half a dozen places by the stones that had raked her. Behind her, the kobukaiba howled at the scent of blood, condemning it as impure, Kazue herself as a source of defilement.

She found herself trapped on a narrow ridge, the trees to her left too thickly placed to let her move among them with speed, the ground to her right a lethal cliff. Kazue ran up and up and up, knowing it offered no kind of escape, but bereft of other options.

And then she came to the top, and realized she had no options at all.

The ground there leveled out, but the safety it offered was an illusion. This was the bald-topped peak above Senzai's hut, and the ridge she'd taken to its summit was the only traversable path. Unless she could dredge out of her past life memories the knowledge of how to fly, she had run herself into a corner from which there was no escape.

If she had ever known how to do that, she didn't retrieve it before the kobukaiba appeared.

Up here, the mountain winds whipped Senzai's hair into a snarled net, fanning out to either side of her like wings. Her face was gaunt, cheeks sunken like those of an ascetic who had fasted for a year. Even her clothing had transformed, becoming looser and more tattered. The unhealthy light of her eyes shone brighter than the moon, and she extended her claws as if preparing to tear Kazue's soul from her body.

This is what I would become.

The realization chilled her to the bone. If Kazue somehow escaped and remained in the mountains, hiding herself away as she had considered, then eventually she would meet the same fate as Senzai. Her spiritual power would grow and turn inward, warping into the malevolence of a kobukaiba, seeking to destroy anything that threatened the balance of the world... which meant any human life that came within her reach.

But what was the alternative? To return to the ise zumi and use a power she dreaded, shattering people's spirits in blind obedience to Heaven's will? Heidoku's screams echoed in her memory, weaving through the kobukaiba's snarls like veins of blood.

Or this, right here. To stand her ground and let Senzai kill her, and hope she could solve this riddle in her next life.

I'm not ready to die. That wasn't fear talking; it was determination. Whatever Tengoku intended for her, she wanted to do it in this life. And that meant she had to survive this moment.

She *could* kill the hag. A yōkai like this was dangerous, but not against a tattooed monk – especially not one with the power of the storm in her hands. Unleashing that, though, would mean annihilating the great promise of Senzai's wisdom.

Her only other weapon was the knot.

The kobukaiba laughed, a low, skeletal sound. *"You will tear yourself apart. You cannot wield what you bear without destroying yourself – and you know it."*

It was true. But Kazue feared destroying herself less than she feared destroying Senzai.

Unless…

Unless Tengoku intended me to use it, not against people like Heidoku, but against creatures like this.

What would enlightened madness do to a yōkai?

Kazue didn't know. But she had spent lifetime after lifetime in the High House of Light, all to learn one fundamental lesson: how to recognize the correct moment in which to unleash her power.

She set her feet against the peak of the mountain, formed her hands into an interlocking mudra, and as the kobukaiba swept toward her, invoked her tattoo.

CHAPTER SEVENTEEN

The world went away.

There was no mountain, no wind, no moon, no stone. No malevolent hag seeking to destroy her.

Only understanding.

She saw without seeing. A cup was before her, plain glazed clay, all the more beautiful for its simplicity – but it was cracked.

She knew those cracks well. The same ones marred her own spirit: power, and the fear of misusing it. Senzai's insight, with her from childhood, was more than simply observation; it was the legacy of previous incarnations, past merit manifesting as ability in the present.

But people did not welcome insight, whatever they claimed. They feared it, resented it, drove it away. And so Senzai had withdrawn, not out of selfishness, but out of generosity, because she had not wished to hurt anyone.

Her caution had only made things worse. She was still human... but if she continued as she was, she would transform irredeemably into a kobukaiba, and be lost forever.

The cracks were there, in Kazue's grasp. Without hands, she

held the cup, and knew she could widen its flaws. Drive them fully open, breaking the clay. Just as she had done to Heidoku.

Just as she had done to herself, once upon a time.

The interlacing knot of her tattoo wasn't a reward for past merit, the way Mitsu thought. No, Tengoku had given her the power to shatter minds because her own had once been shattered: because in a previous life she had spent so much time in meditation, seeking the truth of existence, that she'd fallen to enlightened madness. She knew its beauty and its horror alike – the purity of understanding the world, and the agony of collapsing beneath that unbearable weight.

But a broken cup could be repaired.

There was a hut for the tea ceremony at the High House of Light. Kazue had once assisted a senior monk who received a guest from the Crane Clan, and he had used an ancient set of cups mended by the technique of *kintsugi*: fusing the pieces together with a lacquer into which the artisan had blended gold dust. Kintsugi did not try to hide the damage; instead, it transformed those wounds into a new kind of beauty, golden lines threading through the surface of the clay.

Yes, she could break minds. The difference lay in the material she worked with. Heidoku had not been ready for the insight she gave, and so it destroyed him.

But Senzai was different.

Kazue spoke without a voice, without words.

"The last and the first – are they not the same?"

This was the truth.

Her power was not to destroy, but to enlighten.

Kenshō: seeing the true essence. A glimpse only, a fleeting moment of understanding, the self dropping away to reveal the fundamental nature of things. It required breaking, because a thing without cracks was closed to revelations; that was the purpose of a kōan – to break the usual patterns of thought, opening the mind to new comprehension. And if that mind was ready, then afterward it would be made whole, new gold shining through.

Senzai's mind was ready.

And so was Kazue's.

CHAPTER EIGHTEEN

The wind still whipped across the mountaintop as fiercely as ever, but the crackling energy of the air was gone.

Senzai stood just an arm's length away from Kazue. Her hair floated and tangled in the breeze but had returned to its normal length. Her clothing was the sturdy, practical garb Kazue had first seen. And her eyes no longer glowed.

She caught Kazue before she could fall – which might have saved Kazue's life, given the precipitous drop that surrounded her on three sides.

They sank to the ground together. Kazue wondered, with distant, giddy delirium, whether further mastery of the knot tattoo would allow her to use it without this kind of exhaustion afterward. She felt a hundred times more drained than she had after Heidoku, and wasn't sure how much of that was because she had shown Senzai a glimpse of the true essence, how much was because she had glimpsed that true essence herself, and how much was because she'd fought a yōkai and run up a mountain before opening herself to the universe.

She doubted she would have many opportunities to find out. Now that she truly understood the function of her tattoo, she knew that she could use it for its intended purpose – but only with great caution. Not everyone was susceptible to such an epiphany, and of those who were, not all would survive it. Minds like Senzai's were rare. Anyone who was unprepared to receive that moment of kenshō would almost certainly meet Heidoku's fate.

But even if they did… they weren't gone forever. In the records of the High House of Light she would find the name Togashi Chiaki: the woman she had been in her previous incarnation. Her pursuit of spiritual insight then had led her into enlightened madness, and she spent the last twenty years of her life imprisoned for the safety of both others and herself.

The last twenty years of her life. But not the lives that followed.

"Thank you," Senzai whispered. She released Kazue and crawled backward a small distance, until she could bow to the ground as Kazue had done, earlier that day. "Without you, I would still be lost."

"Please, don't," Kazue said weakly. Her tongue, which had been so eloquent when guided by the tattoo, now felt as clumsy as an arm gone numb. "Without you, *I* would still be lost. Everything you said when you were – before – was true. I let my fear overwhelm me, and was unworthy of this gift. If I had not met you, if you had not been as wise as you are, I might have met the same fate." She managed to command her body well enough to fold herself into a bow of her own.

They both remained there, heads to the ground, until Senzai laughed. "We could stay here all night, fighting to see which of us can be more humble and grateful. But I'm not a monk, and I'm not immune to the cold. Should we go back?"

Kazue groaned as she climbed to her feet. "I *am* a monk, and I would still like to get out of this wind."

She wouldn't have made it down the ridge without Senzai's help. They negotiated it one careful step at a time, because the footing wasn't really wide enough for two women side by side, but if Kazue tried to stand on her own, she had a bad feeling she would pitch headfirst either into the trees or over the ~cliff.

Things became easier once they reached flatter ground. As Senzai's hut came within view, though, Kazue groaned again. "I am so sorry."

In their absence, the building's structural integrity had given way. The roof sagged drunkenly into the gap where she had punched the kobukaiba through the wall. It still stood – more or less – but what shelter it used to offer was significantly reduced, with the wind sweeping through the hole and out the official doorway.

"It was here long before me," Senzai said. "I don't know what hermit built it, but I think it has almost finished serving its purpose."

She led Kazue to the firepit and then lowered her to the ground, unlooping the arm that had supported her on the walk back. "Wait here a moment."

"Yes, sensei," Kazue said reflexively. Senzai paused, but then continued onward to the hut, not saying anything.

When Kazue had asked to be her student, just a few hours before, Senzai had refused. That was the kobukaiba talking,

though – or rather, the isolating impulse that had cut her off
from society and transformed her into a kobukaiba. Now...

Now Kazue had no idea. Her tattoo hadn't granted her any
knowledge of what Senzai had learned in that moment of
kenshō; she only knew that it had ended the transformation,
returning Senzai to her human self. Which meant the hermit
must have decided to end her isolation – but whether that
meant accepting students out here in the wilderness or
traveling once more to settled lands, she couldn't guess. Even
trying made her brain feel tired.

So, she watched, with the fixed stare of someone trying
not to collapse, as Senzai poked around in the hut, testing its
stability. "I think it will stay up for the rest of the night," Senzai
said, emerging once more.

"*Think*," Kazue said with a weary laugh.

Senzai bowed in humorous acknowledgment. "It is the best
guess this humble one has to offer."

Kazue levered herself up again. "I honestly don't care if it falls
on my head. I'm not certain I'll wake up even if it does."

She stopped at the doorway, though, one hand over the
gouges the kobukaiba's claws had carved through the wood.
"You're taking the futon, though. No arguments."

Senzai bowed again. "As you say."

Kazue slept like lead, except for one dream.

In it she saw Senzai in the doorway again, where she'd stood
in her yōkai form when she came hunting Kazue. This time,
though, the moonlight haloed a figure that was serene and at
peace, rather than wild with power twisted in on itself.

"I wish I could offer you a better blessing," this Senzai

murmured. "But your fate is not a simple one, and so I can say only this: that although your power will sometimes bring harm, you must not fear it. The Empire is fast approaching a time when both madness and enlightenment will be needed."

In the dream, those words made sense. But when Kazue awoke, both sense and Senzai were gone.

CHAPTER NINETEEN

Nothing was missing. The cooking pot, the single bowl, Senzai's small collection of tools – they were all still where they'd been the day before. But Kazue felt the difference: the hut was not merely empty now, but uninhabited.

If it weren't for the footprints in the dirt around the fire, she might almost have wondered if the entire thing had been a lengthy dream, or an illusion placed on her by some trickster spirit. But she could see the marks of Senzai's long occupation, and besides, the memory of the previous night was too vivid to be denied. The hermit really had transformed; Kazue really had fought and fled and redeemed her. She had the sore muscles and the sense of inner peace to prove it.

Possibly she was wrong about Senzai having left for good. But she couldn't wait around to find out. However beneficial or even necessary her time in the wilderness had been, Kazue was a samurai, and she had a duty to her lord. A duty she had cast aside for too long already.

She did do one thing before she left, though.

There was a flat-sided stone near the stream where Senzai had

knelt to get water. Kazue was just barely strong enough to dig it
out from the bank and carry it to the hut, dropping it with the
heavy end downward in front of the doorway. Then she took her
knife and, heedless of dulling it, scratched a series of characters
into the surface:

I could not see how
to untie a knot without
beginning or end–
when I asked the mountain wind,
its answer was simply, om.

She bowed before the stone and clapped her hands, offering
up a prayer for Senzai, wherever her path took her.
Then she stood and began her own journey home.

Mitsu didn't run. A senior monk should never be seen running
for any reason other than physical training or battle. Certainly
not in response to a message from one of the novices at the
foot of the peak, saying that someone was on their way up the
thousand steps.

Because he didn't run, he reached the top of the stairs only a
little before Kazue did. But she had her chin down, looking at
the weathered stone in front of her rather than the monastery
above, and so he had a brief opportunity to study her before she
looked up and noticed his presence.

She was thin and dirty, her arms mottled with bruises and
scrapes. Her hair had begun to grow out – but only begun; it was
clear she had continued to shave her scalp during her absence.
That sight gave Mitsu hope.

As did the sight of Kazue at all. Enough time had passed that he'd begun to fear she would never return.

She seemed utterly unsurprised to find him waiting for her. Before Mitsu could say anything, she knelt before him and bowed low. "Senpai. I have come to submit myself for judgment." All the breath went out of Mitsu. Of course she understood. She'd been a member of the order for too long not to realize that there would be consequences for running away.

And she had come back to face them.

So he didn't say anything to welcome her. He didn't tell her how relieved he was to see her or ask what had happened while she was gone. He only said, "Follow me."

Kazue rose without another word. He led her to one of the cells used for discipline, where erring monks meditated on their failures. There were no locks: being at the High House of Light was simultaneously inevitable and a choice. Now that she had returned, Kazue's own sense of duty would keep her in that cell.

"I will bring you paper and a brush," he said as she knelt on the stone floor. "You will write out your report and confession, and I will take them to Hassuno-sama."

"Thank you, senpai," Kazue said softly.

Mitsu turned to go. But he couldn't walk away without asking. "Kazue-san – did you find what you needed?"

The barest hint of a smile touched her face. "Yes. I did."

Breathing in a sigh of gratitude, he went to fetch writing materials.

Hassuno-sama sat with Kazue's report spread on the table in front of her. "Mitsu-san," she said. "What do you think of Kazue-san's situation?"

She had allowed him to read the account. It covered everything from Fuchi Mura to Kazue's return to the High House of Light, and as near as Mitsu could tell, she hadn't spared herself in the account. There was no attempt to apologize or justify, only the simple reporting of facts.

Mitsu chose his words carefully. "I think the Heavens guided her. This Senzai, whoever she is, seems to have been precisely the teacher Kazue-san needed."

"Do you think that is how we should view this?" Hassuno-sama tapped the rice paper. "As Kazue-san following her own path?"

His jaw tensed. That was its effect, yes – and he wanted to lean on the effect, using it to spare Kazue the consequences of her actions.

But they had to consider motivation as well as effect. And Mitsu would be failing her as well as the order if he tried to leave that out.

"No, iemoto-sama," he said. "Our teachings encourage us to follow whatever path is necessary... but I do not believe that was what Kazue intended when she left Fuchi Mura. She reacted out of fear, giving in to one of the three sins. Her fear and her regret over what happened to Heidoku caused her to abandon her duty. The fact that doing so led her to where she needed to be does not erase the fact that she surrendered to weakness."

Hassuno-sama regarded him with a steady eye. "There was a time, Mitsu-san, when you would not have admitted that so readily."

He thought of Heidoku, and the struggle he'd felt over the man's crime. "I feel compassion for her, Hassuno-sama. But compassion must be balanced with other concerns, or in the long run, it will create more problems than it solves."

"Indeed." She folded Kazue's report and set it aside. "Then you know what must be done, Mitsu-san. Tell her to come to the Garden of the Elements at dawn tomorrow."

Kazue bathed carefully, dressed herself in a plain white robe, and prayed.

Then she left her cell and, with the measured strides of meditation, went to the Garden of the Elements.

It was one of the masterpieces of the High House of Light. She had not seen it in this lifetime, but it had scarcely changed. The boulders were a little more overgrown with moss, the flowering plants a little taller, the lanterns a little more weathered. The gravel in the dry garden had been raked into a different pattern. A stream wound through it all, crossing beneath her feet three times on her way to the heart of the garden; the arbors over the bridges were, like the gates she had passed through months before, an opportunity to cleanse herself of the three sins.

At the heart of the garden stood a five-tiered stupa. Like the design of the garden itself, it represented the Five Elements: a cube for Earth, a sphere for Water, a pyramid for Fire, a hemisphere for Air, and the lotus flower of the Void on top.

Mitsu and Hassuno-sama waited for her there, unmoving as Kazue knelt before them. He had instructed her the night before, but Kazue had scarcely needed it; she'd been in his position once, lifetimes ago, overseeing someone else's atonement.

She was a monk, but she was also a samurai. She had fled her duty. A bushi or a courtier or even a shugenja might be made rōnin for a failure like hers, but the ise zumi were never put out of the High House of Light like that.

There was another punishment, though. One that expunged a person's shame, so that they would not carry it with them into the next life.

"Kazue-san." Hassuno-sama's voice was serene and cool. "Do you acknowledge your failure?"

"I do, iemoto-sama."

"What explanation do you offer for it?"

"None, iemoto-sama."

"Why do you come here this morning?"

She touched her forehead to the moss. "To ask permission to expunge my shame with suicide."

Hassuno-sama said, "Granted."

Mitsu stepped forward, bearing a small jade cup in his hands. Kneeling with a grace and lightness unexpected in a man his size, he offered it to Kazue with a bow.

The liquid within smelled faintly smoky, as if it carried the scent of a funeral pyre. In the lessons the novices learned it was called *kiyomizu*: purifying water.

"Drink," Hassuno-sama said. "Die, and be reborn, and return to us cleansed of this shame."

Kazue drank.

Ise zumi were samurai. But when they died, their karma returned them to the High House of Light, through one incarnation after another. Seppuku, the honorable suicide of a bushi or a courtier, would only force the order to go through the long, tedious work of training that soul again.

They had other methods of dealing with such matters.

She saw her life as if from outside: not a sequence of events, as it had been during her gempuku, but a shape laid before her all at once. For an instant she could feel how every piece of it fit together: her flight from Fuchi Mura and her childhood as the daughter of a rōnin mother, the friendships she'd formed in the High House of Light and the animalistic purity of her solitude in the mountains, Senzai and Mitsu, her tattoo and the perilous enlightenment it offered.

Then it faded. One by one the pieces dropped away, dissolving into darkness, until there was nothing left but the Void.

The Void – and herself.

She awoke on the thick moss at the heart of the Garden of the Elements. Golden light flooded the space, the rich warmth of the hour before sunset. The symbolic death bestowed by the purifying water had lasted only a sun's span.

Mitsu helped her sit up. Her body had gone weak again: not as badly as after her gempuku, but enough to make movement uncertain. Whatever was in the kiyomizu, it had a significant effect, not easily shaken off.

"Welcome back," he said, smiling for the first time since her arrival at the top of the stairs.

She tried to respond and found herself coughing instead. He offered her another cup – ordinary water this time – and when she had finished drinking it, another voice came from behind her. "Mitsu-san. We are not yet finished."

Mitsu nodded in acknowledgment, but slipped her a sidelong wink as he did so. Then he rose and came back a moment later with a small writing desk.

Hassuno-sama might not have moved that entire day. She stood patiently until Mitsu had arranged the paper, ink, and brush. Then she said, "The one who failed has died. You are reborn among us, and so it is time to choose your new name."

Unlike a few months before, this time she had not chosen her name ahead of time. She sat motionless with the brush in her hand for a long moment, her mind an unhelpful blank. She could not be who she had been before – and yet who should she be, if not that woman?

The paradox resonated in her bones. Like being an ise zumi: fated to return to the High House of Light, free in every lifetime to choose that path.

She wet the brush and wrote.

Mitsu's eyebrows rose when he came to take the paper from her. But he said nothing, only bore it to Hassuno-sama, who frowned at the characters written there.

Togashi Kazue.

But instead of "one eternity," this time she had written it with different characters. Now it meant "blessed destiny."

"An unusual choice," Hassuno-sama said at last. "But not, I think, an inappropriate one." She returned the paper to Mitsu. "Welcome to the order, Togashi Kazue-san. May you serve the Dragon Clan well."

EPILOGUE

This time Mitsu made no requests. He did not even receive a summons. He was simply walking along one of the porticos that looked out over the deep valleys beyond the monastery when he realized he was not alone.

And in the High House of Light, only one man wore full armor.

Mitsu knelt immediately, pressing his forehead to the boards. With anyone else, it might have been a chance encounter. But this was Togashi Yokuni, the clan champion. He did not idly wander the monastery. If he crossed someone's path, it was because he intended to.

The voice came from above, deep and unmuffled by the mempō that covered his face. "You have changed."

One did not argue with one's clan champion. "Yes, Togashi-ue."

"Though still impulsive, you have gained in restraint. Your actions regarding Kazue-san have shown more wisdom than before."

"I have done my best to serve, Togashi-ue."

His only answer was the rush of the wind. Minutes passed, and Mitsu strained his ears for the sound of footfalls, wondering if the clan champion had moved on – surely if anyone could move quietly in such armor, it would be him. But Mitsu didn't risk a glance upward. He would kneel here until nightfall if he had to.

He didn't have to.

"Yes. You will serve very well." The tone was thoughtful, detached. "I name you, Togashi Mitsu, as my heir."

Mitsu's whole body jerked. One instinct tried to yank him upright; the other, fortunately stronger, kept him pinned to the boards. "Togashi-ue–"

He'd guessed that he was being measured for some new duty. It had crossed his mind that he might become Hassuno-sama's heir, the inheritor of the order's traditions. That prospect had been difficult enough: not to wander anymore. Not to see the Empire in all its glory and disgrace, offering his aid to those who lacked the power to help themselves. Spending the rest of his life here at the High House of Light.

But this… this was worse. Isolating himself even from his fellow monks. Locking his body into that armor.

For one wild instant, he wished he had made a misstep with Kazue. Shown himself to be too reckless and foolish to ever bear more responsibility than he held right now.

Only for an instant. Because he had done what his conscience and sense of honor demanded… and they would not let him flee from this duty.

The clan champion knew that. He would not have chosen Mitsu were it otherwise.

Mitsu forced himself to subside, repairing his damaged bow. "I am not worthy, Togashi-ue, but I humbly accept."

Words. But given enough time, he could make them true.

He would have to.

"Rise, Mitsu," Togashi Yokuni said. "You have tasks to perform still in the outside world. The first is to find the hermit Kazue-san encountered – the woman called Senzai."

Mitsu climbed to his feet, mystified. Kazue had praised Senzai's wisdom... but surely there were many wise people in the world. "My lord?"

"Yes," he whispered, gazing out across the mountains, into distances Mitsu could only guess at. "Find her – for the sake of the Empire."

TALES OF ROKUGAN

PINE AND CHERRY BLOSSOM

BY MARIE BRENNAN

The tracks were easy to follow. Although the southern reaches of the Empire rarely saw snow, it could happen, and this winter was a hard one. Mitsu didn't need his wolf tattoo sharpening his senses to follow the footprints, but he kept it alive anyway. He'd spent four years searching, from one end of the Empire to the other, and he could not stand for losing his quarry this close to the end.

As he drew close, he heard a quiet humming. Through the snow-dusted pines, he saw the mounded shape of a heavy straw cloak and, above it, the head of a woman with her hair pinned in a loose knot. She was using a small hatchet to cut the bark from a pine tree, adding the strips to a bundle at her feet.

Mitsu paused, breathing deeply to steady his pulse. The hatchet wasn't a threat, and Kazue-san had said the spiritual danger was long past. *I might as well start off by being polite.*

He released the energy of his tattoo and stepped out from behind a tree. "What are you doing?"

He'd taken care to ask while she was tidying her pile of strips, so she wouldn't cut herself with the hatchet. But the woman didn't jump in surprise. She only brushed her hair from her face and bowed low. "The inner bark of the tree can be eaten, Togashi-sama. And I'm not aware of any law that prohibits the gathering of bark in this wood."

Given what he'd seen in the nearby village, he didn't have to ask why she was collecting food. And he was easily recognizable as an *ise zumi* – especially for a woman who had met one before. Her face was as described, an oval slightly too long for traditional beauty, with straight, heavy brows, and she was foraging in the wilderness to help others just as he had suspected.

As was what she said next. "Before you do whatever it is you came to do, Togashi-sama, will you permit me to deliver this bark to the village? Mothers there have been starving themselves to give their children more to eat, and it still isn't enough."

It seemed her insight hadn't dulled at all. "Of course, Senzai. After that though, you'll have to come with me to the High House of Light."

Across the Spine of the World, in *wintertime*. But Mitsu had searched a thousand remote forests, flyspeck villages, and city slums these past four years, facing everything from bandits to disease to the questions of interfering officials. All to find this woman. One peasant among millions: the strange hermit who his fellow monk Kazue had met in the remote depths of the northern mountains, whom his clan champion had ordered him to find and bring back, for the sake of the Empire.

She was before him at last. He didn't dare wait for a better season.

Senzai retied her bundle with a rough piece of twine and lifted it to her back. "And if I don't want to go?"

Mitsu said, "I'm afraid I can't allow you that choice."

It didn't occur to Mitsu until later how absurd that exchange had been. Senzai was a peasant, and he was the heir to the Dragon Clan Champion; choice never entered into it. But he hadn't been thinking about rank at all – only the chance to fulfill his lord's order at last.

"Are you going to bind me?" Senzai asked as they began their journey north, trailing Mitsu's packhorse behind them.

"Are you going to run away?"

"I have no plan to do so."

It wasn't a promise not to. Merely an indication that she was willing to go along with him for now. "Not unless you give me reason," Mitsu said, and hoped she would heed the warning. He doubted she could get far before he caught her, but it would be a long, tedious journey north if he had to spend half of it rounding her up.

Senzai didn't shy away from him, or cast her gaze around like she was looking for an opportunity to flee though. She led Mitsu's packhorse quietly for several hours, walking steadily and without complaint, keeping her head down when a Scorpion patrol stopped and asked to see Mitsu's travel papers. When the short winter day faded into grey twilight, they halted at a temple on the bank of a frozen stream, where the monks gave them hospitality for the night.

She was silent through the meal, and he wondered if she was planning an escape in the night. It would be smarter than running away while he was awake. *I wish I had a tattoo that would let me go without sleep,* he thought ruefully. The best he could do was to place himself between her and the door and leave the wolf tattoo active while he slept. It made for a restless night, Mitsu rousing at every small sound, but that was a small price to pay.

Fear was one of the three sins. His mind looked everywhere for something to go wrong, now that he finally had Senzai in hand. Regret was also a sin though, and Mitsu knew which one he preferred.

In the morning, Senzai was still there – and more talkative than before. "You're Togashi Mitsu-sama," she said after they'd walked for a little while. "For an ise zumi, you're unusually famous. I've met a surprising number of people in my travels who have heard of you."

"And you've wandered surprisingly far, for a peasant with no travel papers." He'd chased rumors of her through the lands of every single Great Clan.

Senzai shrugged. "It isn't as difficult as people think. There are fewer threats in the wilderness than in civilization, for those who know their way."

From what Kazue had said, she was more than capable of surviving in the wild. "But most peasants wouldn't risk it without good reason. Why have you been moving around so much? Are you searching for something?"

"I could ask you the same, Togashi-sama."

"You're dodging my question."

She smiled and brushed a strand of hair from her face. "Yes and no. 'Study what the pine and cherry blossom can teach' – isn't that what it says in the Tao?"

"You're seeking Enlightenment then."

"I'd say understanding instead. Humanity may not be the only keeper of Enlightenment, but pine trees and cherry blossoms can't tell me much about people. To understand those, I need to speak with people across the Empire – from the humblest servant to the heir of the Dragon Clan. I imagine you understand that very well."

Was she referring just to his habit of making friends with peasants, or something more?

Mitsu had wondered at first why Togashi Yokuni had chosen him as heir, when he was the most restless man in the order. By contrast, the Champion of the Dragon Clan was an isolated figure, sitting apart from the Empire in the High House of Light.

During Mitsu's search for Senzai though, he'd come to understand. Isolation brought clarity... but it could also bring ignorance and coldness of heart. When the time came for him to don the armor and mask of the champion, Mitsu would need the wisdom he'd gained in his travels, his awareness of the breadth of the Empire, and his compassion for those his decisions would affect.

Mitsu nodded thoughtfully – then scowled. She was more philosophical in her approach than most courtiers, but Senzai was as skilled at deflecting his thoughts as the most silver-tongued Doji or Bayushi. "What happened when Kazue-san used her tattoo on you? What enlightenment did it bring?"

"'The Tao we speak of is the True Tao, yet it is not the Eternal Tao we speak'," Senzai quoted. Then she laughed quietly. "Forgive me, Togashi-sama. I'm not trying to be unhelpful. But I can't reduce what happened to words, except to say: 'The last and the first – are they not the same?'"

He knew that phrase well, from Kazue's report on her encounter with Senzai. It was the koan her tattoo had guided her to speak. But as Senzai had reminded him, the words were inadequate, and always would be; the truth that lay behind them could not be spoken. Whatever moment of enlightenment Senzai had experienced when she heard them, it wasn't something she could communicate to Mitsu.

The clan champion wouldn't have sent me to collect her without a reason. Spiritual wisdom alone was not enough; there were many wise people at the High House of Light. Something about this woman was different.

"If I may ask," Senzai said, "how is Togashi Kazue-sama?"

Another deflection. They had a long way to travel, though, and patience might net him more than pushing. Balancing inaction with action: it was a core lesson of the order. "She's well. She often expresses her gratitude for the wisdom and guidance you shared with her."

Senzai shook her head. "I owe her far more than she owes me. I had lost my way, and without her, I might not have found it again."

And what is your way? he wondered. During her hermitage she'd nearly transformed into a *yōkai*, a spirit creature; she could just mean her humanity. But he didn't believe that was all.

Maybe all would become clear once he got her to the High House of Light. The *li* rolled past, day after day, the ground beneath his feet climbing into the Spine of the World; soon they would pass through to Lion Clan lands, and the teeth of winter. Senzai conversed with Mitsu readily enough, but she might as well have been a koan herself, an impenetrable puzzle, waiting for him to experience a flash of understanding.

Instead he woke one night to discover Senzai was gone.

He leapt to his feet, the energy of the wolf flaring through his senses and his hands clenching into fists. His first thought was, *she lured me into trusting her.* She'd bided her time until they were away from civilization and watching eyes, then made her escape.

Then reason took hold once more. Senzai had survived winters in the Great Wall of the North; she wasn't a fool. They'd sheltered for the night beneath a stony ledge, driven there by a snowstorm that had prevented them from reaching the way station up ahead. That storm had laid down a fresh mat of snow – one that showed her tracks with perfect clarity, even to someone without Mitsu's advantages. She'd made no attempt to hide them.

He sniffed the ground, breathing in her scent. Fairly fresh; she'd been gone less than half an hour. He could catch her easily.

The trail led toward the road, and up into the mountains rather than back down toward the plain. Before Mitsu had gone very far, he heard her voice, muffled by the snow, speaking in a low tone. Wariness sparked again. *Meeting with someone?*

Rather than approach directly, he circled around and found a boulder to scale, allowing him to look down on Senzai without being seen.

The snow lay in a shallow, gleaming bowl between the rocks,

just out of sight of the road. Senzai knelt, heedless of the cold, at the side of a man whose white-crusted clothing said he'd been there since before sunset. The man's arms and legs sprawled at unnatural angles: broken, and badly.

Whatever was going on, it wasn't some clandestine conspiracy. Mitsu slid down the boulder's other side. Senzai's voice continued, soft and soothing, offering comfort to the dying man. But her head came up, and her gaze pinned Mitsu before he could even open his mouth, carrying a wordless command: *Not now.*

She was a peasant, and she'd run away, against his explicit order. But Mitsu knelt and waited.

It didn't take long. The winter air soon finished what those injuries had begun.

When Senzai laid the man's head down at last, Mitsu said, "I recognize him. He was one of the servants following the patrol we saw this afternoon."

Senzai's voice remained low, as if not wanting to disturb the body's peace. "He had angered one of the samurai, very badly. A cruel man. I knew he would take revenge."

"You had a vision?"

She met his eyes. "Not like you're thinking. Not foresight or prophecy. But I understand people." Her gaze fell again to the dead man. "Unfortunately."

Heedless of any defilement from touching the corpse, Senzai arranged the man's broken limbs more decorously, then laid her straw cloak over him and stood. Mitsu brushed the snow off his own knees and said, "It was generous of you to give him comfort. But I have to insist that you not vanish like that again. I thought you'd run away."

"I'm sorry, Togashi-sama."

He thought she was apologizing for having crept out without warning him. But when he began to walk back to their shelter, Senzai didn't move. Her words hung in the cold, still air, and he realized she meant something else entirely.

His voice tightened. "I told you – I can't allow you that choice."

"And I can't go with you," she said quietly. "There are things about the Empire that I don't understand, and I need to. I won't learn them if I go with you to the High House of Light."

"You don't know that."

She gestured at him. "I see it in you. In every detail of how you behave. You want to keep me safe there, and to question me until you understand. But you'll understand nothing that way, and you'll stop me from doing what I must."

"Then help me understand now," Mitsu said through his teeth. "What *must* you do?"

"I don't know."

Lifetimes of monastic training were all that kept him from punching the nearest boulder in frustration. "Senzai–"

"I know the truth of myself, Togashi-sama. That is what I saw, when your sister in the order used her tattoo. But knowing myself is only part of it." Senzai looked down at the dead man, her hair falling to conceal her expression. "I don't understand the Celestial Order. No – I don't understand the *Empire*. Why things are the way they are. I need to answer that question before I can do…"

She trailed off, and Mitsu waited, hands tense. But she only shook her head, breath pluming in a quiet sigh. "Whatever it is I'm meant to do."

"We can help you," Mitsu said. "At the High House of Light. And I have orders from my clan champion—"

This time it was his turn not to finish the sentence. *My orders.*

Senzai stepped closer. "You have realized something, Togashi-sama."

Find her – for the sake of the Empire. That was what Togashi-ue had said, the day he named Mitsu his heir and sent him in search of Senzai. That – and nothing more.

After years of searching, he'd almost forgotten that his orders ended there. His assumptions had filled in the rest of it – the idea that Togashi-ue meant for Mitsu not only to find Senzai, but to bring her back to the High House of Light.

Senzai said, "The foresight of the Dragon Clan Champion is a powerful thing, but not a perfect one. Some day that foresight will flow through you, Togashi-sama – and you will have to make decisions about how best to use it."

Decisions that began now, here at the feet of the Spine of the World.

The answer of a samurai should be to take Senzai with him anyway. It was possible Togashi-ue had indeed meant for Mitsu to bring her there, and if not, then it would be easy enough to let her go afterward. The wishes of a peasant woman didn't outweigh the risk of disappointing his lord.

But Kazue had spoken highly of Senzai's insight. And Mitsu was not only a samurai, but a Dragon; he was not only a Dragon, but an ise zumi. He understood the need to follow one's path.

Mitsu bowed slightly. "Senzai-san. I was instructed to find you, and I believe there was a reason for that. Perhaps you can enlighten me as to that reason. Is there anything I can do to assist you?"

The faintest hint of a smile warmed her face. "You've traveled the Empire, Togashi-sama, far more than I have. Tell me: who is the most wretched person you know of, and who is the most fortunate?"

He gave it careful consideration, even as night deepened around them and the wind sent the fresh snow dancing through the air. *I don't understand the Celestial Order*, she'd said. *I don't understand the Empire. Why things are the way they are.* The most fortunate should be the Emperor, or someone else whose karma had raised them to high status in this lifetime. But that wasn't the case.

"The most wretched," he said, "is a minor courtier in Hakayu Mura. Doji Omocha. She was born to a good family, but lacks all talent and knows it. Her best efforts have brought her nothing but disgrace, for her and her family. She can't even bring herself to ask permission to expunge her shame through seppuku, because she lives in dread of her next incarnation, and the punishments that await her failures. There is no moment of joy in her life, and there has not been for decades – only fear and despair, because she cannot live up to the expectations placed on her."

Senzai nodded. "And the most fortunate?"

"A heimin," Mitsu said. "I don't even know his name. He lives outside of Kōgan Mura, not far from here. Anyone would look at his life and see nothing but hardship and suffering… yet despite that, the man lives content. I asked him once why he was smiling, and he said that he was grateful every day for the miracles of sun and rain, the beauty of the kami, and the hope of the future. That would be admirable enough in any person, but to achieve such peace of mind in circumstances like his? That man is truly blessed."

All of Senzai's previous bows had been mere etiquette, a peasant acknowledging the samurai above her. This time it was sincere. "Thank you, Togashi-sama. Your words have enlightened me."

Not like Kazue's words had done. But he hoped it would be enough.

Mitsu shrugged out of his own straw cloak and offered it to her. "You'll need this. Winter isn't over yet."

She accepted it with gratitude. "May the Fortunes favor your path, Togashi-sama." "And yours, Senzai-san."

Then Mitsu headed for the road north and the High House of Light – alone.

HEART
OF THE
MOUNTAIN

BY KEITH RYAN KAPPEL

Long ago, a powerful mountain spirit looked to the sky and
longed to visit the Heavens. Rooted to the ground as she was,
she raised her mountain home high into the sky so she could
see the kingdom of the gods for herself. Her mountain grew
mighty, visible to even those dwelling above the clouds.

Lady Sun, angry with the spirit's defiant act, sent down her son, the Lord of Flame, to protect the secrets of the Heavens. He fought the mountain spirit, but as the Lord of Flame raised his fiery sword to strike the killing blow, the impulsive god stayed his hand. He was unable to kill the mountain spirit for her curiosity. Instead, the two went inside the mountain, and the Lord of Flame shared his stories of Heaven. The two soon fell in love and were married.

Now living in more of a volcanic crater than a mountain peak, the pair forges wondrous armaments of peerless craftsmanship for the gods from the molten slag. The fire in the mountain's heart has since never guttered or dimmed.

It was the fruits of this passion that had drawn Yoritomo, Captain of Captains, to the mountain's dark and secretive interior. This is where our story begins.

"Any time now, dearest wife!" Yoritomo's attention was focused on the fray around him. He evaded the black-sashed monks' flurries of kicks and drove his fist into the nearest one. Linmei, Lady of the Isles of Spice and Silk, studied a great black stone in the center of the chamber and smoldered instead of answering.

"The kami are restless," Kudaka the Stormweaver warned from beside him. Her lithe arms were as effective at brawling as they were at honoring the spirits. "Linmei's map has 'em scrambling like crabs on a carcass. Can't say I like it."

"Quit your worrying priest," Yoritomo couldn't keep the smile out of his voice as he felled the last monk with a face-crunching knee strike. They would tackle any problem that came their way. The tide comes and goes as it pleases, and just then what pleased Yoritomo most was the thought of taking a spark from the mountain's inner flame.

"Guiding star of my sky? Any luck?" Yoritomo turned to see his wife poring over the scroll. "Oh, I'll guide you somewhere, all right." Linmei grumbled. "Quiet, I'm thinking!"

For hours they'd followed her map, written in the language of the Isles spoken before the Fall of the Kami – the ancestral language of the kōmori. For hours the island's secrets had stymied her: a breakwater gate sealed to entry, ancient roads grown over, and many dead-end tunnels into the mountain. Then they had been set on by the island's guardians, and Linmei's ire had truly begun to boil. By the time they reached this chamber, the sweltering weather seemed pleasant by comparison.

At the center of the room lay a black boulder, wide as a riverboat and shiny as polished silver. Carved into its flat face were images of two large kami and a third smaller one. Surrounding them were two-dozen dials with unfamiliar symbols arranged without a modicum of sense.

Above, the ceiling was a clear quartz dome holding back a lake of boiling magma.

The sickly orange glow of magma lit stone tables, counters, and chests, sparsely

arranged over smooth marble floors. But the furnishings were unimportant: this stone was the only thing left that stood between Yoritomo and his prize.

"Does your map contain some sort of key to open it?" Yoritomo was glad for his wife's presence, for her gift for riddles and ciphers had gotten them this far already. At the heart of the mountain, fire and earth's private secrets lay hidden for only the most daring to discover.

"A key of sorts. It's a star map from our ancestors' farthest travels. We can't see these parts of the Heavens from the Islands of Spice and Silk, so I'm not familiar with the stars," Linmei explained, brushing aside Yoritomo's hand from the dials. "But I've traced the points on the map to represent the constellations on the stone, and it isn't working."

"Is that not the Celestial Pillar of Mweneta?" Kudaka offered as she looked at the constellations.

"Of course!" Linmei's eyes widened, then narrowed. Yoritomo had seen this look many times over the past few years. She would have the seal open soon. "Of course, south is at the top!"

Linmei flipped the map upside down and started busily tracing new constellations. "Fu-Mo-To! Fu-Mo-To! Fu-Mo-To!" a new group of monks emerged from the cavern behind them. One stepped forward, a mountain of a man who dwarfed even Yoritomo's prodigious size.

"You do not belong here," he bellowed. This was their champion!

Yoritomo grinned his most fearsome smile. Kudaka rolled up her green linen sleeves.

Linmei did not flinch from her tracings on the black stone. The monk lowered himself deep into a horse stance. Silence fell over the chamber.

Kudaka mouthed a prayer, then thrust her arms forward. A gale-force wind rushed past Yoritomo toward the monks, who shouted and scattered like gulls chased from a ship's deck.

Fumoto, however, was unmoved.

Yoritomo took two steps and slid toward the monk, letting the current of Kudaka's winds carry him. As he passed between the monk's legs, he struck a blow most would consider dishonorable – or at least impolite – and nimbly rolled back to his feet before delivering a kick to the back of the leg that drove the monk to his knees. Kudaka's winds abruptly ceased, and Yoritomo's arms encircled the monk's head and throat, squeezing with the power of a raging river.

Seconds later, the oversized monk was unconscious on the stone floor.

"I can't believe that worked," Yoritomo grinned. He turned to face the other monks, who quailed at the sight of his flawless martial prowess. Kudaka gestured up a gale, and the monks immediately took flight. The chamber was now empty, but like the pestering seabirds they were, the monks would soon grow bold and return to try again.

"It wouldn'ta worked quite so well on some of us," Kudaka chuffed.

"I am well aware of when there is a woman in my presence Kudaka," Yoritomo answered. "It's why I'm never caught flat-footed!"

"We know you can't resist a pretty face husband," Linmei rolled her eyes.

All brashness, Yoritomo responded. "No one will best me, wife, no matter how beautiful."

"Not the so-called Princess of Pirates?" Linmei's jibe had more bite than expected.

"That was business!" Yoritomo stammered, shock written across his face.

He stepped close to her until only the chart separated them. He gently brushed away some of the soot from her face, letting her unmatched beauty shine through. They locked eyes, and for a moment, shared a secret smile. Then she pulled away, resuming her work on the dials.

"It was just some liquor to celebrate an arrangement," Yoritomo continued. "A little boasting about the time we took that Saamrajya ship, then a quick jaunt to Kirtinaramto to prove that boast, then some more liquor that we stole, a shark hunt, and then a little celebratory liquor.

The rest after that is… hazy, but I know nothing happened between us."

The so-called Princess of Pirates was Damayanti of the Ivory Kingdoms, also known as Damayanti the Red. Some claim that she leads a fleet larger than Yoritomo's. But that depends on which ships you count, and they can hardly claim to rival the Mantis's courage!

"Yoritomo, the heart–"

"Yes, the heart can lead one astray, but if anything had happened, you would know of it." Yoritomo fixed her with his most sincere gaze. She rolled her eyes, as she was so accustomed to doing.

"You're a fool. Look!" Linmei grabbed his wide chin and turned his head toward the mandala. Where the representation of the earth kami stood, a cavity had opened in its rocky torso, revealing a lever. Yoritomo's eyes lit up.

Linmei reached her hand into the figure's chest and pulled the lever. The giant seal in the boulder's face spun and belched an angry blast of heat around its edges. It opened to reveal the jade of heavenly memory: the Heart of the Mountain.

It was beautiful – a flat disc of red jade nearly as large as an open scroll polished to translucency. With this treasure, the prowess, bravery, and honor of the Mantis Clan could no longer be ignored. The Mantis would be respected, not thought of as criminals and pirates, but as equals in the eyes of the Emperor. It would set right all the insults Yoritomo's ancestors had suffered, and they would no longer be forgotten as honorless exiles.

Yoritomo reached in and took the Heart into his hands. "Yoritomo, wait! Don't grab–"

But Kudaka's warning was too late! A sickening crunch drew all eyes to the quartz dome overhead, where a large crack was slowly beginning to spread. Linmei and Kudaka's eyes turned in unison to Yoritomo in aggravation, and even the Captain of Captains shuddered – but only a bit. Yoritomo stuffed the Heart into a satchel.

"We need to run, now," Linmei pointed down the tunnel. Yoritomo nodded and sprinted after her with Kudaka ever at his side. After a minute of racing through the cavern, they reached a fork in the tunnel.

Linmei stopped and scanned her map, which she thought she had remembered exactly.

Unfortunately, she had. "This tunnel isn't even on the map!"

"Fresh air, this way." Kudaka gestured to the right. A loud crash echoed through the tunnel, and a violent shudder passed under their feet, as if something large was passing beneath them. "Let's go!"

Behind them, an eerie orange glow brightened. After a few moments, thick black smoke filled the tunnel, and soon all three were coughing and wheezing. After several complicated twists and turns, they found an air shaft within reach.

The opening was small, but Linmei and Kudaka fit through easily enough. After no small amount of pulling, Yoritomo's broad-shouldered frame passed through as well. They sought refuge on a rocky outcropping above, which extended over the water of the bay where the *Bitter Wind* awaited them. Suddenly, an explosion of lava erupted out of the air shaft, carving a fiery path to the water.

Fresh, cool air had never tasted so sweet. Yoritomo wanted nothing more than to lie peacefully on the outcropping with these two women, their prize now in hand. They could overlook the narrow inlet that circled the western side of the mountain and drink clear water until their stomachs burst. Unfortunately, they had only minutes before the monks who had fled made their way around and caught up to them. Seaward along the inlet, other monks already busied themselves on both sides of the breakwater gate. Below, on Yoritomo's left, the *Bitter Wind* was at half-sail. It would pass the outcropping they stood on in moments.

"Linmei, how are you feeling?" The mountain belched black smoke. Soon, the gates out of the bay would be closed to them.

She sighed between deep gulps of cool air and glared at him. "Like you didn't think this through."

"But we need to get through that gate."

Kudaka gestured to the column of smoke. "I think that gate's the least of our problems." She spat a glob of black ash onto the rocks. "The children of Tenyama, Kagu-tsuchi, and Ryujin're making war o'er that way. None'a that will involve listening to me."

Yoritomo tightened the latch on his satchel. His quest to elevate his clan to greater status drove him on, and he would gladly shoulder any risk to lead his people to that future. But should they not live to see it, would the victory be worth the price? Was this mystery he now held in his satchel worth Linmei's life, or Kudaka's?

Linmei leaned on a rock, still coughing the ash from her lungs and brushing the dust from her kimono. Kudaka had her eyes closed and was trying to calm her breathing.

Yoritomo held himself up as if running from an exploding mountain were nothing more than a brisk jog, but his muscles ached something fierce. His determination and bravery had helped get the Heart into their hands, but his wife was right: he had never thought this through. Now, they needed a plan. "My fearless and cunning wife, what do you think is our best bet off this rock?"

"Why don't you ask Damayanti the Red to solve this problem for you?" Linmei hissed. "What? Nothing happened! It was a business arrangement!" Yoritomo said.

"I know, dammit!" Linmei caught her breath and pushed herself to her feet to stand before him. "That's what I'm angry about! How did you let her swindle you into such poor terms again? You should have consulted me!"

"What's wrong with the terms we got? They agreed to joint raids in Swaramar Bay. Leaving the Kailash Strait to them was more than fair!" Yoritomo responded with equal intensity.

"Joint raids means we'll be fighting them as often as not! And the Kailash Strait gives them direct access to the Venkar Islands, which are their ancestral grounds – we could have gotten a much better deal for access to those!" Linmei glared up at her husband. "This is exactly how we end up in situations like this one."

They continued arguing like this for several minutes. When

those two quarreled, as Kudaka said, it was best to just sit back and let them burn their conflict out. Fortunately, such spats usually don't take place on an angry mountain.

"Linmei, please." Yoritomo finally pleaded. "Can we deal with one thing at a time?" Linmei's sigh was loud and full of frustration.

"Fine. I can get us through the gate; just keep the ship heading out of the bay." She jabbed a finger at his chest. "Next time you conduct business, run it by me first. I don't want you losing the whole fleet to your bravado." She turned back toward the mountains and darted inside one of the caves.

"You can't tell me what to do!" Yoritomo shouted after her, hands on his hips. "I'm a daimyō!" But Linmei was already gone. Yoritomo and Kudaka stood together, waiting for the Bitter Wind to pass below the rocky outcropping.

"Don't you say it," Yoritomo warned. Long moments passed in silence as their glorious vessel drew into sight. The *Bitter Wind* was marvelous, a hybrid of gaijin and Rokugani construction of Yoritomo's own design. Her keel ran deeper in the water than most Rokugani craft, but Yoritomo had achieved a stability and maneuverability any captain would envy. Five broad green square sails can turn the slightest breeze into incredible speed, particularly with Kudaka's help.

"Smooth as a cloudless sail 'cross Dark Water Bay." She was smirking to herself, but he noticed.

"I'm so lucky to have an advocate like you in my marriage." Kudaka made an exaggerated bow.

The ship pulled up below them. Yoritomo waved at his favorite cousin, the dashing Byoki, who was helping the tiller crew at the aft end of the ship to guide it along the rocks.

"Can your old bones handle this jump, or do I need to carry you?"

Kudaka spat at Yoritomo's feet and leapt off the rocks. Yoritomo followed, landing hard and rolling across the deck. Kudaka landed moments after him, as lightly as if stepping off a wagon. The two approached Byoki, loyal crewmate and steady hand, who had expertly guided the ship in their absence.

"Where's Linmei?" Byoki asked. "And what are we going to do about the breakwater gate? They're already shutting it; we'll never get there in time."

"Just keep us off the rocks, cousin, and make all possible speed." Yoritomo clapped loyal Byoki on the shoulder. "Linmei has the gate covered."

Kudaka stood behind them, looking out over the fantail of the Bitter Wind, communing with the kami warring across the inlet. She looked stronger now that she was back on the water.

Yoritomo placed a hand gently on her back, not wanting to interrupt her arranged fingers and mumbled prayers. The inlet waters were choppier than they should be, like a long strip of spiked armor.

Kudaka looked up to Yoritomo, her eyes wide in fear.

A moment later the mountain roared like a tiger! Arcs of orange and black erupted from its peak. Boulders and sprays of lava rained down like a volley of fiery arrows. The water crashed and sprayed in front of the ship as boulders the size of castles slammed into the inlet and filled it with smoke, fire, and stone. Through the haze, the sky glowed like a grim sunset.

"Kudaka!" Yoritomo shouted for her as the ship lurched beneath him. Without visibility, the ship caromed off the new rocky navigation hazards, knocking crew off their feet and chipping the hardened wood of the hull. Kudaka turned and gestured wildly in the hopes of catching the attention of some kami, any kami, but none answered. The crew was struggling to regain their feet. They looked scared. Whatever Kudaka was trying to do, it wasn't working fast enough.

"Hull teams below!" Yoritomo shouted his orders with the unquestionable authority of command. "Main sail at full, douse the rest!" The crew snapped out of their fear at the sound of his voice and attended Yoritomo's orders. He leapt up the aft mast where he hoped to get above the haze and call down bearings.

From his elevated position, Yoritomo could see the gate, already a third of the way shut. It was still perhaps three times as far as Yoritomo could shoot an arrow. Linmei needed to hurry. The ship shuddered as it bounced off another rock, and Yoritomo nearly lost his grip. He scanned what he could see of the water. If they kept to the left, they would soon be out of the rocks and haze.

"Byoki! Thirty degrees to port!" Yoritomo shouted below.

The *Bitter Wind* veered at his command under Byoki's dutiful hand. Then the mountain erupted again. A stream of lava clawed through the air toward the ship, and briefly all Yoritomo could see were red streaks above him.

"Get below!" Yoritomo shouted. "Everyone get below, now!" He repositioned himself, taking cover behind the mast as molten slop peppered the deck and blistering vapor filled the air. A swirl of wind around Kudaka blasted away the acrid smoke; she was safe, and now Yoritomo could see clearly. The ship was running free, with no hand on the tiller. The molten fire had speckled the deck, and the mainsail was aflame. Screams of the men and women that hadn't made it to cover filled Yoritomo's ears. He knew what he had to do, so he grabbed a line and rappelled back to the deck.

But a spray of orange filled his field of vision and his face exploded in pain. The line snapped and Yoritomo slammed into the deck, clutching his face as agony overwhelmed him.

Byoki shouted for his captain, emerging from the relative safety below. Kudaka splashed a bucket of water in Yoritomo's face and the thin line of lava on his right side steamed and fell away. He wiped away the flaky crust and tried to blink away the pain within his head. The skin felt tight and numb, and his vision was blurred.

"How bad is it?" Yoritomo asked Kudaka.

"You just got a little prettier," Kudaka helped him to his feet. "Will you live?"

Yoritomo grimaced, but nodded. Kudaka took the burned rope from his hand. "Good. I'll tend to that later. Your wife'll kill you if we don't make it out of here. Back to it, captain."

The fresh scar only made Yoritomo's grin the fiercer. Still burning, the ship finally emerged from the haze, but they had been thrown off course and were careening toward the side of the inlet. If someone didn't get on that tiller immediately, they'd be wrecked. It swung freely like an angry serpent, covered in flames.

"All hands, return to your stations!" Yoritomo ordered. "Fire teams, get water on the tiller! Douse the mainsail before we lose it and give me full on the rest!" Byoki snatched up Kudaka's empty bucket and dashed away to refill it. But Yoritomo knew there wasn't time to wait.

He leapt across the cooling lava, narrowly avoiding a searing fate as he grabbed the long end of the tiller and heaved with all his might. Willing himself to ignore the searing pain on his palms, he leaned inward, leveraging his entire body to straighten the ship. But the rudder would not budge. Yoritomo yelled with pain and effort, setting his entire self – ambition and pride and cunning and all the rest – against the rebellious current.

The tiller moved.

The ship began to straighten, but then the ship hit a rock and Yoritomo's feet slipped along the deck. For a moment, the tiller began to shift back to follow the current. The rocky wall loomed large before them. But as his hands bled on the tiller, another pair joined them – Byoki set his grip alongside his captain's and their flesh burned together. Then another pair of hands, and another.

"It's not over yet!" Yoritomo's shout was as much for himself as for his crew. He took a deep breath and pushed his focus past the noise of the desperate crew behind him. He took one step, defying the smug Lion, Crane, Phoenix, and even Scorpion samurai that had stood over him, mocking the Mantis, telling him he was not worthy. He defied the assassins that took his family, the imposter he had called father for years. He defied those who impugned his people's honor. Driven on by his crew's devotion, he forced the tiller to bend to his will. He defied all those who had stood in his way and had told him what couldn't be done. Then he had a vision of Linmei, a brief image of his wife nursing a child while studying an old book. Yoritomo grunted with exertion as he took the final step toward her and the tiller steadied.

The ship pointed toward the breakwater gate once again. Kudaka returned with wetted blankets to smother the remaining flames on the tiller while fresh sailors relieved those who had been straining with Yoritomo. The captain's legs collapsed and he sat on the deck in a momentary heap of exhaustion. He stared at his hands, blackened and burnt, and felt the scar newly seared across his face. He made tight fists, letting the pain feed his will to live. To see the Mantis elevated.

"Cousin, we near the breakwater!" Byoki shouted.

Yoritomo took a breath and stood. The gate was nearly closed, and would lock long before they reached it. Monks lit their arrows and nocked them, rows of tiny flames like candles at a shrine. They'd be in range within moments.

"Lengthen those sails," Yoritomo called out. "I want us making all possible speed!" "Cousin, what about that gate?" Byoki was genuinely concerned. "Perhaps we could turn back to a cave, wait out the eruption."

"Linmei is coming." Yoritomo stood and watched the breakwater grow larger. He could make out the details of individual monks' faces now with his eye that wasn't swollen shut.

The gate was seconds from closing when the inlet was suddenly filled with a thousand ear- piercing shrieks. A black cloud erupted from the side of the mountain and stretched toward the breakwater, moving too fast to be smoke. The crew collectively gasped.

"Kudaka, what is that?" Byoki pointed to the unnatural black cloud.

"Not my place t'say," Kudaka shrugged, turning her attentions back to the water.

"That is my wife." Yoritomo smiled so hard he felt the skin crack over his right cheek. She was magnificent. Their children would surely rule all of Rokugan.

Byoki stared at him in surprise.

The cloud-that-was-not-smoke lashed out like a whip, expanding, contracting, twisting, turning. It streamed over the breakwater gate and monks cried out and leapt into the inlet waters to avoid it. It screeched through the sky like a million doomed, angry souls – bats.

Then Byoki gasped in recognition. "A kōmori!"

"Yes!" Yoritomo laughed, all his pain forgotten. "Like in the stories, the yōkai who helped our ancestor Kaimetsu-Uo first survive on the islands."

The gate was now cleared of monks, so the bats that had driven them off dissipated back into the surrounding rocks. All except for amidships, low on the deck, where a thick swarm of the creatures swirled like a waterspout. Yoritomo grabbed a scorched blanket off the tiller and entered the cloud. When the bats dispersed, Yoritomo stood there, his arms around his wife. The crew were terrified, but still had the sense to be grateful for the woman that had made possible their escape.

"Brace for impact!" Byoki shouted. Yoritomo grabbed a line and held onto his wife. The *Bitter Wind* smashed into the unlocked gate. The ship shuddered, but the gate opened. They were free. A great cheer rang out among the crew.

"Linmei," Yoritomo started, brushing a stray hair from her face. "I was wrong to conduct our business with Damayanti without your counsel."

Linmei looked away, toward the south.

Yoritomo put his forehead to hers. "It won't happen again. I swear it." Linmei looked back to him and raised an eyebrow.

Yoritomo's eyes were full of mischief. "After all, how are you going to prove you're half the negotiator I am if all the business is left to me?"

Linmei pulled Yoritomo's mouth to hers and kissed him.

"Y'know, the mantis female eats the head of the male after mating," Kudaka offered. Yoritomo was grinning. They were going to make it out alive. Most of them, anyway. "Let's get some wind in our sails Kudaka."

"It ain't over, yet." Kudaka warned.

A mournful wail filled the inlet behind them, though Yoritomo couldn't tell if it was a horn from the monk's village or the mountain itself as it raged to the heavens. Then a deep, resounding, earth-splitting crack echoed from below. Yoritomo watched as the rate of passing shore slowed, stopped, and then, impossibly, began moving backward.

"Kudaka?" Yoritomo hoped he was wrong.

Her eyes went wide. "Maelstrom!"

"We need wind!" Yoritomo shouted, heaving on a line to open his sails more fully. "Lengthen those sails, keep us ahead of the tide!"

The *Bitter Wind's* sails billowed outward as Kudaka's powers filled them, countering the backward pull of the whirlpool. The ship crept forward slowly. Yoritomo and Linmei worked as one mind, trimming sails and turning them to catch the most wind, trying desperately to hang on against the current dragging them toward certain doom. Byoki manned the tiller, keeping them as stable as any man could as the sea rose against them. Even the mainsail, pocked with holes from lava spray, did its part. For long minutes they labored, the landmarks to either side of the ship unmoving.

The wail sounded again, the trees shook, and the rocks tumbled. Then the current shifted, and the *Bitter Wind* shot forward like an arrow from a bow. A cheer ended early when the ship grazed a rock formation. Then another rock. They were moving far too fast to avoid all the hazards!

But suddenly the rocks disappeared beneath the water. Yoritomo's orders were swallowed up by the sounds of trees snapping and water rushing. Yoritomo looked behind him. He couldn't see the island. The water behind him was higher than his ship.

"Tsunami!" Yoritomo yelled over the roar of water. "Trim those sails, set storm conditions! Extend the leeboards!" As Yoritomo repeated his instructions, Linmei secured a line to him, herself, and Kudaka. The tenkinja whispered a prayer to the gods of the sea that they would make it safely home.

When the wave passed under them, it tossed and pitched the *Bitter Wind* as if it were made of paper. The ship bobbed in the pit behind the wave, sinking until Yoritomo's ears popped.

His stomach flipped until he felt sick. Then they were rising, so fast even his experienced sea legs ached just standing upright. Then the sea finally flattened out, and they were in the Bay of Black Water, the island already small behind them. Even the mountain seemed half the size it had been mere moments ago. A thin whisker of smoke at its nose and glowing stripes of lava along its sides made it seem like a tiger. One they had barely escaped with their lives.

Yoritomo stood next to Kudaka on the fantail, and the pair watched the horizon. "That wave couldn't make landfall, could it Kudaka?"

"Hard to say." She slumped slightly. "Ain't ever easy to see what your actions will do. It's like tryin' to see the ripples from a stone thrown in choppy water. And you like to toss boulders."

Linmei went to Yoritomo and he held her tight. After a long

moment, she broke the embrace to trace the edges of the burn down his right eye and cheek. He gave her a crooked smile. He hoped the scar was as dashing as he imagined. It certainly felt horrific.

Linmei then opened his satchel and removed the jade disc. She flattened the map out, laid the disc over it, and angled it to catch the light. Filtered through the specific red of the unique jade, entirely new symbols and images appeared. As Kudaka joined them over the map, a new puzzle was unfolding. Together, they would solve these puzzles and unlock the secrets of all eleven realms. And next, who knows? Perhaps they will even complete their quest to raise the Mantis and join the Great Clans of Rokugan!

The children sitting near the bench sat in silence for a moment. But the moment passed, and one burst forth with a question, breaking the dam for the rest:

"Didn't Yoritomo get his scar dueling Umineko?"

"How much did it hurt to get burned?"

"Where is the red-jade disc now?"

The children's eyes shone with excitement.

Byoki spun the platter he had been holding up as the red-jade disc and pantomimed casting it into the sea, rocking it back and forth gently as it sank beneath invisible waves. "We lost it when we fought the sea spider. Kudaka threw it into its eye to blind it remember? It fell into the whirlpool, sinking with the monster. I expect it's still down there, a treasure waiting for some new hero to find it. Maybe that'll be you! Now get about your chores."

The children dispersed in a babbling crowd, and Linmei

approached Byoki. "That was quite a tale you spun for the children. They'll be asking to see me turn into a cloud or a bat for days you know, and I won't thank you for that."

Byoki smiled, rubbing the flame-scar on his palm. "Well, they need these kinds of stories. Sets the fire in their bellies, makes them want to find their own treasure. A decksweeper doesn't become a captain in a year. A bunch of pirates don't become a samurai clan in a decade. And it's easy to get too comfortable along the way. Even our champion loves a good tale to remind him what he's chasing. After all, we can't disgrace the memory of everyone who didn't make it by getting lazy now, can we?"

KUROSUNAI VILLAGE

By Chris Longhurst

The fence post was crooked. Katsuo swore quietly under his breath, wrapped both hands around the post and pulled. It came loose from the dry soil too easily; the long summer had baked the dirt into coarse powder.

"Aren't you supposed to be mending that fence?"

Katsuo laid the post on the ground, turned, and gave Tomoko a tired smile. She was standing under a gnarled camphor tree by the side of the path, taking advantage of the shade that didn't quite reach the spot where Katsuo was working. Two buckets of water stood on the ground beside her.

"I don't build like the Kaiu do." He waved at the hole. "It was crooked."

"I know." Tomoko smirked. "I've been watching you sweat for a while." Katsuo rolled his eyes and held out his hand. "Come here."

Tomoko stayed where she was and mimicked Katsuo's gesture. "You come here. It's shadier." Katsuo shrugged. It was true. He crossed the path and kissed her hello.

"Your mother's going to wonder where her water is," he said. Tomoko wrapped her arms around him and rested her head on his shoulder.

"I volunteered to go to the well on the path that runs right by your farm," she said. "She knows exactly where her water is. Besides," she added, "my parents like you."

Katsuo said nothing and held Tomoko close. She had threaded a flower into her hair, its perfume mixing with the scent of camphor from the tree. Looking over her shoulder, beneath the berry-laden branches, he could see the terraced fields of Kurosunai Village, the local wood bordering them to his right, and on the left, the dirt road along which the village's few visitors would come and go. Beyond all that, the wider expanse of Ishigaki Province. Maybe one day he would get a chance to see some of it.

He squinted and shaded his eyes. Tomoko twisted around to see what he was looking at. There were figures on the road. A small group, mounted, bearing pennants, too far away for him to read their crest.

"Samurai?" he said. Tomoko nodded.

"Looks like. Doesn't Yasuki-sama normally come by herself though?"

"Normally. Why would she need–" Katsuo suddenly felt cold. "–It's the still. The barley. It's got to be."

"No." Tomoko pushed away from him. She bit her lip. "Maybe? No. Who would tell them?"

"Take the water to your mother, and let her know that samurai are coming," Katsuo said. "I can't go anywhere until this fence is fixed."

"Make it quick," Tomoko said. She crouched to retrieve her carrying pole, weaving it into the handles of the two buckets and heaving it onto her shoulder as she stood up. "Yasuki-sama still dotes on you like a mother, so you're our best chance of her going easy on us."

Katsuo watched her as she hurried away. No sense of contentment this time, or faint wonder that, of all the boys, she had chosen him ... just the cold coil of fear in his stomach.

Yasuki Hikaru had looked after the village for longer than he'd been alive, and she'd saved him and his family from bandits when he was too young to remember. Since then, she'd come around more frequently to make sure the bandits were really gone, and never really stopped. She'd learned his name and those of the other villagers, watched him and Tomoko and Shiro grow up. Samurai caring about their subjects was somewhat unusual, and it was simultaneously a blessing and a curse.

Diverting the magistrate's attention from the *shōchū* still and the missing barley that fed it had long since become routine. But nothing good would summon a *group* of samurai. Katsuo took a deep breath and turned to the gap in the fence. One thing at a time. First a straight fence, then straight home.

Katsuo trudged down the track toward his home, too apprehensive to feel weary, despite the heavy hammer resting over his shoulder. There were people outside the house: the bulky outlines of his father and mother, the powerful shape of his friend Shiro, chopping firewood – and the sharp lines of Yasuki's traveling clothes and armor. Katsuo started jogging, then forced himself to slow down. Nothing seemed out of place, yet.

Just in front of their home, his dog greeted the samurai with enthusiasm; she crouched to fuss over him, before taking a stick from the firewood pile and throwing it for Takuhiro to fetch. The magistrate was of an age with Katsuo's mother, black hair turning to grey, lines appearing on her face, but even if she dressed in rags one would never mistake her for a peasant. She was too poised, too certain in her own strength, her arms decorated with scars she refused to tell the stories of. In her sky-blue haori, laminated armor gleaming in the sun, she could have been a kami stepping from the air itself. She greeted Katsuo with a casual wave that made his father cringe.

"Katsuo-kun!" she called. "Your father tells me you have been mending fences."

"It is so, Yasuki-sama," Katsuo replied. He let the hammer head drop from his shoulder and bowed low.

"And taking his sweet time about it," Katsuo's father said. "Where have you been, Katsuo-kun?"

"Mending the fence on the goat field father," Katsuo replied. "My first fence post was crooked, so I had to reset it."

"Please look after my horse. I feel the need to stretch my legs.

Katsuo-kun's diligence does you credit," Yasuki said. "You have raised a fine son. A fine son who seems troubled by something. What ails you, Katsuo-kun?"

Katsuo hesitated, then spoke. "I saw several samurai on the road, Yasuki-sama," he said. "I wondered what brought you."

"I came alone." Yasuki frowned. "Can you describe these samurai?"

Katsuo shook his head. "They were too distant, Yasuki-sama."

"Well. I should be present when they arrive, Sanjiro-san."

"Of course, samurai-sama." Katsuo's father bowed as low as he could, but Yasuki was already walking away. She had barely reached the road when Shiro sauntered over and clapped Katsuo on the shoulder, staggering him. He was the same age as Katsuo, but where hard work on the farm had just made Katsuo lean, hard work at the smithy had wrapped Shiro in muscles upon muscles.

"Praise from the magistrate!" His face split into a wide grin. "Maybe she'll see fit to name you as one of her *dōshin* someday!"

"So that he can go traipsing across the entire province on samurai business? No, we need you here in the village Katsuo." Katsuo's father glanced past his son at Yasuki as she walked up the road. "But you said there were other samurai?"

"Yes," Katsuo said. "I think they're here about the still, or at least the barley we've been putting in it."

"You can't know that," Shiro said, although he looked tense.

"Why else would a bunch of samurai come here?" Katsuo said. "They must know we've been shorting them on the barley."

"How?" Shiro pressed. "They're samurai. They don't know how much barley we get in a harvest."

"Someone told them?" Katsuo said. "I don't know. But they're definitely coming."

"Where are the barrels now?" Katsuo's mother interjected.

"The village leader's house," Katsuo's father said. "As long as Yasuki-sama doesn't go in—"

"Where else is she going to go?" Katsuo's mother snapped. Her face curled like a fist. "If she's going to receive other samurai, she's going to do it there. Tell me at least the barrels are hidden."

Katsuo watched the color drain from his father's face. "We were expecting Shin soon…"

Katsuo's mother turned away. She swore, explosively, and Katsuo involuntarily took a step back.

"It's been too easy for too long," his father said apologetically. He shook his head. "Pride has made fools of us all Maki."

"It'll make *corpses* of us all," Maki said. She swore again, colorfully. "Katsuo, Shiro, come with me. We need to keep Yasuki-sama and the others out of that house or we'll all be put to death."

"Would they really kill us?" Shiro asked as they hurried for the paddies. Narrow tracks ran through the rice for unencumbered villagers who didn't want to take the path around, and these would now provide a vital shortcut. "Over shōchū?"

"The samurai would kill us over a bow too shallow," Maki said, "or because they were having a bad day. They would absolutely kill everyone here over barley we've been leaving off the ledger."

"But Yasuki-sama always seemed like she cared about our village." Shiro protested.

"Samurai are human," Maki said. Her face was a fixed mask of tension, all lines and surfaces. "But Bushidō comes from the Kami. They will do what they think must be done, even if it makes monsters of them."

Others in the village had thought along similar lines. When Katsuo, Shiro, and Maki arrived, the village leader and the other older villagers – those not working the fields or attending to other tasks – had gathered and were in the process of greeting Yasuki-sama. The greeting rituals would delay her, but it was clear she wanted to receive the other samurai in the most formal setting the village could offer.

"Where are the other samurai?" Katsuo said as the trio slowed to a casual walking speed. He glanced at his shadow to note the position of the sun. "We saw them at least an hour ago, maybe two."

"Worry about that when they arrive," Maki said. She lowered her voice and pulled the two young men close. "Katsuo-kun, you and I will talk to Yasuki-sama. Shiro-kun, explain things to the others when she is distracted."

She rearranged her face into a pleasant smile and strode toward the samurai, Katsuo trailing in her wake. He tried to match her demeanor but couldn't – Yasuki-sama had easily discerned his earlier anxiousness, and it felt wrong to deceive someone who had never been anything but kind to him. Couldn't they explain? Come to some sort of deal?

"Yasuki-sama," Maki said, bowing low. "May I beg a moment of your time?"

"Of course, Maki-san," the samurai said. She excused herself from the old man she had been talking to. As soon as she turned away, he scurried over to where the other elders were gathering around Shiro.

"Although," the samurai added, "should my peers arrive, I must greet them at once."

"Naturally, Yasuki-sama." Maki bowed again. "My son is old

enough now to choose a path in life, and he wishes to pledge himself to your service. Would you accept him as an *ashigaru*?"

Katsuo dropped into a low bow to hide the shock on his face. An ashigaru? What about the farm? Tomoko?

Yasuki said nothing. Katsuo wasn't sure when – if? – it would be appropriate to straighten himself. The villagers murmured to themselves not far off. Insects hummed. No birdsong, though. Was that an omen?

"Katsuo-kun. Maki-san. Straighten." If Yasuki-sama's voice were a sword, her hand would be on the hilt.

Katsuo obeyed. The samurai's face matched her voice, a gentle mask thin enough that he could see the steel beneath.

"I've known your family for seventeen years," she said, addressing both Katsuo and his mother, "so I will overlook the insult implicit in your deception. But I am hurt. Why are you lying to me?"

Katsuo opened his mouth to say something, but he was immediately cut off by a horrible scream. That was a novel way to distract Yasuki-sama–

Hoofbeats. Who had a horse? Yasuki struck him in the chest, and he fell backward, the breath knocked out of him as he hit the ground. A huge shape whipped between them in a thunder of hooves, right where he had been standing. He scrambled to his feet to see a mounted figure – a mounted samurai! – cutting down screaming villagers. People he knew, people he'd grown up with. Was this samurai justice for using a little barley to make shōchū? Would there be no trial, no ceremony? Just slaughter?

"Get inside!" Yasuki bellowed. "Lock your doors!"

She stood alone at the center of a widening circle. The villagers didn't need her encouragement to run. A handful of unmoving bodies told the story of those who hadn't reacted quickly enough.

Katsuo caught a glimpse of the mounted samurai circling their horse around the smithy, coming back around for another charge. And there, another! Idly cantering her ragged horse into view, *daikyū* in hand, eyes expressionless above the snarling dog muzzle of her helmet. But if they were no allies of the Crab, why were they here? Why were they killing people?

"Katsuo! Inside! Now!"

"But–"

She spared him a glance, and it was all he could do not to drop to the earth and beg forgiveness. There was nothing but death in that look. His. Hers. Anyone's.

An arrow whistled. Yasuki's sword flickered, and the arrow fell aside in two pieces. Katsuo ran.

The door to the smithy was closed. Barred. The next house, too. Everyone was taking Yasuki's instructions to heart. Behind him, he heard hoofbeats thunder, another arrow whistle, Yasuki's *kiai* shout rattling the shutters. He glanced back, but the skirmish had moved out of his sight–

Something rolled under his foot, and he went sprawling across the ground. Looking down, he saw he'd tripped over a head.

He had no idea whose it was. He couldn't see the body anywhere nearby. Something instinctive drove him up and away from it, legs and arms moving of their own accord, hands clawing for grip on a nearby building. He leaned against it, breathing heavily, unable to take his eyes from the gory castoff.

Screams burst from inside the house as though his touch had struck a nerve. The nearby shutters rattled violently against their ties as a heavy weight struck them from the inside, followed by the distinctive, wet sound of a blade in raw meat. Butchery.

"Katsuo!"

Tomoko ran toward him, clothes soaked with blood, eyes wide with horror. Shiro followed close behind.

"Run!" Shiro yelled. "They're in the houses! They're killing everyone!"

"They're in the village center, too," Katsuo shouted back. How many of them were there?

Tomoko crashed into him, flinging her arms around him and crying into his shoulder with great, heaving sobs. The flower in her hair was still there, Katsuo noticed. Petals a little bent.

Shiro was pale, eyes roving, clenching and unclenching his fists. More screams made them all flinch. They couldn't stay there.

A door creaked as it swung open. Katsuo didn't wait to see who was coming out. "Run," he urged, disentangling himself from Tomoko. "*Run!*"

She whimpered, but she moved. Katsuo took off on her heels, and Shiro on his – but Shiro wasn't built for speed. Katsuo heard him shriek and fall, then spit defiance and every obscenity he knew at their pursuer as Katsuo and Tomoko left him behind. Katsuo glanced back as he turned the corner of the next house: Shiro on one knee, clutching his arms to his chest, a samurai in once-green armor standing over him. The samurai split Shiro's stomach side to side with a casual flick of his wrist. Katsuo ducked around the corner, praying to anyone who was listening that he hadn't been seen. Tomoko beckoned from an open doorway, and he ran to join her.

"What's happening?" she said, voice high and tight. Katsuo

shook his head as he closed the door with painstaking slowness and slid the bar home.

"I've got no idea," he whispered. The shutters were still open on the windows into the one main room. If the samurai followed him, he would be able to look right into the house and see them. "We can't stay here."

"Where *can* we go?" Tomoko asked. She bit her knuckles to stifle a sob. Katsuo looked around.

"Out of the back window," he whispered. "Quick and quiet. We can sneak away while he's–"

"And after that?" Tomoko clutched at Katsuo's shirt. He took a deep breath, held her hands in his, forced himself not to glance at the window where the samurai would be passing at any moment. All she wanted was hope. Was for him to convince her that everything could be alright.

"After that, my house. And after that," he cut off the protest before she could say it, "just… away. Anywhere but here. We can do it. But we have to do it now."

She nodded and moved to the back window, climbing nimbly through despite her kimono and shaking hands. Katsuo followed, then doubled back to snatch a large knife from the kitchen before joining Tomoko outside. He handed her the knife. She looked at him blankly.

"If you get a chance, stab him."

"I can't kill someone!" Tomoko said in horror.

"Maybe not," Katsuo said. Cut wood was heaped by the side of the house, and next to that tools – including a heavy maul like the one he had been using to drive fence posts that morning. He picked it up. "Better to have it and not need it though."

A great shout echoed through the village. Something heavy

hitting the ground not far away, wood bouncing off wood. Yasuki still alive, still fighting.

"Go to my house," Katsuo said. "Take the shortcuts. The samurai don't know them and their horses won't do well in the paddy fields."

"Oh no," Tomoko said, shaking her head, divining his meaning. "You're coming with me."

Katsuo struggled to find the right words. Any words.

"Yasuki-sama's fighting them by herself," he said at last, as if it explained anything. "And what are you going to do?" Tomoko pleaded. "You can't fight samurai. You'll die!"

How could he *not* fight them? How could he leave the magistrate to fight and die alone when his presence might make a difference? She'd saved him once – and now he could return the favor.

"Listen." Katsuo tilted Tomoko's chin up to look her in the eyes. "Head back to your farm, get your family, and we can meet at my house. If I'm not along soon, leave without me." Tomoko took hold of Katsuo's arms. "I love you," she said. "I *need* you to know that."

"I love you too," Katsuo said, and he meant it. He kissed her. "But I couldn't go without… knowing."

Another kiai from the village center, this one muffled. Yasuki had taken her own advice and gone indoors.

"Go. Be safe. I'll do what I can."

I'll do what I have to.

Katsuo gave Tomoko a small push, then turned away from her. He dared not look back to see her go.

Movement caught Katsuo's eye amid the stillness of the village center. The door to the leader's house, open and swinging on its hinges. No sign of the samurai, their horses, or Yasuki. No screams. Not a sound save the soft noise of his own footsteps as he approached the door. If the magistrate was anywhere, surely she would be here.

It was only proper that the village leader had the largest house in the village. Almost the whole ground floor was a single open room, large enough for the entire village to gather in if necessary, and well-appointed enough to greet Yasuki, Shin the merchant, or any other honored guest.

Today it held something different. The air was thick with the smell of blood. Two large barrels of shōchū stood where they had been left, unmarked but obvious for what they were. The tatami mats on the floor were soaked with blood, dead bodies scattered where they had been cut down. And at the far end of the room, seated at the village leader's table, was a thing out of nightmare.

It seemed to be a samurai at first glance, armed and armored as a samurai with a skull-faced helm – but as Katsuo watched it move, he realized the skull was its face, skinless, given ghastly expression by what scraps of meat remained attached to it. The monster examined a row of eyeballs laid out before it on the table, holding each in turn delicately between two slender fingers and subjecting it to the scrutiny of its eyeless sockets.

Katsuo froze just inside the doorway. His stomach clenched like a fist. This was no samurai.

This was something altogether worse. Half-remembered tales of childhood terror struggled for his attention. "*If you don't behave, the goblins will get you.*" Was this… thing… some sort of divine punishment for withholding the barley?

The creature replaced the eye it was examining in the row before it and moved on to the next one.

Yasuki was not there. Katsuo made to slip back out of the door but stopped as his roving gaze picked out the slumped form of his mother, curled into a ball not far from the eyeless monster. As Katsuo watched, Maki twitched slightly and whimpered. She was alive!

The monster continued with its macabre inventory.

Katsuo approached his mother with painful slowness. Sweat trickled down his face. His knuckles ached from his grip on the maul. Maki's face was a ruin, but she still took deep, shuddering breaths.

Katsuo forced himself to take the last few steps slowly and silently; the thing seemed blind without eyes. He crouched beside his mother, trying not to notice the horror.

"Say nothing," he whispered, and Maki swallowed a whimper. "It's me, Katsuo. The thing can't see. If we're quiet, we can escape."

"I can see perfectly," came the haggard voice.

Katsuo leapt to his feet, spinning around. The mockery of a samurai was so close to him that he recoiled, tripping over his own feet until his back fetched up against a support pillar. One eye had found a home in the thing's right socket. Its jaw hung slackly open, its deep, sepulchral voice rolling forth without tongue or lips.

It laid one hand on the hilt of its katana. With the other, it pointed at Katsuo's face – his eyes, he realized – then tapped the cheekbone just beneath its empty socket. *Tap tap*, gauntlet on bone.

Katsuo clutched the maul defensively. His bowels felt like ice water. His heart had climbed into his throat, pounding like it might burst.

The mockery closed its mouth with a definitive click. Its katana rung like a bell as it slid from its sheath. It advanced on Katsuo, not even bothering to adopt a *kenjutsu* stance. Katsuo raised the maul, Tomoko's words coming back to haunt him.

You can't fight samurai. You'll die.

An unearthly howl echoed around the room, and a bedraggled shape crashed into the monster, throwing it off balance.

"Mother!"

Maki shrieked like a spirit from Jigoku as she clung to the creature's sword arm with her entire body, spinning the two of them to the ground.

The monster drew its *wakizashi* backhanded with its free hand and jammed it so hard into Maki's chest that Katsuo heard it strike the wood of the floor. Maki spasmed and coughed up blood but clung to the thing with the tenacity of death itself. The samurai-creature paused to get its feet underneath itself, ready to cut itself free of the entangling woman once and for all.

Like driving a fence post. Katsuo's overhead swing blasted the thing's skull to splinters.

The only sign of life when he reached his family's farm was Yasuki's horse still standing patiently outside. Would the abominations kill all the people but leave the horses alive? Katsuo couldn't guess.

"Katsuo-kun!" Tomoko burst from the door and wrapped her arms around him. Then she pulled back. "I found Yasuki-sama. She's here!"

Sure enough, the samurai had followed Tomoko out of the house. Her clothes disheveled, armor bearing the scrapes and dents of combat, otherwise untouched. It was like watching a mountain walk out of his home. Behind her cowered his father, one hand holding the scruff of Takuhiro's neck. The dog whined and bared his teeth, aware that something was wrong. Perhaps he could smell them.

"Yasuki-sama," Katsuo said, bowing. "They're not human. The one I killed had no face. I don't… I don't know *what* they are."

"You killed one?" Yasuki raised her eyebrows a fraction and glanced at the maul Katsuo held. "Impressive."

"I had help." Katsuo couldn't look at her. Her praise reminded him of Shiro, cut down like wheat. "Father… Mother is dead."

Katsuo's father gave a curt nod, his face paling but showing no other reaction. He and Katsuo would do their grieving later.

"They are the Lost," Yasuki said. "Samurai who have been consumed by the Shadowlands. May I see your hammer?"

"It had *no face*," Katsuo repeated as he handed the hammer to the samurai. Spoken aloud, it sounded absurd.

"The Shadowlands spawn every kind of horror," Yasuki said. She seemed distracted as she examined the hammer's head. "Faceless and otherwise. Speak true: did you really kill it?"

"Yes, samurai-sama."

"Then you have done Rokugan a service." She propped the maul against the door frame.

She walked out to the front of the farmhouse, glanced up and down the track, then walked back to the family. For a moment, Katsuo saw an expression struggle to reach her face, but she repressed it. "Now I must also do Rokugan a service."

"Midakai Province isn't far to the east," Katsuo's father said. His voice was weak. "We could find safety there, let the clan know what happened."

"No," Yasuki shook her head. "To halt the spread of the Shadowlands Taint, you all must die."

She drew her katana. The blade caught the sun. "*What?*" Tomoko shrieked. "We *survived!*"

"Katsuo, Tomoko. You are covered in blood. You have been exposed to the creatures of the Shadowlands. The Taint could be taking root in your bodies even now. As a samurai in service to my clan, I cannot permit you to live and spread it further. The most I can offer you is a clean death by my hand."

"What about as a human being, Yasuki-sama?" Katsuo's father asked quietly. "You saved us from bandits. You have watched Katsuo-kun grow up. Is the most you can offer us, as a *person*, a clean death?"

"As a person, it breaks my heart." Not a trace of emotion made it to Yasuki's face. "But my duty is clear. Please. Bow your heads."

"What about jade?" Katsuo asked, grasping for memories of the stories. "We can just be purified with jade!"

A whistle, and the sound of metal in meat. Katsuo half expected to experience his own head falling from his body, but another whistle followed – and this time Yasuki was a blur of motion, sword slicing a barbed arrow from the air. A third arrow, cut from the air once again. It took Katsuo a moment to locate the first: planted solidly in Yasuki's back.

On the road, the dog-masked woman from before was back, daikyū in hand. Now that he knew to look for it, Katsuo could see the Taint in her and her steed alike: their emaciated appearance, their translucent grey skin shot through with veins of black. Almost casually, the woman unstrung her bow and dismounted. She drew her sword and looked down its length, inspecting it for defects, but she did not approach.

"There is no jade," Yasuki said. A tiny waver in her voice. Pain from her wound, or her heart? Blood was blossoming onto her *haori* from the site of the arrow. "The other clans will not sell it to us, and we do not have enough to discharge our duty."

Katsuo fumbled for words. "I… don't understand."

"Neither do they." Yasuki tried to draw a deep breath, and couldn't. She coughed, blood speckling her lips as they curled into a bitter smile. "I have lived long enough that I forgot about mortality. I am going to die here, Katsuo, and I need you to swear me an oath."

"An oath?"

"If your father, or Tomoko – or *Takuhiro* – show the faintest signs of the Taint…you have to kill them. If you show the signs of the Taint…"

"I understand." Katsuo glanced at Tomoko, who was staring with fixed terror at the pale-skinned samurai on the track. Could he kill her in cold blood? "I will."

"Then you will be a better samurai than I." Yasuki reached behind her, and with a gasp of pain broke the shaft of the arrow. "I will spend what remains of my life to purchase as much time for you as I can. Take your family and *run.*"

Katsuo's father approached them. He silently offered Yasuki a maul. She returned her sword to its sheath and took the hammer. Hefting it, she began to walk toward the other woman, who was cutting the air with her sword in the manner of an unschooled bravo.

"I am Yasuki Hikaru of the Crab Clan," she spat, "and you will meet your end at my hands." The woman smirked and shook her head. She lifted her sword in a ready stance.

Katsuo turned to his father. "We need to go." His father

nodded, and the three of them fled with Takuhiro at their heels. Behind them, Yasuki's battlecry rang out one more time.

Katsuo had never traveled this far from his home before. Night had fallen some hours ago, but none of them had wanted to stop. Now, the moon was high, the last heat of the day fading to the chill of night. He sat on the ground, Tomoko wrapped up with him, Takuhiro and his father asleep together on the other side of a small fire. Would the Lost see the fire? Perhaps. But the villagers wouldn't survive the night without it.

"I don't understand," Tomoko murmured. "She was ready to kill us… then changed her mind?"

Katsuo listened to the insects, the crackling of the fire. Somewhere, a night bird was singing. "Samurai are human," he quoted after a while. "She never wanted to kill us. She just thought she had to. That it was her duty."

Because the Crab didn't have enough jade to do their duty *correctly*. Wasn't it the duty of the Kaiu Wall to keep Shadowlands monsters out of Rokugan? The duty of the other clans to give the Crab what they needed? How many villages had the Crab slaughtered to keep the Taint contained?

"Duty," Tomoko said into his shoulder, her voice morose. "I heard what she asked you. Would you kill me? If the Taint got me?"

In the end, Yasuki Hikaru had stayed her blade. Would Katsuo have the courage to kill where she had chosen to die?

"I don't know," he admitted at length. "I wouldn't have thought so, but… would you want to become something like that?"

Tomoko shuddered. "No."

They sat in silence for a while, Katsuo listening to the sounds of the night. Tomoko's breathing became slow and regular as she finally succumbed to sleep, and he laid her gently down on the grass.

He lay on his back next to her, staring up at the stars. The world was broken. Were the Fortunes watching as everything came apart like a cart with a cracked axle? Were they trying to fix it? Was this part of their plan?

"Something has gone terribly wrong." He said the words aloud, as if to test them, and hearing them spoken cemented his conviction that they were true. The giants were fighting, and all he could do was pray that they watched for the ants beneath their feet.

BETTER
TO BE
CERTAIN

By Robert Denton III

Hiruma Shizuyo didn't set her camp until the shadows of the parched landscape no longer matched whatever cast them. Even her own shadow was tall and branched, like a flawed oak stripped to the bark.

This was the game the Shadowlands played.

She sorted her supplies and numbered her cache of arrows with paper blessings tied to their shafts. She left everything on the cart and released the ox to return to the Wall without her. As she watched it go, her fingers brushed the smooth jade pendant hanging from her neck – the one thing that wasn't expendable.

She spent the day setting bell-adorned tripwires and driving standing torches into the cracked ground around the camp. Memorizing the terrain would be futile; it would just shift when she looked away. Only the landmarks she left would remain consistent.

When the sun touched the west horizon, she lit the torches, nose wrinkling at the scent of fish oil and pine. Aching from a day spent in armor, she started a campfire by her tent and planted her tetsubō like a banner. Fair warning. Then, facing the south, she sat and waited.

The wind was barely audible beneath the sliver of pale indigo moon. Nothing stirred beyond her bubble of campfire light, not even the sparse patches of dead grass. After a time, she pulled a stack of cards from her satchel and shuffled them. She dealt herself a single card from the bottom of the deck. An ink-wash depiction of a barbed tapeworm, a diamond of white space forming an inhuman mouth, leered at her from the card.

"Tsumunagi," she said. "Hides in supplies. Kill with fire or smother with jade oil."

The next card off the bottom revealed a hulking creature of muscle and sinew, a yawning toothy mouth where its head should have been.

"Kanu's Oni. Engage from afar. Use jade arrows, or exploit the narrow windpipe."

Another card. A segmented shell and a mass of cockroach limbs capped with human hands.

"Gokimono. Once human. Compelled to extinguish lights. Kill with–"

A bush warbler's whistle rose from beyond her camp. By the end of the trill, it was a human voice, mournful in its wordless cry. Shizuyo raised her eyes. No movement except the flickering shadow of her tetsubō. She inched closer.

Another card. A splotchy human walking in splintered armor, one eye just an empty socket. "Hyakuhei. Animated corpse." She stared into the dancing flames. "Kill as you would a man."

Shizuyo ignored her spine's dull ache and the burn beneath her eyelids as she prodded the traps beneath a morning sun painted a sick shade of purple. An uneventful night spent in her armor left her limbs heavy and stiff. Her body cried for sleep, but it wouldn't be safe until the hour furthest from the Hour of Ox – the hour sometimes written as the Hour of Fu Leng.

Only one trap had caught something: a trembling white and tan fluff with slender ears. The rabbit was tangled in the sling, helpless. It cast Shizuyo a pleading look.

She narrowed her eyes.

The hare twitched, as if trying one last time to wrench free. She slammed her tetsubō down.

There was a wet crunch, like a stomped kabocha squash. She exhaled until any remorse was gone.

It was better to be certain.

The campfire had seen Shizuyo identify thirty-five creatures in her demon deck before a tinny bell clatter broke the silence. In the night beyond, one of the pin-prick torches blinked out.

She strung her bow and collected her arrows. In the distance, something skittered into the light of the next torch. Before the light was extinguished, she barely caught sight of spindly cockroach limbs and human hands.

A cold gasp froze her. The creature had come from the south, the direction of the caravan. Her fingers found her pendant. The jade would kill it. Just one touch...

No. Not if this was it.

Shizuyo readied an arrow and pointed at the next closest torch. She counted to five, then released. The torch went dark. Something screamed.

Another arrow found it at the next-nearest torch. In the one after, she saw the arrow shafts protruding from its glossy plates. Five torches yet to go. Then would be the campfire. And then...

Another arrow. Then another. Again and again. Now it scrambled, faster, closer. Its outline grew against the night sky, blotting out the stars with its darkness. Her racing heart tightened as she launched the last arrow as the final torch, a mere hundred feet away, went suddenly dark.

A shriek. A dull thud. Silence.

Shizuyo carried a piece of the campfire to the horror's motionless body. The arrows were deeply embedded, their written blessings now blank scraps. She could recover none.

She held her breath as she finally brought her makeshift torch to where the killing arrow protruded from the eye of its human face.

It wasn't him.

She tossed the torch onto the body and returned to camp.

•••

Shizuyo startled awake. Ashes floated against a midday sky. She spat a curse. An entire morning wasted, no time to replace the used traps. She cannibalized the cart for firewood as the sun dragged a crimson path into the western ridge. Then she lit the remaining torches. Even with the soreness in her bones, it didn't take long.

Hours dragged in silence, and the campfire slowly ate away at itself. Firelight glinted along the jade pendant as she turned it over. The dreamlike image of the hare slipped into her mind – its prone body and desperate eyes. She shook her head and the vision tumbled away. Maybe it had really been a hare. Maybe it hadn't. The only way to be sure was to use her jade.

A faint bell. One of her surviving traps, far from the remaining torches. Again. She frowned.

She took her tetsubō and stepped into the dark.

The trap was triggered, but there was nothing there. Her fingers brushed clawed grooves in the dirt, numbing with slow realization.

She spun around and sprinted back to the campfire, but she was too late. Her tent blackened in the fiery column, her supplies crackling in the heat. She gritted her teeth at the high-pitched laughter. Goblinoid forms dancing around the flames, their spindly shadows entwined.

Bakemono. Three of them. One tossed her cards into the fire with her remaining torches. It laughed again.

She caught up to it and smashed it with her tetsubō. It went silent.

The remaining two turned, wide-eyed gazes flicking from Shizuyo to their dead comrade. They shrieked.

Her fingers slipped from the tetsubō handle as one charged

into her, knocking her backward. Her armor cracked and the wind was pushed from her lungs. Claws raked her cheek as the thing shrieked, again and again. Her hand darted to her hip, but her wakizashi's sheath was empty. She grit her teeth and tore the frenzied thing away, hurling it into the bonfire.

Screams pierced the night.

She started to roll to her feet, but the last goblin leapt into her chest. Her blade flashed in the creature's hands, slicing through her armor swing by swing. She reached for her tetsubō, but she could only graze the handle. The goblin arched its back, mangled blade above its head, readying a death blow. It roared in triumph.

The jade pendant. She had no choice. She tore it free and crammed it into the creature's maw.

The goblin flailed, shrieking, clawing its face, as if a burning coal were in its mouth. With new energy, Shizuyo lunged for her tetsubō. Spinning, she brought it down. The goblin's head broke like an egg.

Ragged breaths shook her. The pendant was now black, oozing in its ruined jaw.

She smashed its face again. And again. Over and over, until she had only the strength to curse the Fortunes.

It wasn't until dusk that movement on the southern horizon caught Shizuyo's gaze: a thin silhouette limping slowly toward her camp's charred remains, its navy blue cloak tattered and stained. Human.

She rose, watching his slow progress, her heart beating in tandem with his heavy steps.

He didn't look up until the sun was nearly gone, twilight

painting the landscape in purple hues. He froze, spotting her, just a short distance away. His cracked lips parted.

"Mother?"

His eyes, amber like his father's, lit up. The tattered cloak fell as he ran. "Mother! Thank the gods! I thought I would never see you again!"

She narrowed her eyes.

He slowed to a stop, confusion flickering across his face. The tetsubō handle pressed against her palm.

"Mother? What are you...?" He shook his head. "It's me, Mother! Hiruma Kenjirō. Your son!"

She did not react.

His amber eyes searched the ground. "We never reached Hiruma Castle. I'm the only one left. I was determined to survive, to see Yukino again. She is well, yes?" He smiled weakly. "We're getting married in spring. Remember? You insisted on spring..."

Her chest was like a rope twisted too tight. Insects were screaming. The sun bled over the peaks. She didn't recognize his shadow. She didn't recognize hers.

His smile faded. "T-take me to the Kuni shugenja," he stammered. "I am well! I can prove it." He reached for her with pleading eyes. "Mother–"

She slammed the tetsubō into his face. His skull crumpled like a hollow shell. He fell.

Her shadow blanketed his prone body. He jerked, as if trying to see from his now-empty socket. His wet scream broke the night.

The tetsubō came down. Then, only her shuddering heart made any sound.

•••

Shizuyo cradled jade beads as the Kuni shugenja with red and white face paint plucked a black thread from her hair and held it taut beneath his flaring nostrils. Cavalry Master Hida Tsuru sat before her with crossed arms. She lingered on the courtyard gates, lungs nearly bursting from her held breath.

"Is it done?" She nodded. "Are you sure?"

She raised her expressionless gaze. "I made certain."

The wind carried specks of ash across the red sky. Somewhere, a bonfire was burning.

The Kuni snatched the beads and raked a prolonged look over her palms. She didn't flinch. At last, he let her go. "No sign of the taint, Tsuru-sama. Even so, she should be quarantined at the shrine for seven days of cleansing."

"Make the arrangements."

After the shugenja left, Tsuru offered Shizuyo a thin scroll. She accepted it with limp fingers. Inside was her son's new name, the name they would use whenever they remembered him. His old name was tainted now.

"My condolences," he said. "We will erect a marker in his memory. Although the caravan never reached its destination, you should be proud. He died serving the Crab Clan." He rose to leave.

"It looked just like him." She wavered. "It had his voice. It... knew things." Again, she met his gaze. "It even called me 'mother.'"

"That is the game the Shadowlands plays. It wears the faces of our loved ones to sow our hearts with doubt. But that thing was a pretender. It could not have been human." Kneeling again, Tsuru laid his hand on her shoulder. "After all, if it was repelled by the burning pine inside the torches, recoiled from your arrows, and burned at the touch of your jade, then it could not have been your son." Before her paling face, he gave a reassuring smile. "At least of that, you can be certain."

SMALL MERCIES

By Robert Denton III

Western Shinomen Forest, Tenth Century

To pass on, a soul must be at peace. This is why the world was flooded with ghosts. Who meets their end having accumulated enough things, having solved all their problems with an untroubled heart? Preoccupied by endless worries and desires, they don't notice when death comes. The moment passes and they are left behind, invisible and unseen, feeding off the living. Nyotaka was glad to banish them. He had not been born with the ability to see ghosts, but he had learned how after his *gempuku*. For this, he thanked his sensei and the way of the Falcon.

"That's the last of them," he said, flicking his blade. The other *yureigumi*, the phantom hunters, knelt by the fading lights left by their banished foes, whispering prayers for Emma-Ō's attention. "They were probably Forest Killers in life. Damn bandits. They're a pain even when dead!"

Close by, Masaomi laid a scrap from a sutra over a fading ghostly light, murmuring. His other hand fed his sword – a purified katana with a handle wrapped in sacred scriptures – to its sheath.

"Even the mockingbird doesn't waste his chirps," Nyotaka remarked.

Masaomi centered Nyotaka in his mismatched eye, the pale one with the mother-of-pearl shimmer. It was proof of his lineage to Yotogi, the clan founder. Nyotaka could not look upon it without the heat of jealousy.

"We've done them no favors, sending them confused and lost with the additional weight of their new karma. They couldn't help themselves as *ukabarenai* souls." *Those who cannot rest in peace.* "Don't you feel sorry for them?"

So much for the playful jokester he'd known in his youth.

"Does one feel sorry for a shadow? For a breeze?" Nyotaka shook his head. "They are what they made themselves. Emotions without a mind. Desires without a body. If this is a punishment, it is self-inflicted. To slay them is a small mercy. There is nothing human left to pity."

"Nothing human is left?" Once more he felt Masaomi's pale gaze. "Are you so certain?"

"Yes." Nyotaka replied. "In the heart of a samurai, there is no room for doubt."

"Masaomi!"

They jolted at the *gunsō's* bark.

"The others are moving on," the sergeant growled through his mossy beard. "Will you be left behind?"

"No, cousin," Masaomi replied. Then, red-faced, corrected himself. "No, Taguchi-*sama*."

Where Masaomi had only one, Taguchi could see ghosts with both eyes. Yotogi's blood ran stronger in his veins. That was the only reason he was a gunsō. He set his hand on Masaomi's shoulder.

"Remember your task," he said. "The Lady appears perhaps each generation. A chance like this comes but once a lifetime." His face grew stern. "I won't see you squander it!"

"I won't," Masaomi promised. "I'll make father proud."

Taguchi turned, setting Nyotaka squarely in his searing glare. Nyotaka knew why – Taguchi considered him an outsider, a nuisance, and a bad influence on his little cousin. It had been so ever since they were children.

Nyotaka returned the glare. Masaomi was a gentle soul with no ambition to rise in the clan. No one here would look out for him, much less Taguchi and his constant pushing – his preoccupation with titles and glory. He didn't understand Masaomi like Nyotaka did.

The squad continued their march in grim silence. Their lanterns were blue orbs weaving between long gray trees.

Movement above. While he did not possess Yotogi's sight,

his clan's training honed his senses. A nocturnal falcon perched on a low branch, transfixed on something. A field mouse perhaps.

"We've arrived," Taguchi finally said. The others set their lanterns down, pushing the darkness back. In the clearing, a bell hung from a stone arch, turned green with time. Trees surrounded the glen like the bars of a cage.

Had he been here before? Nyotaka listened to the brittle crunch of leaves and watched the shivering branches. All quiet glens looked the same. Perhaps he'd huddled here years ago, during his gempuku.

He had been deep in the Shinomen marshes when his sensei abandoned him, leaving him alone to find his way back. No one had told him this was the rite of passage to become a Falcon Clan samurai. That would have defeated the entire purpose. Some fellow students claimed ghosts had led them back. Others said they were attacked, spirits chasing them through haunted woods. For Nyotaka, his gempuku was just another unremarkable night. He could barely remember it at all.

He'd been at the top of his class before that night. But now Masaomi was on the rise, forced into increasingly risky, dangerous missions. Nyotaka conducted only lonely patrols, lighting the lanterns of the Valley of Spirits every night on his own. Nyotaka had been left behind, while Masaomi was pushed ahead where Nyotaka could not protect him.

But not after tonight. As the others formed a circle around the bell, Nyotaka moved beside Masaomi and glanced at his troubled face, his wounded expression.

Taguchi produced a small mallet and struck the bell with a

dull ring. As one, the squad turned to the east, waiting. In the branches above, the falcon watched them all.

"There!"

A crimson light peeked between layered trunks, moving, growing closer. The gathered samurai shifted nervously, a few exchanging whispers until Taguchi shushed them.

Masaomi will never forgive me for this. But Nyotaka didn't care. Masaomi was not made for crawling the swamp, his beautiful heart hardening with each new horror. Surely he would understand. Eventually.

A short figure entered the clearing in a halo of crimson light, the red lantern swinging from a bamboo staff. The pale woman wore a style of layered robes that Nyotaka had only seen before in old paintings inside his father's study. She crossed in graceful silence, not even the crunch of fallen leaves.

"I am Toritaka Taguchi, sergeant and phantom hunter of the Falcon Clan." He bowed low. "We come as you summoned, Honored Lady."

Nyotaka's mother once told him that the Lady appeared to the first Falcon and many others since. Whether she was a ghost herself, an immortal sorceress, or simply the great-great-granddaughter of the woman who guided Yotogi, none could say for sure.

"A new threat comes," she whispered.

Taguchi straightened. "The Falcon are ready."

The lantern threw long shadows across her porcelain face. "A willful, ancient soul has escaped the Realm of Hungry Ghosts. It dwells in a palace within these woods, drawn to something within."

"We can depart at once," Taguchi offered.

"Only one may go," she warned. "More, and it will smell you coming." She looked from one wondering face to the next. "Which of you is willing?"

Taguchi cast a glance at Masaomi, who tensed, ready to accept this task on behalf of the Falcon.

I'm sorry, Masaomi. I hope you'll understand.

"I will!" Nyotaka announced, pushing past Taguchi's stunned face before Masaomi could even speak. He fell to a knee. "I am Toritaka Nyotaka, head of my class! I am ready to honor the pact!"

Silence. She didn't even acknowledge him. The others exchanged confused looks. Masaomi, face pained, just looked away.

"Forgive him," Taguchi hissed. "He forgets himself."

Nyotaka sprung up. "P-please! I am faster, quieter, a better swordsman!" Each word stabbed at his heart, but worse was the thought that Masaomi might face the danger alone. "Give me the chance, my Lady! And I will—"

"How long has he been following?" she asked.

"Since we entered the forest," Masaomi croaked. "I...I let him."

Nyotaka spun. "No! I came of my own will! Do not blame—"

The Lady's face softened. "Poor thing. You don't remember how it happened, do you?"

His gempuku night. Turning a corner, his sensei gone. Dropping his sword. Where had it fallen? He didn't have it even now...

"It's my fault," Masaomi spoke. "I took the fire striker from his bag, so he would be lost in the dark." Moisture welled in his eyes. "It was only a joke."

That night had been so cold. What had happened afterward? He couldn't remember returning. Couldn't remember…

The Lady smiled. "Your regret reminds me of *him*, Masaomi. So I do you this favor."

She lowered her lantern. A chorus of gasps. Now they all could see him. Nyotaka drew his gaze slowly down his translucent hands, where the red light now passed through, and down to his legs where his feet vanished into darkness. His sword was gone. His armor was gone. Taguchi shook his head. Where there had surely been anger in his eyes before, Nyotaka now recognized pity. Pity for the dead.

"He knows what he is now," Taguchi said. "It's time, Masaomi. Make your father proud."

The Falcon blade was in Masaomi's hand. "I'm sorry," he said, a wet gleam in his pale eye. "I won't forget you."

"It's not true," Nyotaka murmured. "I still feel. I…"

The blade fell. From above, the falcon scooped the field mouse with its claws and carried it past the canopy, into the darkness beyond.

TRUST ME

BY ROBERT DENTON III

Late Summer, Sagisōmine Shrine in Crab Lands

The week since Tadaka's last visit had not changed Azusa much. Her broom sweeps were a little slower, her careful walk a little weaker, her complexion slightly more pale from the time spent indoors. But her brown eyes still sparkled, and she still hummed like a bush warbler. The same dog greeted Tadaka, a massive puffy bean of white with stick legs, bouncing around Azusa's every step. And her smile was the same, the one unchanging detail throughout his visits in the past few weeks.

He startled her with a bare footstep into the shrine's foyer. Then her eyes lit up. "Tadaka-sama!" she chimed, instantly aglow with new energy. "You are early. I expected you tomorrow." She bowed deep as the dog barked happily in an excited circle, bounding snout-first into Tadaka's shins.

"Happy greetings, Priest Azusa," he replied, offering her a bow. "You are looking better since last time."

The young woman's smile grew wry against her pallid face and sunken cheeks. "Liar," she joked.

Azusa's hand shook as she scooped her ladle into the tea powder. The dog hovered over the kettle, taking occasional nips at the rising steam. Tadaka tried not to notice the overwhelming light, dozens of melting pale sticks spreading wax roots across the shrine floor, a virtual ring of flame.

"Forgive all the candles," Azusa said. "My sight has been darker lately." Hands shaking, she tried again with the ladle.

"When did that begin?"

"Just a few days," she admitted.

Not good. "I should start visiting daily."

"No! Don't trouble yourself on my account!" Her braids danced as she shook her head. "I can manage! I am getting better, I think. I hardly have any nightmares anymore. And it's been days since–"

A hand spasm. An echoing clatter. Powder scattered across the floor.

"Damn," she cursed.

Tadaka took the dropped ladle. "Let me."

Azusa rubbed her wrist and stared into a candle flame as he prepared the tea. The whites of her eyes were like aging paper, yellowing and spotted.

"Where are all the attendants?" he asked.

"They didn't want to get sick," she replied. She must have noticed his mouth twitch into a frown, because she hastily said through a smile, "Don't be mad at them. I told them to go. There is no reason we should all get sick!"

His stomach churned with the boiling water in the kettle, his face hot like the glowing coals. His task would be easier now that Azusa was alone, but even so, it wasn't fair. Hadn't she been like a mother to them all?

"Is this normal?" she asked, rubbing her wrist. "The locking joints…"

"Are you drinking cold liquids?"

"No!" she insisted. "Just hot tea. Like you said."

"No cold liquids," he repeated. He kept his voice flat, matter of fact. "The disease will attack your joints. Your bowels. You will get weaker." He hesitated. "I suspect it will get worse before it gets better."

A technical truth. But not the whole one.

"Do you think I can do it?" She was staring deeply into that dancing petal of flame. "Or do you think it would be better…?"

To get it over with. To end it.

Tadaka thought for a long time.

"I remember a shrine keeper who never fled," he finally said. "Just fifteen, facing down an angry *goryō* without flinching!"

Her pallid face flushed and smiled. "I merely stood behind you, and held your ofuda."

Her shy, admiring eyes brought heat to his face. And shame. Such thoughtless trust...

Loud barking. The dog hunched facing the far corner, growling, unleashing harsh shrieks again and again.

"Tazu! Stop that!"

The dog obeyed Azusa's admonishment, pulling away, but Tadaka's gaze lingered there.

"Are you taking your medicine?" he asked. "Is it working?"

The light recoiled from that dark corner, where the dust and cobwebs gathered thickly, coating the walls, the ceiling...

She nodded. "It helps me sleep. But it is a dreamless sleep."

"Sometimes that is better," he murmured.

"Bad luck out," Tadaka whispered, sweeping another dust cloud out of the shrine. He hadn't done this since he was a boy, but his bones remembered the proper way. He found that he enjoyed it now that he was older. Something simple to clean, for once. Immediate, obvious results.

Methodically he swept the shrine, floors and ceiling both. But he didn't sweep the dark corner. That he left grey and furry, dust motes suspended in the crack, like spores...

When he finished, he returned to Azusa's flat mattress and the smell of burning sage and incense. Tazu hadn't left her side. Her hand rested on his head, occasionally scritching his white fur.

"It is finished," he told her.

"I'm sorry. You shouldn't have to do that. It's beneath you."

"There is no priest-work that is beneath me." Tadaka leaned in so she could see his smiling eyes. "I enjoy it."

"You're still wearing that cloth," she observed.

He pulled back, fingers absently touching the sash concealing his lower face.

"Is that the new fashion?" she asked without guile. She chuckled. "It makes me think you're hiding something."

"I will make your medicine now," Tadaka said.

The rice paper stuck to the fog-root as he unwrapped it. The dog sniffed it once, then drew back, gagging. Slowly Tadaka ground a piece into an acrid paste, nose wrinkling at the smell, then carefully measured a portion to stir into Azusa's hot tea.

"Can we add a little more?" she asked. Her eyes were unfocused, dull.

Tadaka frowned and wrapped up the remaining root. "We must be careful with this. The right amount will dull the pain and help you sleep. Too much…"

She sighed. "Right."

Too much would kill her. She knew that already. It was Azusa who had taught Tadaka this, shown him were to find it, back when he was just an apprentice, and she just a shrine keeper under his sensei's Kaiu friend.

"It's just that the nightmares have come back," she said.

Tadaka stirred her tea.

"When I dream," she told him, "I forget my entire waking life. I don't remember anything while I am sleeping. It is as if the dream is all I've ever known. Until I awaken, and then I remember. 'That's right, I am the priest Azusa.'" She paused a long time. "If I die during a nightmare, it would be as if the nightmare were my entire life. I would die without remembering my actual life, the people, or the things that brought me joy. It would be as if all I ever knew were terror."

Black cobwebs in the filthy corner.

"That won't happen," Tadaka said, setting the cup beside her. "Trust me."

Azusa sat up as he tucked the root away. In her open palm stood a tiny origami dog. Tadaka's gaze flicked between Tazu and the paper figure. The resemblance was uncanny; she'd even captured the way his tail flopped when he was pleased.

"This is for you," she said.

The weight of her kindness pushed him down, buckling his legs and twisting his stomach. The guilt was cold, like the wet smack of a crashing wave. It was all he could do to remain standing. "I cannot accept this," he began.

"Why? I made it to thank you."

"Obligation warrants no thanks," Tadaka said. He winced. It was his sensei's favorite saying. He used to hate it. How easily it came to him now.

"Even so, this is specifically for you."

"I do not suit it," he said, realizing too late that she might interpret his words to mean that she didn't know him well enough to craft a suitable gift.

If she did, she didn't show it. "Then you should give it to *her*." To Tsukune.

Azusa's eyes were without guile. Without judgment. "She must be worried about you. When was the last time you wrote her?"

Weeks. Ages. Letters came for him, but he didn't reply. He'd wanted to, but it never seemed right. She'd only worry about him. She had enough to worry about now.

Again he regarded the origami. It was the sort of thing she would like. But it was barbed kindness, wasn't it? His eyes went to the dark corner, where the dust motes stirred.

"I'm sorry," Azusa said. "I didn't mean–"

"She would love it," Tadaka said, accepting the gift. It felt heavy somehow in his calloused hands.

It was curious how the filth never spread from the corner. It was a thick cocoon now, grey stuffing and fuzzy threads, a gradation of light into coal-shade. Just the sight of it made Tadaka long for a bath. But it never reached too far beyond. It clung to the crack. As if tepid. Cautious. Waiting.

"Tadaka-sama?"

Azusa's voice was a mere whisper. She couldn't see except for right before her. There was dust on her sheet and mattress. She stank of unwashed skin.

"I am still here," Tadaka said, setting her new dose of medicine beside her.

"Have you seen Tazu?" Concern flickered across her face. "He's normally begging for food by now."

Tadaka lifted his gaze down the hall, out the open door of the shrine, to rest on the unmoving slumped pile of white fur there, dry lips pulled back from canine teeth amid the buzzing of flies.

"I am sure he is fine," he replied. "Dogs know how to survive."

"The root isn't working," she said suddenly. "The nightmares are back. Every night." She paused. "Tadaka, do me a favor. See to the village's late harvest festival? They have no one else to do it."

Tadaka set the unwrapped fog-root by her bedside and leaned in. "Azusa-san, listen to me. You are in the worst of it now. But if you endure it, you will get better. Do you understand?"

A weak smile spread on her slight face. "Yes, Tadaka-sama. I trust you."

When Tadaka turned away, he left the fog-root behind.

Azusa stirred awake near the Hour of the Ox. Tadaka could tell from how her breathing changed, from the soft sobs escaping her lips. He remained still, but in the dark and with her failing sight, there was no chance that she would see him. He sat silent and watched. Waiting.

Slowly her shaking hand slid from under the sheet, grasping the sticky fog-root. Tadaka watched as she brought it to her lips. Even in the dark, he could see the glittering of her tears.

She bit into it. Tore chunks away and swallowed. Again and again.

Until it dropped from numb fingers, and her body thrashed beneath the sheet, her head striking the wood floor with a bone-cracking thump, over and over, pale froth pouring from her mute, screaming mouth. She vomited on her face. Then, it was blood.

And then, with a final shudder, she was still. Her skin tightened around her lips, curling back from her red-specked teeth.

Tadaka waited.

The darkness in the corner stirred. The dust fell away, spreading its filth in a cloud. A thin segmented leg dangled from the darkness of the ceiling. Then, fell. A heavy thud struck the wood beside Azusa's still body. Clawed hands scraped her cheek. The shaft of moonlight through the window glinted wetly off its extending tongue, a red strap of bloated flesh, barbed with curled teeth. With a wet slap, the tongue dropped into the pooling blood beneath Azusa's head, curling to lap it up.

Tadaka stood.

Pale orbs shot open. A razor maw parted in surprise.

"Accept this offering," Tadaka said, and he let the jade light pour from his hands.

The shrieks echoed across the empty plains. Beneath them throbbed a woman's sobs.

Tadaka slowly turned the fragile origami dog. The paper was dirty, the corners wrinkled and bent. It was intact, but it seemed ruined to him now. Again he repeated his prayer, that Azusa's soul might know peace. He could barely hear his own whispers above the shrine's cracking wood and flames, an impromptu pyre blotting out the stars.

"You are wasting your time," Kuni Yori said. "She'll never find peace. Not now."

Tadaka turned, swallowing the lump in his throat. Yori's Kabuki-painted face was lit in bronze hues. Carefully he rolled the barbed tongue into a tight coil, folded it in leather, then tucked it into his satchel.

"You did well," the Kuni said. "From this tongue, I can make protective talismans for eight, perhaps nine Crab warriors. You did a great service to the Crab, and therefore the Empire."

"She didn't have to die like that," Tadaka started.

"Then we wouldn't have the tongue." Yori patted his satchel. "A peasant's life for such a prize is a fair trade."

"I could have banished it instead," Tadaka insisted. "At any time, I could have–"

"Yes, and it would have just gone somewhere else. It could reappear anywhere in the Empire. A family's den. A child's bedroom." A knowing pause. "The quarters of the Phoenix Clan Champion."

Tadaka's blood soured.

"It can only be truly killed while it feeds," Yori concluded. "This woman was a hermit. A peasant. No family. No standing. Better her than another, yes?"

His words made Tadaka gag. As a shugenja, as an Isawa of the Phoenix, he found the notion revolting. A person's value was more than who they knew, or whether they had children, or their possessions, or status, or fame. Azusa hadn't deserved to be bait, her pain and confusion in her final moments all but ensuring that she'd awaken in Gaki-dō, the Realm of Hungry Ghosts, a damned soul. At the very least, she'd deserved a peaceful end.

But there was another voice, pragmatic and deeply buried, that agreed with Yori. Nine Crab warriors could be protected now. A monster was gone. Better one woman than dozens of others. Better a peasant than someone important.

"There is darkness in your heart."

He thought he might throw up.

"I did not think a Phoenix would have the stomach for this work," Yori said. It was meant to be a compliment. "You have proven me wrong, Master of Earth. Tomorrow, I take you to Hiruma lands. I will teach you what I know."

The heat left Tadaka as he followed. This wouldn't be the last distasteful thing he would have to do. But the Kuni did these things regularly, and they were the only ones who knew how to push back the darkness. For the good of the Empire, Tadaka had to learn. He had to bring their ways back to the Phoenix. No matter what.

Tadaka tucked the origami away. *It will be worth the cost,* he thought. *Do not worry, Tsukune.*

You can trust me.

WHAT COST
A DREAM

By DG Laderoute

"I dreamed," Doji Toin said, clutching his bamboo flute, "that I have a son."

Yūgure's head, silhouetted against the crackling bonfire, tilted slowly to one side. "And do you do *not* have a son, Toin-san?"

"No. I have two lovely daughters, but no son. I always thought I–" He shook his head. "No, I have no son."

He felt Yūgure's gaze on him, a keen awareness emanating from the deep shadow beneath a broad, conical hat.

"Why did you come here, Toin-san?"

"You know–" Toin began, then looked down to the damp soil upon which he and Yūgure sat cross-legged. Although he couldn't, for some reason, clearly remember *how* he'd come to be here, he knew *why* he had. He looked back up at the unseen face, framed by the inconstant glare of the bonfire beyond. "You know why I am here."

Again, slowly, Yūgure tilted his head, this time the other way. "Do I?"

"Yes, I ... I want you to teach me music. Music as good as that which you taught me last time. Better even."

The *jingasa* lifted slightly, and Toin could see Yūgure's mouth – thin, pale, lifted in an even thinner smile. "Well, then, *better* it shall be."

Yūgure took the flute from Toin, raised it to his lips, and began to play.

His first note was the wind across the Doji Plains.

Now it was Doji Toin who slowly tilted his head, as the music unfolded from that first, pure note. Sweeping away from the Doji Plains, Yūgure crafted the ocean, beating upon the shores of Rokugan... thunder, grumbling along the desolate peaks of the Spine of the World Mountains... water, plinking softly into hidden, mossy pools deep in the Shinomen Mori. Toin could only marvel at the richness of tonal colors Yūgure coaxed from the flute, rendering its simple handful of notes into an endless spectrum of sound–

But.

But, just on the edge of hearing, Toin thought he heard

something else. Something… formless, cacophonous, a blur of discordant, shrieking notes, an arrhythmic pounding of drums–

"Toin-san?"

Toin blinked. "I… I thought I heard–" His voice caught on the word *music*. Whatever he had heard – if he'd actually heard anything at all – it hadn't been music but, somehow, it also had.

The thin lips beneath the jingasa smiled once more. "Would you like me to play the piece for you again?"

Toin stared for a moment, then shook his head. Just like last time, he remembered every movement of Yūgure's fingers, every nuance of breath, as though he'd just played the piece himself. As though he'd known it all his life. "No, that will not be necessary."

Yūgure bowed and offered the flute back to Toin, who rose, suddenly anxious to leave… to be anywhere else. He nonetheless paused to offer a bow in return.

"I… appreciate this, Yūgure-san."

The smile widened. "I know you do, Toin-san."

Toin turned and hurried from the clearing, from the fire, from the enigmatic man he knew only as Yūgure, and that wild, atonal music that he might, or might not, have even heard at all.

Toin opened his eyes, blinking, gasping. Sitting up, he flung his gaze around, seeing only darkness–

"Toin-kun?"

He turned to the voice. "Rina?"

His wife smiled through the wan moonlight filtering in from the terrace. "Who else would it be, here in your bed?"

Toin stared into his wife's question until her smile began to fade. He forced a smile of his own. "I was… dreaming."

"I know. You called out a name – Yuma, your grandmother. You were dreaming of her…?"

Toin shook his head. "No. I dreamed… that we had a daughter, who we had named Yuma, *after* my grandmother."

Rina looked down at the futon. "You dreamed first of having a son, and now, a second daughter." She smiled again, but now it was wistful and sad. "Had we, I would have been pleased to name her Yuma."

Toin just nodded. Rina patted his arm.

"You were too good at tonight's recital," she said. "So much effusive praise has unsettled you."

"Next time, I will try to be less good."

"Well, it will certainly be difficult to play something *better* than you did tonight." She patted his arm again. "Now though, it is time to sleep."

They settled back onto the futon, but Toin could only stare into the darkness.

Rina was wrong. It would not be difficult for him to play his flute better than he had at tonight's recital.

It would be impossible.

As before, Toin couldn't quite remember how he had come to be here, in this gloomy clearing where the bonfire flared and snapped. What he did know though, was that he needed Yūgure to play another tune for him, one with which he could entertain the court of Kyūden Doji. His last performance had raised expectations for his next one to new heights; there had been a hint that he might even play before the Clan Champion.

Yūgure smiled through the dim nightglow. "So, you seek music that is even better *still*, Toin-san."

Toin nodded. "Please," he said, handing over the flute.

Yūgure raised the instrument, and began to play.

The piece was… beyond beautiful. Tears rolled down Toin's cheeks, despite the skirling dissonance that so clearly wafted in from beyond the firelight… despite the hints and glimpses of liquid movement in the darkness that accompanied it.

Toin held his wife's hand as they passed through the gate of Kyūden Doji. The castle's wall had been hung with a multitude of silver and gold lanterns, pushing back the warm softness of the summer night.

"So you are to perform for none other than the Clan Champion," Rina said, squeezing Toin's hand. "I am so proud of you, Toin-kun."

Toin nodded, but said nothing. After a moment of walking among the cherry trees that lined the road to the castle gate, he felt Rina's smile darken into a frown.

"Does something trouble you, my husband? Your performance tonight moved, well, virtually *everyone* to tears. And now, you are not only to perform for our esteemed Champion, you may even be selected to play for the Imperial Court itself."

Toin took a deep breath, tasting the fragrance of azaleas and hibiscus on the warm night-air. Another shakuhachi performer, a Kakita, had played tonight immediately following Toin. He had found his own eyes stinging, brimming with tears as she had played, so intense was the desolate passion woven through her performance. But only one of them would be endorsed by the Champion to perform at the Imperial Court in Otosan Uchi – and Toin could not deny the Kakita's formidable talent. It went far beyond mere technical mastery of the shakuhachi; the Kakita had been no mere artisan, but a true artist.

She had, in fact, been as good as he was, and perhaps better.

Stopping on a bridge vaulting over a placid stream, Toin turned to his wife, intending to say these things to her... to tell her of his doubts, and seek the reassurance she invariably managed to make sound convincing. He'd even formulated the words, but when he began to speak, something altogether different came out of his mouth.

"Rina, why did we never have children?"

She blinked, apparently just as taken aback by the question as he was. "You had your music, and I had my art."

He looked down into the water, painted with moonlight and the glow of lanterns from the castle. "I dreamed that we had a daughter."

"And a son. Yes, you told me of this."

He looked at her. "No. A *second* daughter."

Rina looked into the night, and said nothing for a moment. Finally, she turned back, her eyes bleak. "Perhaps you are coming to regret the choices you have made in life."

Toin quickly shook his head and squeezed *her* hand. "No, no, of course not. I regret none of my choices." He offered her the most sincere smile he could. "*None* of them."

She smiled back and they resumed walking, but neither of them spoke any further along the way back to their guest house.

"Ah, then you will need something most special to perform for your Champion," Yūgure said.

Toin gave a slow nod, and thought of the Kakita and her

splendid music. "Yes," he said. "Special. It must be the best performance I have ever given."

Yūgure reached for the shakuhachi flute. "Then let us give you such a piece, suited for such an auspicious occasion."

The wild, dissonant blare and pound of shrill notes and harsh drums almost, but didn't quite drown out the breathtaking splendor of Yūgure's music. Indeed, despite its mad discordance, it somehow managed to thread its way seamlessly among Yūgure's clear notes, as though rhythm and discord each teetered on the verge of becoming the other. Even the random crack and spark of the bonfire seemed to meld itself into the sound, weaving a magnificent whole. It was as though the untamed cacophony was the raw stuff of music, the primal source from which all of it was ultimately woven. And now Toin saw there was, indeed, movement all around them, half-seen dancers flinging themselves wildly through the darkness.

And then it was done, leaving only silence and the crackle of the fire. Yūgure offered the flute back to Toin with a bow. The Doji, sobbing, had to wipe brimming tears from his eyes before he could accept it.

Toin stopped on the bridge vaulting the placid stream, and stared along the watercourse. Lantern-light reflected from the looming walls of Doji Castle, glowing brightly from the mirror-still water, edging lotus and water lilies with soft highlights. He liked this little bridge, especially on such a gentle summer night as this, and often came here after a performance in the court to stand quietly, and simply breathe.

It was a moment of both placid tranquility, and great triumph.

He could still hear the Clan Champion's words that had echoed through the court.

"You shall play for the Imperial Court in Otosan Uchi, Doji Toin-san. Bring to that esteemed place the beauty of your music, that all might enjoy what is, I dare say, as near to perfection as any I have ever heard performed."

The Champion had even wiped at an eye, once. The Kakita, meanwhile, had made a particular point of coming to him and offering a deep bow of congratulations.

A great triumph indeed.

But Toin had no one with whom he could share this triumph. He had given his life wholly to his music, having never taken a wife, or raised a family, and that tempered his joy with wistful sadness. He had only ever dreamed of such things.

"You seem hesitant, Toin-san," Yūgure said. "Surely you wish to play music fit for the Imperial Court… for the Son of Heaven himself."

He nodded. "I do, but…"

The jingasa tilted against the blaze of firelight. "But?"

"But… I dream of… of a wife. Of a family I never had." He looked into the night. "Just dreams though. At least, I *think* they are dreams–"

"But you have almost gained that which you sought, Toin-san, when you first came to me."

"I do not… remember that," Toin replied. "I do not remember seeking you at all–"

"Oh, but you did," Yūgure replied. "You sought perfection in your music. It is all that has ever truly mattered to you. And now, you have almost achieved your goal." The smile widened, loomed closer. "You stand within reach of the very perfection you so crave. Having come so far, will you truly falter now?"

Toin looked at his flute, the bamboo polished smooth by years of handling, of playing. The firelight gleamed against its barrel, making it glow as though with intense heat.

"No," he finally said. "I have given…" He took a breath. "I have given my life for this." He looked back up, at Yūgure. "My performance for the Imperial Court… it must be perfect."

"And so it shall be, Toin-san."

He offered over the flute, but Yūgure shook his head.

"You do not need me to teach you," the smiling mouth said. "You already know what you must play."

He hesitated, frowning. But… he did. He *did* know. Lifting the flute to his mouth, he blew, sounding a note. Another. A third.

Then more, the notes smearing into a discordant, atonal skirl, a rhythmless succession of disconnected tones, rising to a piercing shriek, plunging deep into a basal abyss. What he played was chaos, utterly formless, and utterly perfect for it.

ABOUT THE AUTHORS

ROBERT DENTON III lives in the New River Valley of Virginia with his wife and three spoiled cats. He's written extensively for the *Legend of the Five Rings* setting, including dozens of short stories, contributions to the 4th and 5th Editions of the *Legend of the Five Rings Roleplaying Game*, and his first novella, *The Sword and the Spirits*. As an author of tabletop roleplaying games, his works include *Tiny Taverns: A Slice-Of-Life Fantasy Roleplaying Game* and the underwater fantasy setting *Destiny of Tides*.

twitter.com/ohnospooky

MARIE BRENNAN is a former anthropologist and folklorist who shamelessly pillages her academic fields for material. She recently misapplied her professors' hard work to *Turning Darkness Into Light*, a sequel to the Hugo Award-nominated series The Memoirs of Lady Trent. As half of M A Carrick, she is also the author of *The Mask of Mirrors*, first in the Rook and Rose trilogy.

swantower.com
twitter.com/swan_tower

D G LADEROUTE is a freelance writer with a long history with *Legend of the Five Rings*. He started playing the card and roleplaying games in the late 1990s, and did stints editing the official fan publication – *The Imperial Herald* – and as brand manager for L5R with AEG. He contributed extensively to the 4th Edition of the roleplaying game, and to work on L5R under Fantasy Flight Games, writing many of the game's official pieces of fiction, and for the 5th Edition. He has contributed to various roleplaying games, including *7th Sea* and *Infinity*, with more freelance projects upcoming. He also has two published contemporary fantasy novels, *The Great Sky,* and *Out of Time.* The latter was shortlisted for the 2013 Prix Aurora Award for Best Young Adult Novel. He lives in Ontario, Canada, with his wife and the obligatory writer's cats.

KEITH RYAN KAPPEL is a former Naval Intelligence Specialist who served at Naval Space Command and aboard the USS Theodore Roosevelt (CVN 71). After his service, Keith earned his BA in Creative Writing from Columbia College Chicago. When not writing, fiction or for the tabletop gaming space, Keith teaches writing for games online at his Adventure Writing Academy.

twitter.com/krkappel

CHRIS LONGHURST is an author and game designer from Oxford, England who wields his pen like a sword and his sword like a pen. He usually loses duels.

twitter.com/potatocubed

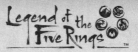

Legend of the Five Rings™

Brave warriors defend the empire from demonic threats, while battle and political intrigue divide the Great Clans.

EVAN DICKEN   MARIE BRENNAN   DAVID ANNANDALE

Follow dilettante detective Daidoji Shin as he solves murders and mysteries amid the machinations of the Clans.

JOSH REYNOLDS   JOSH REYNOLDS   JOSH REYNOLDS

The Great Clan novellas of Rokugan return, collected in omnibus editions for the first time, with brand new tales of the Lion and Crane Clans.

WORLD EXPANDING FICTION

Do you have them all?

ARKHAM HORROR

- ☐ *Wrath of N'kai* by Josh Reynolds
- ☐ *The Last Ritual* by S A Sidor
- ☐ *Mask of Silver* by Rosemary Jones
- ☐ *Litany of Dreams* by Ari Marmell
- ☐ *The Devourer Below* ed Charlotte Llewelyn-Wells
- ☐ *Dark Origins, The Collected Novellas Vol 1*
- ☐ *Cult of the Spider Queen* by S A Sidor
- ☐ *The Deadly Grimoire* by Rosemary Jones
- ☐ *Grim Investigations, The Collected Novellas Vol 2*
- ☐ *In the Coils of the Labyrinth* by David Annandale
  (coming soon)

DESCENT

- ☐ *The Doom of Fallowhearth* by Robbie MacNiven
- ☐ *The Shield of Daqan* by David Guymer
- ☐ *The Gates of Thelgrim* by Robbie MacNiven
- ☐ *Zachareth* by Robbie MacNiven
- ☐ *The Raiders of Bloodwood* by Davide Mana *(coming soon)*

KEYFORGE

- ☐ *Tales from the Crucible* ed Charlotte Llewelyn-Wells
- ☐ *The Qubit Zirconium* by M Darusha Wehm

LEGEND OF THE FIVE RINGS

- ☐ *Curse of Honor* by David Annandale
- ☐ *Poison River* by Josh Reynolds
- ☐ *The Night Parade of 100 Demons* by Marie Brennan
- ☐ *Death's Kiss* by Josh Reynolds
- ☐ *The Great Clans of Rokugan, The Collected Novellas Vol 1*
- ☐ *To Chart the Clouds* by Evan Dicken
- ☑ *The Great Clans of Rokugan, The Collected Novellas Vol 2*
- ☐ *The Flower Path* by Josh Reynolds *(coming soon)*

PANDEMIC

- ☐ *Patient Zero* by Amanda Bridgeman

TERRAFORMING MARS

- ☐ *In the Shadow of Deimos* by Jane Killick
- ☐ *Edge of Catastrophe* by Jane Killick *(coming soon)*

TWILIGHT IMPERIUM

- ☐ *The Fractured Void* by Tim Pratt
- ☐ *The Necropolis Empire* by Tim Pratt
- ☐ *The Veiled Masters* by Tim Pratt *(coming soon)*

ZOMBICIDE

- ☐ *Last Resort* by Josh Reynolds
- ☐ *Planet Havoc* by Tim Waggoner
- ☐ *Age of the Undead* by C L Werner *(coming soon)*